I0761830

Revenant Prince

KAVORA
SHAVHALLA
VIHAARA FOREST
TARSI
JAKHAT
VALMANDI
MAYUKA RIVER
ADRATI RIVER
SHARMOK
CHATANDA
HAYATHU
SULAR DESERT

HARI
LIBERA
OSELIEN
DEVEAURAL
MALFRAM
ATREA
N
ERYTHYR

ALSO BY T. A. HERNANDEZ

THE CURSE OF SHAVHALLA TRILOGY

Tethered Spirits
Revenant Prince
Riven Empire

THE SECRETS OF PEACE TRILOGY

Secrets of PEACE
Renegades of PEACE
Survivors of PEACE

OTHER WORKS

Calico Thunder Rides Again
Whispers of Shadow and Starlight

Revenant Prince

T. A. Hernandez

This book contains varying degrees of the following:
Mild language, violence, depictions of death, references to self-harm and suicidal ideation, exploration of trauma and mental illness, discrimination, torture, and imprisonment. Please read safely and responsibly.

REVENANT PRINCE

Cover art and design by T. A. Hernandez

ISBN: 978-1734033021

THE STORY SO FAR

A MAN NAMED AMAR TRAVELS THE EMPIRE OF KAVORA WITH HIS TWO companions, a musician named Mitul and a Sularan warrior named Saya. Together, they seek answers about Amar's mysterious immortality, which allows him to return to life each time he is killed...but without any of his previous memories. They enlist the help of a girl named Kesari and the Spirit Tarja she is Bonded to, a fiery being named Lucian.

Meanwhile, orphaned refugee Aleida and her Spirit Tarja Valkyra pursue Amar, believing his immortality could save Aleida's brother from a fatal illness. They attack Amar and his companions, and Amar and Aleida are both wounded in the fight. While Aleida escapes, Mitul and Saya beg Kesari to save Amar using her magic. Experiencing traumatic flashbacks, Kesari is unable to do so, and Amar dies.

The others carry his body to the home of a Tarja named Tamaya who may hold some of the answers Amar and his friends have been searching for. While there, Kesari asks Tamaya to break her Bond with Lucian, but Tamaya refuses and urges Kesari not to pursue this.

When Amar returns to life the next morning, he has no recollection of who he is or anything that happened previously. He panics and tries to leave, but Mitul stops him and explains his immortality and memory loss. Tamaya suggests that Amar may be cursed, and she encourages him to seek help from a powerful Tarja named Jameson, who lives in Atrea. She indicates that Jameson may also know how to break the Bond between Kesari and Lucian. The group sets off for Atrea together.

Having recovered from her injuries, Aleida breaks into Tamaya's home and interrogates her about Amar and the others, even going so far as to torture the old woman. She leaves feeling guilty but resolves to do whatever it takes to save her brother.

Aleida and Valkyra follow Amar's trail through Kavora. While in the city of Valmandi, Aleida breaks the curfew enforced on all Visan refugees and is arrested. Valkyra arranges her escape with the help of

Magistrate Ashaya. Aleida is disturbed by Valkyra's connection to Ashaya, who is a known friend of Nandini Kumar, the woman responsible for the invasion of Aleida's homeland.

Saya leads Amar and the others through the Sular desert. They come upon a group of Kavoran poachers harvesting mesala flowers, and Saya drives them off. She later explains that the Kavorans' excessive harvesting of the mesala plant threatens the Sularans' way of life. Through a rite of passage known as haseph, Saya hopes to strengthen her people's ability to defend and preserve their way of life using the same curse that has made Amar immortal. Amar warns Saya against this, but she insists it may be the only way to prevent her people from declining.

Aleida and Valkyra stop in the town of Chatanda, where Aleida's brother Tyrus lives under the care of a healer named Hasan. Hasan advises Aleida to stay in Chatanda, saying Tyrus will not live much longer and that she should be with him in his final days. More desperate now than ever, Aleida leaves to continue hunting Amar.

Kesari leads Amar and the others to her home city of Deveaural. There they visit the Wizard Jameson, and he agrees to try restoring Amar's memories. Kesari ventures into the city and runs across a belltower. A vivid flashback triggers a panic attack, but Saya and Lucian are able to calm her. Kesari tells Saya about a tragic accident she caused two years prior when she accidentally set fire to the tower. Fifty-three people died, including her brother Rajiv, and she ran away, vowing never to use her magic again. She decides to go see her family now. Her parents welcome her with open arms, but her younger sister Navya remains upset with her for leaving.

Several days later, Kesari and Lucian assist Jameson as he performs the spell that will restore Amar's memories. Through this process they learn that Amar's curse is connected to Shavhalla, an ancient city now in ruins and said to be haunted. Jameson also reveals that he's found a way for Kesari and Lucian to break their Bond, but Kesari realizes this is no longer what she wants. She decides to accompany Amar and the others to Shavhalla, leaving her family behind once more but promising to return again. They depart by ship and begin sailing north.

Aleida arrives in Deveaural and questions Jameson about Amar. The wizard reveals that he has gone to Shavhalla. Aleida and Valkyra hire a ship of their own, and they decide to bring Jameson along as a guide.

While at sea, Kesari begins using her magic again. Aleida's ship eventually catches up to theirs, and a naval battle ensues. Amar and his companions are victorious and sail on. Aleida, Valkyra, and Jameson abandon ship, make their way to shore, and continue their journey on foot.

Amar and the others make landfall and begin a trek through the forest to Shavhalla. When they reach the ruins, they discover stone statues and eerily preserved skeletons which come to life each night, animated by the spirits of the dead. They make their way to the palace, where Amar remembers how he was cursed.

Six hundred years prior, Amar was the prince of Shavhalla and the son of a cruel warlord. The warlord conquered, stole from, and enslaved many people, including a young woman named Mahati. Mahati went to the palace hoping to curse the warlord but instead found Amar. Out of time and options, she cursed him in his father's place, binding his soul to the physical world until he could atone for the atrocities of war.

Amar tells the others about this realization, and they seek more information in the palace records room. There Saya also discovers what she has been looking for—a journal describing Amar's curse and potentially the means to replicate it.

Aleida, Jameson, and Valkyra reach the outskirts of Shavhalla. Valkyra scouts ahead for Amar and the others, leaving Aleida alone with Jameson. He tells her what he knows of Nandini Kumar's demise, suggesting that she may not have actually been killed after she betrayed the empress, but instead became a Spirit Tarja. He also suggests that Valkyra lied about the contents of a recent letter from Hasan, and he offers to read it to Aleida himself. She agrees. The letter reveals that Tyrus has passed away, and Aleida realizes Valkyra is actually the spirit of Nandini Kumar. When Valkyra returns, she confronts her, and Valkyra severs the Bond between them. As Aleida fades into unconsciousness, she witnesses Valkyra forcing a new Bond with Jameson.

Amar finds Mahati's bones in a cell and determines she must have used the last of her life to fuel the curse that now lays over Shavhalla. He gathers her remains and carries them out of the city with the others. They come across an unconscious Aleida, and Kesari uses her magic to heal some of the damage from her Bond being severed. Amar lays Mahati to rest, and the blue spirit lights in Shavhalla rise into the night sky. The curse over the city is broken, but Amar knows his own curse remains intact.

Aleida regains consciousness and is alarmed to find herself amongst Amar and his companions. She tells them what happened and pleads with them to help her defeat Valkyra. Killing Jameson would be the easiest way to do this, but Kesari and Amar do not want to harm the wizard and insist on trying to trap Valkyra instead. They continue through the forest without seeing any sign of the pair, and when they stop to rest, Amar translates the records Saya took from Shavhalla.

The following night, Valkyra attacks using Jameson as her puppet. Kesari manages to create a barrier that will trap them both. Before she can close it off, Aleida charges in with Amar's sword, attempting to kill Jameson so Valkyra will die, too. Valkyra stops her and gains the upper hand, ensnaring all of them and then knocking Kesari unconscious.

In exchange for his friends' safety, Amar offers to go with Valkyra. She puts the others to sleep before taking Amar deeper into the forest. Once there, she forces Jameson to stab him, then severs her Bond with the wizard. Jameson dies. Amar realizes Valkyra intends to make a Bond with him instead, which would allow her to share his immortality. He knows he's dying and will come back to life without his memories, at which point Valkyra will be able to lie to him about everything and potentially manipulate him into killing his own friends. He manages to ingest a magic-inhibiting fungus called daravak before he dies, hoping this will buy his friends some time.

Kesari and the others regain consciousness the following morning. They find Jameson's body, as well as a pool of blood they realize is Amar's. They decide to split up. Mitul and Aleida will search for Amar and determine what Valkyra's plans are. Saya will go to Hayathu to finish her haseph, and then she, Kesari, and Lucian will travel to Deveaural to recover Jameson's research so they can restore Amar's memories again.

In the final scene, a young man named Savir travels to Valmandi. He doesn't remember his past, but he's been told he is Prince Savir, the long-lost heir to the Kavoran throne. He formed a Bond with his guardian, Valkyra, who died when they were attacked on the road. They both hope Savir's memories will return, but if not, Valkyra reassures Savir that he needn't worry. She has planned for everything…

Part I

The Dragon & Her Prince

SAVIR

"WHO ARE YOU?"

It wasn't the first time Valkyra had asked the question, and Savir had an easy response ready. He kicked at a rock in his path and answered with the flat tone of memorized recital. "My name is Prince Savir Akraja Jai Sharma."

The name itself still didn't seem to fit, but the royal title, at least, was comfortable. Perhaps that made him conceited. He couldn't remember anything about himself, and yet he dared to call himself a prince? But in all his desperate graspings at the memories he'd lost, that title was the only thing that made sense. He couldn't explain why, but the surety it brought was like a tether connecting him to his past. He clung to it, hoping if he held on long enough, it would lead him to the rest of his history.

Perched on his shoulder, Valkyra gave a low hum and brushed her long, silky tail over his back. The sunlight filtering through the trees above dappled their path and danced across Savir's vision as he walked. Despite the abundant shade, the air was warm and muggy—a typical autumn day in Kavora.

He snatched at the thought, trying to pull up the recollection of some other autumn from his earlier life. After a few seconds, he gave up. There was never anything personal associated with the knowledge his mind carried, a fact that only left him discouraged if he dwelled on it too long.

"What else?" Valkyra asked, drawing his attention back to her original question.

He sighed. She wanted more than his name. After all, a name was only a small part of a person's identity, and if Savir wanted to remember who he was, he needed to know his own story. She'd been telling it to him in pieces for the last two weeks, and she would often ask him to repeat it back. They both hoped that in doing so, the memories he'd lost would return.

Ideally *before* they reached Valmandi.

"I'm the rightful heir to the Kavoran Empire," he replied, "believed to be missing or dead for seventeen years. After my father died, assassins were sent to kill me and my mother. She discovered this plot and arranged for me to be taken away from the palace. I was raised in secrecy and safety in the Vihaara Forest by her trusted maidservant—that's you—until I came of age and could take my place on the throne."

Valkyra nodded her approval. "Good. And then what?"

"We were attacked on our way to Valmandi. You were killed, I was injured. I lost my memories, and you…" He gave her a sidelong glance, conjuring up the very earliest memory he had—her spirit hovering in front of him the morning he'd regained consciousness. She'd appeared as a woman then, her features hard and square, but beautiful. The Bond they'd formed had allowed her to take on a physical form, but not a human one. Now, she was a small, feathered dragon, her fur pure white and her eyes a gleaming silver.

"You became a Spirit Tarja," he said. "But I'm not supposed to tell anyone that." According to Valkyra, very few people had known she was a Tarja when she was still alive, and she'd been no one of great consequence. Better to let everyone assume she was nothing more than a well-trained pet. That way, she could continue to watch over and counsel him discreetly—something that would be even more critical now that he'd lost his memories.

He tested his newfound magic, shooting tiny sparks of lightning from his fingertips. Bonding with Valkyra meant his life would be shortened by half, and she had presented the alternative choice that he go to Valmandi on his own and leave her spirit to fade away. In the end, it hadn't been much of a choice at all. Savir needed her. Besides, the ability to use magic like any natural born Tarja was turning out to be a gratifying tradeoff.

A stray tendril of lightning crackled more violently than he'd intended and stung the end of his nose. He let out a yelp and quickly closed off his connection to his altma. It slid back down to some quiet place in his core, latent for now but still within reach.

Valkyra cleared her throat in a way that sounded very much like a growl. "Are you *quite* finished with your games, Your Highness?"

Savir stuffed his hands into his pockets. "Sorry."

Her claws dug into his shoulder ever so slightly, but she didn't launch into one of her usual lectures. Instead, she simply resumed testing him. "What's our plan when we reach Valmandi?"

"We're going to meet King Bhajan and Queen Indira," he recited flatly. "My mother's parents. We need them to back my claim to the throne before we bring it to Empress Dashiva's attention." That was the part he dreaded most. There were so many ways for things to go wrong, even if he hadn't forgotten his entire past. "How am I supposed to convince them I'm the prince, anyway? We should at least wait until my memories return."

"We're *not* waiting," Valkyra hissed.

He stopped in his tracks. "Why not?"

"Because we've waited too long for this already. I gave up *everything* to make you a man I'd be proud to see on the throne. We've been hiding in the shadows like peasants all this time when we should be living safely and comfortably in the palace."

He swallowed some of his ire at that reminder. If they'd been safe in the palace, they wouldn't have been attacked out here in the forest. Valkyra would be alive, and he'd still have his memories.

She brushed a soft, feathered wing across his cheek. "That throne is rightfully yours, Savir. You deserve better than *this*." She swept her foreleg out to gesture at the trees around them, the mud on his boots, the flat coin purse and empty sheath at his belt. "More importantly, the people of this country deserve better. Your rule is what will solidify the bond between Jakhat and Valmandi to truly unite the empire. Your mother knew that. It's why she sent you away, so you could be safe until your time came. That time is now."

He shook his head. "Maybe so. But they're going to have questions about where I've been the last seventeen years, and I can't remember anything before the last two weeks."

"What does that matter? You can make it all up, spin your own story however you'd like. You were barely more than an infant when we left the palace, and once we were gone, no one else was around to watch you grow or make those memories with you. They're not going to know any better."

"But *I* will. I can't just lie about this—not when taking the throne could impact the entire empire." He crossed his arms tight, fingers pressed hard into the flesh of his arms. "How can I even be sure *you're* not lying to me?"

The question had been swimming through his thoughts for days, a constant, lurking shadow he hadn't dared give voice to until now. Valkyra's silver eyes narrowed, but she didn't flinch or immediately try to reassure him. She said nothing at all, and Savir's heartbeat seemed to echo in the silence between them, louder even than the birdsong coming from the trees.

When he couldn't stand it any longer—the quiet or her stare—he lowered his gaze. "It's just, I don't—"

"Shh," she cut him off, eyes darting away from his face to something farther down the road. "Someone's coming."

He heard them before he saw them, a trio of voices laughing and exchanging vulgar banter. Three men came around a bend and over a small rise, and Savir began walking toward them, sticking to one side of the path to let them pass on the other. The one who spotted him first nudged his two companions, and all their laughter ceased as they began whispering to each other instead.

"Careful," Valkyra murmured in his ear, but Savir didn't need the warning. His last encounter with a stranger on the road had left her dead and him with an injury that cost him his memories, and these men didn't have a particularly friendly look about them. They spread themselves out across the entire width of the path like wolves blocking their prey's escape. One was already reaching for the hatchet hanging from his belt—the kind meant for chopping wood, but it was still sharp enough to kill a man.

Savir swept his cloak back to reveal the flintlock pistol at his hip, which hung opposite his empty scabbard. The blade itself had been lost at some point during his previous fight, and neither he nor Valkyra had been able to find it. But the pistol was already loaded, and his fingers curled around its stock with the ease of something done thousands of times before.

"Let me pass," he called out to the three men. "I don't have anything valuable on me, and I don't want any trouble."

"People always say that," said the man with the hatchet, swinging the weapon up to rest on his shoulder. "But everyone's got *something* of value, in the end. That pistol of yours looks handy. And I bet that dragon would fetch a few hundred jitaara at least. Give them up, and you can be on your way. We don't want trouble, either."

Savir raised his pistol halfway and pulled back the hammer in warning. His companions drew their own weapons—a curved dagger and a blunderbuss with a flared barrel.

"Come on, boy," said the first man. "You've only got one shot in that pistol, and there are three of us. Make the smart choice."

They were right, and the introduction of the bandit's firearm would have complicated matters under normal circumstances. But there was one small detail they weren't accounting for, and that meant the odds were still very much in Savir's favor.

"Take your time," Valkyra whispered. "Focus your energy. Strike only when you're ready."

Savir made a show of considering the bandits' offer. With a resigned sigh, he finally muttered, "All right," and bent to set the pistol on the ground.

Altma buzzed against his skin like a hundred droning bees, stronger than any of the magic he'd dared conjure before now. He couldn't contain it, didn't know how to control it, so before it could escape him entirely, he did the only thing he could. Stretching his hands out, he let the energy burst from his fingertips.

Blue lightning crackled between him and the three bandits. Valkyra leapt from his shoulder as a shot rang out. Savir toppled back, uncertain whether the force he felt was from the bandit's bullet or from the recoil of his own magic. His vision swam with jagged phantoms of blinding blue, but there was no pain, and his searching hands found no wet blood on his clothes or body.

"Get up!" Valkyra yelled, wings fanning his face as she fluttered in front of him. "You missed one."

He rose shakily and looked up just in time to see the blurry image of a man charging toward him, weapon raised above his head. Savir's body moved of its own volition. Instinct allowed him to narrowly dodge the blade's deadly arc. Another attack followed, and he rolled to one side, toward the gleam of what he thought was his pistol still on the ground. He swept it up and took aim, pulling the trigger before the man could get close enough to strike.

The body toppled forward with a groan and a thud and then went very still. The other two men lay equally motionless.

Dead.

He should have been shocked. He should have been horrified. After all, he'd never killed anyone before.

Had he?

As his heart settled back into a normal rhythm and the rest of his vision cleared, all Savir felt was a reassuring sense of calm. He was alive, and they were not. They'd attacked him, and he had defended himself. It was that simple.

Valkyra settled onto his shoulder once more, perched upright as she pressed her forelegs to her chest. Her claws sunk in deep and withdrew something, which she held out to him. "A souvenir," she said with a hint of amusement.

The small, round ball dropped onto his palm, its metal surface smooth and unbloodied. Though her spirit had a physical form, Valkyra wasn't alive in the same sense he was, so the shot she'd taken for him had caused no real damage. Still, the fact that she'd automatically jumped in to save him was touching, and he suddenly felt even more foolish for having questioned her motives. She'd been nothing but helpful and supportive from the moment he regained consciousness and had given him every reason to trust her. If not for her, he might still be wandering around trying to figure out who or where he was.

He exchanged the undamaged shot for a cartridge in his pouch and reloaded his pistol, hoping he wouldn't have cause to use it again. Two separate run-ins with brigands such as these was more than enough for a single journey, and all he wanted now was to make it to Valmandi in one piece.

"Let's go," Valkyra said. "It will be getting dark soon, and if anyone comes looking for them, we'll want to be somewhere else."

Savir set off down the path once more. A few minutes lapsed in silence before he cleared his throat and spoke to her again. "Thank you for protecting me back there."

"I'll always protect you, dear."

His face burned with shame. "I'm sorry about earlier, for accusing you of lying to me. It's just that...well, this is all *so much.*"

"I know," she said softly. "And it was a fair question. Of course, I want you to trust me as you once did, but trust takes time, and it's built on all our past experiences. Without your past, you can't be sure of anything. I'm so sorry it came to that. I wish I could have done more to protect you back then."

She'd already given up her life for him; what more could anyone have done? He brushed his hair out of his face with one hand. "What if I never remember?"

"I believe you will, in time. And if not, that will be a great tragedy, but one we'll get through together. The same as we've always done."

A bitterness rose in the back of his throat. He simultaneously recoiled from and took comfort in her certainty, in the calm sense of closeness she brought to every conversation. She knew him when he didn't even know himself, and there was something so unfair about that he wanted to scream. He squeezed his hands into fists, nails digging into his palms, and clamped down on his frustration before it could break free.

"What is it about these lost memories that's really bothering you?" she asked. The question would have seemed patronizing if not for the sincerity in her voice.

"Everything," he replied. "Who am I without them? What if I'm not the same person I used to be? What if I can't be a good ruler?"

"Hm," Valkyra murmured. "Close your eyes."

"Why?"

"Try something with me. Please."

He hesitated a moment but stopped walking and did as she'd requested. The forest's yellow-green light faintly permeated his vision.

"I want you to imagine what makes a good ruler, a good man. The kind of man you want to be."

The man who came to mind was both vague and distinct all at once—a figure shrouded in shadow, but he got the sense this was a specific person. He couldn't remember any such person, of course, and there were no clear physical features, but there was an awareness of who this man was at his core. Kind, gentle, brave, selfless. Strong, not necessarily in body, but in spirit. Happy, hopeful, loyal. A good man.

For a few moments, it seemed the beginning of a song began to play in Savir's mind, until Valkyra spoke again.

"You may not remember who you were before, but that doesn't mean you can't still be a good man. A good *ruler*. And it starts by taking on the responsibility you were born to. You know that, don't you?"

Savir opened his eyes and nodded. He *did* know, and though he couldn't control if or when his memories returned, he could control what he did next. The only choice that made sense was to keep moving forward.

And so, with Valkyra's comforting weight on his shoulder, he put one foot in front of the other and continued down the road toward Valmandi.

ALEIDA

THE TREMORS WERE GETTING WORSE.

Or at least, that was how it seemed whenever Aleida did anything with her hands. Water now seeped through her tunic where she'd spilled on herself while trying to take a drink. She scowled as she struggled to fit the stopper back into her canteen, but her fingers wouldn't cooperate. It didn't matter how careful she was, how still she held the rest of her body. Her hands hadn't stopped shaking since Valkyra had severed their Bond and left her for dead.

She'd never be able to draw or paint again.

The ache wrought by that knowledge felt dull next to the gaping chasm of grief over losing Tyrus, but after everything else she'd suffered, it seemed a cruel final blow—one inflicted by a merciless god who must find amusement in her misery.

Or perhaps this was punishment for everything she'd done in pursuit of her goals, dozens upon dozens of sins, wrongdoings, and questionable choices. Not least of which was abandoning her brother to suffer and die alone while she chased an impossible cure for his illness. If her pain was nothing more than Artex's justice, maybe she deserved it.

Or maybe there was no Artex at all.

That almost would have been more comforting, but after so many years of clinging to the faith she'd grown up with, casting those beliefs aside now would have been like ripping out her own heart.

If only she could do that, too. Get rid of her heart and all the anguish it carried.

"Are you coming?" Mitul's voice drifted from somewhere ahead.

She'd lost him through the trees and quickened her pace, wincing at the twist of a cramp in her gut and the throbbing in her skull. She suspected the physical pain was a lingering symptom from the trauma of her Bond being severed. With the dogged pace Mitul was setting and no time to rest or heal, that pain had only worsened. Perhaps that was why her tremors were worsening, too.

She caught sight of the older man on the narrow path. Ahead of him, the Adrati river cut through the trees, sunlight gleaming off its surface. They would have to cross it, but it wasn't particularly fast or wide at this point, and Aleida was a good swimmer. She couldn't say whether the same was true for Mitul.

He pulled his graying hair into a ponytail at the base of his skull and turned. Dark eyes met hers from beneath furrowed brows, and his jaw was set with the same tightness it had held since Amar went missing. She knew his concern was for his friend rather than for her, but his expression softened a little as she stopped beside him. "Do we need to rest? You don't look so good."

As much as she would have liked to take him up on the offer, she forced herself to shake her head. "I'm fine. Let's keep going."

"First we need to decide which way." He pointed to the river. "We could follow the Adrati south to Valmandi from here, or cross it and head west to Jakhat."

She frowned. Was he thinking of changing their plans? "I thought we'd decided on Jakhat."

"Did we?" he said a bit tersely. "Is that where Valkyra would take Amar? You didn't seem too certain before."

Aleida's shoulders tensed. "I never claimed to be certain. You asked what I thought she would do, and I told you. It's not like I can read her mind, but it's the best guess I have."

"A guess," he muttered. "Based on what, exactly?"

"For starters, I know her better than you or any of your friends."

The fact that she hadn't known Valkyra very well at all in the end still gnawed at her, but the statement remained true all the same. "You said that yourself."

"I did. I just want to be sure. Or at least, as sure as we can be."

"She probably wants power," Aleida said. "Or revenge. In either case, what better place to go than Jakhat? Those who wronged her are there, and she may still have connections to people who can help her regain power." Her stomach churned at the very idea. Nandini Kumar—the woman Valkyra had been before her death—was partially responsible for the invasion of Vis, and the last thing Aleida wanted was for her to rise to any position of authority again. The continued existence of her spirit in this world was injustice enough.

"Jakhat," Mitul mused, staring out across the river. "I suppose it does make more sense than anything else. Come on, then." He shifted the straps of the bags on his shoulder—his own satchel along with Amar's pack. The immortal man's sword stuck out from the top, embellished hilt glinting in the sun. Its sheath and belt had gone with Amar himself.

The river was slow and only chest-high in the middle, which made the crossing easy enough. Once on the other side, they stopped briefly to refill their canteens, then continued at the same unrelenting pace.

Aleida was stumbling over her own feet by the time they made camp. A few hours of daylight remained, but Mitul laid down his bags at the base of a nearby tree and began to arrange a circle of rocks for a fire. She suspected he'd only chosen to stop because he'd noticed her energy flagging, but he had the decency not to say anything, and she was too exhausted to insist they continue. Instead, she tossed her own pack down and went to help him.

They worked in silence until they had a decent blaze going, and Mitul mixed rice, herbs, and dried fish in a shallow pan for their supper. They also ate the last of some berries Aleida had foraged the day before. As the fire burned low, he took out his saraj and began to play a somber tune, something he'd done nearly every night during their travels together. Though his songs were all melancholy, the music seemed to soothe him. His body would relax, and some of the tight lines in his face smoothed away.

It was like her art, a safe and comforting release for the turmoil within her. She wished she had that now—she certainly needed it—but she couldn't bring herself to even make an attempt. Not when she'd lost so much control of her hands.

She glanced down at them, shaking in her lap even as she clasped them together. Rage flared within her like embers in a gust of wind.

It was Valkyra's fault—all of it. Everything Aleida had lost and suffered could be tied back to *her*. If not for the fact that the deceitful Spirit Tarja was dead already, she would have sworn to kill her. Since that wasn't an option, she would settle for wiping her from existence entirely.

The quiet whisperings of conscience brushed against her brooding thoughts. Vengeance was not Artex's way. Artex was a god of love and creation, not malice and destruction.

But she was no longer Artex's disciple. If he was real, he had abandoned her when she needed him most, and she hated him almost as much as she hated Valkyra. She was finished with gods and faith. Vengeance and fury would be her faith now, and retribution her only prayer.

Beneath that fury was something else, cold and dark and full of teeth. As a Tarja, she'd learned to be mindful of her emotions. Doing so helped to create the harmony between mind, body, and spirit that was necessary to channel altma. But she was no longer a Tarja, and if she went anywhere near that cold, dark feeling, it would swallow her whole. Anger was easier, an old friend that had been blazing within her for years. It burned, but it also strengthened her, and she needed that more than ever now. It was the only thing carrying her forward.

A sudden shriek from the trees broke through her musings, and a discordant note sounded as Mitul startled. A dusky brown shape flew toward them, large black eyes locking on to Aleida. Feros landed atop her knee, his talons pricking her skin. She dislodged him unceremoniously, which earned her a sharp nip from his beak and a few scratches on her arms. Damned savage bird. What was he even doing here? Tyrus couldn't send her any more letters.

"Is that a strix?" Mitul asked, watching the creature with a mixture of fascination and caution. "I've never seen a tame one before."

Aleida scoffed at the idea of Feros being considered *tame*, but she supposed that for Tyrus, he had been. She'd never been quite as enamored with the beast. Quite the opposite, actually. They tolerated each other for the sake of a mutually beneficial arrangement where Feros carried messages and Aleida occasionally provided him with a free meal. With Tyrus and the rest of her family gone, however, she had no more use for the strix. In fact, his presence was only an unwanted reminder of her grief.

He was scratching at the pan they'd used to cook in, and Mitul bent closer to get a better look. "He's handsome, in an eerie sort of way."

"He's a menace, is what he is," she muttered, holding out her arm. "Come here, you brute."

Feros' head swiveled around to look at her, his eyes as dark and round as two starless holes in the night. He squawked once, then fluttered over to perch on her arm. Aleida fumbled at the lid of the tube between his wings, but her shaking fingers couldn't open it.

After a few seconds, Mitul stood and took a tentative step toward her. "Will he mind if I help?"

She shrugged. "You can try."

Feros shrieked at Mitul and fanned his wings out wide, but he settled at Aleida's sharp hiss and allowed the man to relieve him of his parcel. The bundle of papers rolled inside was thick, and Mitul handed them over to her without looking at them.

"Go on, then," she said to the strix, raising her arm a little to encourage his departure. "Get out of here."

He leapt into the air but didn't go far, settling on the branch of a nearby tree to watch them. Mitul went back to his saraj and resumed playing, and Aleida stared at the papers in her hand. With shaking fingers, she pulled away the string binding them and unrolled them in her lap.

The top page was a letter scrawled in Hasan's slanted handwriting. She glanced over it, unable to read the words, and set it aside. Beneath that were pages and pages of drawings she'd sent to Tyrus over the last two years, their own unique way of keeping in touch after she'd set out on her quest.

A hot lump burned in her throat as she flipped through each one.

He'd saved everything she'd ever sent him. She had her own bundle of pages like this, letters and drawings from him to her. They'd all been ruined during the battle at sea between her hired pirate crew and the ship carrying Amar and his friends, but she'd kept them anyway, believing they were all she had left of her brother.

Now, she had these, and she wasn't sure whether she wanted to hug Hasan or curse him for sending them. These pages showed all the love and joy she and Tyrus had shared, but the sheer number of them revealed all the time she'd wasted, days and weeks and months that she'd left her brother alone. Her vision blurred, and despite her best efforts, a few tears splashed onto the top page.

"Bad news?" Mitul asked.

Aleida ignored the question and hurried to roll up the papers again. She could look through them later—somewhere private where she wouldn't risk having a full breakdown in front of Mitul or anyone else.

It was only after she'd stuffed the roll inside her pack that she realized she'd forgotten to bundle up Hasan's letter with the rest. She picked it up and glanced across the low flames at Mitul. Before she could think too much about it, she asked, "Do you know how to read?"

He kept playing. "Well enough. Why?"

"Could you teach me?"

His fingers stopped moving. He set down the saraj and put a few more branches on the fire before answering. "We need to get to Jakhat as soon as possible. I don't want to lose any time or get sidetracked on things that aren't important."

"You can teach me while we walk. Or at night, when we stop to rest."

"To *rest*. And to sleep. Not to further strain ourselves with mental exercises."

Aleida folded up the letter and stuffed it into her pack. It was a stupid idea anyway, and she was already relying on his help more than she would have liked. "Fine. Forget I asked."

He didn't say anything for a few seconds, and the only sound between them was the quiet crackle of fire snapping at the branches. She tried to put the idea out of her mind. It wouldn't change anything anyway—not now. It was too late for that.

"I'm sorry," Mitul said, leaning forward with his elbows on his knees. "I shouldn't have been so dismissive. It's clearly important to you, even if I don't understand why."

She clenched her jaw, unsure how to explain or if she even wanted to. Her illiteracy was part of what had allowed Valkyra to manipulate her. That wasn't the only tactic she'd used, and even if Aleida had been able to read, the dragon likely would have found some other way to control the situation. Still, that one personal shortcoming nagged at her, like a splinter burrowed beneath her skin. If only she'd learned to read as a child. If only she'd paid more attention to Hasan's lessons.

If only.

It was too late to change things now, but she didn't want to carry that weakness the rest of her life, haunted by the reminder of what it had cost her.

"You saw the letter," she said at last, referring not to Hasan's newest one, but the one that had come before. They'd all seen it, lying beside her on the forest floor when they found her. It was how they'd known her name before she'd been able to tell them.

Mitul's gaze was made more intense in the flickering firelight. "I did."

"She lied to me about what it said. I couldn't read, so she made something up, made me think Tyrus was still alive."

"Tyrus is your brother?"

"Yes."

He nodded. "I'm very sorry for your loss. I should have said that sooner. We don't know each other very well, but no one should have to go through what you did."

Aleida forced down the knot in her throat. The cold dark within her yawned wider, threatening to close its jaws around her. She couldn't talk about this, certainly not with a man who was scarcely more than a stranger. Instead, she let her rage fill her up until there was nothing else. "You have no idea what I've been through," she hissed. "You know nothing about me."

If he was at all taken aback by her tone, he didn't show it. "Don't I?" He clasped one hand over his wrist, thumb running across the thin band of silver and turquoise he wore there. "You were willing to do anything to save your brother. I know something about what that's like."

It took her a few seconds to realize who he must be talking about. "Amar's not your brother."

"You don't have to be blood to be family."

She grunted and went back to staring at the fire. "Then be glad yours is still alive."

"Yes, thank the skies. I'm truly sorry yours isn't."

The cold bit deep into her chest. She bowed her head, vision blurred, shoulders trembling. Mitul walked around the fire to sit near her. He said nothing, but having him there was a small comfort. She let a few tears fall, then sniffed and dried her face on her shirt.

"I don't read very well," Mitul said quietly. "But I'm happy to teach you what I can, if it will help."

She managed a small, thin smile. "Thank you. I think it will."

KESARI

KESARI SHIELDED HER EYES WITH ONE HAND AND STARED OUT across the sand to the rock formations jutting upward, their rough surfaces as bright and orange as Lucian's flames in the waning afternoon sun. She could just make out the blocky shapes of tents at the edges of the oasis settlement. More than three weeks had passed since they'd parted ways with Mitul and Aleida, but finally, Hayathu was within sight. The sturdy pair of horses they'd bought early on in their journey had made travel both faster and easier than before, but Kesari was looking forward to a proper meal and a good night's rest once they reached civilization.

Saya looked less enthusiastic. She reined her horse to a stop and took a long drink, eyebrows pinched in the middle. Kesari drank from her own canteen and gave the young woman a sidelong glance. "We're almost there," she said in her best Sularan, which she'd been practicing as they traveled.

Saya inhaled a deep breath and nodded. "Almost."

Kesari nudged her horse forward, but when her friend didn't follow, she stopped again and twisted in the saddle to look back.

"I think she's frozen," Lucian murmured quietly in her ear.

"Shh. Give her a minute."

They waited in silence, but Saya did indeed appear frozen. She stared ahead, unblinking, one hand resting on the saddlebag that held the handwritten book she'd taken from Shavhalla. It would be her haseph offering to her tribe, marking the completion of the pilgrimage she'd been on for more than two years.

If accepted, that was. As Saya had explained, there was a chance the tribal leaders—including her own mother—would reject her offering. The thought made Kesari's insides twist, even though the outcome would have no direct bearing on her. She could only imagine how Saya herself must feel. It was no wonder she needed to pause a moment before completing this last stretch of their journey.

So they waited. Lucian entertained himself by humming a jaunty little tune that sounded like one of the shanties they'd heard aboard the *Vindicator*. Kesari simply watched Saya, and when the waiting became too much, she blurted out the words she hoped would be most helpful. "I'm here with you."

Saya gave her a slightly confused look, and Kesari thought she must have misspoken. Her Sularan was getting better, though it was still more difficult to speak than it was to understand. She switched to Kavoran to better explain herself. "I know how important this is, and maybe you're scared. But you're not alone. However this turns out, we'll be right there with you." She shrugged. "Or maybe you're not scared. I've never seen you afraid of anything. But still, I'm here."

"You are, and I'm very glad for that. Thank you." She clicked her tongue at her horse and pressed her heels into his sides. Kesari's mount fell into stride beside hers, and they headed toward Hayathu at a steady walk. "And for the record," Saya added, "you *have* seen me afraid."

"When you were seasick on the *Vindicator*?" Lucian suggested. "Or when we were attacked by those spooky statues in Shavhalla?"

She laughed a little at his teasing, but when she spoke, her voice was somber. "A little, yes. But also when Valkyra and Jameson had you trapped in those roots, Kes. I thought she was going to kill you."

Kesari swallowed against a rush of her own fear at the memory, but with it came the bitter taste of shame and guilt. She'd been so helpless. She could have used her magic to stop them—she'd certainly tried. But fear had overwhelmed her, and when the others had needed her most, she'd failed them all.

"I'm sorry," she said.

"For what? It's not your fault."

"I should have done something more. Fought back or held the barrier longer. We had her trapped, but then I—"

"Then Aleida ruined everything," Saya cut in with a sharpness not directed at Kesari. "You're not the one to blame for any of it. You did your part." She sucked in a breath. "Skies, maybe Aleida was right. If we'd killed Jameson, we could have been rid of Valkyra, too."

Kesari shook her head vehemently, though she could understand Saya's point. Things might have gone very differently if they hadn't concerned themselves with saving the poor wizard. Still, after mulling it over these past few weeks, she was glad they'd chosen not to go down that road. Despite the unfortunate outcome, she couldn't justify giving up on a man who'd helped them so much. At least they'd *tried* to save him.

And lost Amar in the process.

Your fault, whispered that self-disparaging voice in the back of her mind. She pushed it away, focusing on Saya's words instead. *You did your part.* And she had, as best as she could. It hadn't been enough, but next time, her best would be even better. *She* would be better. Stronger. Braver. More capable.

Except...what if that still wasn't enough?

"I guess it doesn't matter," Saya said. "It's done. All we can do now is deal with the consequences."

They rode along as evening turned to dusk, and small lights began to appear all around them. Most were blue, the faint glow of the mesala flowers native to the desert. Directly ahead, a few orange campfires flickered and grew. One seemed closer than the others, off to their west a little and well outside the settlement. Saya tugged her horse's reins in that direction, veering off the straight line they'd been making toward Hayathu. "Come on. I think I know who that is."

Not long after, they came upon a small encampment consisting of a single ghayat-hide tent, a bird roasting over a campfire, a dun colored horse, and a man sitting cross-legged atop a woven blanket. He turned to look at them as they approached. His features were even sharper than usual in the firelight, and his teeth gleamed like a fox's when he smiled.

"Do my eyes deceive me, or is that Saya hàs Seda approaching my camp?" Zefar asked in Sularan, and Kesari was pleased to realize she could understand everything he'd said. Her friend's full name might have confused her until recently, but she'd since learned about Sularan naming conventions and the custom of passing down their lineage through the mother's given name. 'Hàs Seda' simply meant, 'born of Seda.'

"It's me," Saya replied, stopping her horse at the edge of his small encampment.

The mercenary stood up to greet them. "And have you finally returned home, or are you only here for another visit?"

"Is that what you'd prefer?"

He shrugged. "I can't say I didn't enjoy the commotion you stirred up last time."

She swung herself down from the saddle and strode over to him. "I'm sorry to disappoint you, then. My haseph is finished. I'm back."

He beamed wider, then did something Kesari never would have expected. He put both hands on Saya's shoulders and pulled her into a tight hug. "Welcome back." He murmured something else to her, but the words were too quiet to make out.

They broke apart as Kesari slid from her horse, and Zefar nodded to her and Lucian. "And you brought friends again."

"You remember Kesari and Lucian?"

"Of course. The Tarja girl and her fiery companion—how could I forget?" He motioned to the roasting bird. "Supper's almost ready, if you care to join me. There isn't much, but I'm a decent enough cook. Or were you planning to continue on to Hayathu?"

"We'll stay," Saya said quickly. When Zefar raised an eyebrow at her, she rolled her eyes. "I've been gone for two years. What's the rush now?"

He gave her a sly grin and a quick wink. "Stay until morning if you'd like."

They attended to their horses, tethering them near Zefar's to allow them to graze on the patches of wild grass in the area. Zefar checked the roasting bird and, once satisfied it was finished, divided it between himself, Kesari, and Saya. There was also a starchy vegetable Kesari had never tried before but thoroughly enjoyed.

While they ate, he caught Saya up on the latest happenings in Hayathu, including the many antics of her younger brothers. Kesari and

Lucian exchanged a few amused smiles as they listened, both fondly remembering their interactions with the boys on their last visit.

"Ah, and I almost forgot," Zefar said. "Hazim returned from his haseph last week."

Saya leaned back and stretched her long legs in front of the fire. "Did he? It will be good to see him again."

"Your brother?" Kesari asked, trying to remember which one he was. There were several, and they all looked alike. As hard as she'd tried, she hadn't ever managed to figure out exactly who was who.

"The oldest," Saya said. "You never met him. He was away the last time we came through. What was his offering?"

"No idea," Zefar replied. "I didn't attend his ceremony."

She let out a sigh. "Of course you didn't."

He crossed his arms, his face suddenly tense. "What did you expect? He doesn't want anything to do with me, as he's made very clear several times."

"That's just his pride. You have to keep trying."

"I *have* tried—you know that. With all of them."

"They're only children. They don't know any better."

"Hazim's finished his haseph. He's a man now. He knows exactly who he wants to associate with, and I'm not on that list."

"He's still your nephew. My father would have wanted—"

"Your father's dead," Zefar snapped. "I'm tired of being rejected by all his brats simply because tradition says I'm not worthy."

"Not all of them," Saya said quietly.

For a moment, a wounded look passed over the man's face. Then his jaw tightened, and he stood abruptly. "Not all. Not yet anyway. But you'll be taking your place among the tribe soon, and what then?"

"I'm not going to—"

He made half an attempt at a smile. "Save us both the trouble and spare me the promises, all right? You're going to be the masahi someday, and I'm just your disgraced outcast uncle. Even if you won't admit it now, you're better off denying me. I'd be selfish to want anything different." He turned and started to walk away, out into the chill vastness of the desert.

"Zefar, stop," Saya called after him. "Don't walk away. Where are you going?"

He raised a hand to them over his shoulder and kept walking. "A man's got to piss somewhere, and I'd prefer it not be in front of guests."

Saya muttered something under her breath and continued to stare after him. Eventually, Kesari tried to fill the awkward silence with an obvious question. "So…he's your uncle?"

"Yes, you failed to mention that before," Lucian chimed in.

Saya rubbed at her temples with her fingertips. "He's an outcast. I'm not really supposed to consider him family anymore. And I didn't think Amar would appreciate that little connection, seeing how Zefar once killed him."

"A fair point," Lucian conceded.

"I'm sorry about your father," Kesari said. "I had no idea."

"It's all right." Her voice made clear it was very much *not* all right, but Kesari could understand that. More than two years had passed since Rajiv's death, and though the pain was now easier to bear, she doubted she'd ever get past it completely.

"He was sick," Saya added. "Not physically, but in his mind, his spirit. At least, that's how my people see these sorts of things. I think Atreans call it melancholy."

Kesari nodded. She'd heard the term before, though she didn't know much about it.

"He fought it for a long time, for me and my mother and brothers. We thought he'd recovered, or at least learned to cope with it. But then he jumped off the cliffs there." She pointed to the sharp, dropping silhouettes near Hayathu, no more than jagged shadows against the star-filled sky. "It nearly broke our family."

"That's awful. I can't even imagine. I'm so sorry, Saya."

She ran a hand along the sash draped over her shoulder and tied around her waist. Its color was the exact same shade of red as the haseph markings painted on her face. "This was his. He wore it on his haseph. So did Zefar, and I'll give it to one of my brothers next. It's not enough, but at least it's a reminder of him to carry with us."

"I'm sure that will mean a lot to them."

"Maybe. Or maybe they'll think it's tainted, since it once belonged to an outcast." She glanced in the direction Zefar had walked and shook her head. "He and my mother never got along, and after my father, it only got worse. I think they both blamed each other on some level. But I want my brothers to know Zefar the way I do. Especially the youngest ones. They were too little to remember our father very well, but Zefar is...not like him at all, actually, but he made me feel like I still had some piece of him here with me."

Kesari glanced at Lucian, who in some ways had fulfilled the same role for her after Rajiv's death. At times, that had been more painful than helpful, but in the end, it had aided her healing. It still did. Perhaps that was part of why Saya held such affection for Zefar, despite his obvious faults and bad manners.

They watched the fire burn low, lost in their own thoughts, and Kesari's eyelids began to droop. She stifled a yawn.

"You should get some rest," Saya said. "We can leave first thing in the morning. It won't take long to reach Hayathu from here."

Kesari stood and dusted the sand off her pants. She *was* tired. After retrieving her pack and blanket, she pulled on Rajiv's coat for a little extra protection against the cold and laid down. "Goodnight, Saya," she said, but the warrior did not reply. Zefar hadn't returned, and her golden eyes still watched the distant sand and rock.

She would be all right; of that, Kesari was certain. For as long as she'd known her, Saya had been as strong and solid as the desert cliffs all around them. If anyone could handle whatever came tomorrow, it was her.

SAVIR

UPON ARRIVING IN VALMANDI, SAVIR AND VALKYRA RENTED A ROOM at an inn where they could rest and prepare for an audience with King Bhajan and Queen Indira. Valkyra claimed to know someone who could help them get that audience, but she shared few details. Instead, she kept Savir's attention focused on presentation, making sure he looked the part of a prince in everything from his dress and appearance to his bearing and manners.

It was a tall order, considering how disheveled he was after a few hard weeks on the road. A hot bath washed away the dirt and sweat, but he had no suitable attire to change into. This issue was soon rectified when Valkyra took him to a local tailor to buy new clothes. She didn't say where she'd obtained the necessary funds, and he didn't ask, though he suspected they'd been stolen during one of her nighttime flights through the city. They chose a few pieces that were durable and well-made, finer than his previous attire but mostly functional and only modestly decorated. They also picked out a more stylish outfit he could wear to the palace, something befitting a noble if not a prince.

In the days that followed, Valkyra continued to instruct him in proper court manners and the social customs he'd be expected to follow. It was mostly a refresher; according to her, she'd taught him these things all his life, and some of it seemed to come back naturally. But there was a lot of information to keep track of, especially when it came to all the names and histories of important players in Kavoran politics, including his own family.

Just as she'd done during their travel here, she would spring her questions on him when he least expected it, a test to make sure the knowledge was truly ingrained. This morning over breakfast, it was, "Tell me your family lineage."

Savir took a drink to wash down the bite he'd just finished. He could recite the names in his sleep at this point, but as he'd quickly learned, she wouldn't let the question rest until he'd answered to her satisfaction. "My father was the late Emperor Akraja, elder brother to the current ruler, Empress Dashiva. My mother was Princess Priyani of Valmandi, daughter of King Bhajan and Queen Indira." He proceeded to run through the rest of his lineage on both sides of his family going back three generations.

"Very good," she said, giving him a curt nod. "Now tell me about the relations between Jakhat and Valmandi."

"Past or current?"

"Both. After all, the present is inextricable from the past, is it not?"

He held back a sigh and gave the answers she wanted—answers a prince would be expected to know. Valmandi had once been a sovereign nation encompassing much of what was now southern Kavora. At that time, the Kavoran Empire had been rapidly expanding, both through forceful invasions and as smaller nations and cities ceded their territory in exchange for Kavoran resources and protection. Valmandi had resisted this expansion at first but eventually came to an agreement with the empire. The royal family kept their land, titles, throne, and some level of regional jurisdiction, but they were ultimately subject to imperial rule.

Despite this formal hierarchy, Valmandi still held great power within the empire, both in military strength and in their influence with other nobles. The city also controlled key travel and trade routes connecting Kavora to the rest of Erythyr, making it an integral part of the economy.

"It was hoped that the marriage between my parents would strengthen Valmandi's connection to the imperial throne," Savir said.

"But tensions worsened when my mother died, especially since Empress Dashiva may have been the one who hired assassins to kill both of us."

He should have been upset, knowing his throne and his mother had been stolen from him in such a violent manner. Perhaps it *had* upset him, before. Now, he couldn't particularly bring himself to care. He'd come here to reunite with his maternal grandparents, and eventually to secure the imperial throne. But if he stopped to consider whether that was what he wanted, his confidence wavered. It was what he was *supposed* to do, and there was no denying that the title of prince felt familiar.

But that didn't mean he *wanted* it.

"That's only speculation," Valkyra said, but the chill in her voice made it clear she believed the rumors. "Empress Dashiva is a cunning woman, and a snake if I ever met one. With her brother childless, she was secure in her place as heir to the throne—that is, until you came along. She would have wanted to make certain you never took her place." She ruffled her feathers and arched her long neck, regaining whatever composure she'd lost to bitter emotion a moment before. "But you must take care with your words, dear. There are certainly more diplomatic ways to phrase such accusations. In fact, better not speak them at all. At least for now."

"I know that," he said, unable to keep some annoyance out of his voice. He wasn't a completely ignorant child. Though without his memories, could he really blame her for sometimes treating him like one?

She dipped her head and curled her tail over her front claws, speaking in a softer tone. "We must tread carefully, Your Highness. You *are* the rightful heir to the throne, but convincing the rest of the empire of that fact when you're believed to be dead will be no easy feat. There can be no missteps."

He knew that, too, and the pressure he felt only increased with each passing day. Sleep proved difficult most nights, and he would often toss and turn, his mind wandering through questions about his unknown past and worries about what came next.

When he did sleep, there were dreams—or at least, he thought so. Upon waking, he could never latch on to any of them. There were only snippets of lingering emotions and vague images, and half the time, he couldn't be sure what they were. Whenever he tried to understand what they meant, they would vanish, and he was left wondering if he'd really seen or felt anything at all. He borrowed a quill, ink, and paper from the innkeeper and took to jotting down whatever came to him immediately upon waking, hoping the dreams could provide some connection to his missing memories.

On their fourth night at the inn, he woke from such a dream, the last remnants flickering from his mind like a dying candle. He kept his eyes shut and tried to cling to it. The only thing he could picture in his mind was a flash of red. Nothing more.

Before he could roll over to write down that singular detail, something in the room clicked. He cracked one eye open to see Valkyra unlatching the window. She sometimes went out while he was sleeping, but whenever he asked where she'd gone, she simply said she was attending to other business. Savir guessed most of that business involved arranging his meeting with the king and queen, but he would have appreciated a few more details. Including who she was working with, and how they planned to prove he really was the long-lost prince—not only to Valmandi's rulers and all the rest of Kavora, but to Savir himself. Despite her reassurances and the trust she'd earned from him, some doubts lingered. He needed more than her word. He needed evidence, solid and irrefutable.

He kept his breathing slow and even, watching through the narrow slits of his eyelids as she slipped through the window and closed it behind her. Then she hopped down from the sill and vanished from sight.

Savir was out of bed and clambering out the window himself before he could stop to question what he was doing. He kept as quiet as he could, not wanting Valkyra to know he was following her, though he couldn't have explained why. He hadn't even stopped to put on his shoes, and the press of the cold ground against his feet chilled his entire body.

Looking to either side, he searched for some sign of her. The streets were quiet and empty this late at night, but a few lamps still burned with magical orbs of light to provide decent visibility. A set of tiny, clawed footprints cut through a patch of dirt ahead, and he jogged in that direction.

A few streets later, a pair of murmured voices drifted from nearby. Valkyra's smooth alto was immediately recognizable, and Savir stopped running to sneak in closer. The other voice was deeper, a bit nasally and with the highborn accent Valkyra was always trying to get him to mimic.

He paused at the end of a nearby alleyway, peering around the corner of a building. A tall, cloaked figure stood facing Valkyra, who was perched on a barrel at waist-level. Savir couldn't make out the man's face very well in the shadows, but he sounded nervous. "Are you sure it's not too soon? If this goes wrong, we—"

"That won't happen, so long as you do your part," Valkyra cut in. "You have the journal, don't you?"

"Of course. And the medallion?"

"I've got it. All that's left is to present the boy to the king and queen. They'll do the rest."

"What if they don't believe it?"

"People believe what they want to believe. They'll make it true, and that's all we need. Let me see the journal."

For a few seconds, all was quiet. Savir shifted his weight from one foot to the other, trying to give each one a brief respite from the cold ground. He blew softly into his hands to warm them.

"You've done well," Valkyra said. "The writing matches perfectly."

"Are you sure he's ready?" the stranger asked.

"As ready as he can be. You've arranged an audience?"

"Yes, four days from now, right before they take their afternoon meal."

"Good. I'll bring him to you that morning, then."

"I'll be waiting."

With the conversation seemingly about to end, Savir jogged back to the inn. He quickly hoisted himself inside through the window, rolled into bed, and pulled the blankets over his shoulders, trying not to shiver as heat slowly seeped back into his body.

That man must have been who Valkyra had been working with all this time, but who was he, and how did she know him? Savir didn't like that they'd held this meeting in secret. Why not tell him about it? What significance was there in the journals and medallion they'd mentioned? And what did it mean that the writing matched perfectly?

He had no answers, but he'd soon be getting some if Valkyra planned to bring him to the stranger. And after that, to the palace.

He tucked his knees up a little closer to his chest. *Was* he ready for that? Would he ever be? Perhaps the only way to find out for sure was to go through with it. A queasy feeling swirled inside his stomach, and this time when he shivered, it was not from the cold alone.

He closed his eyes and tried to fall back asleep. It was only when he heard the sound of fluttering wings behind him that he realized he'd forgotten to close the window.

A gentle weight pressed against the bed near his feet. "Savir?" came Valkyra's low voice. "Are you awake?"

There was no point in pretending otherwise. She already knew, and he had the sneaking suspicion that this was yet another kind of test. He pushed himself up on one elbow to look at her.

"Why is the window open?" she asked.

"I heard you go out," he replied. Didn't the best lies include some piece of the truth? "I wanted to make sure you could get back in."

"I'm perfectly capable of opening windows on my own."

He shrugged and forced out a yawn, trying to appear sleepy and nonchalant. "It was getting too warm in here, anyway." He flopped back down on the pillow before she could respond, trying to put an end to the conversation and whatever suspicions she might have.

It shouldn't have mattered. He should have been able to tell her that he'd followed her and ask about what he'd overheard, but he couldn't bring himself to do it. She had her secrets, so he would keep his own, at least for now.

She shifted on the bed at his feet. "Let me know if you get too cold, and I'll close it for you."

He was cold already, but he said nothing, even though it meant he lay there shivering in the dark for the rest of the night.

KESARI

BY MORNING, WHATEVER TENSION HAD STRETCHED BETWEEN ZEFAR and Saya the previous night had faded to a cool aloofness. They didn't speak except to exchange the most basic of pleasantries. Saya asked for Kesari's help in reapplying her haseph markings, and afterward they readied the horses to leave while Zefar busied himself with tidying his camp.

Kesari mounted her horse. Saya was about to do the same, but she paused and turned to face her uncle. "You'll come to my ceremony, won't you?"

"Only if you want me there," he replied, not meeting her gaze.

"Of course I want you there. Skies, why do you always have to be so difficult?"

Zefar stiffened, set down the blanket he'd been folding, and strode over to her. "All right. I'm an ass, and I'm sorry. Is that better?"

Saya pursed her lips. "I'm not going to shun you after this. You know that, right? I don't care about the traditions."

"You should."

"Well, I don't." She crossed her arms. "I expect to see you there when they clean these marks from my face and tell me my haseph is finished."

The mercenary's mouth stretched into a sneer, and he motioned to the scars on his own face. "And what if they *don't* accept your offering?"

"All the more reason for you to be there."

He sighed and took a step closer, clapping one hand over her shoulder. "I wouldn't miss it."

"See you tomorrow, then." She hoisted herself up onto her horse, and together she, Kesari, and Lucian rode to Hayathu.

Upon their arrival, they were enthusiastically greeted by all seven of Saya's brothers. Kesari recognized six of them from her previous visit, but not the seventh. He stood some distance from the others, watching quietly as they laughed and clung on to Saya, all chattering excitedly. He was a bit taller than her and had the slightly disproportioned frame of a boy becoming a man. Hazim, Kesari assumed—the one who'd recently returned from his own haseph.

Once Saya had disentangled herself from the others, she approached him. They clasped each other by the arm briefly, and she said a few words to him in Sularan. Hazim barely returned her smile, though he was friendly enough when she introduced Kesari and Lucian.

They made their way to the masahi's tent on a rocky ledge that sat higher than the rest of the settlement. Many of the Sularans stopped what they were doing and followed them in twos and threes, until they had a sizable crowd trailing them. Saya waited outside while one of her brothers went in to get their mother, and when the woman emerged, the commotion around them died down to a quiet murmur. The masahi exchanged a few words with her daughter before embracing her, and Saya relaxed into her arms.

Afterward, they both stepped forward, facing the gathered onlookers, and the masahi raised Saya's hand high with her own. "My daughter has returned from her haseph at last!" she called out in Sularan. The onlookers cheered, and Saya's grin widened. After a few seconds, the masahi raised her other hand to silence them. "The council will now gather so that she may present her offering."

A few people approached the masahi's tent. Saya gestured for Kesari and Lucian to come forward as well. They'd previously discussed how valuable their expertise could be, considering the magical nature of Saya's haseph. Magic was uncommon among Sularans, and their understanding and use of it was solely for healing and spiritual practices. Kesari and Lucian still didn't have a solid understanding of curses, but given what they'd seen and experienced with Amar and Shavhalla, they had as much knowledge to offer on the subject as anyone.

Kesari slipped through the crowd and made her way to Saya's side. Lucian hovered between them. "Are you ready?" he asked, though it was unclear which of them he was talking to.

Saya nodded resolutely. Kesari's nod was more hesitant. She wasn't sure what the Sularan council would ask or how exactly she was supposed to help, but for Saya, she would do whatever she could.

They followed the others inside the tent, which was even larger than it had appeared from the outside. There was another entrance at the back, which had been left open to allow for some airflow in the stifling heat. Cushions were arranged in a half-circle at the center of the room, and all but Saya and Kesari took a seat on them. The council itself was made up of four people: the masahi, a young woman dressed all in white, an ancient woman with long gray hair, and another individual who was tall and thin with androgynous features.

"You can sit there for now," Saya said, gesturing to an empty cushion beside the old woman. Kesari took her place with Lucian floating over her shoulder, and all eyes turned to Saya as she withdrew the book she'd taken from Shavhalla. They'd reviewed it together several times during their journey in preparation for this moment. Inside were handwritten notes about Amar's curse, including theories for replicating it and Amar's translation of the Shavhallan writings.

The masahi motioned for her daughter to speak, and Saya took a deep breath before beginning her presentation. Kesari had heard her quietly rehearsing it to herself many times and knew enough Sularan to understand the basics of what she was saying. She started by explaining the purpose of her haseph and what she'd set out to find: a means by which her people could ensure their own safety and the continuation of their way of life. She highlighted the need for this by pointing out that Kavora's armies were powerful enough to conquer the Sularans and take over the desert at any time—something that seemed increasingly likely given their history of conquest and their poor adherence to existing trade agreements.

Saya's offering, however, could give her people a significant advantage in such a conflict, for she had found a means to make them all but invincible: an ancient and powerful type of magic that even the

Kavorans didn't know. At this point, she held the journal up for dramatic emphasis. "We can use this magic to make ourselves immortal."

The councilors' expressions shifted from astonishment to skepticism, and they began to ask questions. Saya answered each of them in turn. Kesari had a difficult time keeping up with the conversation, but it seemed there was some concern about the nature of this ancient magical practice, specifically the fact that it was a curse. Centuries ago, curses were believed so dangerous and powerful that they'd been forbidden in most societies, and all knowledge of their creation was systematically eradicated.

When the conversation began to die down, Saya gestured to Kesari and Lucian, and all focus shifted to them. "The council has some questions you might be able to answer better than me," she said in Kavoran.

Kesari stood awkwardly, limbs tingling with nervous energy as she went to Saya's side. Quickly, the young warrior ran through introductions. "These are my companions, Kesari Eves from Atrea and her Spirt Tarja, Lucian. You've met my mother, Masahi Seda, and these are our other council leaders."

Kesari bowed slightly. "It's a pleasure to meet you all."

None of them returned her greeting, instead launching straight into their questions. The woman in all white was the first to speak, a heavy accent filling her Kavoran with breathy whispers. "Can you confirm that this man Saya has spoken of is indeed immortal?"

"Yes," Kesari replied. "Sort of. That is, he does die, but he doesn't stay that way. He comes back to life."

"A *new* life," the old councilor said in a loud but quavering voice. "One where he has none of his prior memories. It's too dangerous, I think, throwing away all the knowledge and wisdom of our past experiences so casually."

"Not everyone would have to take this curse upon themselves," Saya said. "Only those who volunteered. The rest could help them remember, make sure their pasts aren't entirely forgotten." The masahi gave her a sharp look, and she quickly added, "That is, if this offering is accepted."

"I still don't like it. The ancestors would not be pleased."

"Don't the ancestors want us to preserve our ways and traditions for the generations that come after us? How can we do that if the Kavorans take our land and strip it of all its resources?"

The councilor in white frowned. "You may be right, but this is not an immediately pressing issue. Empress Dashiva seems to have grown tired of conquest these past several years. Not since the invasion of Vis has she truly sought to expand her territory."

"Not a pressing issue, but a looming one nonetheless," said the third councilor, speaking for the first time and drawing the others' full attention. "How feasible is this, truly? I imagine a curse takes a great deal of power and skill to replicate. Is this even something we *could* do, should we decide we want to?"

Kesari exchanged a look with Lucian, unsure how to respond. He floated forward a little to address the council. "That's a difficult question to answer without knowing the exact strength and skill of all the Tarja among your people. However, I do believe it's possible, especially with further study and practice. The key element of a curse seems to be the source it draws on."

He drifted closer to Saya. "Open that book for me, will you? Let's find Amar's translations." He scanned the hastily scribbled words. "Ah yes, there it is. According to the scholar who wrote this, 'a Tarja must draw on the blood of their own body and the *jhivan* of their spirit…' Sorry, it looks like he forgot to translate that bit. *Jhivan* must be the Shavhallan word for altma."

"The same as what we would use to perform any other kind of magic," said the masahi.

"Correct. However, it seems the use of the Tarja's own blood is what makes a true difference. An unpleasant business, to be sure, but not one that requires a significant sacrifice. Amar told us the young woman who cursed him simply cut into her palms."

The youngest councilor scowled. "Self-mutilation and blood magic. I don't like it."

"What about the memories?" Saya's mother asked. "Is there any way to prevent the curse from taking those, or to get them back?"

"Memory loss wasn't ever mentioned in the curse or in the scholar's writings," Lucian replied. "It could be they simply didn't know about it at the time of writing. Or it could be an accidental instability in the magic, something never intended to be a part of the curse."

"We can get the memories back, though," Saya said. "A Tarja in Atrea did it for Amar, and Kesari's going to learn how to do it herself. Maybe she could teach our Tarja, once she learns."

Kesari swallowed. She still wasn't sure she'd be able to master the technique Jameson had used to restore Amar's memories, and that was assuming they first managed to retrieve his notes and research. She nodded anyway. "I'll help however I can."

The woman in white let out a huff. "I don't understand why we're even entertaining this notion when the Kavoran threat is practically hypothetical."

"I disagree," the masahi said. "Saya is right. The Kavorans have a long history of taking what they want by force. We've managed to keep them at bay so far, but that could change at any moment. Already their merchants steal our mesala, ignoring the trade agreements we've set. Any decisive action we take could invite retaliation, but the ghayat herds are dwindling, and before long, so will our people. We'd be foolish to wait until soldiers are at our borders to find a solution."

This seemed to stifle the rest of the young woman's protests, at least for now.

Masahi Seda spoke to the councilor on her left, who seemed to be the most knowledgeable among them when it came to magic. "You've long advocated for us to place greater importance on magical practices and training, but the concerns raised here today are reasonable ones. Using this power does seem an extreme step to take, especially if we can't contain it. We would be the first to bring curses back to Erythyr, but it would only be a matter of time before that knowledge spread. Including into Kavora."

"We would do our best to prevent that, of course," the councilor replied. "We could teach the practice to only the most trusted of our own Tarja and advise them to guard its secret closely. But you're right; in time, information would spread. Perhaps that's a problem for another day—one we can address *after* we've ensured the safety of our people and our lands."

The masahi nodded, leveling her gaze at her daughter once more. "Thank you, Saya. We appreciate your offering and the information your companions have shared. However, I'm afraid we cannot accept it yet. Our final decision will require more consideration and study. Please hand over the book, and then leave us. We have much to discuss."

Saya's jaw tightened, disappointment shining in her eyes as plain as the high noon sun. She approached her mother with slow, even steps and handed her the book, then turned away. Kesari and Lucian followed her out of the tent, where a few of her brothers still lingered, waiting for an update.

They didn't get one that day, nor the day after. Zefar arrived expecting to witness Saya's completion ceremony but seemed less surprised than most upon learning of the council's deliberations. "Half the time, they don't know their brains from their asses," he said in a tone that was possibly meant to be sympathetic.

In response, Saya only blinked, and he shrugged. "Even I wouldn't wager on them being fool enough to deny your offering. They'll sort it out."

And they did, though it was well past dark by the time Masahi Seda came to deliver the verdict. The warrior stood, motioning for Kesari to come with her, and together they approached. Lucian remained with Zefar.

"We've come to a unanimous decision," the masahi said, speaking in Kavoran as a courtesy to Kesari. "Unfortunately, the offering you brought back isn't something we plan to use. Not immediately, at least, and perhaps not ever." She shook her head, and the mantle of leadership seemed to fall away, replaced by the quiet concern Kesari had so often seen in her own mother's face. "This curse is a very dangerous thing, Saya. Surely you know that."

The young woman's jaw tightened, and she raised her chin. "I know. And I wouldn't have brought it if I didn't truly believe it could help our people. For a long time, I wasn't sure I *should* bring it."

"So why did you?"

"Because the decision was a bigger one than I could make on my own."

Masahi Seda gave her daughter a slight smile and tilted her head. "You've grown more than I realized in your time away from us."

Saya's expression smoothed into something carefully neutral, but her hands remained clasped tight behind her back. "I'm sorry to have wasted the council's time. With your permission, I'd like to continue my haseph and seek out a more worthy offering."

"When did I ever say your offering was unworthy?"

Saya exchanged a quick glance with Kesari. Her gold eyes glimmered in the moonlight, wide and hopeful.

"We will accept your offering," the Masahi said, "and we'll hold on to those records. They may well serve us in the future."

Saya spun to Kesari with a wide grin and threw her arms around her shoulders. Kesari hugged her back. It was good news, perhaps the best outcome they could have hoped for. The curse wouldn't be used until it was absolutely necessary, which reduced some of the associated risks and concerns, if only temporarily. And Saya's two-year quest was ending in success. She would be fully accepted into her tribe with all the honor she deserved.

"The council does have one request," Seda added. "For now, we'd prefer to keep the nature of your offering a secret. As we've established, it's dangerous. We don't want it falling into the wrong hands."

"Of course," Saya replied. "That's reasonable."

"Aside from your companions here and the two others who were traveling with you, who else knows of this?"

"There was a Visan girl. And an Atrean Tarja, but he's dead. Zefar knows a little. His information is what first led me on this search."

She made no mention of Valkyra, who was, by Kesari's estimation, the greatest potential threat. However, it was unclear how much Valkyra knew or cared about Saya's haseph specifically.

Masahi Seda looked past them to where Zefar sat some distance away from the rest of the tents, his silhouette dark against the night sky. "Ask him to keep your secret. He respects you enough to honor that request. Then you must sever your ties with him. You were a child before, and the tribe was willing to overlook your associations. They will not be so forgiving now."

"He's my uncle," Saya said firmly. "I won't turn my back on him for the sake of some cruel tradition." She did, however, turn her back on her mother, effectively ending the conversation.

Kesari gave the woman an awkward look. "I'm sure she…" The rest of her words failed her. "Well, sorry."

The masahi sighed. "I'm not surprised. She's always been strong-willed." She reached into the folds of the sash at her waist and withdrew a small, beaded pouch, which she handed to Kesari. "Thank you for watching out for her on your travels. It comforts me to know she had such strong, loyal friends by her side."

Kesari wasn't sure she would have described herself as strong, but she dipped her head in a slight bow anyway and opened the pouch. Inside was a handful of finely ground powder, pale blue and faintly shimmering in the moonlight. She thought she knew the answer, but she asked anyway. "What is it?"

"Mesala. When ingested, it will enhance your Tarja powers for a short time."

Kesari knew it was a more generous gift than she could fully appreciate, given the delicate balance between the mesala plants, the ghayat herds, and the Kavorans who harvested more than their share of the flowers. For a moment, she considered refusing it, but that might have been perceived as an insult. This mesala was freely given, not stolen, and she might need it to bring back Amar's memories. She closed the pouch and tucked it carefully inside her pocket. "Thank you. I'll treasure it and try to use it wisely."

"That is all we ask." Seda returned to her tent, and Kesari hurried after Saya, who had already begun conversing with Zefar and Lucian.

She'd just finished explaining the council's decision when Kesari joined them. Zefar did not take the news well. "What right do they have to decide that? Offerings are always presented to the tribe for final approval."

"Not this time," Saya said. "And I think it's the right decision."

His eyes narrowed. "What exactly did you bring back?"

She considered this for a few moments, then shook her head. "I'm sorry. The less information you have, the better."

He crossed his arms. "*I'm* the one who told you about the immortal man in the first place."

"I don't want anyone else knowing. It's too dangerous."

"Oh, well pardon me, then," Zefar scoffed. "I didn't realize you'd grown so mighty and wise out there in the world. I suppose I should be grateful you're here to protect us all from our own ignorance. After all, it's not as if *I* have any experience with dangerous things."

Saya rolled her eyes. "Don't take it personally. It's my haseph, which means it's my responsibility to protect it. That's all I'm trying to do."

"And it has nothing to do with shutting me out? Putting the dishonorable outcast back in his place?"

Kesari winced at the accusation, but Saya simply glared at him. "How can you even think that?"

"How could I not?"

"You know me better than that. I thought we trusted each other."

"So did I."

Saya's eyebrows pinched together. She opened her mouth as if to say something else but closed it again just as quickly. Kesari and Lucian exchanged an uncomfortable look and began to edge away, toward the tent they'd been offered to sleep in. This wasn't a conversation either of them needed to hear.

But apparently, the other two had said all they wanted to, because a few moments later, the sound of Saya's footsteps sinking heavily into the sand followed behind them.

ALEIDA

THE GRAY CLOUDS HANGING OVER JAKHAT DID NOTHING TO improve Aleida's already sour attitude toward the city when she and Mitul finally arrived. She'd spent a fair amount of time in Kavora's capital when she was younger, and her bleak memories of the place came back now with bitter clarity.

The last time she'd been here, she and Valkyra had been tracking down information about a mysterious man who couldn't die—a man whose immortality might save Tyrus from the fatal illness he'd recently been diagnosed with. They'd stayed here for the better half of a year before they were able to get a lead on his next suspected location, and the search had been excruciatingly tedious.

Before that, she and Tyrus had been in Jakhat together, only twelve and nine years old. They'd traveled to the city with a larger group of Visan refugees hoping to find work and a new start. Not the most ideal place to be, considering it was from this very city that Empress Dashiva and her advisors had sent their invading armies. But a lack of options meant the displaced Visans couldn't afford to be particular, and Jakhat's promise of decent pay and shelter was a boon many couldn't refuse.

As it turned out, Kavoran law prohibited child labor for anyone under fourteen, and Aleida and Tyrus wound up cold and hungry on the streets before too long. They scraped by at the brink of starvation for almost a year before they were caught stealing apples from a trader's cart. Rather than handing the two of them over to the city guards, the trader took them back to his employer in Chatanda with the idea that they ought to work off their crime. That employer was Hasan, who instead sheltered and cared for them as if they were his own children. A fortunate change in circumstances, to be sure, but Aleida still remembered well those cold, tear-filled nights huddled together under shop awnings, praying that Artex would show them mercy.

Both times in this city, she had been desperate, and as the familiar sights and sounds began to surround her, so too did that desperation, as strong and stifling as if it had never left. The only difference now was that it was accompanied by the aching abyss of her grief. Both times, she'd failed Tyrus, and now he was gone forever.

As for Artex, she was no longer sure he or any other god had ever been there to hear her prayers at all.

She kept close to Mitul as they walked, weaving their way through the lively commotion of the winding streets. The city was a sprawling spider's web, the roads like so many threads connecting each other and leading in toward the center, where the imperial palace sat on a green hilltop. Bulbous domes capped its three distinctive towers. The two smaller ones rose up on either side of a larger tower in the center, the top of which boasted a few additional decorative curvatures before tapering to a point. The entire structure was a pristine white with gold accents. It was said that an entire team of Tarja labored daily to keep it looking polished and new, and the inside was more luxurious still.

Aleida had always thought the palace looked out of place, sitting up there on the hill in stark white when the city below was full of color. Kavorans everywhere tended to dress in bright colors and patterns, but in Jakhat, that was especially true. Merchants and traders hawked their wares from garish carts and stalls in a competition to see who could best attract the attention of passersby. Even the buildings were colorful, with doors painted in bold hues and vibrant murals adorning the exterior walls. It was all a little too much for Aleida's taste, and the city held too many bad memories for her to ever grow fond of it, but she could appreciate the locals' love for color and art.

As they walked, Mitul scanned their surroundings like he was searching for something. Amar, perhaps, though it seemed unlikely they'd simply run into him and Valkyra out here. He glanced back at Aleida occasionally to make sure she was keeping up. She was, though it was difficult. The man seemed to have a sixth sense for navigating the tangled streets, and she nearly lost him in the crowd a few times. "Can we slow down?" she finally asked. "Where are we going, anyway?"

He stopped and turned around, blinking as if he were coming out of a daze. "I'm not entirely sure. I mean, I know where we are, but…I have no idea where we should go."

She frowned. The plan was to find Amar, of course, but they hadn't ever talked about *how* they would go about that once they reached Jakhat. The city was huge, and with only the vaguest idea of what Valkyra might be plotting, Aleida didn't know where to start looking.

Her stomach rumbled loudly, and she became acutely aware of a warm, spicy scent wafting from a building behind Mitul. "How about something to eat, for starters? We haven't had anything since this morning." It was well past noon now, and with the excitement of reaching Jakhat wearing off, hunger was hitting her full force.

Mitul glanced back at the building she pointed to. They made their way inside, found an empty seat, and ordered two bowls of the stew being served that day. It arrived minutes later, piping hot and with a rich, meaty smell that made Aleida's mouth water. She dug in immediately and burned the roof of her mouth, but didn't care enough to stop and wait for it to cool.

"Any good?" Mitul asked, raising an eyebrow at her. He was still stirring his with a spoon and fanning the steam away with his other hand.

She nodded vigorously, unable to speak through another mouthful.

The edges of his mustache lifted with his smile. "Good." They ate quietly for a few minutes before he broached the subject of their current predicament. "So, we're here in Jakhat, hopefully the same place Amar and Valkyra are. What's next?"

She washed down her food with a drink of water. "I don't know. What do *you* want to do?"

"Well, you thought she might try to use old contacts here to achieve whatever goal she's after. In that case, we should start by looking at the people she was close to, especially anyone wealthy, powerful, or well-connected."

"That's a good idea."

Mitul leaned forward and tilted his head to one side as if waiting for more.

"What?" she asked.

"Who was she close to? What connections did she have?"

Aleida snorted. "How am I supposed to know?"

He opened his mouth as if to argue, then shut it again and took a deep breath.

"Look, I'm sorry, all right?" she said. It came out more defensive than sincere, but what had he been expecting from her? "I wish I had more information to go on, but she lied about *everything*. I might know her better than you, but I still don't know much."

"Then we need more information," Mitul said. "About Nandini Kumar—who she was, who she was friends with, where she spent her time. People and places she might seek out now to set her plans in motion. So how do we get that information?"

He spoke the question softly, more to himself than to her, but she considered it anyway. He was right; they needed to know more than they currently did. And given Nandini's prior social standing, the rich and powerful among Jakhat's citizens would be the best sources of information. The problem was that neither of them were in a position where they might have access to those people.

Not yet, at least. But if they could insert themselves in places where they might rub shoulders with that crowd...well, that would be a start.

"How good a musician are you really?" she asked.

He looked slightly offended at the question. "You've heard me play."

She shrugged. "You sound fine to me, but I don't know enough to judge."

He finished the last of his stew and leaned back in his chair. "I don't like to boast, but I'm good. Very good. I might have made a name for myself here if things had gone differently."

"Did you ever play at any parties or gatherings? You know, the kind rich people have."

"Many times. Why do you ask?"

"That might be a way for us to get the information we need, if you can build enough of a reputation for yourself. If you're invited to play at those events, you can get closer to the people who run this city. Nandini Kumar must have known some of them. At the very least, they'll know if anything big happens, and maybe that will help us." If Valkyra was trying to reclaim her power or take revenge on those who'd wronged her, she was bound to stir up big, important happenings at some point.

Mitul mulled over the idea for a few seconds. "I suppose that could work."

Aleida crossed her arms. "What about it *doesn't* work? Do you have a better idea?"

"No, it's a fine plan. I'm just impatient. Worried about Amar. He's lost, and he doesn't know who he is. This is exactly what I've always tried to prevent." He let out a low, humorless chuckle. "I don't know what I expected. That we'd come here and find him and rescue him right away? Even if we already knew where he was, we'd have to wait and collect more information, form a better plan. Preferably one that involves Kes and Saya once they get back."

So many pieces still left to put together, and they'd barely begun. Aleida could understand his impatience, the way every passing day probably felt like a lifetime to him as long as Amar's condition remained uncertain. It had been the same for her with Tyrus.

"For what it's worth," she said, "I don't think he's in any danger of physical harm with Valkyra. She's more likely to try and manipulate him with lies and false kindness than brute force. It's what she did to me."

"Yes, but look how Jameson ended up."

Aleida winced at the memory of the wizard's mangled corpse. "That was different. She was out of options when she forced their Bond, and he was a Tarja already. None of that applies to Amar. I'm sure he's fine."

Mitul nodded, slow and uncertain. "I hate to think of what she might make him do, and how he'll feel about it once he remembers. *If* we manage to bring his memories back at all, that is."

"We will." The foreign softness in her own voice was enough to shock her back to her senses. Damn it, what was she doing? Mitul had been kind enough during their time together, but the last thing she needed was to start feeling sorry for him or letting herself get attached. He was a means to an end, nothing more. All she needed was for him to do his job so she could take her revenge and deliver the punishment Valkyra deserved.

She cleared her throat and scowled at him across the table. "Pull yourself together. Sitting here worrying isn't going to help anything."

"You're right." He rolled his shoulders back and sat a little taller in his chair. "What about you, then? Are you planning to take up an instrument too, or do you have some hidden musical talent I don't know about?"

She shook her head. "I'll try to get myself hired by someone wealthy or noble. Lots of them have Visan servants. I'd fit right in."

"That's hard work, and the pay isn't much. Are you sure?"

"I'll be in a perfect position to hear whatever they're gossiping about," she said. "And if you keep teaching me how to read, I might even be able to do a little snooping. The letters and records they keep could hold valuable information."

"Oh, of course." Mitul laughed a little. "What harm could possibly come from violating your employer's privacy?"

"I won't get caught."

He sobered instantly. "Oh. You were being serious."

She rolled her eyes. "Once again, I'm open to any better suggestions you might have."

He sighed and ran a hand over the top of his head. "And once again, I have none, which is starting to make me feel rather old and useless, to be honest."

"Then get up." She slid her empty bowl aside and rose from her chair. "We've got a lot to do, and the sooner we get started, the better."

And so that was exactly what they did. Before they left, Mitul rented a room at the inn, which was called the Serene Star. He offered to get one for Aleida, too, but she only allowed him to pay for a couple of nights, hoping she'd have a job by then and that whoever hired her would have some kind of servants' quarters or other accommodations.

That way, she could stay nearby and befriend the other servants in the household, who might be useful sources of information themselves.

After that, they made their way deeper into the city to set their plan in motion. Mitul used the last of his coin to buy new clothes for them both. He needed to make himself more presentable to the patrons he was trying to attract, and all of Aleida's attire was more than a little worse for the wear. The clothes he bought her were nicer than any she'd had for a long time, and despite her misgivings about anyone viewing her as a charity case, she took them gratefully.

Once they'd both changed, they found a street corner in an affluent district with heavy foot traffic, and Mitul began to play. Aleida was impressed by how quickly the coins started to fill his pockets, even if it was only a few jitaara at a time. While he played, she kept an eye out for passing servants running errands for their employers. A few Visans were among them, and each time she spotted one, she approached and asked about potential opportunities for work. By the time the sun set, Mitul had enough coin to pay for another two week's stay at the inn, and Aleida had four promising leads for a job.

It took another two days before she found someone willing to hire her, but the position was as good as she could have hoped for. She'd be working in the kitchens for a prestigious merchant—hard, dreary work, but since the man had dealings all over the city and beyond, there would be many comings and goings from other traders, shopkeepers, and nobles looking for new business ventures. Surely someone would eventually have information that could lead them to Amar and Valkyra. At the very least, Aleida would learn of various ties between powerful people in the city. She could pass that knowledge on to Mitul, and in time, he'd be able to ingratiate himself to those connected to Nandini Kumar.

The slow tedium of the process ahead made Aleida want to scream. She might have been comforted if she had some guarantee that it would work, but there was none. Before, she might have prayed for divine assistance and clung to her faith, believing—*knowing*—that Artex had prepared a way for her. But that was before Artex had failed her. Before she realized Artex may not even be real.

All she could count on now was herself.

SAVIR

SAVIR HAD NO INTENTION OF COMMENTING ON VALKYRA'S clandestine meeting with a stranger in a dark alley, but he was curious to see how long she waited to divulge the news of his upcoming audience at the palace.

As it turned out, she waited until almost the last minute. "My contact on the royal council has arranged a meeting with the king and queen," she said to him one afternoon. "He'll take us to the palace tomorrow morning."

He raised an eyebrow. If she knew someone on the royal council, she had powerful connections indeed. "Who is he?"

"Magistrate Ashaya."

Savir mentally ran through the names and titles he'd spent the last week memorizing. Dev Ashaya had recently been appointed the Advisor of Law on the Valmandi royal council, but prior to that, he'd served Empress Dashiva in Jakhat. He'd been removed from the position three years ago due to a personal connection with Nandini Kumar, a powerful Tarja who was imprisoned and eventually executed for conspiring against the empress.

"He knew your mother well," Valkyra added, "He always held a deep respect for her, which means he's likely to stay loyal to you. He has what we need to prove your identity, and he can attest to the fact that your mother sent you away to safety on the night assassins came."

"You arranged all of this without telling me?"

She ruffled her wings and brought her tail forward to curl demurely over her claws. "You've had more important things to worry about. It wasn't anything worth troubling you over, so I made the arrangements myself. Besides, it was always our plan to seek his help once we arrived here."

Heat flared through Savir's chest and bloomed across his face. "I don't remember that," he growled. "I don't remember any of the plans we made before. All I know is you've been sneaking out in the middle of the night, not bothering to tell me what's happening."

Valkyra lifted her chin, her silver eyes filled with calm resolve. "Yes, I have. Because you are the *prince*, Savir, and not just any prince. *The* prince—the one who's been missing for seventeen years. A legend out of song come to life. Do you have any idea what that means to the people in this city? If they knew you were here, you would not have a moment's peace, and we would lose all control of the way your return unfolds." She stood up, tail lashing behind her like a cat's. "Bhajan and Indira *must* be the first to find out, not only because it's what's fair and right, but because you need their acceptance and their protection if this is going to work. So yes, I have been *sneaky*. Perhaps I should have kept you more informed, but again, I thought you had enough to worry about already."

Savir crossed the room to the window and stared out, his entire body thrumming with restless energy. "You should have told me," he said, but the words felt empty. That wasn't the problem—not really. Beneath his ire was something smaller but no less consequential, squeezed up tight against his ribs like a frightened animal. "It's too soon. I'm not ready."

Valkyra fluttered over and landed gently on his shoulder. Her weight there was familiar in a way that was becoming more and more a comfort to him. "I'm not sure anyone truly *can* be ready to do what you're about to. But you're ready enough, and that's all we need. You'll figure the rest out along the way."

He snorted. "You have no way of knowing that."

"Yes, I do," she said with serene confidence. "Because I know *you*, Savir, and because I'll be right there with you every step of the way."

"Even when I mess up and make an ass of myself?"

She swished her tail across his shoulder. "Especially then."

At her reassurance, some of the tension within him melted away. He still had his doubts, but Valkyra was so certain, so steady, and for now, that was enough. He might not be able to trust his own judgment, but he could trust hers, at least in this.

"I have something for you," she said, gliding from his shoulder to a bag hanging on a nearby chair. She crawled inside and rummaged around, emerging a few seconds later with a gold chain in her claws. Savir stretched out his hand, and she dropped it into his palm.

Hanging from the chain was a round medallion, intertwined leaves engraved into both sides. A tiny ruby gleamed in the center. He held it up, recalling the mention of a medallion when he'd eavesdropped on her conversation with Magistrate Ashaya. But what was its significance?

"It belonged to your mother," Valkyra said in response to his questioning look. "She gave it to me the night she sent you away with me."

Savir's studied the necklace in the sunlight. The medallion and the journals—two items that were somehow important to proving his identity.

All that's left is to present the boy to the king and queen.

"Is this how you plan to prove I'm really Prince Savir?" If so, it didn't seem like enough.

"We have stronger evidence, but this certainly helps. Your mother once told me it was a birthday gift from her own mother. Which means the queen will recognize it, and that lends another layer of legitimacy to your claim." She caught his eye and inclined her head toward the table. "Now then, are you ready to continue your lessons, Your Highness?"

He wasn't, but he needed to, especially considering his impending visit to the palace. With a resigned sigh, he fastened the chain around his neck and tucked the medallion under his shirt. "I guess I am."

They made their way to Magistrate Ashaya's estate early the next morning, before most of the city's residents had begun their daily business. Savir was dressed in his finest attire, a surprisingly comfortable outfit made of soft, black silk with gold leaves embroidered at the collar. A red sash draped over his left shoulder, and around his neck hung the gold medallion that had once belonged to his mother. The whole ensemble remained concealed beneath a drab gray cloak, and no one gave him so much as a second look as he passed.

Ashaya lived in the middle of the city, and on the way there, they passed by the temple the king and queen had renamed for Princess Priyani. A large mural of her adorned the wall facing the nearby palace, and Savir couldn't help but stare at it as he walked by.

"She was very beautiful, your mother," Valkyra said softly. "You don't look much like her, but you do have her eyes."

It was almost impossible to see that in the painting, given how the artist had depicted her with her eyes closed, but Savir liked the idea of it.

When they reached the magistrate's home, a man was waiting for them outside the door. "That's him," Valkyra whispered as they approached. "Dev Ashaya, honorable magistrate of Valmandi and the royal council's Advisor of Law."

Ashaya was taller than most men, including Savir, but otherwise unremarkable. His face was round and plain, his clothes simple. On the whole, he looked almost out of place standing there in front of the ornate double doors of his home, surrounded by a lush garden that must have required the attention of a whole team of servants.

"Your Highness," he said in a voice Savir immediately recognized from his late-night conversation with Valkyra. "It is the honor of my lifetime to finally meet you. Your mother was so dear to me, and I have long hoped the rumors of your survival were true, but to see you here now—" He blinked rapidly as if warding off tears. "Words cannot express how happy it makes me."

Savir tried not to show his annoyance at the man's adulation. Perhaps it was to be expected, though he certainly hoped he wouldn't always be met with such over-the-top sentiment. "It's an honor to meet you, too, Magistrate." When he said nothing more, Valkyra pressed her claws into his shoulder a little, jogging his memory. "And, of course, I'm very thankful for all you've done."

"Your gratitude is appreciated but quite unnecessary, Your Highness. It's my pleasure, truly." The man took half a step forward and gestured to the street at the edge of his property. "Shall we head for the palace? They'll be expecting us soon."

Together they set off. It wasn't far, and Savir took a few deep breaths to calm his nerves as they approached. Valkyra nuzzled her cheek against his. "You'll do great," she whispered reassuringly. "I have every confidence in you."

He wasn't half as certain as she was, but he held his head high and tried to fake it anyway. The magistrate spoke to one of the guards posted at the main gate while another quickly searched them for weapons. He didn't disclose Savir's identity and said only that he was accompanying Ashaya to a formal audience with the king and queen. There was some grumbling about whether the pet dragon should be permitted entry, but the guards eventually gave in and allowed them all to pass. From there, Savir followed Ashaya down a wide stone walkway that cut across the grounds. Branching paths wound through a maze of well-groomed hedges and flowers of all different colors.

The palace itself was even larger than Savir had expected. Stone pillars carved with intricate designs stood to either side of an enormous doorway. Inside, a red carpet stretched down a hallway and up a wide staircase to the second floor. Tall arch windows sent sunlight spilling onto the polished tile floors, and sections of the wall were adorned with carvings like those on the pillars outside, depicting various animals and creatures from legend.

A painting stretched across the ceiling above, showing a blue sky and fluffy white clouds. Three figures clothed in billowing robes circled each other as if they were dancing, their hands outstretched but not touching. Savir recognized them instantly—another piece of knowledge his mind seemed to have retained though he couldn't specifically remember where it had originated. The figures were meant to represent mind, body, and spirit, the three elements of balance connected to all life and the world's creation. It was these same three elements that Tarja brought into harmony within themselves to channel their altma.

There should have been a fourth figure—one to represent life itself. Jhivan, it was called. But Kavoran myths and studies on magic's origins always left that out, instead focusing only on the other three elements.

Savir frowned as he considered this piece of knowledge his mind had dredged up. He was no scholar of magic or ancient myth, so where had he learned that?

"Come along, Your Highness," Valkyra whispered in his ear, and only then did he realize he'd slowed to a near standstill.

He hurried to catch up with Ashaya, who was now at the bottom of the stairs talking to a footman. The man gave Savir a dubious look and all but sneered at Valkyra perched on his shoulder. "May I take your cloak, sir?" he asked, more a strong suggestion than a question.

Savir removed the garment and passed it over. Upon seeing the finer clothes he wore beneath the cloak, the footman's demeanor shifted from disdain to curiosity. He glanced at Magistrate Ashaya, who gave a gracious smile, then straightened and motioned to the stairs. "Follow me, please."

Halfway up to the second floor was a wide landing. From there, the stairs split off and curved around to either side. The footman led them up, then to a set of double doors at the center of the hallway. A pair of guards in polished steel armor and red capes stood outside. With a nod from the footman, they opened the doors to a long, open room with upholstered chairs along the walls facing inward. At the far end stood a broad dais. Panels of fabric in red and gold draped down the wall and over the ceiling. The center of the dais held a single throne, wide enough for the two people on it to sit comfortably.

The walk from the door seemed to take an eternity, giving Savir plenty of time to study the faces of King Bhajan and Queen Indira. His grandparents. They were more ordinary looking than he'd expected. Their clothes were only slightly more elegant than his and surprisingly practical in fit and style. The queen wore a dainty gold tiara with small points all along its edge and a single round ruby at its center. The king's crown had larger, stronger points and a matching ruby. A short beard gave his jaw a strong, square look.

At the bottom of the dais and off to one side stood one of the tallest men Savir had ever seen. He appeared to be somewhere in his early fifties, his hair shaved away to leave only a graying beard, which was trimmed to a neat point at his collar. He wore the same uniform as the other guards they'd seen, but his position near the monarchs, along with the red cloak draped over one shoulder, seemed to indicate some elevated status. His eyes were two chips of obsidian set in a mask of stone, and they remained fixed on Savir from the moment he entered the room.

"Your Majesties," Magistrate Ashaya said, stopping near the foot of the dais to bow low. "Thank you both for granting me this audience. I know you're terribly busy, but as you'll soon understand, this couldn't wait."

The king stared past Ashaya to Savir. "I must admit your request intrigued me, Magistrate. And who else do we have the pleasure of meeting today?"

"Before we make any introductions, would you honor one more request? The information I need to share is for your ears alone. If you'd be so kind as to dismiss your staff and your guards, I would very much appreciate it."

Bhajan stiffened. "Our ears alone, *and* this stranger you've brought with you."

"He won't be a stranger for long. Please. I wouldn't ask if it weren't of the utmost importance."

The king and queen exchanged a look. She gave a slight shrug, and with that, Bhajan nodded to the half-dozen people lingering in the corners of the throne room. Most dispersed quickly and quietly, but the guard with the red cloak remained where he was.

"Tarik will stay," Bhajan said, glancing at the man. "Now tell us, what is the purpose of this meeting? And who is your new friend?"

Ashaya stood a little taller and swept one arm out to indicate Savir. "This," he said, "is your grandson."

At this, Tarik coughed into his hand, but stiffened when the magistrate cut him a glare. There were a few moments of tense silence, and Savir held his breath, half-expecting to be thrown out of the palace at any moment. Then Queen Indira gasped, reaching out to clutch her husband's sleeve. "Bhajan, look at him. He's the right age. He's wearing Priyani's medallion."

The king's eyes narrowed, which only made his stern expression more severe. "Come closer, boy."

"Wait," Tarik ordered, stepping forward before Savir could move. "I must insist on searching him for weapons before this conversation continues."

"Diligent as always," said Bhajan. "Go ahead."

Savir didn't point out that he'd already been searched at the main entrance; he doubted that would dissuade the guard of his precautions. The older man moved in, towering over him like a scowling statue. He patted down Savir's arms and torso first, then bent to check his legs and boots. "I'd prefer if you'd left the dragon outside," he murmured, his voice low and gravelly.

"I can take the dragon, sir," Ashaya chimed in. He held out an arm, and Valkyra immediately hopped from Savir's shoulder onto it. "She's really quite well-behaved, but I think we can all appreciate your vigilance."

Tarik rose, his expression still cold and intimidating, as it was no doubt intended to be. He backed away, and Bhajan motioned for Savir to approach.

Savir walked forward until his toes pressed against the first step of the dais. He bowed in the manner Valkyra had shown him during their lessons. "It's wonderful to meet you both. I've waited a long time for this day."

Bhajan said nothing, but Indira's eyes glimmered with something between hope and fear. Savir straightened, waiting patiently for them to take in the news and process what they were seeing. At last, the king spoke to Ashaya. "We've had more than a few frauds declaring themselves our daughter's son over the years. None were ever vouched for by someone as trustworthy as you've proven yourself to be, but even the most loyal men can be deceived by these pretenders."

"Of course, Your Majesty," Ashaya replied. "You are wise to be cautious. But as you said, I've proven myself trustworthy. Please trust me now. Hear the boy's story, then hear mine. I can prove he is who he claims to be."

Bhajan leaned forward. "All right, then. Let's hear it."

Savir cleared his throat and began his tale. It was the same one Valkyra had told him—the one he would have grown up hearing but had since forgotten, along with the rest of his memories. He told of how his mother had discovered the plot to end her son's life, how she'd entrusted her maidservant to take him away to safety. He spoke of how that maidservant had raised him as her own, preparing him to take back his throne when he came of age. Finally, he told them of their journey to Valmandi, their assailant, and Valkyra's death.

He didn't mention the fact that she was now a Tarja Bonded to him, or that he'd lost his memories during the attack. Both details complicated his credibility, as she'd put it. Savir was inclined to agree, though the omission of such significant facts made him squirm a little.

"After that," he said, "I came here and sought out Magistrate Ashaya. Our original plan was always to meet with him before coming to see you."

Ashaya stepped forward and took over. "Of course, when the boy showed up, I had my doubts. But then I heard his story, and I began to piece together some of the details from my own memory of that time. For example, the way the funerals were managed."

"What of it?" the king asked.

"Forgive me, but I always thought it strange that Savir's body remained in Jhakat to be cremated, as is their way, yet the princess' body was returned to you, alone."

Bhajan stiffened, and Indira's face contorted as if the memory of that day was still painfully fresh. "They should not have been separated like that," he said. "But I can't fault the empress for wanting her nephew to receive the same funeral rites as all his ancestors."

"It was gracious of you to be so understanding," Ashaya said. "But I suspect Dashiva had other reasons to insist on cremation."

A muscle in Bhajan's jaw tightened. "What are you suggesting?"

"To be perfectly candid, Your Majesties, the empress is and always has been an ambitious woman. It's no secret she was dissatisfied when her brother finally produced an heir, thus annulling her right to inherit the throne. There have even been speculations that she may have been behind the assassinations of Priyani and Savir."

"There have been," Bhajan said evenly. "Though to speak such things aloud would be considered treasonous in some circles."

"Surely not in *this* circle. Forgive me, but I've heard you voice similar concerns yourself...under the right conditions."

Bhajan's lips stretched in a tight smile. "Remind me never to drink with you again, Magistrate."

Ashaya continued with the point he was making. "Whether or not she orchestrated Prince Savir's death, she did benefit from it. I'm not a man prone to believing in conspiracy theories, but I do have to wonder if her insistence on private cremation was meant to avoid any close inspection of the boy's body."

"You're suggesting it was some other child's body."

"It's more than a suggestion. It's a hypothesis based on evidence and observation." He gestured to Savir. "All of which implies that this young man may indeed be your grandson."

Bhajan's face remained unreadable, but he shifted a little closer to the queen. She clasped his hand tight and sat up a little taller on the throne. "You said you had proof?" Her voice sounded shaky, and her gaze continued to flit back to Savir. The cautious longing in her eyes was pitiable, and he had the sudden and inexplicable urge to comfort her. Instead, he stayed where he was and focused on Ashaya. He was curious to see this evidence as well. It wasn't something he and Valkyra had ever discussed.

"I have a letter," the magistrate said, digging into the pouch on his belt. When he pulled his hand free, he was clutching a small book. "And this—your daughter's journal."

Indira raised her free hand to her mouth, but not before Savir caught sight of her chin quivering.

"Where did you get that?" Bhajan asked, rising from his throne and beckoning Ashaya forward.

"It was stored away in Jakhat along with the rest of her things. I went to great pains to retrieve it after her death. It was always my intention to give it to you someday, but..." He hesitated, arm halfway outstretched to pass the book to Bhajan. "Well, I wasn't sure if it would be a welcome gift or only a painful reminder."

"All reminders are painful," Bhajan said dryly, taking the book. "We want to remember anyway."

"My humblest apologies, then. If I made an error in judgment, it was only because I wanted to avoid hurting you further." He pointed to a folded sheet of paper jutting out from the edge of the journal. "That's the letter I received seventeen years ago, written by the maidservant who saved your grandson. It was passed along in secret, and neither I nor the person who gave it to me knew how to send a response back to her. If you open the book to that page, you'll also find the relevant entry from your daughter's journal."

Bhajan remained standing and opened the book. He flipped past the letter to study the passage Ashaya had indicated.

Indira rose and went to his side. "What does it say?"

"It's from the week after Savir was born," Bhajan murmured.

"'He's perfect,'" Indira said quietly, and it took Savir a moment to realize she was reading the journal aloud. "'I still can't believe he's mine. I keep staring at him, trying to memorize him in this moment. His hair is thick and black like mine, and sometimes he scrunches up his little forehead in a way that makes him look exactly like my father. His fingers are so delicate, and he has a little birthmark forming on the back of his left hand, right between his finger and thumb. One day, too soon, those hands will be bigger and stronger than my own. Maybe then, I'll be able to look at that mark and remember this moment, when he was a tiny babe asleep in my arms. I don't ever want to forget this.'"

Indira's voice was a half-whispered quaver by the time she reached the end of the passage. She and Bhajan both looked at Savir with the same question burning in their eyes.

He didn't wait to be asked or invited. He simply walked up the steps of the dais and held out his left hand, and all three of them stared down at the mark his mother had described. It was small, not even as big as a single jitaara coin. Savir had paid it no mind before now and had barely even registered its existence. But there it was, another piece of evidence that he was who he professed to be, even if he couldn't remember most of his life before now.

And yet, it was only a birthmark, one any number of young men in Kavora might have had. So how significant was it, really, as proof of his identity? When he glanced at Tarik, standing off to one side but watching intently, Savir saw those same misgivings reflected in the guard's shrewd eyes.

He blocked out his remaining doubts before they could fully seep back in. Maybe he'd never have more solid proof than this. It had to be enough, especially combined with everything Valkyra had told him, Ashaya's backing of her story, and the speculations they'd discussed regarding the young Prince Savir's death—or rather, his disappearance. The pieces all fit.

Didn't they?

The king was staring at him, and Savir met his gaze, doing his best to ignore the sound of his own thundering heartbeat. For a few breathless moments, he was terrified Bhajan was going to accuse them all of lying and have them arrested to face execution.

Instead, the man stepped forward and brought his arms up to wrap tight around Savir's shoulders. Indira joined their embrace, choking out a sob as Bhajan spoke, his voice low and rough with emotion.

"Welcome home, Savir."

KESARI

KESARI STOOD ALONGSIDE SAYA'S BROTHERS TO WATCH THE ceremony that would mark the completion of the young warrior's haseph. Zefar lingered at the edge of the gathered crowd, maintaining a respectful distance and seemingly unphased by the dark glances and disgruntled mutterings occasionally cast his way. The masahi and the rest of the council faced them all, squinting against the brilliant sunrise. The only person missing now was Saya.

She came from the east a few minutes later, holding a shallow bowl of water in both hands. The crowd parted down the center to let her through. Her red haseph markings were bright and unmarred against her deep bronze skin, and a single braid hung down the center of her back. She flashed Kesari and Lucian a quick smile as she passed.

She approached her mother first, and Masahi Seda spoke loud enough for all to hear. "Today is a joyful day. At long last, my eldest child has returned from her journey with an offering worthy of our people. Her haseph is complete." The crowd responded with loud cheers, and Kesari lost most of the masahi's next words through the noise. Shouts of jubilation turned to confused murmuring, and even Saya's brothers began to exchange concerned looks.

"What's happening?" she asked Halos, who stood next to her.

"She's not going to tell us what Saya's offering was," he replied in

Kavoran. "That's unheard of."

Hazim, towering over her, leaned down to say, "*You* know what it is though, don't you?"

She swallowed, struggling to produce an appropriate response.

"It wasn't our decision," Lucian said. "We're only respecting your leaders by keeping that knowledge to ourselves."

Hazim let out a dissatisfied grunt but straightened and returned his attention to Saya and the council. She had shifted to one side so that she was now standing in front of the elderly ancestral guide, who dipped a cloth into Saya's bowl of water and used it to wash away the half-circle painted around her eye. "We praise the sun for shining on your path and protecting you from danger."

Saya sidestepped to stand before the next woman. With delicate fingers, the young healer wiped away the line that ran down the center of her chin. "We acknowledge the path that led you to a worthy offering and brought you safely home."

Finally, the warrior returned to her mother, who removed the last markings below her right eye. "We thank you, Saya hàs Seda, for bringing an offering worthy of our people, and we invite you to be one with us for all the rest of your days."

Saya raised the bowl of water to her head and poured it over herself. The rest of the Sularans cheered, none louder than Saya's seven brothers. Music broke out somewhere behind Kesari, drumbeats so loud they seemed to reverberate through her very core. A sudden and fierce surge of pride rippled through her as she watched her friend, whose smile seemed more radiant than the sun itself.

It wasn't long before the Sularans broke into song and dance, and Kesari was swept forward by a wave of boys as they rushed their sister, asking questions and congratulating her excitedly. Saya responded to them cheerfully enough, but her attention seemed split as she searched the crowd. Her brow creased a little when she didn't find who she was looking for.

"He was here," Lucian said. "I'm not sure where he went, but he saw you."

Some of the worry left her eyes, but her expression wasn't quite as exuberant as before.

The celebrations continued for the rest of the morning. There was singing and dancing and storytelling, and the mouth-watering aromas of a feast began to fill the settlement. Everyone wanted to speak to Saya, and Kesari was content to sit back and watch her bask in the attention. She and Lucian played games with some of Saya's brothers and the other children, and she even let them talk her into using her magic for a few simple tricks, which delighted them.

Saya found them again once the feast began. They sat at the edge of the oasis' central feature, a giant pit plunging down to a large pool fed by an underground river. While they ate, they watched some of the children dive fearlessly into the water to swim.

"Your people certainly know how to throw a party," Lucian said.

"Perhaps a little too well," the young woman replied with a laugh. "I'm already exhausted, and this will probably last all day."

Kesari nudged her in the shoulder. "Congratulations again."

"Thank you."

An idea that had been building in her mind all morning finally took shape, and she blurted it out before she could stop herself. "You should stay if you want to. I know we planned to continue and help Amar together, but you have a family here, and so many other people who care about you. They need you." For a split second, her own family's faces flashed through her mind. "After all the time you've been gone, do you really want to leave them again?"

Saya shrugged. "Amar's something like family, too, and right now, he needs me more. Needs *us*." She took a long drink of water, then added, "Besides, someone should make Valkyra pay for murdering poor Jameson, not to mention all the other damage she's caused."

"I think Aleida might have first claim to that honor," Lucian said.

"Aleida's half the reason we're in this mess to begin with."

"I wonder how she and Mitul are doing," Kesari mused.

Saya grunted. "I don't envy him. The three of us got the better deal when it comes to traveling companions, but if anyone can put up with that girl's wretched attitude, it's him. Skies bless him, the man has more patience than—"

She stopped mid-sentence as a series of shouts and disgruntled voices drifted their way, and they all looked to see what the commotion was about. A few Sularans—Hazim among them—were dragging another person into the center of the settlement. Numerous flailing limbs and general thrashing made it difficult to see who the person was, but when they forced him onto his knees in front of Masahi Seda, his face became clear.

"Zefar," Saya hissed. She was up and running to him in an instant. Kesari followed, and they pushed their way through the gathering onlookers until they stood beside the masahi, looking down at Zefar.

The scarred mercenary glared up defiantly but stayed on his knees, which may have had something to do with the two spears poised directly under his jaw. The hands of those who'd dragged him forward still pressed down on his shoulders and neck.

Hazim stepped forward, holding aloft a small book—the very same one Saya had brought from Shavhalla. "We caught him in my mother's tent, trying to steal this."

Murmured questions and whispers of disapproval rippled all around them as the masahi took the book and tucked it into a sash at her waist. Zefar's eyes flicked to Saya, and for a moment, he looked almost apologetic. Then the glare returned. "That offering is meant for the entire tribe," he said to Seda. "You have no right to keep it to yourself. We all deserve to know what it is and why you won't share it."

She raised her chin and stared down her nose at him, lips tightening in a sneer. "*You* are not a part of this tribe. You deserve nothing from me or from anyone here."

Zefar wrenched an arm free, and the tip of a spear cut through the skin at his neck. A thin trail of blood began to trickle down as he pointed to Saya. "She gave up two years of her life to bring back a worthy offering. Not just anything—something that could truly make a difference for our people. Now you want to hide it away, discard all the sacrifices she made to bring it here."

"It doesn't matter, Zefar," Saya hissed.

If he heard her, he gave no acknowledgement. "I may not be a part of this tribe, but there are people I care about who are. I'm not going to stand by while you make decisions alone that could impact all of us."

"The council decided," said the masahi. "Not I alone. That's the purpose of having a council, is it not? To make decisions for the good of the tribe."

"*With* the input of the tribe. At least, that's how it's supposed to be. Otherwise, we're no better than the Kavorans with their monarchs."

There were more murmurings through the crowd, building to a tension so heavy it was almost suffocating. Kesari stood rigid beside Saya, who watched her mother and her uncle intently.

"He's right," someone called out, and all heads snapped to look at who the speaker was. It was a woman, older than Saya but not by much. She held a baby on one hip while a toddler clasped her other hand. "How can the council say they speak for the people if they don't even know what the people want? And how can we decide what we want if we don't have all the information?"

Before, no one had seemed willing to align themselves with Zefar, perhaps because of his outcast status. But with these words from one of their own, there were a few more vocalizations of agreement. Saya exchanged a nervous glance with Kesari and Lucian, then turned back to her uncle. His sly grin broadened, and he straightened a little, a challenge burning in his golden eyes.

"The council has already made its decision," the masahi said. "It was not an easy one, but we all agreed it was the right one. What Saya brought back could be extremely dangerous in the wrong hands, and we cannot risk that. If we decide at some later time to use it, then of course, we'll welcome the tribe's input. But until the time is right, we will hold it for safekeeping."

"Who are you to decide when the time is right?" Zefar shouted.

"I will say no more about it!" She stepped forward until she loomed over him. "Time and time again, you have refused to accept the rules and customs of our people. Despite your status as an outcast, we have allowed you to continue living among us as long as you kept your distance and stayed out of our affairs. Clearly, you are no longer willing to do that. You are banished, Zefar hàs Yaratha. If I ever see your face within the borders of our lands again, I'll kill you myself." She nodded to Hazim and a few other men. "Get him out of my sight."

They grabbed him by the arms and hauled him to his feet. As soon as he was standing, he spat on the ground in front of Masahi Seda.

Hazim immediately elbowed him in the gut.

Saya took a few steps forward, then seemed to think better of it and stopped. Her hands balled into fists as she watched them escort Zefar away, but he did not look back at her or anyone else. She stayed like that even after he was out of sight.

"What does it mean, that he was banished?" Kesari asked quietly. "He was already an outcast."

Saya's fists were still clenched, and her words came out low and tense. "Yes, but he was still permitted to live here in the desert and have some minimal contact with members of the tribe. To trade or engage in other necessary interactions. Now he can't even do that. He'll have to leave the desert, and he'll have a target on his head if he ever comes back. Anyone caught associating with him could also face consequences."

Kesari didn't like the sound of that. Saya had made it very clear that she had no intentions of severing ties with her uncle once her haseph was finished, but surely, this would change things. Even if she stuck to her previous resolution, communication between them would be far more difficult…and potentially dangerous. And of course, gone were the hopes she'd expressed that Zefar might be able to build some relationship with her brothers—his nephews.

Unable to change any of this and unsure of what to say that might help, Kesari linked her arm through Saya's and leaned against her in a gesture she hoped was comforting.

The rest of the crowd began to disperse. Masahi Seda came to her daughter's side and whispered something in her ear. Saya's body relaxed a little, but when she looked at Kesari a few moments later, her eyes were full of rage and tears.

Saya and Lucian woke Kesari long before sunrise the next morning, so early she wondered if it was still the night before. "Is something wrong?" she mumbled.

"No, but we should leave," Saya replied. "I want to put some distance behind us before the day gets too hot."

It was the middle of autumn now, but as she'd experienced during the journey here, the desert heat was still merciless this time of year. She set about gathering her belongings and stuffing them into her bag. Saya had already packed and stood fidgeting in the doorway, eager to leave. She went to check on the horses, and Kesari quickened her pace.

"What's wrong with her?" she whispered to Lucian.

His mouth flickered through the flames in a jagged grimace. "I'm not sure. She and her mother had some more words last night. I don't think it went well."

"You didn't eavesdrop on their conversation?"

"I do have *some* manners, you know."

She snorted and returned his playful smirk.

Saya returned a few seconds later, again lingering near the door. "Are you ready?"

Kesari nodded and hoisted her pack over her shoulders. They exited the tent and found Saya's family there waiting to send them off. A couple of the boys were yawning and rubbing at their eyes, and the two youngest—the twins—dozed off while being held, one in his mother's arms and the other in Hazim's.

One by one, Saya bid them farewell. It was a quicker affair than the last time Kesari had watched them part ways, hurried along by Saya's impatience to get moving. Kesari was still trying to thank the masahi for her hospitality when Saya climbed onto her horse and motioned for her to do the same. Then they were off, trotting across the sand and into the desert until Hayathu disappeared from view behind them.

When they slowed to a walk, Lucian voiced the same question Kesari had been wondering. "Any particular reason you were in such a hurry to leave?"

The scowl Saya had been wearing all morning deepened. "I didn't want to be there anymore."

"Clearly. But why?"

"Because of the way she banished Zefar. He raised a legitimate concern, and for that, he was sent away."

"He made a scene and tried to steal from the council. I thought that's what he was banished for."

She shook her head. "The entire tribe's in turmoil over my haseph. I don't even know which side is right. All I know is that *I* caused the conflict. I got Zefar banished, and I brought back an offering that's so dangerous our leaders don't know what to do with it." She let out a snarl of frustration. "And now I'm running away from the problem like a coward."

Kesari frowned. Saya was anything but a coward. "You always planned to leave again so you could help Amar. This isn't running away. And trust me, I would know the difference." The memory of Deveaural's burning clocktower flashed through her mind, but she didn't let it take hold long enough to hurt her.

Saya immediately seemed to realize what she was referring to, and her eyes went wide. "Oh Kes, I'm sorry. I didn't mean to imply that *you*—"

"I know. It's all right. Besides, I think sometimes we *need* to run away, to protect ourselves." That was all she'd been trying to do, wasn't it? Maybe that made her a coward, but it made her a survivor, too. "It doesn't have to be forever," she added.

"No, I guess it doesn't."

Kesari smiled at her friend, then set her sights on the horizon and the home that lay beyond it.

SAVIR

SAVIR AWOKE IN A LARGE ROOM WITH EXTRAVAGANT FURNISHINGS, including the most comfortable bed he'd ever had the pleasure of sleeping in, at least as far as he could remember. It took a few moments to remember where he was—in the palace—and the knowledge of what the day might bring left him jittery and unable to fall back asleep, despite the early hour.

An entourage of servants began to come and go not long after, offering him a hot bath and help getting dressed and something to drink and something to eat and something for his pet dragon and all manner of other things he was used to taking care of on his own. He let them draw a bath but then dismissed them as politely as he could, preferring to wash and dress on his own. Once finished, he sat on his bed, wondering what on earth he was supposed to do with himself now, but this question was mercifully answered by the arrival of yet another servant summoning him to breakfast. With the king and queen. His grandparents.

It still felt strange to think of them like that.

The meal was a rather awkward affair which mostly involved them peppering Savir with questions about his upbringing. Since he couldn't actually remember that period of his life, he tried to keep his answers vague. Fortunately, Bhajan and Indira seemed almost as afraid of him as he was of them—or at least afraid of scaring him off—so they didn't pry too much. By the time the meal was over, he was anxious to escape, but he waited politely as they continued to talk with him.

"We're so grateful you're back," Indira said, giving him a watery smile across the table. She'd already teared up twice that morning telling stories about his mother, and the fondness in her eyes now made him want to hide under a rock. "I know this must be very strange and overwhelming for you, but I hope you'll be comfortable here. It's a wonderful opportunity for all of us. We get to be a family again."

Bhajan nodded in agreement. "You must understand, Savir, after all that's happened, our first concern now is for your safety. There are guards all throughout the palace, of course, but I've asked Tarik to personally take charge of your security."

The old guard had been standing near the door but approached upon being summoned by the king. His expression remained as hard and cold as it had been the day before. "It will be my honor to serve you."

"I'm afraid I didn't properly introduce you yesterday, given all the excitement," Bhajan said. "But Tarik Apti is one of the most honorable men I've ever known and has been a loyal guardian to me and your grandmother for many years. Decades, even, but don't let his age fool you. He could best a dozen younger men in a fight without breaking a sweat."

Tarik did not refute the compliment, and Savir thought he caught a glimpse of a smirk somewhere beneath the man's thick mustache. He wasn't sure he liked the idea of someone following and watching him so closely, but he couldn't very well argue against his grandfather's wishes. He was the prince, and there were certain expectations and precautions that came with that title, whether he was ready for them or not.

They finished breakfast, and Indira suggested a stroll through the palace gardens, followed by a fitting with the royal tailor. Bhajan was busy attending to other business throughout the day, but the queen seemed eager to spend some time with her long lost grandson, and Savir had nothing else to do. Tarik trailed behind them while they walked, keeping a respectful distance to allow them some private conversation.

After the fitting with the tailor, he made some excuse about feeling tired and asked to retire his room, hoping for a few minutes of solitude.

Or, at least, with only Valkyra to keep him company. Tarik followed, of course, and Savir tried not to let on how hopelessly lost he was as he wandered through the palace. It was an enormous building, with dozens of winding hallways and an outrageous abundance of staircases leading to various wings and towers. At last, he was certain he'd found the right room, but when he stepped toward the door, Tarik stopped him.

"That's not your room."

Savir sucked in a breath and turned around stiffly. "Would you mind pointing me in the right direction, then?"

The guard lifted an eyebrow. "I was wondering how long it would take you to ask. This way."

They set off down the hall together, walking side by side now. "Thank you," Savir murmured.

Tarik merely grunted in response. They descended a flight of stairs that Savir couldn't remember ever having gone up, and after a few more turns, they stopped outside another door. He reached for it, but again, Tarik's voice made him pause.

"I'm going to speak freely, boy. I don't care whether I have your permission to do so or not, but I'd suggest you pay attention."

Savir crossed his arms and shifted back around to face him. "All right."

"I've served King Bhajan since before you were born, and do you know how many Prince Savir imposters I've seen? Go on, take a guess."

"I don't know. Maybe ten?"

"Nineteen. They started showing up not long after we buried the princess, little boys dragged in here by con men looking for a quick ride to wealth and power. And that's only the ones I know about. Dozens more never got through the front gates. Nineteen times, I had to watch the king and queen get their hopes up only to have them dashed to pieces. You can understand why I'd have a hard time being convinced by assertions such as yours."

Savir could see where this was going, but rather than argue, he simply nodded and waited for Tarik to continue.

"Their safety is my top priority. You had better not be deceiving them."

Valkyra tensed on Savir's shoulder, but he kept his expression carefully neutral. "You saw the evidence yourself, and if the king and queen have turned away nineteen imposters already, you know they can't be easily fooled."

"Grief and pain make fools of even the best of us," Tarik replied flatly. "Your *evidence* is no guarantee that you are who you say you are."

Savir raised his chin. "And you have no proof that I'm deceiving anyone." He yanked the door open, intending to leave the guard and his accusations behind.

Tarik put one large hand against the door and pushed it firmly shut, staring down at Savir with a scowl. "I will give you this one opportunity to back out. If this is some scheme, you may gather your things now, and I'll escort you from the palace myself, free and unharmed." His eyes narrowed, both scrutinizing and threatening. "But if you stay and I find out you're lying, I'll make sure you regret it."

Looking into the older man's hard, black eyes, Savir had no doubt he meant it. "It's a good thing I'm not lying, then," he said. "Now please, it's been a long morning, and I'd like to rest a while."

Tarik backed off, and once Savir was safely inside his room, he shut and locked the door behind him. Valkyra hopped from his shoulder to land atop the plush bed in the center of the room.

"I don't think I can do this," he said. His heart was pounding after the tense exchange with Tarik, and he felt on the verge of a breakdown. He knew now that he truly was the prince, but knowing that and playing the part were two very different things.

"You're doing fine," Valkyra reassured him. "It's overwhelming right now, and that ill-tempered guard certainly isn't helping matters, but it will get easier. You'll get used to all of this, and—"

"No, I won't!" He let out a snarl and grabbed at his hair with both hands. She still didn't understand. Without his memories, he was little more than a shell of himself, and a shell of a man was not fit to rule anyone, let alone an entire nation. "You spent years preparing me for this, and I know you expected me to come here and be ready. But I'm not. How can I be, when I don't remember *anything*?"

Valkyra stared at him for a moment, unblinking, then sighed. "You're right."

He wasn't sure how he'd expected her to answer, but it wasn't like that. "What?"

"You're right. You're not ready." Her tail lashed once behind her, and she inclined her head toward the door. "But *they* are. The king and queen, Magistrate Ashaya, the other advisors. The people of this country. They're all ready for you to take back your throne, Savir. Are you going to give up already simply because this is harder than you imagined?"

"I'm not giving up," he snapped, and he was almost surprised at the surety in his own voice. "I just—I don't know how to do this. Any of this."

"That's all right. You don't have to know it all right now. No one who matters expects you to be perfect. You'll learn. It will be hard, and you'll make mistakes, but there are so many people who want you to succeed, myself included. I'll guide you as best as I can every step of the way, as will Ashaya, and the king and queen. They love you so much already. Can't you see that?"

Savir snorted, recalling the feel of Indira's hands gripping his as they walked through the garden. "Maybe a little too much."

"What did you expect? They're your grandparents, and all this time, they thought you were dead. Let them have their joy."

For the next two days, that was exactly what Savir tried to do, allowing Indira to fuss over him and share endless memories of his mother, taking Bhajan up on an offer to practice swordsmanship in the courtyard each morning. And when the king told him of the special council he'd arranged with his advisors to officially announce Savir's return, he tried to look pleased rather than ill.

That morning, he dressed in the outfit Indira had helped him pick out for the occasion and followed Magistrate Ashaya to the council chambers. Tarik accompanied him, but posted himself outside the door. Valkyra sat rigid on Savir's shoulder, and they garnered curious glances from the six others already sitting around a large circular table in the center of the room. Ashaya motioned to an empty seat for Savir. The chair immediately to his left was obviously King Bhajan's, slightly elevated with a high back and a plush red cushion on its seat.

To his right sat a woman dressed in blue and green. She seemed young for a royal advisor, possibly in her mid-thirties, and she eyed him—and Valkyra—with a particularly keen interest.

“I don’t believe we’ve met,” she said in a low purr. “I’m Chayani Sha, Advisor of Magic.”

Savir was acutely aware of the others all watching him intently, but Bhajan entered at that moment, and he was spared from having to say anything. The king wasted no time in addressing the matter at hand. After introducing Savir as his long-lost grandson and rightful heir to the imperial throne, he launched into an explanation of the validity of those claims, paying no mind to the bewildered looks on his advisors’ faces. Magistrate Ashaya supported the story and presented the same evidence as before. The advisors posed many of the same questions Bhajan himself had asked upon first meeting Savir, and all were answered as thoroughly as possible. All the while, Savir listened, apprehensive, his gaze constantly roving to avoid looking any of them in the eye for too long.

When the discussion died down and Bhajan sat back in his chair, a long silence lingered. It was Chayani Sha who spoke first, her eyes flitting once more to Valkyra. “And the dragon…is it…” She hesitated, eyebrows scrunched together as she searched for the right word. “Friendly?”

It was the first time any of them had asked him something directly, and he wanted to make a good impression with his answer. He suspected she really wanted to know why he’d brought his pet to their assembly but didn’t wish to offend him. Before he could formulate a response, Magistrate Ashaya came to his rescue. “As I’m sure you’ve all noticed, the dragon is a well-behaved companion animal, and Prince Savir is very fond of her. The situation he finds himself in now would be overwhelming for any of us. Surely we can grant him the small comfort of keeping her close.”

The other advisors exchanged a few looks, and Savir added his own explanation. “She was a gift from the woman who raised me. I have nothing else left of her now.” For good measure, he reached up to scratch Valkyra affectionately under the chin. She responded in kind, leaning into the caress of his fingers like a purring kitten.

King Bhajan cleared his throat. “We have more important matters to discuss than my grandson’s pet.”

“Indeed,” said the man seated next to Ashaya. He had small, shrewd eyes and a pockmarked face. "What *is* your intention, now that the prince has returned?" He leaned forward to fix his gaze on Savir, bringing his hands to rest on the table in front of him. "Or perhaps I should be asking *you*, Your Highness."

Savir had been wondering the same thing himself, and there was no sense in trying to pretend he had a plan. "I'm not sure, but I trust the wisdom of the king and this council to guide me."

The look Bhajan gave him was one of pride, and Savir began to relax a little. So far, so good. He'd at least managed to avoid saying the wrong thing.

"By all rights," the king said, "Savir should be the one sitting on the imperial throne, not Dashiva. Once we announce his return and present the evidence to her, she'll have to step down."

The advisor's nose crinkled. "Step down? The empress is a proud, ambitious woman. Surely you don't think it will be so simple."

"I have to agree with Lord Vasu on this," Ashaya said, nodding to the man. "Even if she's willing to accept the evidence as truth, I doubt she'll relinquish her crown to Savir. It's far more likely she'll try to discredit him and any who dare stand with him."

Bhajan stood. "You're right. What I should have said was that if she won't step down, there will be consequences. I am fully prepared to go to war with Jakhat if necessary."

The statement was hard and resolute, leaving no room to question whether he was bluffing or exaggerating. No, he was absolutely serious, and that sudden understanding chilled Savir down to the bone.

"I don't want to start a war," he said, and all the attention in the room shifted his way. He squirmed in his chair, trying to appear taller, stronger, more prince-like. "If that's where this is going to lead us, perhaps I shouldn't lay claim to the throne at all."

Bhajan put a hand on his shoulder. The coldness in his eyes was gone now, replaced by something deeper, warm but also sad. "Your birth and eventual rule were meant to strengthen the bonds between our two cities." His steely gaze swept over the rest of the room, jaw tightening with emotion. "I could never prove it, but I've long suspected Dashiva herself was the one who stole that future from us. She took my daughter's life. She's a murdering thief and a liar, and the throne does not belong to her. I will not sit here in submissive fury any longer—not when I have a chance to restore the future we were supposed to have."

Savir wasn't sure what to say to that. This man—his grandfather—had lost something precious and irreplaceable. His grief was tragically clear, his intentions honorable, and Savir wanted him to have the promised future he'd spoken of.

But not at any cost.

"I don't want people fighting and dying because of me."

Bhajan's lips pressed together, and he gave Savir's shoulder a firm squeeze. "Then let's hope Dashiva has more honor and sense than we're giving her credit for."

From there, the meeting turned to planning and preparations. Everyone had some idea or suggestion, and even if Savir had known what to say, he wouldn't have been able to get a word in. He was alarmed by how quickly they all seemed willing to go along with the worst-case scenario Bhajan had presented. War was something he still hoped to avoid, but the king and his advisors treated it like an inevitability.

The Advisors of Grain and Coin began taking detailed notes on how much money, food, and other supplies they needed to stockpile in preparation for a conflict, and the Advisor of Secrets shared intelligence on which high-ranking military officers might be persuaded to ally with them. Lord Vasu, the Advisor of Diplomacy, identified several other powerful allies they might find among Kavoran nobility and provincial leaders. General Khan, the Advisor of War, was already drawing up battle plans and strategies for an incursion. At one point, Chayani Sha suggested various methods for amplifying the abilities of their Tarja soldiers, which included the use of mesala harvested from the Sular desert. That idea made Savir particularly uncomfortable, though he couldn't pinpoint why.

By the time the meeting ended, dinner was almost ready. Bhajan seemed eager for the chance to talk with his wife and grandson in private, but Savir excused himself before the meal was served and retired to his room. The serene and noiseless emptiness of the space was a much-needed comfort. He sprawled onto his bed with his arms behind his head, still trying to process everything the day had brought. A headache pulsed at the front of his skull, and his chest felt tight, like he couldn't quite take a full breath. He tried anyway, inhaling and exhaling long and deep until the thoughts racing around his mind slowed.

"You did well in there," Valkyra said, curled up on the blanket beside him. "The advisors all seemed quite impressed with you and willing to back you as the rightful heir to the throne, which is exactly what we need."

"It has nothing to do with me," Savir muttered. "They're only going along with Bhajan."

"Give them more credit than that. Your grandfather is no fool. He's chosen advisors who will guide him well, not puppets willing to follow his every whim. I told you from the start—the people of this country are still loyal to *you*. They want to see you on the throne where you belong."

"What if that's not what *I* want?" Saying it aloud made his stomach churn. He was a prince, wasn't he? That had always felt right, more than anything else he knew about himself. The title of Emperor didn't seem to fit in quite the same way, but still, he was meant to rule. A part of him *wanted* to rule.

But not if it meant plunging the country into a civil war.

Valkyra spoke to him like a mother scolding an irritable child. "I understand your reservations, Your Highness, but being a leader often means that your wants don't matter—not in comparison to your responsibility. You *are* the rightful emperor of Kavora, and as such, you have a responsibility to the people of this country, including the ones who just declared their support for you."

"Shouldn't my responsibility be to keep my people alive and safe, then?" Savir said. "A war's going to make that difficult."

"We don't know for sure that it will come to that. And even if it does, you must see the bigger picture. This is about justice and setting a precedent. There are laws and policies regarding succession for a reason, including to ensure that usurpers can't seize power and throw the empire into chaos whenever they please. Which is exactly what Dashiva did seventeen years ago."

"Seems to me she's been a decent ruler since then," he muttered. "Maybe it's better if we let her be."

"Even if that were true, it's no longer an option. You heard Bhajan in there. Do you really think he's willing to let this go? Do you think any of them are?" She took a few steps closer, arching her long neck to look down at him. "People know you're alive now. Already, whispers of your return are spreading through the city, and if word hasn't yet reached the rest of the country, it will soon."

"I guess that means it's too late to run off to the woods and become a hermit."

"You've already spent too much of your life as a hermit in the woods. And besides, that's not what you *really* want, is it? You're not the sort of man who runs from a challenge or abandons the people who are counting on him. And the people of this country will be counting on you, Savir, once they know you're alive."

He sat up and ran his hands over his face. Everything she was saying made sense, and yet…

And yet what? He wasn't sure, but somewhere in the back of his mind, misgivings lingered.

Valkyra jumped onto his shoulder and nuzzled her cheek against his. "Your concerns are noble ones, Your Highness. You want peace, which shows an admirable level of care and compassion for your subjects. That's exactly what will make you a great ruler—one worthy of your people's respect."

"I guess," he mumbled.

She lowered her voice to a near whisper, but her words were resolute. "Power brings possibility, Savir. Imagine all the good we can do once you're crowned."

ALEIDA

In spite of her low expectations going in, servant's work turned out to be even more tedious and exhausting than Aleida anticipated. The one thing that made it a little more tolerable was the fact that many of the other servants were also Visan, and there was a certain level of comfort in that. She hadn't had any consistent interaction with so many of her own people in years, and the simple joy of being able to converse in her own language was a gift. They laughed while they worked and shared stories of the old days, before the invasion, and though the reminders of home were still painful, it was soothing to work alongside people who shared so much of her history and lived experience.

Their employer had a small bunkhouse on one of his properties, and that was where Aleida stayed, along with some of the other hired help. One of them was a young woman about her age named Sabina. They usually worked in the kitchens together, and Sabina made great efforts to befriend her. Aleida enjoyed her company well enough and treated her amicably, but she maintained a solid wall around anything too personal. She wasn't here to make friends, nor did she want any.

A few nights a week, if she happened to finish her work before dark, she would visit Mitul at the Serene Star. It wasn't long before he was hired to play at a renowned scholar's retirement party, which resulted in several more requests to perform at various gatherings over the next few weeks. It was a good start to his side of their plan, and as his reputation grew, they hoped he would receive invitations from some of the city's more prominent citizens. They already had a few names of people who might be connected to Nandini Kumar, but so far, they hadn't interacted with those individuals directly.

On the nights Aleida visited, Mitul continued with her reading lessons. He was a patient teacher, offering abundant praise when she succeeded and only the gentlest of corrections when she made a mistake. The indecipherable markings she'd seen on signs and notices throughout the city were slowly becoming more recognizable. She practiced whenever she could, even going so far as to secretly borrow some of the books from her employer's library. Books for children, mostly, with colorful illustrations on the cover and simpler words inside. Even those were a challenge, but she was improving.

One night, about two weeks after Aleida had been been hired as a servant, Sabina entered the bunkhouse with a glint in her eye and an extra bounce in her step. Aleida had quickly learned this often meant she had some story or juicy bit of gossip she was eager to share, and considering she'd spent the day waiting on their employer and his business partners during a meeting, that seemed likely now. She hummed a jaunty little tune to herself as she unbound her hair and began brushing it.

"How was your day?" Aleida asked casually, not looking up from the book in her lap. The trick to getting Sabina to talk was to show just the right amount of interest—enough to let her know you were curious, but not so much that you seemed overly eager.

"Fine," Sabina replied with a coy little smile, then carried on with her humming.

Aleida raised her eyebrows but kept reading.

One of the older women barked at her from the other side of the bunkhouse. "Oh, tell us what it is already. You've clearly got something to share."

Sabina's eyes gleamed as she set the brush down and dramatically cleared her throat. "I have it on good authority that Prince Savir is alive."

The old woman harrumphed. "So does everybody else and their mother."

Sabina put her hands on her hips. "I'm serious. They were talking about it today in their meeting. A few of them are from Valmandi, and they say the prince is living in the palace. He has been for weeks now."

"Probably some imposter," Aleida muttered. She shut her book and slid it under her pillow. It was too hard to concentrate on the words when everyone else was talking. "I'm sure there have been plenty of those over the years."

"Exactly," said Sabina. "And the king and queen haven't entertained any of them until now. This one is the right age, and one of the merchants said he heard it from the Advisor of Coin herself that there's proof to back up his claim. They're treating him like a full member of the royal household. He wears a crown and all."

"Why isn't he here, then?" one of the other women asked. "If he's the real Prince Savir, isn't he the rightful heir to the throne?"

"Does the empress know he's back?" said another.

"Don't be daft, of course she knows."

More questions and speculations were thrown out in a whirlwind of conversation, but after a few minutes, all attention returned to Sabina. She watched and listened with a satisfied smirk, as if she'd been hoping for such drama all along.

"What else did they say?" the oldest among them asked. "Surely there was more."

Sabina shrugged. "They were mostly concerned with how his return might affect their business. One of them—I think he sells fabrics—said the queen invited a tailor to do a fitting. Said the tailor told him Prince Savir was pleasant enough, but a little strange. Quiet, didn't talk much. Apparently, he has a pet dragon he takes with him everywhere."

Aleida's blood went cold. "A pet dragon?"

Sabina nodded. "Yes, a little white one, he said. They were talking about investing in breeding programs, seeing how pet dragons will probably be in fashion once everyone learns about his."

She went on, but to Aleida, her voice was only a distant droning. A little white dragon, Prince Savir returned, a young man who seemed the right age. If she was remembering Kavoran history correctly, Prince

Savir and his mother had been killed seventeen years ago, when he was still a toddler. That would make him almost nineteen now.

Amar could easily pass for nineteen.

Grabbing her cloak off the end of the bed, Aleida stood. She made for the door, ignoring the questions that followed about where she was going and what she was doing.

Was *this* how Valkyra intended to make her grab for power? They'd always assumed she'd killed Amar and then formed a Bond with him, taking advantage of his memory loss to manipulate him into doing her bidding. But this went far beyond what any of them could have guessed she might do.

She needed to talk to Mitul immediately. Valkyra had destroyed thousands of lives when she was still alive, and that wasn't including the personal hell she'd put Aleida through. They couldn't let her regain any shred of the power she'd once held.

If she intended to make a play for the throne using Amar, it was all the more critical that they rescue him.

By the time Aleida arrived at the Serene Star, the moon was up, and the sky had darkened. She waved to the innkeeper, who'd become accustomed to her comings and goings over the past weeks, and headed up the stairs to Mitul's room.

When she reached the top and rounded the corner, however, she stopped short. A man stood outside his door—someone she didn't recognize. Abruptly, she pulled back, retreating a few steps so she was of sight. A knock sounded from down the hall, and she peered around the corner to watch.

Who else could possibly be calling on him at this hour? She tried to get a better look at the man, but his profile was half hidden beneath a mane of dark curls that hung around his ears and the nape of his neck. He had broad shoulders and a sturdy frame. His clothes were simple in design but stylish and made of fine silk, so whoever he was, he must have money, or he wanted to make a good impression. Perhaps some nobleman's manservant come to hire Mitul for a performance. Hopefully, their business wouldn't take long. She shifted back and forth on the balls of her feet while she waited.

There was a creak as the door swung open, then silence. Aleida couldn't see Mitul, but he must have been standing on the other side of the threshold.

"Can I come in?" The man had a deep, friendly voice, and the easy cheerfulness in it gave the impression that he was used to smiling at everyone he met.

It took Mitul a few seconds to respond, and when he did, he stumbled over the words. "O-of course."

The man stepped inside, and the door thumped softly shut behind him.

Aleida waited a few seconds, but between her eagerness to tell Mitul what she'd learned and her curiosity about his strange visitor, staying put quickly became unbearable. She padded down the hall and took up a position outside the door, leaning against it to listen.

The stranger was speaking, his words only slightly muffled through the wood. "—heard you were in the city, I had to come see for myself. Call it a morbid curiosity."

"I meant to pay you a visit," Mitul replied with that same faltering hesitation. "But I—well, I wasn't sure I'd be welcome."

"Why not?"

"I didn't think you'd want to see me."

"Why wouldn't I want to see you?" The man chuckled a little. "It's been so long. No need to dwell on the past. Not the unpleasant parts, anyway."

"I guess not."

Aleida thought she could hear a note of sadness in his voice, or maybe something more bitter. Whatever it was, this stranger seemed to elicit some emotion in him, and apparently, they had a history. Who was he? And why was he seeking him out now?

There was another brief silence before Mitul spoke again. "You look good. From all I've heard, you've done quite well for yourself these last ten years."

"Has it really been that long? The time goes by so quickly. But yes, I've been very fortunate."

"I'm glad. Every time I hear your name or see your work…" He trailed off for a moment, and Aleida pressed her ear against the door a little harder to make sure she could still hear the conversation. "Maybe I don't have the right to say so anymore, but I'm proud of you. You've made all your dreams a reality. It's very impressive."

"Thank you. That means a lot, coming from you." The stranger's voice was softer now and had lost some of its carefree amusement. "I've missed you."

"I've missed you, too."

Aleida scrunched her mouth to one side, not wanting to interrupt but seeing no other way to accomplish what she'd come here for. Clearly, these two still had some catching up to do, but that could wait. She had far more important things to discuss with Mitul. Sucking in a breath, she knocked.

"Excuse me for a moment," Mitul said. A few seconds later, he opened the door, smiling when he saw her. "Aleida, come in. I was just talking with an old friend."

He stepped aside to let her through, and she nodded to the stranger, who stood in front of the window. He offered a slight bow, black curls sweeping across his forehead as he bent. His smile was easy and warm, and the way it touched his eyes made him look much younger than he probably was.

Mitul stepped forward to make introductions. "This is Aleida. Aleida, this Kamaal Ruman."

Kamaal Ruman? Surely it couldn't be. Her eyes drifted to the man's hands, the flecks of colored paint that hadn't been scrubbed from his skin, the pigment that lingered at the edges of his fingernails. He was the right age, and he was dressed in attire befitting a nobleman…or a famed artist.

Kamaal Ruman, her idol, standing here in the last place in the world she would have expected.

And she was a stinking, disheveled mess after a long day of servant's work.

Her cheeks flushed, and she bowed her head to hide her shame. Then, remembering herself, she bent at the waist to show her respect. "I'm such a pleasure to—happy, I mean—" Skies be damned, why couldn't she get out a coherent sentence? "It's such an honor to meet you."

Kamaal's grin widened. "And you as well. It's an honor to meet any friend of Mitul's."

"I didn't mean to interrupt," she stammered, even though that had been exactly what she'd intended. She only felt bad about it now because of who the stranger turned out to be. "I can go, if you're still talking."

"That's all right," the artist replied. "I was the one who showed up unannounced. I'll go. But I'd like to extend an invitation to you both, if that's all right."

"Of course," Mitul said.

"Stop by my studio sometime. I'd love to show you some of the pieces I'm working on, for old times' sake. It's in the Lower Gardens district. Most of the locals know it. They can point you in the right direction."

"I'd like that. *We'd* like that, I mean." He glanced at Aleida and tucked in his bottom lip, looking mildly flustered.

"Good. It was wonderful to see you again, Mitul. You look well." His hand started to reach forward, and the other man took half a step toward him. At the same moment, they both froze, staring at the empty space between them.

"Goodnight," Kamaal said, whirling suddenly and heading for the door. "Aleida, it was lovely to meet you."

She barely managed to stammer out a dazed, "You, too," before he was gone.

Mitul stood there for a few seconds, hands pressed flat against the door. His shoulders rose and fell as he took a deep breath.

"That was Kamaal Ruman," Aleida said, still awed and speaking more to herself than to him.

"Yes, it was." Despite apparently knowing the man, Mitul seemed no less shaken than she.

He said nothing more and walked over to the window to stare at the street below. Aleida joined him. They both watched as the artist stepped out of the Serene Star and disappeared around the next corner.

Part of her wanted to rush after him, or better yet, reverse time so she could redo their entire interaction. Anything would have been better than *that*. How many times had she pictured herself in that very situation? She'd rehearsed what she might say if she ever by some miracle met the man, but when that impossible opportunity had come, she'd made a complete fool of herself.

In an effort to distract herself from her embarrassment, she asked Mitul, "How do you know him?" The familiarity between them was obviously more than a passing acquaintance, and that was curious in and of itself. She'd never thought of him as anything more than a wandering musician, and certainly not someone with connections to one of the most famous artists in Kavora.

"We were lovers, for a time. More than that. Partners."

It was perhaps the last response she'd expected, but their not-so-subtle dance between distance and intimacy suddenly made a lot more sense. "When?"

"Ten years ago. We were together for five." His voice dropped a little lower. "Hard to believe it's been so long. He looks almost exactly the same."

"Why did you—" She stopped herself before she could finish the question. Curiosity gnawed at her, but it wasn't her place to pry into the details of his personal life.

"Why did we end things?" he finished for her. She nodded, and he sighed. "It was my decision. Amar was setting out to find answers about his curse, and I couldn't let him go off alone. Not when he might die somewhere along the way and forget everything."

"You went with him instead of staying with Kamaal?"

"It's not like he had anyone else. He's my brother. What else was I supposed to do? I'm sure you understand."

Aleida swallowed against the sudden tightness in her chest as Tyrus' face flashed through her mind. She did understand, all too well.

"Kamaal thought he might come with us, even though his career was finally starting to take off. It was everything he'd ever wanted, and I couldn't let him give it up to go wandering all over Erythyr with no end to our quest in sight. So I left. In the middle of the night with only a letter to say goodbye." He shook his head. "In hindsight, I probably should have found a better way to handle the situation. After all these years, I assumed he must hate me for the way I left things. But tonight, he shows up here, and he's…" He trailed off, shaking his head again.

"He was happy to see you."

"Yes, but that's Kamaal for you. He never let things get him down for too long. He was always happy, so full of life and joy." A smile tugged at his lips. "It was the one thing I loved most about him."

The way he spoke about the man, Aleida suspected a flicker of that love still resided in Mitul's heart. But she hadn't come here so they could dwell on his past. "I heard something today I thought you should know," she said. "It's about Amar."

Quickly, she recounted the rumors Sabina had shared. At first, Mitul wasn't convinced, reminding her that there had long been rumors of Prince Savir being alive, waiting for the right time to come home. Once she told him about the prince's pet dragon, though, the pieces fell into place for him, too. He began pacing, saying nothing for a long time, but clearly the cogs in his mind were spinning as fast as Aleida's.

"It has to be him, right?" she asked.

"Probably."

"We should go to Valmandi and see what other information we can gather. I can be ready to leave tomorrow morning."

Mitul stopped pacing and went back to staring out the window. Aleida stood next to him, tapping her finger against the sill impatiently.

"Actually, I think we should stay here," he said. "The rumors may be slower to reach us, but we'll still hear them. If he's going to assert his claim to the throne, he'll have to come here and present himself in person. The empress likely will have heard of his return already. She'll want to invite him, assuming King Bhajan isn't already making arrangements to send him."

"Why wait for all that when we could be in Valmandi in two weeks?"

"And then what? If that's really Amar, we still don't have a way to get him back, especially not if he's holed away in the palace surrounded by guards. Even if we did, he won't remember us." He shifted around, leaning against the wall on one shoulder. "Saya, Kes, and Lucian are probably still making their way to Deveaural. They won't be back for another two months, so either way, we'll be waiting, and I don't see the point in rushing off when Amar and Valkyra could just as soon be coming here. Besides, we need to verify it's really him before we do anything."

Aleida still didn't like the idea of staying put—it felt too much like doing nothing—but she could see his point. She crossed her arms. "Fine, but we can't wait forever. If she gets Amar on the throne, he'll be even harder to reach than he is now, and I don't want to think about what she could do with so much power. We have to stop her."

"I know. I want that as much as you do, if only to save Amar. But we need the others' help to make this work. We have to be patient."

Aleida pursed her lips. Patience had never been one of her strengths, but she didn't have much choice right now. It seemed the days ahead would be filled with more servant's work, which meant she ought to be returning to the bunkhouse. Mornings always came too early. "All right, then. I should get going."

"It's late," Mitul said. "You shouldn't walk back alone. I can go with you, or you're welcome to stay here."

"I'll be fine on my own." She backed away from the window, and her stomach let out a loud rumble.

Mitul raised an eyebrow and stared pointedly at her. "Have you eaten anything tonight?"

She didn't answer. She hadn't, and lunch had been only a few bites of leftover kitchen scraps snatched in between scrubbing dishes. She was famished, but she'd been hungry before, and she didn't need anyone taking care of her.

"That's a 'no,' then," he said. "Come on. Supper ended a while ago, but I've befriended the cook. She'll make us something if I ask nicely."

"I'm fine," she grumbled. "I don't need your charity."

He raised an eyebrow. "Charity? Is that what you call one friend trying to take care of another?"

"We're not friends."

"Aren't we? Well, that's a disappointment. Oh well, charity it is then, I suppose. But I'm not letting you leave here hungry, and I really do think you should take my bed for the night. It's very late, and you look like you could use a good night's sleep."

Still somewhat reluctant but too drained to protest, Aleida followed him out the door and down the hall. "Where are you going to sleep, then?"

"Oh, I doubt I'll be sleeping much at all, after today's emotional whirlwind. Too much to think about." He glanced at her over his shoulder. "I know I come across as the strong, impassive type who never lets anything get to him, but beneath that stone exterior, I do have a rather sensitive heart, you know."

Aleida snorted and rolled her eyes. The man wore his feelings as plain as a badge on his chest for all to see. Friends or not, that was something she'd come to appreciate about him. After the betrayal that had come from Valkyra's companionship, his simple honesty was a welcome change. There was never any guessing about where she stood with him or how he felt about something; she just knew.

If she *were* looking for a friend—and she certainly wasn't—she could do a lot worse than a friend like Mitul.

SAVIR

AFTER HIS INITIAL MEETING WITH THE ADVISORS OF VALMANDI'S royal court, Savir's days became much busier, full of social engagements, lessons in politics and military strategy, private meetings with important players in the area, and dozens of other princely duties. It was all quite mentally exhausting, but Valkyra often praised his instincts and insisted he was taking to everything naturally.

This was a comfort to Savir, and though he didn't always enjoy his many obligations, he did make every attempt to learn and grow from them. He also found that having something else to occupy his attention kept him from fixating on his missing memories. They still nagged at him, but not as much as before, and the persistent feeling that he could handle his royal responsibilities grew stronger as he learned to embrace the role of prince. Perhaps, in time, he'd feel more certain that he was meant to be emperor.

Rumors about him spread faster than a plague. The Advisor of Diplomacy, Lord Vasu, immediately suggested a letter be sent to Empress Dashiva to officially announce Savir's return and arrange a meeting. There were significant debates between Bhajan and his council about what should be included. In the end, nothing regarding succession was stated outright, but the matter was implied and should thus be on the forefront of Dashiva's mind.

The letter went out with their fastest rider, and in the days they waited for a response, Savir spent what little free time he had with his grandparents. Now that the initial awkwardness of first introductions had worn off, they were all able to relax and settle into a more natural rhythm. Savir came to enjoy Queen Indira's quiet sense of humor and endless stories. She had a sharp mind for strategy and taught him all her best tricks for winning a complicated game called Samud that was favored by Kavoran nobles. The stories she shared of his mother almost satisfied his craving for some connection to his past. They often ate lunch on the highest balcony of the palace together, which looked out on the nearby temple with its mural of Princess Priyani.

"Kamaal Ruman painted that, you know," the queen said to him one afternoon as they sat there.

"So I've heard," Savir replied. "It's lovely."

"Yes. It was right after she died, long before Kamaal's name was known throughout the empire. He was so kind and gracious about it. He spent several days talking to us about her and how we wanted her portrayed." She took a sip from a delicate glass cup. "He asked about putting you on there, too, but we couldn't bear the thought. People were already speculating that you still lived. Mostly gossip, of course, and it wasn't something we could really allow ourselves to believe. But I suppose a part of me hoped it was true, and having you painted up there would have been admitting it wasn't."

She put a hand over his, patting it gently, and he returned her smile with one of his own. After a few seconds, he brought up the topic he'd been wanting to discuss with her for a while. "Grandfather said he suspects the empress arranged my mother's death. I can understand why she'd want me dead, but why her?"

The queen's lips pinched together as if she'd tasted something sour. "I'm sure Priyani was nothing but a loose end, which makes her murder all the more deplorable. She didn't need to die."

"If you both suspected Dashiva was behind it, why didn't you say anything all this time?"

"Your grandfather wanted to, but I talked him out of it. What would have been the point? You were gone. Our daughter was gone. Nothing we said would have changed that, and it likely would have only stirred up trouble with Jakhat."

Savir twisted the gold signet ring they'd given him and cast a glance at Valkyra, who was perched on the edge of the balcony. "I'm afraid that's what it's going to do now."

"So am I." She patted his knee gently. "I know you don't want a war, Savir. Neither do I, and for all her faults, I don't think Dashiva does, either. But if she won't step down, you *must* take a stand. There are things worth fighting for, and this is one of them. It's not about the throne. It's about what's right and fair."

Savir thought about her words for days after, trying to decide whether he believed them enough to justify a war, if it came to that.

And skies above, he hoped it wouldn't.

The empress' reply to their letter came one morning while Savir and Bhajan were sparring in the courtyard, which had become a part of their daily routine. It was something Savir looked forward to each morning, and he was good at it. Great, even. Bhajan was surprisingly strong and had decades of experience over him, but neither he nor any of the guards who'd tried had managed to best Savir yet.

Tarik was always present and sometimes took a turn sparring with him. Though he was a better swordsman than all the other guards, even he hadn't managed to win a bout—something that brought Savir a smug sense of satisfaction, given the coldness of their prior interactions. Today, the man seemed to be in a particularly aggressive mood, throwing everything he had into the fight until it crossed the threshold of intense training exercise into unfriendly duel territory.

A series of rapid blows pressed Savir backward across the courtyard. Despite the age difference that should have given him the advantage, there was no chance of competing with Tarik's sheer size and strength, forcing Savir to instead rely on speed and skill. He had plenty of both, but he was beginning to suspect Tarik had been going easy on him until now. Ragged breaths escaped his lungs as he dodged yet another blow, and he couldn't tell for certain whether he only imagined the murderous look in the older man's eyes.

Finally, he managed a quick maneuver that put him behind Tarik. He pressed the dull tip of his practice sword against the guard's back. "Got you," he said, the words coming out in a strained rush.

Tarik gave a curt nod and dropped his own sword, and Savir thought the duel was finally over. But as he lowered his weapon, Tarik spun around with one fist raised. In the blink of an eye, it was engulfed in flames and coming straight at Savir's face.

He stifled a cry and jumped back. Tarik was a *Tarja*? But of course, that made sense. Any guard with the advantage of magic would have been assigned the most important tasks from the beginning of their career, and that included protecting the royal family. Savir was only annoyed with himself for not making the assumption sooner.

The flaming fist stopped mere inches from Savir's face, and it took a great deal of restraint to stop himself from channeling his own altma.

"Tarik!" Bhajan called out, hurrying over to them. "That's enough, don't you think? You're supposed to help train the prince, not scare him to death."

"This is training," Tarik said, letting his fist fall and extinguishing the magical flames. "He ought to remember that swords and guns aren't the only weapons at an enemy's disposal. You can't always know who you're really fighting. It's important to stay on guard, always, no matter how good you are or how many enemies you've defeated."

Bhajan stepped closer and quickly looked Savir over. "A useful lesson, I suppose," he said, "though with you around, he shouldn't have to worry about fighting anyone."

"That is the plan, Your Majesty, but even the best plans go awry sometimes. It's better to be prepared for everything."

"A lesson I won't soon forget," Savir said, and meant it, though not only in the way Tarik had intended. He'd used the same trick on the bandits he and Valkyra had encountered on their journey, and he could use it again if needed.

A footman approached them then, trailed by a second man dressed in an ensemble of pure white accented with emerald green. His sleeve bore a patch depicting a large tree with hanging vines, the insignia of the imperial throne.

"An emissary sent by the empress herself," Bhajan whispered to

Savir as they put away their practice swords. He was already wearing his king's demeanor again, which was how Savir had begun thinking of the stiff decorum and strong bearing he seemed to don whenever he was acting as the monarch of Valmandi. That was most of the time, but there were moments, like during their morning sparring, when the king part of Bhajan fell away and he was simply himself—Indira's husband, Savir's grandfather, a reserved man who laughed a little more and spoke a little softer.

Together, they approached the emissary, who bowed to Bhajan in greeting. "Pardon my interruption, Your Majesty." He gave Savir a smaller bow but did not address him directly. From inside his jacket, he produced a letter with a green wax seal. "Her Imperial Majesty Empress Dashiva requested this be delivered to you both right away. Please take whatever time you need to discuss it with each other and with your advisors. I shall await your response."

Bhajan nodded. "Yes, of course. Thank you."

With that, the emissary bowed and followed the footman back up the stairs and into the palace. Bhajan waited until they were both out of sight to open the letter. He held it close, lips moving noiselessly as he read. Savir had a difficult time making out the flowing script over his shoulder, and though he was curious, he didn't want to snoop.

When he'd finished reading, Bhajan held the letter out to Savir. "I'm going to gather the advisors. Meet us in the council chambers, and invite your grandmother, would you? She'll want to be involved."

An hour later, they all sat around the table, listening as Bhajan read the empress' letter aloud. After a rambling preamble expressing her skepticism in the most diplomatic way possible, she got around to inviting Savir to the imperial palace. This was framed as a friendly opportunity to get acquainted, though she obviously wanted to judge the evidence of his claim for herself.

The invitation had been expected; at some point, he would have to meet his aunt, and since Dashiva was unlikely to leave the security and comfort of her home, he would have to go to her. The concerns that most seemed to trouble the council now lay in everything the letter did *not* say.

"What are her intentions for the boy once he gets there?" General Khan asked, speaking as if Savir wasn't even in the room.

"A good question," Chayani Sha said. "She wants evidence that the prince is the legitimate heir but makes no mention of what will happen after. If she's convinced by that evidence, does she plan to cede the throne or keep it for herself, even when our rightful ruler is standing before her?"

"She won't give up the throne," said the small, short-haired woman at the end of the table. Her surname was Khatri—Savir had never heard a given name—and she was so quiet he often forgot she was there except for the rare moments when she spoke up. Her voice was a soft rasp befitting her title, the Advisor of Secrets. "Already, she's sent spies to find out what evidence we have, likely so she can refute it."

"What's the point of sending the boy at all, then?" the Advisor of Coin asked. "If the empress won't step down, we should to focus our energy on preparing for whatever comes next."

On the other side of the table, Lord Vasu leaned forward. "I agree, but we can't simply refuse an invitation from the empress. His Highness will have to go, if only for the sake of diplomacy and public perception, both of which are going to be critical no matter which path we take going forward. If we show we've done everything we can to appease the empress, any conflict that breaks out will be a clear result of her own refusal to cooperate and not our lack of effort."

Queen Indira sat up a little taller, lacing her fingers together in front of her. "*If* he does go—and I'm still not convinced he should—how are we going to ensure his safety? What's to stop Dashiva from having him killed once he's in her home where she has complete control?"

"Tarik will go with him, of course," said Bhajan. "Along with several more of our own guards."

"It would be very unwise for the empress to attempt any such thing," Vasu reassured them. "Prince Savir is already well loved by the people, and he hasn't even made a public appearance yet. He's a legend. If any harm were to befall him in Jakhat, even an accident, there would be a public outcry, and that would only reflect badly on Dashiva."

Savir wasn't sure what to make of this assessment of his popularity. It was true that he'd made no formal public appearance since arriving at the palace, but he'd had several brief conversations with servants, tailors, cooks, messengers, and others who all lived throughout the city. He'd expected some talk and gossip to spread, of course, but the idea that people had any strong opinion of him after so little interaction was disconcerting.

Bhajan shifted in his chair to better face Savir. When he spoke, his voice was somewhere between the assertive tone of a king and the gentler one he used when he was simply a grandfather. "What do you think, Savir? This is about you. We all have our ideas and opinions, but yours are the ones that matter most right now."

He was acutely aware of the many pairs of eyes suddenly fixed on him. Ideas and opinions had been percolating through his mind since the moment the letter arrived, but it was only now that he was able to gather them together into any kind of coherent form. He knew he had to go to Jakhat; that part was easy. He needed to meet his aunt, even if his grandparents were right about her trying to kill him all those years ago, and Savir himself still wasn't entirely convinced that was the case. She certainly had both means and motive, but that didn't mean she'd done it. Regardless, she was another connection to his past, and maybe meeting her would give him some answers. More importantly, it might prevent a war.

"I want to go," he said. "As soon as possible." If he could show her he wasn't a threat and didn't want to destroy everything she'd built, then perhaps they could come to some sort of compromise. "I'd like to see if we can find some way to avoid a conflict."

Magistrate Ashaya gave him a skeptical look. "Your Highness, that's very noble, but—"

Savir cut him off. "I won't renounce my claim to the throne. I *am* the rightful heir, and this empire and its people are my responsibility. It's for that exact reason I don't want a war. I'll do everything I can to prevent one, as long as I don't have to concede what's right."

The room fell silent, and whatever protests Ashaya or the other advisors might have had were withheld. Bhajan smiled at Savir and nodded approvingly. "Well said, Your Imperial Majesty."

Indira rose to her feet and took Savir's hand. "Long live Emperor Savir!" She pulled him up from his chair so that he was standing beside her, and the call was taken up by the other advisors to ring through the council chambers.

"Long live Emperor Savir! Long live Emperor Savir!"

Valkyra's claws dug into his shirt as she brought her mouth to his ear, adding her own whisper to the others' cheers. "Long live Emperor Savir."

ALEIDA

NEWS OF PRINCE SAVIR'S UPCOMING VISIT TO JAKHAT SPREAD through the city quickly, and like everyone else, the servants Aleida worked with were all abuzz with excitement.

"Do you reckon the king and queen will come with him?"

"I hope so. Maybe we'll get the day off for the coronation."

"Who said anything about a coronation?"

"A couple of palace guards mentioned it in the market yesterday."

"Oh, what do they know? We can't be talking about putting him on the throne already."

"I heard the empress is going to throw a ball to welcome him."

"Why would she do that? She doesn't even believe it's really him."

"It *has* to be him. Why would she invite him here if he wasn't the real Prince Savir?"

"Maybe so she can get rid of him."

"Sabina, hush!"

"What? She tried it before, didn't she?"

"You can't say things like that."

"Oh, don't get your knickers in a bunch. No one who matters is around to hear. Besides, I don't care if he's real or not. I only want a chance to see him. I hear he's handsome."

"Too handsome, too rich, and too powerful for the likes of you.

Now get back to your washing or we'll have no clean dishes for supper."

Aleida tuned into every whispered rumor, hoping to learn something that would help her and Mitul confirm that the revenant prince was actually Amar. When she went to the Serene Star that night, she presented the few ideas she'd come up with.

"Maybe we can catch a glimpse of him when he rides into the city. I bet he'll have a whole procession, so if we get close enough—"

"*If*," Mitul said. "And only *if* we're in the right place at the right time. The streets are bound to be crowded. It won't be easy, and I wouldn't be surprised if he's hidden in some carriage all the way to the palace."

Aleida had considered this as well and agreed with his assessment. They needed to get closer. "If there's a ball or a feast of some kind, they're going to need extra servants. I could volunteer." She frowned. Once she'd spoken it aloud, the idea sounded silly. The regular palace staff knew how to handle events like this and would likely have everything covered. If they needed any outside help, they'd have people in mind already—people who had to be vetted well ahead of time for security purposes.

Mitul shrugged and continued plucking at the strings of his saraj.

She continued with one final suggestion. "They're going to want entertainment. Maybe you could go."

He raised an eyebrow. "I've made a decent name for myself with the local merchants and lesser nobles, but I doubt I have enough prestige to earn an invitation to the palace. Besides, we could be spotted by Valkyra that way, and the less she knows what we're up to, the better."

Prestige and anonymity, or at least no obvious connection to the two of them. If only they knew someone like that who had the social influence needed to get close to this supposed Prince Savir.

She jumped out of her chair, prompting a concerned glance from Mitul. "What? Why are you smiling like that?"

She tried her best to drop her grin, but most of it stuck anyway. "I know exactly who can help us."

The following evening, Aleida and Mitul found themselves lost in the Lower Gardens district on the east side of the city. It was getting dark, and after wandering down half a dozen nearly identical streets, Aleida's patience was waning. "You never went to see him after he invited you?"

"He invited both of us," Mitul replied. "It would have been rude for me to show up alone."

She rolled her eyes. "I just happened to be there. He really wanted *you* to come, and if you'd gone already, we wouldn't be lost now."

For at least the fifth time that night, he slowed to check his reflection in a glass window, smoothing his graying beard with nervous fingers. "It's not so simple."

She stifled a snort. "Well, if *I'd* been the one personally invited to his studio, I'd show up at the first opportunity. You realize he's one of the best artists in all of Erythyr, right? Do you have any idea what people would give to see where he creates his masterpieces?"

"I didn't know you cared so much about art."

"Of course I care about art! It's everything. It—" She cut herself off as heat crept over her neck and face. She'd said too much already, but under the scrutiny of his gaze, she felt she needed to elaborate. "I used to draw a lot. Kamaal Ruman was always someone I looked up to. Someone I wanted to be."

"You *used to* draw?" Mitul's voice hung heavy on the past tense.

She held up her shaking hands by way of explanation.

"Ah. I'm sorry."

The look in his eyes was more kindness than pity, but it still made Aleida's stomach clench. She shoved her hands back into her pockets. "That's how I tracked you all down, you know. I drew you. First it was only Amar, based on how Valkyra described him. But after we fought, I drew all of you from memory. I'd show the pictures everywhere we went, asking if anyone had seen you and knew where you'd gone next. Someone always recognized you."

"That's impressive. You must have been quite skilled."

"I was." She'd always been so hesitant to admit it before, but now that her skill had been stolen from her, the words came freely. Pride tasted as bitter as bile in her throat and stung at her eyes. "I was *really* good."

"Have you tried to draw anything lately?"

Aleida stepped in front of the nearest passerby, ignoring his question. She didn't want to talk about it, and they needed to figure out where they were going. "Excuse me, sir, can you tell us where Kamaal Ruman's studio is?"

The man pointed back in the direction they'd come from. "You need to go that way. Take a left at the next street and you'll find it. It's a small, blue building. He's painted flowers all around it."

She turned around quickly and heard Mitul thanking the man behind her. A few minutes later, they stood in front of the building he'd described. It was small compared to others in the area but spacious nonetheless. The blue was a few shades lighter than a clear noon sky, and the flowers were all different types, covering the entire bottom third of the building in various hues of yellow and orange. It might have looked dowdy and inelegant if painted by another artist, but in Kamaal's distinct style and detailed rendering, it was stunning. Aleida's insides warmed looking at it, as if she were standing outside on a clear summer day, happy and well-rested without a care in the world. That was, of course, not her reality at all, but she couldn't help smiling a little as she stood there admiring his work.

"Maybe we should come back tomorrow," Mitul said. "It's getting late. We don't want to bother him."

She shook her head. Whatever nervousness was making him hesitate couldn't stop her—not now. Her pulse quickened with the anticipation of seeing the inside of the studio, and besides that, they needed Kamaal's help. Before Mitul could talk her or himself out of it, she approached the door. He reluctantly followed and, with a deep breath, raised his hand to knock.

Kamaal answered after a few seconds. His gaze flicked over Aleida briefly but stopped to linger on Mitul, and a grin pulled at one corner of his mouth. "I was starting to wonder if you'd ever show up. Did you get lost, or were you really that nervous to see me again?"

Mitul smiled back sheepishly. "A bit of both, I suppose."

"Well, I'm glad you're here now. Come in."

They stepped into a sprawling room that seemed to take up most of the building. Drapes were drawn over large windows that would allow for plenty of natural light when opened, and there was a slanting skylight overhead through which a few stars were visible in the darkening sky. A simple set of wooden stairs led up to a small loft which held a bed and a low table.

Canvases covered nearly every inch of visible wall space, some with finished paintings and some mostly blank. Aleida's focus danced across all of them, caught between an eagerness to take them all in at once and a desire to give each one the time and attention it deserved. Dozens of portraits were mixed in amongst paintings of flowers in every color of the rainbow. Scattered around the room in a seemingly haphazard fashion were more plants than she could name—bundles of dried blooms hanging from the ceiling, flowers in vases next to brushes and bottles of paint, and leafy green beauties spilling from pots of all shapes and sizes. Many were already depicted in Kamaal's paintings, and others were starting to take shape on the canvas.

Aleida's focus eventually settled on a small painting hung at eye level. Unlike the rest, it had been framed, and the ocean scene it depicted was one that felt so familiar she could almost feel the spray of the sea on her face and the wind in her hair. She drew closer and stood there staring at it, barely noticing the approach of the two men behind her until Kamaal spoke.

"The cliffs of Libera in Vis. You've seen them yourself, I assume?"

"Yes. I was born in Libera. My brother and I used to climb those cliffs every summer." Something tugged at her, but she couldn't tell whether it was joy or pain. Both emotions were so blended for her now she couldn't distinguish one from the other, because the things that had once brought her joy were the same things that now brought her pain. A memory echoed in her mind—Tyrus' laughter as he dove into the sea, the rush of water as she followed him to plunge below its frothing surface.

"It was a beautiful city," Kamaal said, his words dragging her back to the present. "I was fortunate enough to spend some time studying there, before the invasion."

"I know. One of your paintings hung in the church my family and I attended." She didn't mention how often she'd sat and studied it, vowing to herself that she would someday create something even half as impressive. That dream was gone now, as was the painting. "It was probably destroyed in the invasion."

"It was only a painting," he replied softly. "There were so many losses far greater than that."

Her throat went tight and sticky at his acknowledgment of what she and her family had personally suffered. Kavorans didn't often speak of the Visan invasion, and when they did, it was framed as something unavoidable, a natural order of the world. For them, Vis had only been another piece of land to be conquered and added to their empire. They didn't think about the tragic costs involved, or if they did, they avoided talking about them.

But not Kamaal.

Some of the tension in her stomach uncoiled. She hadn't realized it until now, but a part of her had feared he'd turn out to be unworthy of the pedestal she'd placed him on. She'd been disappointed by people too many times to not be skeptical. So far, though, the man seemed decent enough.

"Aleida draws too, actually," Mitul chimed in behind her.

She stiffened. Not that. He could have said *anything* but that. She shot him a glare, but he only raised an eyebrow, seemingly oblivious to her embarrassment.

"Oh, really?" Kamaal asked.

"No, not really," she blurted out before he could say anything else. "Not anymore."

"Why not?"

Her cheeks warmed, and she wished with all her might that the ground would open to swallow her. It wasn't enough that she'd lost her ability to draw and paint; now, she had to explain it to the one person whose skill she most admired. After a few more seconds of flustered silence, she raised her hands, which were trembling more violently than usual. "I can't even hold a stick of charcoal very well anymore, much less control it." The words came out like stones, cold and heavy on her tongue.

She stuffed her hands back into her pockets where she wouldn't have to look at them and tried to refocus her attention on the painting. When she stole a glance at Kamaal, however, he was still watching her, and the kindness in his gaze cooled some of the hot embarrassment roiling through her.

"Why did you become an artist in the first place?" he asked.

She'd never felt confident enough to claim that word, that label. There was so much weight to it, especially coming from him. She had no training except what she'd taught herself, and how much could a poor fisherman's daughter from a now-ruined city really know about fine art? Who was she to profess any expertise in the presence of someone like Kamaal? "Oh, I was never a *real* artist," she said. "Not like you. But I enjoyed drawing."

"Why?"

"It made me happy. And when I wasn't happy, it calmed me, gave me peace." She thought of the drawings she'd sent Tyrus and the ones he'd sent back to her, and of long hours spent by the hearth as a child, sketching in the dim firelight until the last embers had died away. "I guess there was always something in me that wanted to make art."

"And is it still there?"

She had to consider the question for a few moments, but at last, she nodded. "I think so. But my hands—" She bit down on her bottom lip to stop its sudden quivering.

"Sometimes we need to find new ways to continue doing what we love," Kamaal said. "If that creative spark is there, then let it shine."

"It's not the same," she replied bitterly.

"No, it isn't. But I think you'll find a way, when you're ready and if you want to. A true artist always does." He looked straight into her eyes when he said the words—*a true artist*—and even though she still had trouble seeing herself that way, it seemed he had no doubt. He gave her a quick wink and turned back to Mitul. "I'm afraid there's not much else to see, and I don't often entertain guests here, but I'm happy to get you a drink if you'd like."

"No, that's all right. We won't stay long. We actually had a question for you. More of a favor."

"Of course. What is it?"

Mitul started by giving a brief history of his recent travels with Amar, including the trip to Atrea to get his memories back and then to Shavhalla, where they'd learned the truth about his curse. Having heard the story before, Aleida quickly grew bored and stepped away to wander the rest of the studio, admiring Kamaal's work as she went. Seeing so many of his paintings here in various stages of completion provided an enlightening look into his process, and she relished the opportunity.

Eventually Mitul got around to their suspicion that the returned Prince Savir was actually Amar, which led to the favor they needed to ask. Aleida tuned back into the conversation but stayed where she was, pretending to examine a large fern hanging from a basket in one corner.

"We have every reason to believe it's him," Mitul said. "But we have to be absolutely sure, and we need to know what kind of state he's in."

"You're worried he's being controlled by the Spirit Tarja," Kamaal said.

"Yes. If not directly, then through her manipulations. And if he truly believes himself to be Prince Savir, rescuing him is going to be a lot harder than we imagined. Neither of us have any chance of getting close to him, but you…" His voice faltered for a second, and when he spoke next, the words came out in a sudden rush. "I know I don't have the right to ask you for anything, but if you could arrange to see him and make sure it's really him, I would be grateful."

Aleida shifted slightly to better see Kamaal's response. He stood facing Mitul with his arms crossed, brows drawn together and mouth taught. Not a frown, exactly, but something close to it. She couldn't see Mitul's face, but his shoulders were slumped, and there was a stiffness in his posture that reminded her of when he'd spoken of leaving Kamaal all those years ago. He still carried some part of that heartbreak with him.

It had cost him a great deal to even come here, she realized, and even more to ask this favor. Before she could stop herself, she stepped forward and cleared her throat. "It was my idea," she said, her voice too loud but effective in drawing their attention. "I'm sorry. I didn't mean to presume. I'd never ask for anything like this if it weren't important. The Spirit Tarja, Valkyra—she's the one who left me like this." Again, she held out her shaking hands. "She promised she'd help me save my brother's life, but she lied, and I never even got to say goodbye to him. Her real name is Nandini Kumar."

Kamaal's brows furrowed. "The empress' former advisor?"

Aleida nodded. "She was behind the invasion. She's the reason my parents are dead. If she's using Amar to regain even a small part of her former power, I hate to think of what she might do next. I can't let her get away with everything she's done, and I don't know any other way to confirm our suspicions. Please, will you help us?"

His eyes had softened a little listening to her, and he shared a quick glance with Mitul before responding. "What would you have me do?"

"Go to the palace and offer to paint Prince Savir," Aleida said. "Or him and Empress Dashiva together. Something to commemorate the occasion of their first meeting. You've done paintings for her before, haven't you? And for other members of her court?"

"I have, and I'm sure she wouldn't refuse the offer. But what do I say to Amar if it is him?"

"Nothing," Mitul replied. "We only want to know. If it is him, he won't remember you. Skies willing, it won't be him at all, and we can continue our search elsewhere."

"Elsewhere?" Kamaal's head tilted to one side. "I can't say I hope the same. I was beginning to like the idea of you staying here a while."

Mitul looked down at his feet and said nothing, but he couldn't quite hide the creases that formed at the corners of his eyes when he smiled.

The artist chuckled and shifted his attention back to Aleida. "Of course I'll help. I once considered Amar a friend, but even if that weren't the case, the integrity of the empire is at stake. How could I refuse such a noble proposition?"

"Thank you," Aleida said, bowing in the traditional Kavoran show of appreciation.

Mitul also offered a slight bow. "Yes, truly. I appreciate your help more than words can express." He motioned to the door. "I suppose we should get going. We've taken up enough of your time for one night."

Kamaal tilted his head. "Have you? I certainly hope you'll consider taking up more of it another night, then." Again, the comment was met with a half-concealed smile from Mitul and a responding chuckle from Kamaal at his bashfulness. "Aleida, it was good to see you again. The next time you stop by, you should bring some of your work. I'd love to see it."

"Oh, that's all right," she replied, flustered once more. "You really don't have to look at it."

"I want to. I'm always curious to see what young new artists are doing. Promise you'll bring it?"

"All right, I will. Promise." She almost felt she could lift off the ground and fly if she wanted to, but she forced her hopes to remain firmly grounded. Most likely Kamaal would forget all about the request, and even if he didn't, someone as skilled as him wouldn't find much to be impressed by in her work.

Still, she clung to the kindness of his words and the small praises he'd offered as if they were a rare treasure. All the way back to the bunkhouse, one piece of their conversation echoed in her mind again and again.

You'll find a way, when you're ready and if you want to. A true artist always does.

She thought she could almost believe that.

KESARI

THREE WEEKS AFTER LEAVING HAYATHU, KESARI, LUCIAN, AND SAYA arrived in Deveaural on a gray day that smelled of rain and seawater. A storm hadn't yet broken, but heavy clouds and flashes of lightning in the distance warned of one soon to come. They rode into the city at a brisk pace, hoping to retrieve what they'd come for quickly and put a roof over their heads at Kesari's family home before the rain started.

Their journey had been quick and uneventful. Once they'd left the desert and transitioned to colder climates, the chill of autumn in its prime reminded them that winter was fast approaching, and they were due to meet Mitul and Aleida in two months. Kesari took to wearing Rajiv's old coat again—a practice she'd abandoned after she and the others had left Shavhalla. Its warmth was still a comfort, though wrapping herself in it was now a matter of practicality rather than emotional soothing.

They reached Jameson's tower late in the afternoon. Kesari and Lucian were discussing how to get past any lingering enchantments the wizard might have left when Saya reined her horse to a stop. She pointed to the base of the tower across the street, where a uniformed man armed with a rifle stood guard. A couple of others were coming out the front door, carrying boxes full of Jameson's belongings and loading them into a wagon. They went back inside, presumably to retrieve more. The wagon was already half full, and Kesari recognized more than a few of the oddities it contained from their previous stay at the tower.

She slid off her horse and was about to approach, but Saya stopped her with a hiss. "What are you doing?"

"They're taking all his stuff. We need to get what we came for before they cart it off."

Saya shook her head. "They're not just going to let you go through his things."

"It's an investigation," Lucian said, drifting a little closer. "We can't get involved."

Kesari frowned, still not understanding.

"Jameson's been missing for almost three months," Saya said. "They must have figured out something happened to him, or that he's not coming back. If they realize we were some of the last people to have seen him, they'll have questions, and we'll be delayed while they sort everything out. It could take ages, and we might end up suspects."

"We didn't do anything wrong," Kesari said. "It was Aleida who got him killed, not us. Why not tell them what happened?"

Lucian's dark eyes widened in the flames. "Oh yes, let's tell them. 'You see, sir, the Wizard Jameson sent us to a mystical city straight out of old legends so we could break our immortal friend's curse. Then the mad Visan woman chasing us captured Jameson, and her Spirit Tarja somehow forced a Bond with the poor wizard. *That's* what killed him. We have no proof of any of this, so you'll have to take our word for it. Oh, and do you mind us poking around and taking some of his things while we're here?'"

"Oh, all right. You don't need to be so sarcastic about it."

"But I *live* for sarcasm—you know that."

She sighed. He was right, as usual, and that was without factoring in her own history of setting fire to the clocktower. Once the investigators learned that, she would lose all credibility and goodwill she might have had with them.

A twinge of guilt made her eyes sting with the threat of tears, but she fought them off. There was no time for that now. One of the guards was watching them rather intently now, and if they didn't move, he'd be on his way to ask why they were loitering.

She returned to her horse and hoisted herself into the saddle. Just then, the two men who'd gone back into the tower emerged with a few more boxes.

"That's the last of it," the taller one said.

"You sure?" asked the man posted outside.

"Aye. Only the furniture left, but we'll have to leave that for now."

"All right. Let's haul this lot off, then."

Kesari turned her horse around and followed Saya back toward the main street, whispering to Lucian as they went. "Go with them, but stay out of sight. Find out where they're taking his stuff, then meet us back at home."

"Aye aye, captain." He shot into the sky to keep watch over the wagon from above.

Rain began to fall as Kesari and Saya ventured into the quieter fields on the outskirts of the city. By the time they reached their destination, it had become a downpour, but Kesari's drenched state didn't stop her mum from pulling her into a tight embrace the moment she opened the door. Her dad joined in a few seconds later. There was no sign of Navya.

Dad insisted on tending to their horses himself, and Mum ushered Kesari and Saya inside to warm themselves. She went back to the stove where she was cooking supper, and Kesari pitched in to help. She answered a never-ending stream of questions about her travels while Saya sat by the fireplace, wrapped in a blanket. Dad kept her company once he'd finished with the horses.

Lucian returned as Kesari was setting the table, floating down the chimney and popping out through the fireplace so suddenly it startled both her parents. They all had a good laugh about it, which was a relief to Kesari given how strained and argumentative the relationship between Lucian and her father had often been. Like most Atreans, he had little experience with or understanding of magic, and it had taken him a long time to come around to the idea that his daughter had traded half her life to form a Bond with a Spirit Tarja. Truth be told, she still wasn't sure he'd fully accepted it, but at least he'd dropped the outright hostility toward Lucian.

After exchanging a few more pleasantries with the man, Lucian came to hover beside her. "They took everything to a guardhouse near the docks," he murmured softly. "The one south of the fish market. It's not very big, but it's locked up tight."

She pouted at the stack of plates she carried. They were going to have a hard time retrieving what they needed if that were the case. "Is there any other place Jameson might have kept his notes?"

"Maybe, but the ones we need are definitely in there. I went inside the guardhouse to take a peek once everyone left the room, and I found the book he was writing in while trying to figure out Amar's curse. I'd have carried it out myself right then except for, you know, all this." A long tendril of flame flicked out and moved to gesture at the rest of him, barely corporeal and no more capable of carrying objects than a real fire.

"I don't suppose they'd give it to us if we asked nicely."

"We can't do anything that will raise questions or draw suspicion. Jameson was an important figure here. Judging by the conversations I overheard, they suspect foul play. They'll want to pin his disappearance on someone."

Which left stealing as their best option—something she was not looking forward to.

Before she could contemplate exactly how they were going to pull it off, her mum wrapped an arm around her shoulders. "It's so nice to have you back. How long do you think you'll be staying?"

The question was quiet and careful, with a slight tremor that jabbed at Kesari's heart. Her sudden disappearance two years prior had left her family wondering where she was and worried about her safety. Now, her parents were relieved simply to know she was all right, but they wanted more than that. They wanted her back home. The softness of Mum's voice belied a fear that if she pressed too hard, asked for too much, she would push her daughter away.

She wouldn't, of course, but Kesari still couldn't give her the answer she wanted to hear. "I'm not sure. Not very long. The man I was traveling with before—he's in trouble, and I think I might be the only one who can help him." With Jameson dead, who else would perform the magic needed to restore Amar's memories? Once they had his book of notes and returned to Kavora, they could perhaps enlist a more experienced Tarja's assistance, but Kesari had a unique familiarity with

Amar and with the process Jameson had previously used. She needed to stay involved until the situation was resolved.

Besides, she didn't yet feel ready to come home. She'd done a lot of healing during her time away, especially since joining Saya and the others. But the weight of her mistakes was still a burden here in the house that would forever be darkened by Rajiv's absence. She glanced at her arms and could clearly picture the crisscross of scars hidden beneath her sleeves. Her own internal light was brighter now than it had been when she left, but not yet strong enough to keep that darkness at bay, and she couldn't let herself be swallowed up by it again.

She set down the last plate from her stack and threw her arms around Mum's waist, squeezing tight, the way she used to when she was a little girl. "I'm sorry. I miss you—all of you, but I…" Her words caught on a lump in her throat. "I can't stay here. I'm not ready."

Her mother pulled back and placed both hands on her cheeks, staring into her eyes with warmth and understanding. "It's all right, little one. We'll be here whenever you are."

She managed to hold back brimming tears and followed Mum to the stove. "Where's Navya? I thought she'd be home by now." It was getting dark outside, and the storm had intensified to include a fierce wind and loud bursts of thunder along with the downpour.

The smile slid from Mum's face, and she exchanged a worried look with Dad. For a few seconds, neither of them would answer the question. Something was wrong, but what?

"Navya's been staying out late most nights," Dad said at last. There was more to it than that, but he wasn't elaborating further.

"Why?" she asked.

"Running amok," he replied with a scowl. "We had to pick her up from the guard station last week after she was arrested for vandalizing a shop. I thought she'd straighten up after that, but she was right back out the next day with the same friends who got her into trouble."

"Nothing we say or do seems to make a difference," Mum added. "She's angry all the time. Some of it seems like normal growing up. But these new friends she has are a tough lot, children who've lived a hard life and not had as much parental support as they probably need. Some don't have parents at all." Her chin began to tremble. "I suppose that's why she was drawn to them. We certainly haven't been the most involved parents these last few years."

"We did the best we could," Dad murmured. The words came out like he'd said them a hundred times before but still wasn't convinced they were true.

Mum shook her head. "She was hurting. We should have paid more attention."

The weight that had been pressing in on Kesari grew heavier. They'd all been hurting, and she was the reason for that hurt. She'd killed Rajiv. She'd abandoned Navya. She'd left their parents grieving the loss of not just one child, but two. She had no doubt that they'd done the best they could under the circumstances, but *she* was the one who had created those circumstances. And Navya had suffered for it, the last, lone child overlooked amid their parents' grief.

She took a few deep breaths in an attempt to quiet her racing thoughts, but it didn't help much. The old guilt and self-loathing clamped down on her painfully, and when they all sat down to eat, her attention kept wandering to the empty place across the table where Navya should have been. Saya mercifully took over most of the dinner conversation, but Kesari's parents kept casting worried glances in her direction, and at the door, as if they hoped Navya would come strolling in at any moment.

She didn't, and even though the spicy dish her mother had made was one of Kesari's favorites, to her, it didn't taste like anything at all.

KESARI

KESARI FOUND IT DIFFICULT TO SLEEP IN HER OLD BED THAT NIGHT, not because she wasn't tired or comfortable, but because she couldn't stop her mind from circling around her troubles—past, present, and future all included. Despite talking it over with Lucian earlier, she was still half convinced Navya's struggles were a direct result of her own mistakes. Then there was Jameson's research and the challenge of stealing it. Even if they managed to pull that off, she wasn't certain they'd be able to restore Amar's memories. They still didn't even know what state he was in, or where he was, or how to help him without Valkyra thwarting their every move.

There was nothing she could do about any of those concerns now, and sleeping would have been a far more productive use of her time than worrying. Somehow, that knowledge only made sleep more elusive.

She was finally starting to drift off somewhere in the early hours of the morning when a noise startled her awake again. Her eyes snapped open and immediately found Lucian, who'd drifted toward the door. On the other side of the room, Saya kept dozing peacefully.

"What was that?" Kesari whispered.

"Probably nothing," Lucian said. "Your mum or dad getting something from the kitchen. Go back to sleep."

She closed her eyes again, but there was another thud followed by a hissed curse in a voice she recognized immediately. She slipped out of bed and tiptoed quickly to the door.

When she opened it, the figure on the other side jumped and cursed again. Navya froze when she saw Kesari, her mouth opening slightly and her dark eyes glinting in the glow of Lucian's flames. A small bag was open in her left hand, and the right held a few fresh carrots and turnips Mum had picked from the garden earlier. She appeared to be in the process of filling the bag with them.

"Are you…sneaking into your own house?"

"Shh," Navya hissed. "You'll wake them up."

Kesari frowned. "You've been out all night. Do you have any idea how worried—"

"Shh!" Her voice was more insistent this time, and she cut a quick glance at their parents' bedroom door. "Not here." Stuffing her handful of vegetables into the sack, she crossed to the front door and stepped out. Kesari followed, but Lucian stayed behind to let them talk privately.

"What's with the bag and sneaking around?" she asked quietly once they were outside.

"It's for my friends. Food's hard to come by, for some of them, and Mum always harvests more vegetables than she knows what to do with. They might as well fill some hungry bellies."

"She'd give them to you if you asked. You don't need to slink in here in the middle of the night. They worried when you didn't come home, you know."

Navya laughed, a low, harsh sound that was more caustic than amused. "Oh, did they? And I suppose you're the expert on that, aren't you? You kept them worrying for more than two years when *you* didn't come home."

The words hit like a blow to the stomach, and it took Kesari a few seconds to recover. Navya, meanwhile, wore a tight but smug smile. Her eyes burned with the same anger she'd hurled at Kesari during her last visit.

"You're mad at me, and you have every right to be. But don't take it out on them." She jerked a thumb back at the house where their parents still slept. "Or yourself. They told me what kind of friends you've been running around with, the trouble you've gotten into. What do you think's going to happen if you keep that up?"

"What do you care?" Navya spat back.

"You're my sister. Of course I care."

"The same way *they* care because they're my parents, right?" She scoffed. "Blood doesn't mean anything. Rajiv died, and you left, and they stopped noticing me. They were too upset about the children they lost to pay attention to the one they still had."

"Grief is messy," Kesari replied. "They dealt with it as well as they could."

"That's not good enough!" Navya clenched the bag tighter in her fists. "I have a new family now—people who actually care about me and understand what I've been through."

"You call that a family? They got you arrested."

"So what? They'd never abandon me—not the way *you* did." She drew in a choked breath and jutted her chin out. "What are you doing here anyway? Didn't you have something important to do with *your* new friends?"

It took every ounce of patience Kesari possessed to swallow the arguments she still had for Navya. She wouldn't listen anyway, and her abrasiveness wasn't entirely unjustified. "I did, but things went wrong, and one of them is in even more trouble than before. We came back here looking for a way to save him, but…" She shook her head. This was nothing Navya cared about or needed to know.

"But what?" she pressed, raising an eyebrow.

"It doesn't matter."

"Fine then, keep your secrets. You and Rajiv never used to tell me anything. Even with him gone, it's still the same."

Kesari rubbed at her brow and held back an exasperated sigh. She'd almost forgotten how petulant her younger sister could be, but beneath the cutting words, there was a genuine pain she wanted to ease if she could. "There's a book of notes that belonged to the Wizard Jameson. We need it, but we can't get it now because it's locked up in some guard station near the docks with the rest of his things."

"Near the docks?" Navya repeated, her eyes now bright and alert instead of glaring.

"Yes," she confirmed, recalling the specific location Lucian had told her about. "South of the fish market."

"That's perfect!" She cocked her head to one side. "Please tell me you're actually using your magic these days."

Kesari lifted one shoulder in half a shrug. "A little. Why?"

"Because," Navya said, her grin as sharp as a sword's edge. "I think there might be a way we can help each other."

"I don't like this," Saya said the following evening as she and Kesari stood in the long shadow of the belltower. Lucian hovered between them, all three watching the square for Navya and the friends she was bringing to meet them.

"I don't like it either," Lucian said, "but it's the best idea we've got."

"We're not committing to anything yet," Kesari reminded them both. "We're just going to hear them out."

Saya crossed her arms and pointed to a trio of approaching figures. "Here they are."

Navya was the shortest among them, positioned between another girl who looked to be about Kesari's age and a lanky young man with skin as pale as ivory. Confident, purposeful strides gave the impression that he was the one in charge. The tails of a well-worn but once elegant coat fanned out behind him, and shaggy hair hung loose beneath the brim of a bowler hat perched crookedly on his head.

Navya quickly made introductions between the two groups, and a few handshakes were exchanged. The girl's name was Emma, and the young man called himself Nemo. He held on to Kesari's hand a few seconds longer than was comfortable, staring at her with narrow green eyes beneath skewed brows. "So you're the witch then, eh?"

Kesari would have preferred 'Tarja' but didn't bother to correct him. Atreans had all sorts of names for magic users even though there weren't many among them, and most were convinced each term meant something different. Witches were usually mysterious figures who could hurt or heal depending on their mood. Not quite as crafty and evil as a sorceress or as pure and benevolent as a priestess, but somewhere in the middle. That was close enough to what a Tarja really was.

She pulled her hand away. "I am."

Nemo raised an eyebrow. "Never met a witch before. You're younger than I pictured."

She ignored the comment. "Navya says you need to get into the guardhouse near the docks?"

"We do. They took something from us, and we need it back. 'Course it's a real challenge for any ordinary person to get in without being caught, but a witch? I'll bet you could do it in your sleep."

"Not exactly. Not with all those guards in there."

"Perhaps that's where I can be of service."

The plan they came up with was simple enough. Nemo and his crew would create a diversion nearby—something big enough to draw out most of the guards. Once they'd gone, Kesari, Saya, and Lucian would sneak inside the guardhouse, using Kesari's magic to bypass any security measures they might encounter. They'd find what they needed, take it, and get out before the guards came back.

"What sort of diversion are you planning?" Lucian asked.

"Leave that to us," Nemo replied. "We've got a few tricks up our sleeve, haven't we?"

Navya and Emma both nodded, and Kesari couldn't help feeling a little unsettled by the mischievous glint in her sister's eye. The way Nemo talked, heists like this were routine for him and his crew. It was no wonder Navya was getting into trouble, hanging around with this lot.

Not that Kesari herself was any better. Here she was, getting them both wrapped up in an illegal scheme that could go wrong in at least a dozen different ways. A fine example she was to her younger sister. Oh yes, very fine indeed.

At the very least, perhaps she could mitigate some of the damage. "If we do this, Navya stays out of it."

He shook his head. "I need one of my own people with you to make sure you get what we asked for. I was going to send her—someone we can both trust."

"If we get caught, I don't want her around. She's not getting arrested again."

He shrugged. "So don't get caught."

"I'm not taking her." Navya shot her a glare, but Kesari ignored it. "Pick someone else."

"Fine," Nemo grumbled after they'd stared each other down for a few seconds. "Navya stays with me, and Emma'll go with you."

Kesari wasn't thrilled about having another person to worry about, but she could understand his insistence that she bring one of his own crew. He didn't trust them, and he had no reason to. Of course, they had no reason to trust him, either, but if they could both get something they wanted out of this arrangement, that was a solid enough foundation for a temporary partnership. She reached out to shake Nemo's hand again, sealing the deal.

He squeezed her fingers harder than was necessary. "We'll meet back here in three days. That should give all of us enough time to prepare. Sound all right?"

"Sure."

"Good. I look forward to working with you."

They all started to walk away, and Kesari called out to her sister. "Wait, Navya. Aren't you coming home?"

All three stopped, and Nemo and Emma both smirked at the younger girl. There was something mocking in the way they looked at her, and it made her stiffen. She hunched her shoulders. "No. And I don't need you babysitting me or telling me what to do."

"All right. But Mum and Dad want to see you. You should at least come by later."

The other two snickered. Navya stared down at her feet, brows drawn tightly together. "Just leave me alone." Kesari wasn't sure whether she was talking to her or the others. She shot Kesari one last glare, then shoved past Nemo and Emma to continue walking across the square.

The two of them followed, making a show of holding back laughter as if they'd just witnessed the funniest thing in the world. In high-pitched voices, they taunted her.

"Aw, do Mummy and Daddy miss their little girl?"

"Best hurry home so you don't miss your bedtime story."

"Shut up," she growled.

Kesari had half a mind to go after them, but that would likely only make the teasing worse and drive the wedge between her and Navya deeper. She clenched her jaw in frustration and watched until they disappeared from view. "Come on," she said to Saya and Lucian. "Let's go home."

On the way, she explained the plan again to Saya, who'd had a difficult time following her conversation with Nemo in Atrean. Once she'd finished, Saya asked, "Are you sure you want to do this?"

"We have to, don't we? We need to get Jameson's notes as soon as possible. Mitul and Aleida will be expecting us back in Valmandi before too long."

"And you're all right with using your magic to break into the guardhouse?"

She bit her bottom lip. She suspected what her friend was really asking was whether she could manage it. Channeling altma tended to be more difficult in high-stress situations, and they couldn't afford for anything to go wrong. The last time Kesari had tried to use her magic in a tense situation, it had failed her, and Valkyra had managed to take Amar captive.

Who would pay the price if she failed this time?

"You still have the mesala my mother gave you," Saya added quietly. "If you need it."

Kesari didn't want to waste such a precious resource on something she should be able to do on her own, especially not when she might need it for more important things later. Like bringing Amar's memories back. "No, I'll be fine," she said, forcing as much confidence into her voice as she could manage. "I can do this."

Lucian darted in front of her with a wide grin. "You're damn right, you can. Of that, I have no doubt."

SAVIR

PRINCE SAVIR'S GILDED CARRIAGE ROLLED INTO JAKHAT IN THE LATE afternoon, drawn by four black horses with plumed feather headdresses and followed by an entire entourage of guards, envoys, and other staff. Naturally, this drew the immediate attention of everyone around, and crowds soon lined the streets to watch the procession as it made its way to the imperial palace. Their cheers rose in volume when Savir briefly dared to draw back the silk curtains and peer outside. Some made as if to rush the carriage, but they were quickly dissuaded by the guards' stern looks and barked commands.

He closed the curtains and leaned back against the cushions in his seat, trying unsuccessfully to get comfortable. His clothes were too scratchy, and his shoes pinched at the toes. The crown on his head was a cumbersome band of thick bronze that kept slipping down his brow. Bhajan had gotten it resized for him before he left Valmandi, but it still didn't seem to fit quite right.

Or maybe his discomfort was more a result of the attention coming his way. This entire parade was a spectacle he would have rather avoided, but his grandparents—and their entire council—thought it best he make an entrance worthy of his station. He knew people would be eager to see him, but he hadn't understood to what extent until now. There were so many of them, and he couldn't help wondering how their lives might be impacted by whatever came from this meeting with the empress.

Perhaps he'd never be able to fully appreciate the weight of that responsibility, but it was one he would not—could not—let himself forget.

Magistrate Ashaya sat across from him, and Valkyra lounged on a cushion beside him. "They're all so excited to see you," she said, her silver eyes wide and gleaming.

"And they'll be equally thrilled to see you on the throne," Ashaya added.

Savir doubted the empress herself was so eager to be replaced.

The procession took a winding path to the center of the city and began a gradual ascent. Through a narrow gap in the curtains, he glimpsed the imperial palace at the top of a hill, its trio of polished white domes reflecting the sunlight. Clenching and unclenching his fists a few times, he tried to release some of the tension building within him.

"She's your aunt, dear," Valkyra said gently. "She should be pleased to see you. This is a happy reunion."

A happy reunion. Perhaps if he kept that optimistic perspective, it would manifest itself into reality.

The carriage stopped, which Savir could only assume meant they'd arrived. He straightened the crown on his head once more, prompting a stern look from Ashaya, who'd told him to stop fretting with the confounded thing at least half a dozen times already. "Are you ready, Your Highness?" he asked.

"I think so."

"All right then." He smoothed out his robe, adjusted the hems of his sleeves, and opened the carriage door. Savir waited until he'd stepped down to exit himself, and Valkyra fluttered out behind him, alighting in her usual spot on his shoulder. Tarik dismounted the horse he'd been riding and fell into step behind them.

Savir's mouth started to open as he took in the sight of the palace, which appeared to be at least three times the size of the one in Valmandi and much taller than it had seemed from the city streets below. Its white stone looked as solid and pristine as the day it had been cut, with nary a crack, blemish, or smudge of dirt to be seen. A wide set of stairs led up to the doors, and on a broad mezzanine halfway up stood several guards and a woman dressed in finery that put Savir and the rest of his entourage to shame.

For half a second, he thought she must be the empress, but she was too young, perhaps only ten years older than him. She wore a draping, floor-length gown of pale gray and white with silver embellishments embroidered along the edges. Her shoulders were bare, one partially concealed beneath the sheer fabric of her headdress, which cascaded over her long, black hair to her waist. Her jewelry was made of pearls and glistening blue stones set in silver, and she wore more of it than anyone Savir had ever seen.

Magistrate Ashaya was the first to speak, coming to rest two steps down from where the young woman stood. "Princess Jasala, how lovely to see you again." He bowed low, and Savir followed suit, causing his crown to slip a little. He straightened it in what he hoped wasn't an obvious show of clumsiness.

The princess returned their bows with a slight dip of her head. "It's a pleasure to see you as well, Magistrate. And you must be Savir." The warmth of her smile almost made him fail to notice the way she'd left off his royal title. "I'm sure you'd all like to rest after your long journey, but my mother is quite eager to meet you. She requested that I bring you to her before you're shown to your rooms. If it's not too much trouble, of course."

"No, of course not," Ashaya replied. "We'd be honored."

"Excellent. My people will see to it that yours are given fitting accommodations. You are, of course, welcome to bring your own guards along, though we did increase palace security in preparation for your arrival."

"Thank you," Savir replied.

His grandparents had warned that Dashiva and her inner circle were not to be trusted under any circumstances, and whatever misgivings Tarik still had about him, he seemed to take his duty seriously enough. He took a step closer to Savir now, his shadow long and dark over the white stairs. "I'm sure your existing safety measures are sufficient, Princess, but I'd feel better seeing to His Highness' security myself, if you don't mind."

"Of course," Jasala replied. "You can all follow me, please." She walked up the steps, her movements all fluid grace with her dress trailing like liquid silver behind her. Savir and Ashaya followed, and when they reached the top, a pair of uniformed guards opened the entry doors to let them through.

Jakhat's palace couldn't have been more different from the one in Valmandi. Where that building's charm lay in the intricate details and patterns adorning every surface, this one's majesty could be seen in its clean lines and sharp angles. Windows all around allowed natural light to fill the entry, bouncing off the white stone surfaces to create an almost glowing effect. Shades of blue and green offered the only splashes of color amongst the alabaster. The blue came from geometric tiles lining a pool of clear water in the center of the large entryway, while the green came from the various plants decorating the window ledges and balustrades. There were hanging ferns, draping ivy, and leafy vines, with some bearing white flowers to match the pale stone of the palace itself.

It was undeniably beautiful, the most impressive edifice Savir had ever seen—not that he could remember seeing many. A structure befitting the ruler of an empire.

But there was something aloof and impersonal about it, too. He much preferred the colorful warmth of the Valmandi palace. Perhaps, when he was emperor, he could inject some of that warmth here.

A shiver ran up his spine as his mind caught on the thought. *If* he became emperor. Not when. It wasn't a surety yet.

"Are you coming, Prince Savir?" Ashaya called from a set of stairs on the other side of the fountain, where he and Jasala had paused to wait.

He hurried to catch up. "Sorry. I was admiring the architecture. It's incredible."

Jasala nodded. "It is, though I'm not sure it compares to the palace of Valmandi. I always enjoy seeing all the beautiful adornments and figures carved into its walls. I discover something new every time I visit."

"Do you visit often?"

"I used to, when I was a girl. Though, regrettably, I haven't had a chance to go back since the late empress passed."

His mother. In Valmandi, she was always called Princess Priyani, not Empress, even though that had been her official title after her marriage. He couldn't be sure why, but he liked to think it was his grandparents' way of keeping alive the memory of the daughter they'd known best—the princess beloved by her entire city, before she'd been swept away to give the emperor an heir.

"Here we are," Jasala said, motioning to a door ahead, and Savir did his best to stay poised and calm. He'd hoped to have a little more time before meeting the empress, but here they were, and he'd only have one chance to make a good first impression. With any luck, Dashiva would be just as congenial as her daughter had been thus far.

Jasala knocked on the door softly and spoke, raising her voice a little to be heard on the other side. "Mother, it's me. I've arrived with our guests. Shall I show them in?"

"Yes, please," came the muffled reply.

She opened the door and led them through to a luxurious sitting room. A large window had been left open to overlook a flower garden and, below that, the city. The rest of the walls bore several paintings framed in gold. A low table and several cushions sat in the center of the room, along with a pair of plush sofas. In one of these sat an aging woman with gray hair twisted into an elaborate knot at one side of her head. Her blue gown had a loose, robe-like fit and was far less extravagant than Jasala's, but the gold crown on her head was unmistakable.

"Your Imperial Majesty," Magistrate Ashaya said, making the lowest bow he could without toppling over. As they'd practiced, Savir bowed as well, though not as deeply. He was still a prince, after all, and the rightful heir to the throne, which meant Dashiva should have been bowing to *him* instead. But there was a big difference between formal rules and common courtesy. He was in her home at her invitation, and she was still—for now—the empress.

She gave Ashaya no attention at all but regarded Savir with dark, hooded eyes and pursed lips. Her gaze swept over him from top to bottom several times, her expression flat and unreadable. Savir kept his own face equally neutral and tried not to think too much about the pounding of his chest or the thin sheen of sweat starting to form on his brow. His crown seemed to be slipping lower one slow hair's breadth at a time, and he willed it to stay put.

After several long seconds, Dashiva spoke. "So, you're the boy claiming to be my long-dead nephew. Come closer so I can get a better look at you."

He stepped forward a few paces, but the empress motioned him closer still, until his toes were mere inches away from hers. She straightened a little and leaned forward, peering up at his face. The scent of a strong perfume filled his nose, something floral and woodsy. He avoided inhaling too deeply and waited for her examination to end.

"Your dragon is staring at me," she said, eyeing Valkyra with a wary look. "I don't like dragons. I've heard they can be good pets, but I've also heard far too many stories of them turning on their masters. Has she ever bitten you?"

"No, Your Majesty."

"Hm. Well, you be careful. Treacherous creatures, dragons, and far more clever than any beast has a right to be."

Savir held back a smirk at the thought of what Valkyra must think of her observations. "Thank you, Your Majesty. I'll be careful."

She leaned back against the sofa and tilted her head. "You don't look very much like your father. Or your mother, for that matter. I suppose you have some proof of your identity or King Bhajan never would have suffered things to go this far."

"The proof is here, Your Majesty," Ashaya said, producing Princess Priyani's journal with a flourish. "I've marked the relevant passages, and I also have this letter from the maidservant who took young Savir into hiding and raised him."

Dashiva took the journal, glancing at the folded letter poking out from the edge of the cover. "And where is this maidservant now?"

"I'm afraid she's no longer with us." He cast a rather pitying look at Savir. "She and the prince were attacked on their way to Valmandi. She didn't survive the encounter."

"How tragic," Dashiva said, though she didn't sound very sincere.

"Indeed. If I may, there's a particular passage in the journal that will—"

Dashiva held up a hand to cut him off. "I will review the information you've provided in my own due time, Magistrate. I expect you're all very tired from your journey. Jasala will show you to the rooms we've prepared for you. Please make yourselves comfortable and enjoy all the pleasures the palace has to offer."

"Of course." Ashaya stepped back and bowed once more. "Thank you. We are most grateful for your hospitality."

Savir bowed, too. They headed for the door where Princess Jasala was already waiting.

"Oh, and Savir?" the empress called.

"Yes, Your Majesty?"

"Kamaal Ruman has offered to do a painting of the two of us. I accepted, of course. As you can see, I'm rather fond of his work." She gestured to the paintings hung on the surrounding walls, and it was only then that Savir realized they were all done in the same distinct style. Most incorporated floral elements, including a portrait of a much younger Dashiva surrounded by flowering jasmine vines. "Apparently," the empress continued, "he wants to commemorate the occasion, and it would be a great honor to have someone of his renown capture our images for the ages. I arranged for him to come by tomorrow morning so we can sit for him. It will be a good chance for us to talk and get to know each other better."

"Thank you. It would be a great privilege."

"Good. Do make sure you find something more suitable to wear, would you? And don't bring the dragon."

"Of course. Good day, Your Majesty." He dipped his head slightly and followed the others out.

Once he and Valkyra were alone in his assigned room—a large space that came with a whole host of servants he'd promptly dismissed—he sank into a chair and took the crown off his head. The tight breath that had been caught in his lungs all morning came out with a whoosh, and he stretched to release the lingering tension in his muscles. All in all, his first meeting with his aunt had been—

What? It was impossible to judge with any certainty. He wouldn't have called it a success or a failure; both words seemed too extreme. Dashiva hadn't exactly welcomed him with open arms or even acknowledged that he was her nephew, but the accommodations she'd provided were certainly fit for royalty. And she wouldn't have accepted Kamaal Ruman's offer to paint them if she weren't at least entertaining the idea that he was her nephew.

Unless, of course, she was only using that as an opportunity to trap him in a room for hours and interrogate him. What was it she'd called it? *A good chance for us to talk and get to know each other better.* Suddenly, he was very much dreading tomorrow morning's appointment with the famed artist.

"I don't think she liked me very much," he said to Valkyra, spinning his crown around in his hands.

"No, but you didn't really expect her to, did you?"

He frowned and shook his head. He hadn't, but that hadn't stopped him from hoping. "I just thought it would be easier if I could make her like me."

"There's still time for that," said Valkyra, but they both knew time wasn't the problem. He was a threat to Dashiva's rule, and no length of time spent ingratiating himself with her was going to change that.

Still, he had to try. "Maybe after she's seen the evidence, she'll be more accepting. There's got to be some way to work this all out peacefully."

Valkyra inclined her head and ruffled her wings a little. "I do hope you're right, dear, but if Dashiva won't step down, you must be strong enough to take back what's rightfully yours."

He swallowed, suddenly nauseous. What ugly consequences would come from taking that path?

When he didn't respond, she brushed her tail over his hand. "You want to be a fair ruler, don't you? Strong enough to do what's right and stand up for your people when they need it most? It starts with this. You have to stand up for yourself first, or how can you be strong for anything or anyone else?"

"I know."

"So you'll fight, if it comes down to that?"

He looked at his hands, which always gripped a sword so comfortably and seemed more adept at fighting than anything else. Now they held a crown, and despite its weight and the clumsiness of its fit, the title that went with it still felt right. He *was* a prince, and though he wished to avoid any conflict over who sat on the throne, how could he deny that part of himself and let a usurper continue her rule unchallenged?

"Yes," he said. "If it comes to that, I will fight."

He wasn't entirely sure he believed himself.

Part II

The Musician & the Artist

16

ALEIDA

ALEIDA STOOD AT THE WINDOW IN MITUL'S RENTED ROOM, watching passersby in the lamplit street below and searching for broad shoulders and curly hair among them. Mitul paced behind her, stopping occasionally to look outside. His fingers kept twisting the turquoise cuff around his wrist, and he worried at his bottom lip with his teeth.

"He should be here any second," he said, a phrase he'd repeated so often in the last two hours it no longer held any meaning. Aleida only nodded in response, though she was sure he'd been talking to himself more than to her.

They were waiting for Kamaal, who'd been scheduled to present himself at the imperial palace first thing in the morning to begin his painting. He'd agreed to meet Mitul and Aleida at the Serene Star once he left the palace to confirm whether Prince Savir was actually Amar. Aleida had come over as soon as her workday ended, hoping to find the artist already present with news, but he still hadn't arrived. It was well past dark now, and with every passing second, they both grew more impatient, though she seemed to be handling the delay much better than Mitul. The man's nerves were obviously being strained by this whole affair, as evidenced by the frenetic pacing and the untouched plate of food on his table.

In an effort to distract herself and pass the time, Aleida opened the leather parcel in her hands and looked over its contents. Inside were the drawings she'd created during her travels across Erythyr these past three years. She doubted Kamaal would even remember that he'd asked to see her work, but she respected him enough to at least honor the request.

Many of the drawings had been severely damaged by seawater during her escape from the sinking *Hound's Hatred*, but the ones she'd sent to Tyrus and that Hasan had later returned were in better condition. Toward the back of the parcel, she also kept the letters her brother had written to her, many with drawings he'd done himself. All of those were damaged beyond repair, little more than smudged ink and charcoal she couldn't decipher even though she'd become a decent reader. All except for a single letter at the back—the one Hasan had written to tell her of her brother's passing.

She ran her trembling fingers over the paper's surface, worn with creases and dried tear stains. Before she could stop herself, she let her eyes drift over the words, and the first line jumped into her mind with ease.

Dear Aleida, I am very sorry to tell you that your brother—

She snapped the parcel shut before she could continue, already sensing the dark pit of grief opening within her, threatening to drag her in. This was not the time or place.

She went back to staring out the window and caught a glimpse of black curls disappearing under an awning at the inn's entrance. "I think he's here."

Mitul shifted his pacing closer to the door. When the knock came, he flung it open and ushered Kamaal inside with a quick wave of his hand.

"It's him," the artist said before the question was even asked. "You were right."

Mitul threw his arms around Kamaal's shoulders, and Aleida couldn't be sure whether the choked sound he made was a laugh or a sob. Kamaal whispered something in his ear and rubbed one hand over his back. They stayed that way for a few seconds, and when they broke apart, Kamaal took both of Mitul's hands in his and gave them a squeeze. "You found him. It's going to be all right."

"Thank you." Mitul's voice was rough with strained emotion.

"Thank you for going to see him."

"Of course. I was happy to do it."

"How did he look? Was he hurt or confused? Afraid?"

"No, he seemed fine. Healthy, happy enough. He didn't recognize me at all, but that's to be expected, given what you've told me about his memories. From what I could tell, he fully believes he's Prince Savir, though I'm less certain the empress believes the same. She asked him a lot of questions, particularly about his childhood. He made good efforts to answer, but it felt more like he was reciting a story than sharing his own memories."

Mitul's resumed his pacing once more, twisting his hands together with nervous energy as he walked.

"Was there a white dragon with him?" Aleida asked.

"No," said Kamaal. "At one point, I saw a dragon with another man—someone from the Valmandi delegation, I'd guess."

Aleida opened her leather parcel again and flipped through the pages until she found the one she was looking for. In her haste and clumsiness, a few of the others fell out and fluttered to the floor, but she paid them no mind. She held up the paper to show Kamaal a series of small, charcoal sketches depicting Valkyra, which she'd sent to Tyrus more than a year prior. "She would have looked like this. White with silver eyes, about the size of a half-grown kitten."

Kamaal's brows lifted a little as he studied the drawing. He bent to pick up the pages that had fallen on the floor, gaze lingering on a portrait of Amar. Aleida's stomach flipped as he studied her work, but it wasn't entirely uncomfortable. Despite how much she admired him and knew her skills didn't match his, she recognized that, with time and practice, someday they might have.

But not anymore. Any skill she might have had was rendered meaningless now that her hands were so uncooperative.

He passed the pages back to her. "These are quite impressive."

"Thank you."

"You've clearly worked hard to cultivate your talents. It would be a great tragedy for you to give up art forever—one I'm sure Artex would weep over."

He said it gently, likely with the intention of encouraging her, but irritation prickled within Aleida at the mention of her god, and she bowed her head to keep it from showing on her face. If Artex had wanted her to be an artist, he wouldn't have taken away her control over her hands and fingers. If the good, benevolent creator she'd once believed in was real at all, he would have heard her prayers and intervened to save her brother.

"Do *you* believe in any god?" she asked quietly.

"Occasionally. I did always like the Visan idea of a god who's an artist. Of course, I'm an artist too, so perhaps that's only hubris."

When she looked up at him, he winked, but she did not return his smile. Her trembling fingers curled more tightly over the edges of the papers in her hands.

Mitul stopped his pacing to stand at Kamaal's side. His eyes remained blank and unfocused until Kamaal reached out and squeezed his hand. "I'm sorry about Amar. I know this is exactly what you feared might happen to him."

"It's worse," he said with a sigh. "The whole reason I stayed with him all these years is because I didn't want him to die out there alone and forget everything again. But he did die, and each time I was there to remind him who he was. This time, though—" He ran his free hand over his graying hair. "He's being manipulated by a cruel and powerful enemy, and there's nothing I can do."

"Nothing you can do *yet*," Kamaal said gently. "You have a plan. Your friends are coming back, and they'll know how to restore his memories so you can get him away from the dragon."

"This never should have happened. I should have stopped her. If I were a warrior or a Tarja, maybe I—"

Kamaal shifted around to face him head-on. "Shh. None of that, now. You are perfect exactly as you are. The world has enough men of violence and power. Humble musicians with soft words and gentle hearts are just as admirable and far more precious, and if Amar were here now, he wouldn't stand to hear you put yourself down like that."

Some of the worry lines on Mitul's brow faded a little, but he kept hold of Kamaal's hand in both of his as if it were a lifeline.

"What are we going to do now?" Aleida asked.

"I don't think there's much we *can* do until Saya, Kes, and Lucian come back," Mitul said. "We should keep listening, trying to find out more. Did you get any sense of whether Amar is planning to stay here?"

Kamaal shrugged. "For a little while, it seems. Beyond that, it's hard to say. The empress didn't seem particularly friendly toward him, and of course, we've all heard the rumors that she'll deny him as the prince outright."

Mitul's frown deepened as he shook his head. "To break his curse, he's supposed to atone for the atrocities of war, and now he might end up right in the center of a new one. He's a pawn in a game he shouldn't even be playing."

Aleida's mind felt sluggish as she tried to come up with some other solution—something better than standing by helplessly and waiting. It wasn't so much that she cared about Amar's fate; she didn't know him well enough to care and had spent the better part of the last three years viewing him as little more than a prize to hunt. But she'd seen firsthand what could happen when the desires of the powerful stirred up conflict, and Valkyra was not above furthering her ambitions through an all-out civil war. Aleida had no goodwill for Kavora or its people as a whole, but that didn't mean she wanted to see the innocent among them suffer the same violence she'd witnessed in the Visan invasion. More than that, she couldn't stand to see Valkyra succeed in any of her plans. She had to be stopped. She had to pay for everything she'd done, not only to the people of Vis, but to Aleida specifically.

And then there was Mitul. Looking at him now, the hunch of his shoulders and the twisted set of his mouth, something inside her cracked. Here was a man who was terrified for his brother and trying desperately to save him. He had every reason to hate her for her role in creating this mess, but all he'd ever shown her was kindness.

She needed to do something, but there was nothing *to* do—not yet. Mitul and Kamaal had both been right about that. With Valkyra so close to Amar and likely keeping a watchful eye on everything and everyone around him, they had to be careful. They would probably only get one chance to rescue him, and they weren't prepared for that yet.

"At least we know where he is now," she said. "He may be in the worst place possible, but he's not lost anymore."

Mitul said nothing, and she couldn't tell whether her words had helped or only made things worse.

She glanced at the window and the streets outside, which had grown even darker in the time they'd spent talking. Her workday began before dawn, and she was already longing for sleep. "I need to go. I'll see you tomorrow?"

"Sure," he said, but his voice sounded distant.

"Thank you for your help," she said to Kamaal.

"Yes, of course. Thank you for allowing me to see some of your art. It was truly a pleasure. I hope you'll consider pursuing it again, whenever you're ready."

Aleida wasn't sure she'd ever be ready, but she nodded anyway and went to leave the room.

The two men followed her but lingered in the doorway, and she caught a piece of their conversation as she walked away.

"Stay. Please."

"Are you sure?"

"If it's not too much trouble. I don't know if I can stand to be alone right now."

She glanced over her shoulder at them. Kamaal raised one hand to the side of Mitul's face. "It's never too much trouble, you know that. I'll stay."

They stepped back inside, and she heard the soft *thunk* of the door closing as she descended the stairs.

KESARI

"WHAT'S TAKING THEM SO LONG?" KESARI ASKED, GLANCING OVER her shoulder to the guardhouse across the street. The question was directed mostly at Emma, who ought to have some idea of what Nemo and his crew were planning for a distraction, but the young woman only shrugged and went back to picking at her fingernails.

Saya sat on a low stone wall dividing the dockside market from the walking path below. Lucian hovered above them all, barely noticeable as a tiny glow the size of a candle's flame. They'd been waiting here in the dark for at least an hour, and Kesari's impatience grew with each passing minute. Had something gone wrong already?

She tried to distract her mind from worst-case scenarios by studying the various ships docked nearby, classifying each one by type and making up names for them. It was a game she and Rajiv had often played, though he was always better at coming up with ship-worthy names than she was.

There were lights on some of the vessels, made by fires and lanterns that hadn't yet been doused. As she watched, one of these lights seemed to grow, but it was far enough in the distance that she couldn't be sure what had caused it. The same happened on a closer vessel, the glow expanding so quickly this time that she was certain something was wrong. "I think that ship's on fire."

"Looks like it," Lucian replied.

Emma stopped picking at her nails and sat up straighter, but she wasn't watching the fires. Instead, she was focused on the guardhouse.

A bell sounded from somewhere down the path, closer to the burning ships, followed by another nearby. Several passersby shouted, and within seconds, a dozen guards had poured outside, rushing past on their way to assist with the fires.

"And that's our cue," Emma said, jerking a nod at Kesari. "You ready, witch girl?"

"Wait—this was *you*?" She pointed to the orange flames, which had spread to a third vessel now.

"Me? 'Course not. I'm here with you lot."

"You know what I mean."

The young woman remained unruffled. "You needed a diversion, and now you've got one."

A chill slipped down her back, but it was quickly overpowered by burning rage. "You set those ships on fire! Do you have any idea how dangerous—what if there are people on them? And the damage—you can't just—"

"What's wrong?" Saya asked in Kavoran.

"*They* started those fires!"

The warrior's eyes widened, and she exchanged a concerned look with Lucian, who had floated down to hover at Kesari's side.

"Let's get on with it," Emma snapped. "Those guards will be back before too long, and we need to be gone by the time they arrive."

She took a step forward, but Kesari grabbed her by the arm. Judging by the way Emma winced, her grip was stronger than she'd meant it to be, but she didn't care. "Where's my sister?" she hissed. "If you've gotten her into any kind of trouble, I—"

"How am I supposed to know?" Emma yanked her arm away.

"Is she on one of those ships?"

"Probably. And all her efforts are going to mean shite if we don't get what we came for. Now come *on*."

A bright glow seemed to fill Kesari's vision, and all sound became muffled beneath a deafening *whoosh*. She couldn't breathe. What if the fires kept spreading? What if Navya couldn't get off the ship? What if she—

She floated backward, away from herself, away from here and now. Rajiv. The fire. The clocktower. Her fault. *All* her fault.

Someone grabbed her hand—Saya—and a voice spoke against her ear—Lucian. She snapped back to the present and sucked in a deep breath, then another and another, concentrating all her attention on the flow of air in and out of her lungs.

"I'll check on Navya," Lucian was saying.

"I'll go with you," Saya added.

"She's probably fine, but if not, we'll do what we can to help her. You focus on this. Get that book of notes, get out, and come find us."

He was right, and Kesari needed her magic to pull this off, which meant she couldn't afford to come apart.

But *skies*, it was hard to hold herself together sometimes. Impossible, even.

"Deep breaths," Lucian said. "You can do this. Use the mesala if you need to."

"Go," she whispered, and before her terrified heart could send her chasing after him, she whirled around and ran for the guardhouse.

"Finally," Emma muttered, hurrying to catch up.

They approached from the rear of the building, where the door was locked but unguarded. Kesari had been practicing a means for getting past that door with Lucian, but she hesitated now, one hand reaching for the pouch of mesala in her pocket. The plant was supposed to enhance a Tarja's power and help them channel it with ease—something she could use assistance with right now, especially given the tangle of nervous energy within her. They needed everything to go smoothly, and if she couldn't control her magic, she was useless at best and a liability at worst.

A familiar self-doubt began to creep in at the edges of her thoughts, but she was more practiced now at fighting back. She was also a more practiced Tarja, and breaking into the guardhouse was something she'd prepared for and knew how to do. She didn't need mesala. She just needed to trust herself.

She let her hand fall back to her side and faced the door with squared shoulders. "I can do this," she whispered, repeating Lucian's earlier words to herself. "I am *not* useless."

"Sure," Emma said, drawing out the word slowly. "Are we going in now?"

Kesari channeled her altma, forming a man-sized barrier around the door to muffle the destructive blast that followed. The latch broke, along with a sizeable chunk of the door itself. It swung open freely when she pushed it.

Emma stepped through with a low whistle, staring down at the broken latch and splintered wood. "Damn, that was incredible! I wish I had magic."

"Shh." Kesari gathered up the latch and as many chunks of wood as she could see. She passed a handful over to Emma. "Help me with this."

"What are we doing?"

"We don't want anyone to know we were here, right? We have to put it back together. Look, that one goes there."

Emma pressed a long shard to the spot Kesari had indicated. "You can do that?"

"Yes, but it's much easier if all the pieces are placed more or less where they belong. Now hurry, and be quiet."

She glanced over her shoulder periodically as they worked to align each piece, fingers splayed in awkward angles to hold everything. They were in an antechamber with an open doorway, but no one came through from the main area beyond. Once all the wood was fitted into place, Kesari pressed the metal latch into position and took a breath.

She stayed like that for a few seconds, eyes closed, taking stock of everything happening for her internally. The fear, the anger, the worry, the memories from her past. She let them drift through her like leaves caught on a breeze, noticing each one but never allowing it to overwhelm her. She had a job to do, and that was the only thing she could control right now. This job, this moment, this door that needed fixing.

She channeled her altma in a slow, steady stream, maintaining a level of control that would have made Lucian proud. The wood began to shift a little beneath her fingers, the cracks narrowing and then melting away altogether as the door became whole again.

It only took a few seconds, but when she pulled her hands away, Emma stared at her as if she'd built an entire house by herself. "Brilliant," she muttered.

Kesari couldn't help smiling a little at that. She led the way to the other side of the antechamber, pausing for a moment to survey the area. There was a long hallway with a set of stairs in the middle. According to Lucian's directions, they needed to go up those and into the first room on their left, which shouldn't be locked but would still require some care to get into. It was right next to a larger room with a few holding cells, and those were never left unattended. Even if the guard on duty didn't spot them, anyone occupying the cells might and then alert said guard, intentionally or not.

"Stay right behind me," she instructed Emma. "And keep quiet."

They went to the steps and took each one slowly, bodies pressed against the wall. When they were high enough to get a decent view of the floor above, Kesari paused. A guard sat in a chair near the entryway to the larger room, positioned at an angle that would allow him a decent view of the cells as well as the outer hallway, though his attention seemed more focused on the book in his lap. Kesari could also see three holding cells from where she stood, possibly with room for a fourth at the far end, out of her line of sight. Only one of them appeared to be occupied.

She channeled her altma again, focusing the energy into her hands as she crept forward. Her view of the room expanded to reveal a fourth cell that was fortunately empty. A window with closed wood shutters caught her eye, and it was toward this that she directed her magic. The shutters flew open with a clatter, and the guard nearly dropped his book as he jumped to his feet.

The noise caught the prisoner's attention as well. Both he and the guard were so distracted by the window that they didn't see two young women slinking across the hall behind them. Kesari opened the door to the room they sought, and they slipped inside without either man noticing.

She produced a small, dim orb of light to illuminate the space and sent it floating ahead of her. There were rows and rows of crates, boxes, and shelves, all containing items presumably recovered over the course of multiple investigations. Lucian had said all of Jameson's things were stacked together in one corner, and it didn't take Kesari long to spot them. There were more books than any one person ought to own, along with equipment for his experiments and assorted colorful oddities she recognized from his tower. She sorted through the books as quickly as she could, picking out all the green ones to check for the notes he'd written while figuring out how to restore Amar's memories. After several failed attempts, she found it—a small but thick journal with worn pages and numerous ink and tea stains.

Emma waited in silence at the door, watching the crack of light beneath it for movement. Kesari approached with the book in hand and put out her light, then channeled altma into a barrier surrounding them both so they could talk without being overheard.

"I've got what I need."

"Good," said Emma. "Now to get what *I* came for."

"And what's that, exactly?"

"It's in there." She jerked a thumb toward the wall—the one this room shared with the holding cells.

Kesari shook her head. "We can't go in there. What about the guard?"

"Can't you put him to sleep or something?"

"If I do that, he's going to know someone was here."

She flashed a roguish grin. "He's going to find out anyway when one of his prisoners goes missing."

Understanding fell over Kesari like a cold, wet blanket. Emma wasn't here to retrieve some*thing*, but some*one*.

18

KESARI

SHE STAYED FROZEN FOR A FEW SECONDS, HER MIND SCRAMBLING TO fit in this new puzzle piece and determine how best to proceed. This must have been why Nemo had been so insistent on her bringing one of his own people. Breaking a prisoner out of their cell was far riskier than stealing evidence. He'd withheld his true intentions until the last possible second so she'd agree to go along with the plan.

For a moment, she was tempted to walk away from the whole thing. But Nemo had Navya, and that was all he needed to ensure Kesari's cooperation. If she didn't bring him what—who—he wanted, there was no telling what he might do. He'd been willing to set ships ablaze simply to create a diversion. She wouldn't put it past him to hurt Navya, or turn her in to the authorities and let her take the fall for starting those fires.

Kesari's barrier wavered under the volatility of her emotions. She recovered quickly, pausing a moment to listen in case the guard had heard anything, but there were no approaching footsteps or any other sound to indicate that he had.

"Why did you let me go to all the trouble of fixing that door if we were going to make our presence known anyway?" she muttered, still trying to come up with a new plan.

Emma shrugged. "Why not? It's not every day I get to see a witch at work."

"I'm not a witch."

"Sorceress, then?" She gestured to Kesari's face. "I couldn't see it before, but now you're getting that sort of evil look in your eye. No offense intended, of course. Don't turn me into a toad or anything."

"Let's just get on with this. I assume we need to free the man in the cell?"

"He's the one."

"You stay here, then. I'll take care of it."

She kept the barrier around herself and pushed the door open a crack to peer out. The guard was back in his chair and had started reading again. Perhaps it would be best to simply put him to sleep, as Emma had suggested, but that would require getting close enough to touch him. It was also something she'd never attempted before, though considering she'd recently been on the receiving end of such magic, she thought she could replicate it. The memory of that night in the forest made her shudder—Jameson's cold hands pressed against her forehead, Valkyra staring down at her, her useless attempts to channel her own magic and stop them.

The barrier around her fell away. *I'm safe now*, she told herself, repeating the words over and over until they felt true. *I'm in control.*

Instead of reforming her barrier, she attempted an illusion. She knew it was working when Emma's mouth dropped open, and she looked down to see her own arms and legs wrapped in gray shadows that matched the darkness of the room. It wasn't a perfect disguise; she was certainly still visible to anyone looking right at her. But she was far less noticeable, and that would hopefully buy her the few seconds she needed to get close to the guard.

She pushed the door open a little wider and stepped out, creeping toward him like a cat stalking a mouse. Air filled her lungs and pressed tight against her chest as she took the last few steps, breath held, preparing to redirect her altma to a new task.

The guard looked up right as she was reaching out to press her hands against his forehead. "Oi! What the devil?"

In an instant, the illusion slipped away, and there she stood, fully visible. The man started to stand, but she lunged for him, channeling her altma before she even touched him. The moment her hands made contact with his skin, he slumped to the floor, jaw slack.

Kesari's breaths came in shallow pants. He appeared dead, but the steady rise and fall of his chest assured her he wasn't. She doubted he'd stay asleep for long, given her lack of experience with that particular spell. The quicker they could get out of here, the better.

"Come on," she hissed, and Emma soon appeared. She stepped over the guard's body with an awed look, then turned her attention to the man in the cell.

"Well, that was certainly something," he said with a mellow lilt that immediately reminded Kesari of Nemo. Upon closer inspection, he bore a striking resemblance to the young man, though he was perhaps a little older. "Now are you going to get me out of here, or just stand there gawking?"

"Keys," Emma said, stooping to retrieve them from the belt of the fallen guard. She fumbled with them for several seconds, trying to find the one that fit the lock, but finally, the cell door swung open and the man stepped out.

"We're done now, right?" Kesari asked, glancing out the open window to the docks. The orange glow of firelight still blazed against the night sky, and she was anxious to find Navya.

"Yes," Emma said. "Thank you, witch. You were incredible."

Kesari strode past them without so much as a sidelong glance. She flew down the stairs and through the hall as fast as her legs would carry her, bursting into the cold night air with determined purpose. Get to Navya. Protect Navya.

And maybe punch Nemo in the nose once that was done.

She reached the docks breathless and wild-eyed. Lucian found her first, dropping out of the sky to hover in front of her. "She's all right," he said, and Kesari drew in what felt like the first full breath she'd taken since the ships started burning. "Nemo had her and a few others set the ships on fire. All unoccupied, thankfully. But the fire spread fast, and Navya got lost. Saya was able to pull her out."

"Where are they?" Kesari scanned the faces of the gathered onlookers, but she couldn't see her friend or her sister anywhere.

"Navya wanted to go home, so Saya took her."

"Good. And where's Nemo? He and I need to talk." She'd never considered herself a violent person, but she was so furious right now he'd be lucky to walk away unscathed.

"He's waiting for you nearby," Lucian replied. "I can take you to him, but first, you might consider helping with these fires. They've managed to stop them from spreading farther, but they're having a hard time putting them out."

"And what am *I* supposed to do about that?" she snapped. She knew the answer already, but she was still riding a wave of fear, anger, and exhaustion, and the sooner she could unleash it all on the person responsible, the better. But Lucian was right. She *could* help with the fires, and given her involvement in this whole situation, she probably should.

Something within her recoiled at the idea, an opposition so strong she nearly choked on it. "I can't," she said, and the words brought back every dark thing she'd felt during the two years she'd wanted to rid herself of her magic. She may have begun accepting herself as a Tarja again, but she still hadn't so much as attempted anything involving fire, nor did she want to. Fire had gotten her brother killed. Fire was unpredictable and uncontrollable. Fire was impossible.

Except that wasn't true. Before the clocktower, she'd been quite good at channeling her altma to create and control fire. It was a skill Lucian had possessed and nurtured during his life as a Tarja, so it came more easily to Kesari once she'd formed a Bond with him. The only thing holding her back was her own fear. A well-founded fear, perhaps, but one that was now preventing her from helping people.

All she had ever wanted to do with her magic was help people.

Lucian's dark eyes met hers. "You *can*," he said quietly.

I can.

Pushing her hair out of her face and summoning every last scrap of courage within her, she hurried to the nearest ship. She planted herself firmly before it like it was some demon straight out of one of her nightmares. Heat radiated onto her face, and rather than trying to fight the old memories that swept her up, she let them in. There was no point in pushing them back or trying to shut down the emotions that came with them. They were a part of her. Those events had happened, and she had survived them, just as she'd survived every destructive thought and impulse that had come after, screaming at her to give up and die.

She had something to live for now. She always had—so many things. Her family, her friends, her dreams for the future, and most of all, herself.

She was a Tarja, and that was a powerful thing to be in a place like Atrea where magic was so rare. She could use that power for good now, even if it meant braving her worst fears.

"You're ready," Lucian said, calmly reassuring her of what she already knew.

She focused on the flames in front of her and channeled her altma. Before, when she'd used her magic to control fire, the flames had always been ones she created herself. Fueled by altma, they often burned brighter and hotter than ordinary flames. This fire had not been magically conjured, so when she sought to manipulate it, it responded faster and more easily than she'd expected. Her surprise at this caused the altma within her to slip away, and the flames began to grow once more. A quick adjustment was all it took, and she was able to douse them a little at a time.

Some of the onlookers took notice and began to talk excitedly amongst themselves. Kesari ignored them, moving swiftly to the next ship where the fire was biggest. A team of guards drew buckets of water from the sea and passed them to their comrades on the deck above, but they were clearly losing the fight. Kesari stepped up to the ship, and one of them shouted at her to stay back and let them work. She ignored him, repeating the same process as before to put the fire out.

"That's it," Lucian said in her ear. "You're doing wonderfully."

She *was* doing wonderfully, and where once the very idea of that power might have terrified her, now it gave her courage. There was still a small, underlying fear—a respect for her own magic and the knowledge of what could happen if things went wrong. But fear and courage could exist at the same time, and she had found the balance. She was in control.

The guards stopped working and watched in awe as the flames died down. When she was finished, they gathered around her, offering their thanks in accented Kavoran and asking where she'd come from. They didn't realize she was Atrean like them; her clothes, brown skin, and magic made them assume she was from Kavora. She let them keep that assumption and brushed their questions off. As quickly as she could, she extricated herself, leaving them to salvage whatever was left of the ships and their cargo.

"Where's Nemo?" she asked Lucian as they walked away.

"Follow me." He bobbed ahead of her, and she followed his glow through the dark. They approached a cluster of buildings crammed together at the edge of the docks, heavy with shadows but still offering a clear line of sight to the smoldering ships. It was exactly the sort of place she might have expected to find the young man, lurking in the dark to watch the chaos he'd created.

Her jaw tightened, and despite her exhaustion, the altma within her flared up once more. That bastard had nearly gotten her sister killed. He'd sent Kesari on a mission without telling her what she was getting herself into, and things could have gone so much worse than they did. She didn't know what she'd do to him once they found him, but she still had half a mind to hurt him. It would be so easy, with her power. So easy, but if she lost control…

The very idea terrified her.

If only Saya were here. Saya was strong and imposing, good at sending a message, making sure people knew not to give her or the people she cared about any trouble. But Saya wasn't here, so Kesari would have to make do without her.

A figure clad in all black stepped out of the shadows, and she inhaled sharply. Nemo grinned at her, a savage smile that for a moment made her feel like a mouse cornered by a wildcat. But she was the wildcat now. Nemo had put her and her family in danger, and there had to be consequences for that.

"Emma was just here," he said smoothly. "Along with my brother, thrilled to be a free man once more. Thank—"

She channeled her altma and thrust her palm against his sternum. With a grunt of pain, he stumbled back against the wall. She held him there, hands steady, focused less on Nemo and more on the magic within her. She had to keep the balance. The purpose of this was to make him understand how serious she was, not to permanently damage him. With great care, she engulfed her free hand in fire and raised it to his face.

He struggled but couldn't escape. The air beside her warmed as Lucian moved in to hover there, big as a dog and twice as intimidating. Nemo paled, his wide eyes clearly reflecting the hellish glow of Lucian's flames. "Now, hold on, witch. You—"

"Shut up," Kesari snarled, bringing her face a little closer to his. "It's my turn to talk, and you're going to listen carefully because I won't say it again. What you did tonight was dangerous and stupid, and I was stupid to go along with it. Navya trusted you, so *I* trusted you, but we shouldn't have. If you so much as speak to her again, I'll find you, and I can't promise to show this much restraint next time."

She brought her fingers together, causing the flames around them to rise and sputter. Nemo turned his face away and pressed one cheek against the wall in a futile attempt to get as far away as possible. Kesari didn't enjoy his fear, but it served a purpose, and if he was as smart as he seemed to be, he wouldn't dare go near her sister again.

She let the flames burn a few seconds longer, then snapped her fingers. The fire vanished, but Nemo still flinched at the sound. She released him and backed away, shaking her head as he slid down the wall and onto the ground.

Guilt twisted knots in her gut, and her legs felt too shaky to keep her standing much longer, but she managed to hold herself tall as she walked away. She did not look back or allow herself to second-guess her actions, not even when her eyes began to sting with unshed tears.

"They left me." Navya sobbed into Kesari's shirt once they were both back at the house. "I got separated from the others, and the fire spread so fast, and they just left me."

"I know." She stroked the girl's hair gently, the strands as black and wavy as her own. "But you're all right. You're safe."

Navya kept crying. It was a long time before she spoke again, and when she did, her voice was listless, as if all the raw emotion had been wrung out of it along with her tears. "I thought they'd never abandon me."

Not the way you *did.*

The harsh words Navya had flung at her that first night drifted through her mind. She wrapped her arms tighter around her sister's shoulders and squeezed. "You know I didn't mean to abandon you, right? It was never about *you.* I couldn't stay here, but I know I hurt you, and I'm so sorry for that." She pulled back a little and shifted around to look Navya in the eye. "You don't deserve to be abandoned. I love you, and I know Mum and Dad do, too. I'm sorry we haven't loved you the way you needed to be loved."

Fresh tears welled in Navya's eyes. Her bottom lip trembled as she opened her mouth to say something, but no words came out. Instead, she leaned against Kesari's shoulder once more, clinging to the fabric of her shirt until sleep overcame her.

They stayed in Deveaural for another two weeks after that, partly to make sure Navya didn't have any more contact with Nemo and his crew, but mostly because Kesari wanted to at least try and mitigate some of the damage her family had suffered. Two weeks wasn't long enough to undo all the hurt of the past two years, but it was all she could spare. She still had things she needed to finish, and other people who were counting on her.

"You could come with us," she said to Navya one night after they'd gone to bed. Saya was already asleep, the sound of her long, deep breaths drifting from the other side of the room.

For a long time, there was no answer, and Kesari thought Navya must have fallen asleep, too. That may have been for the best. She hadn't thought the idea through very well or discussed it with Lucian, who stared at her with wide eyes and no sign of his usual jagged grin. Still, it felt like the right thing to say, an offer of support and relationship rather than the separation they both knew was coming.

"I don't think I should," Navya said at last. "Adventuring was always something you and Rajiv wanted to do."

"It could be something you and I do, if you wanted."

Again, there was a long pause before she answered. "Thanks, Kes, but I think I'll stay here. It's home, you know? I've never really left before, and I don't think I want to. Not yet. But I'll be here the next time you come back. You are coming back, right? Like last time?"

"Of course. I'll always come back."

The next day, she sent Saya and Lucian on a walk and gathered the rest of her family together to have a conversation they should have had years before. Many conversations, really. About Rajiv and the hole he'd left behind, about Kesari running away and the pain she'd caused, about Navya and the way she'd been forgotten, about the parents who loved all three of their children but carried their hurts and their losses like dead weight. Grievances were aired, apologies were exchanged, and everyone shared promises and hopes for the future. By the end, they'd all cried more than once, and Kesari's heart ached with the pain of old wounds reopened. But in the process, those wounds had also been cleaned out and bandaged properly, and perhaps in time, with more conversations and more opportunities for connection and understanding, the wounds could heal. For all of them.

When it was time to go, she felt torn. The last time she'd come home, she'd known for certain that she couldn't and didn't want to stay. This time, though, a part of her *did* want that, and as she readied her things and embraced each of her family members in turn, the pull grew stronger. Not strong enough to hold her here, but enough to let her hope that the next time she returned, she'd be able to truly call it home again.

She picked up her pack along with Rajiv's coat. The weather was getting colder, and she'd left it out in case she needed it, but a better idea occurred to her now. She walked outside to where her family waited to see her off, hugged Mum and Dad, and held the coat out to Navya. "Here. You should hold on to this."

Her sister reached out but did not take it, instead letting her fingers brush over the faded blue fabric. "It's not going to fit me."

"It never fit me very well either, but it's warm, and it's seen me through some rough times." She took half a step closer and pressed the coat into Navya's hands. "Keep it. I don't need it anymore."

The girl draped the garment over one arm and wrapped the other around Kesari's waist. "Be safe out there."

"I will. Don't go getting yourself into any more trouble while I'm gone."

Navya's mouth quirked up on one side, and she winked. The expression made her look almost exactly like Rajiv. "No promises, but I'll do my best."

With that, Kesari swung herself up into her horse's saddle and waved goodbye. Saya nudged her own horse into a walk, and Kesari followed, glancing back only once to see her family still watching her.

"Something wrong?" Lucian asked, drifting a little closer to her shoulder.

She turned to the road ahead. "No. I think they're going to be all right."

"They will be," he agreed. "And they'll still be there waiting for you when you're ready."

SAVIR

SAVIR DID NOT SEE EMPRESS DASHIVA FOR A LONG TIME AFTER Kamaal Ruman's visit. Nearly two weeks had passed since, and she seemed to be making every attempt to avoid both him and Ashaya, which didn't bother Savir half as much as it did the magistrate.

"We've come all this way at *her* request," the man blustered over tea one afternoon, "and she can't be bothered to tell us what she thinks of the journal or the letter I gave her. She hasn't even asked to inspect your birthmark, and I'd think she'd at least want to see that."

"I'm sure she got a good look at it while the two of them were sitting for the painting," Valkyra said, as calm and unruffled as ever. "She *has* reviewed the information, I'm certain. But she'll want more time to verify it for herself and plan her next move accordingly. We must be patient."

"Her next move should be stepping down from the throne," Ashaya muttered. "Everyone knows that."

Valkyra let out a soft hiss. "You'd do well to mind your tongue while we're in Her Majesty's palace."

"You're right. I'm sorry."

Savir took a sip of his tea and looked between them. The more he saw of their interactions, the stranger he found them. Ashaya often deferred to Valkyra for guidance or, more often, out of what seemed to be respect—the kind of respect a man might offer his liege or mentor. It made little sense, considering Valkyra had been only a maidservant while Ashaya had always held some higher position of power within the court. But there was much about Valkyra that remained a mystery. At the very least, she must have been a powerful Tarja to have been capable of taking on her current form. Perhaps that explained the man's deference toward her.

In stark contrast to the empress' apparent lack of interest in her guests, Princess Jasala took it upon herself to be a most gracious hostess. She showed Savir around the palace and dined with him at the end of each day. They often played Samud or other games together, and Jasala would tell him stories of her childhood and what she remembered of his parents. When he suggested that she must have better things to do than keep him company, she simply replied, "Better than becoming reacquainted with my cousin? I think not." Her reference to him as her cousin was a good sign that she believed his identity was legitimate, though she gave no opinion on what she thought should happen as a result.

It was unfortunate, Savir thought one night as he prepared for bed, that his return had cast doubt on Jasala's place in the line of succession. He'd grown to like her in the time they'd spent together. She had a sharp mind and a sharper wit, but it was never cruel or mocking. She carried herself the way a ruler should—something Savir was still trying to figure out himself. And she was kind, even to him, though she certainly had reason not to be.

Perhaps it would have been better if he'd never come here to disrupt things. Jasala had been preparing to rule all her life. So had he, apparently, but he couldn't remember it, which meant he was starting over, so far behind that he might never catch up. At this point, the only thing that made him more suited to rule than her was that it was his birthright, and what did that matter, really?

A sharp knock sounded at his door. He finished pulling on his nightshirt and answered it to find Tarik standing there. "The magistrate is requesting to see you. Shall I let him in?"

Ashaya leaned out to make himself visible from behind the guard's broad frame. "Pardon the intrusion, Your Highness, but there's a matter I'd like to discuss, if you don't mind."

"All right," Savir replied, standing aside to let him in. What the man could possibly have to discuss at this hour, he had no idea.

Ashaya gave a slight nod to Valkyra, who was curled up at the end of the bed, and made his way across the room to the opposite wall. At first, he seemed to be admiring a painting hung there, but then he stepped closer and began examining the wood panels to either side. He pressed on the corners and ran his fingers under the edges, muttering to himself all the while.

"What are you doing?" Savir asked. When Ashaya didn't respond, he posed the question to Valkyra. "What's he doing?"

"I believe he's looking for—" Her words were cut off by a soft scraping sound, and the panel Ashaya had been prying at slid back and sideways into the wall. Behind it lay only darkness—some kind of tunnel or passageway. "For that," Valkyra finished. She stretched her legs and ruffled her wings, then hopped onto Savir's shoulder. "Come along, dear. We have a meeting to get to, and we don't want to be late."

Savir scowled, looking between the passageway and the magistrate, who stood by patiently with his hands clasped behind his back. He wasn't sure who to yell at, Ashaya or Valkyra, and eventually settled for neither, though he resented them both for keeping this from him. He didn't even want to give them the satisfaction of seeing his curiosity, so instead of asking any of the numerous questions on his mind, he simply strode forward and entered the tunnel.

The magistrate squeezed past him to lead the way, and it took Savir a moment to realize that he carried no lantern or a torch, but rather an orb of magical light he seemed to have produced himself. "You're a Tarja?" Savir blurted out, curiosity getting the best of him before he could stop himself.

"Yes. I thought you knew."

"Valkyra never mentioned it."

Ashaya held the light aloft and forward to illuminate their path. "It's not really worth mentioning. I've never been half as skilled a Tarja as her."

"He's only being modest," Valkyra murmured in his ear. "He's very skilled. He could have taken the Advisor of Magic position from Chayani Sha, if he'd wanted to."

"But I didn't. My mind and my talents are much better suited to matters of justice and the law."

Savir tucked this new piece of knowledge away and followed the magistrate, quickly losing track of the narrow, twisting corridors they walked. The journey was not a long one. Within minutes, they found themselves standing before a section of wall with a small symbol carved into it. Savir didn't have time to see it clearly before Ashaya pressed his fingertips against it. A thin seam of light formed a large square against the darkness, and the wall slid away to reveal a small room lit by a single lantern.

"After you, Your Highness," he said, motioning to the door he'd created. "Mind your head."

Savir had to stoop to avoid hitting his forehead, so he didn't get a good look at the person holding the lantern until he'd straightened again. She was taller than him, with a broad frame and a face most would have considered beautiful, even with its numerous scars. A burn dusted one cheek and a thin slash crossed the other. A smaller nick ran from her chin into her lower lip. Her most prominent scar was a jagged thing that trailed up from beneath her collar and over her jaw, splintering off in several places in a way that reminded Savir of lightning or a bare tree branch. A scar made by magic, most likely; no blade or bullet would leave such a mark.

Beautiful, and fearsome. Even before he saw the double flintlock pistols at her waist, he knew this was not a woman to be trifled with, though the weapons certainly added to that overall impression.

"Prince Savir," she said in a low, gravelly voice that made her seem suddenly much older than she appeared. "It's an honor to meet you."

"And you as well," he said, glancing sidelong at Valkyra. Who was this woman?

The dragon stayed quiet, maintaining her role as a mere pet, so it was Ashaya who finally made the introduction. "Your Highness, this is Avani Muraka, general of the imperial Tarja military forces. She wanted to meet you in person."

"And in secret?" Savir asked, raising an eyebrow.

"I'm not the one who proposed secrecy," Muraka replied. She tucked her short black hair behind her ear and stared pointedly at Ashaya.

The magistrate straightened. "Yes, well, given the nature of our conversation, I thought it best to use some measure of discretion."

"And what exactly is the nature of this conversation?" Savir asked. A faint unease was beginning to prickle at the back of his neck, and he glanced past the general to the door on the other side of the room. A quick escape, should he need one.

"Treason," Muraka replied flatly. "Or at least, that is what the *honorable* magistrate is proposing." Her emphasis on the word made it hang in the air like a mockery rather than a compliment.

Ashaya shifted uncomfortably, his tongue darting out to swipe across his lips. He was obviously intimidated by her—anyone in their right mind would be, just looking at her—but after a moment, he seemed to recover. "It isn't treason when he's the rightful emperor."

"I don't see a crown on his head."

"Not yet. Which is precisely the point of this meeting. You served Prince Savir's father faithfully for years. For generations, your family has served this country's rulers, always loyal, always protective. You can't tell me you're content with seeing a usurper on the throne."

Muraka sighed and crossed her arms, looking bored with her eyelids half closed. "Empress Dashiva was the rightful heir to the throne until the boy came along. I don't see how that makes her a usurper."

"Would you maintain that belief if she *stays* on the throne, knowing now that Savir has returned?"

She gave no response, but the muscles around her mouth twitched a little, and her gaze focused in on Savir's left hand. He knew what she was looking for, and he raised the hand a little higher so she could better see the birthmark there.

"You've seen the journal," Ashaya continued. "And now you've seen the evidence up close. You know he truly is Akraja and Priyani's son. Dashiva must abdicate and allow Savir to take his rightful place. If she doesn't, then *she* is the one committing treason."

Muraka's mouth pressed into a thin line, and she remained silent for a few seconds. "She won't abdicate," she said at last. "If it were only her, she might be convinced, but not with Jasala in line to inherit the throne." She shook her head. "The empress is obsessed with creating a lasting legacy. Everything she's done during her reign has been to that end. Jasala is supposed to carry on that legacy, and I'm certain Dashiva would rather go to war than see her daughter stripped of the future she was promised."

This was exactly what Savir had feared. "You're a general. Can't you counsel her against war?"

She lifted one shoulder. "I can try, though I doubt it will work. Besides, I'm still not convinced I should. The empress has been an adequate leader, and Jasala has the potential to be an even better one. Whether you're the rightful heir or not, why would I want some unknown and untested boy to rule instead?"

It was a fair question, and one Savir wanted to take care in answering. Before he could finish forming a response, Ashaya spoke again. "Your Highness, would you mind demonstrating something for the general?"

"Demonstrating what?"

"Channel your altma."

At this, Muraka tilted her head, dark eyes boring into him. Seeing no reason not to, Savir obliged, taking a moment to focus inward before drawing on the altma within himself. He held up both hands, fingertips touching and then drawing apart. Between them, tendrils of lightning danced and crackled, casting a blue glow through the room that illuminated Muraka's smile.

"You're a Tarja," she said once he'd cut off the lightning and let his altma settle.

"Yes." He left it at that rather than explaining how he'd come by his abilities.

"The empress didn't mention anything."

"No one knows. Only us here."

"Not even King Bhajan and Queen Indira?"

"No."

Ashaya interjected again. "His Highness thought it best to keep this ability hidden, at least for now. It's been a long time since we've had a Tarja on the throne, and people have strong feelings about such things. Were the knowledge to spread, it would only complicate the situation. We trust you can keep his secret?"

She shrugged. "I can, but why tell me at all?"

"Because you of all people ought to have a vested interest in seeing another Tarja in power. Think of all the advancements that were made the last time we had a Tarja emperor. Funding for research, training academies, expeditions to study magical practices in other lands, the creation of the same Tarja army you now lead. Magic has never been a priority for Dashiva, but with Savir on the throne, we could continue to advance our knowledge and harness its power."

Savir had never given much thought to what policies or goals he might pursue as emperor, but he didn't disagree with Ashaya's words. Magic was a useful tool, and one of Kavora's greatest strengths as a nation. Why shouldn't they focus on developing that strength further?

Muraka was still mulling this over, but after a few seconds, she nodded. "You make a compelling argument, but you're still dancing around the real purpose of this clandestine meeting, and I'm running out of patience. What do you want from me?"

Savir had been wondering the same thing.

"Our apologies, General," Ashaya said with a slight bow. "We certainly don't want to waste your time. To put it plainly, we're simply trying to get an idea of who our allies might be. As you said, the empress isn't likely to give up her power, and if war breaks out, we'll need all the friends we can get. Friends who can help us end things quickly, before there's too much bloodshed."

Savir inhaled sharply. What was the magistrate thinking with that suggestion? Even if they were ready to prepare for war—and he certainly wasn't—they couldn't go around boldly declaring their intentions to Dashiva's top military leaders.

He opened his mouth to contradict Ashaya, but Valkyra dug her claws sharply into his shoulder, and he swallowed his words. "Wait," she said, her voice barely a whisper against his ear. "Watch and see."

Muraka's hand drifted to one of her pistols, and the smirk that spread across her face was a dark, monstrous thing. "Well, Magistrate, you certainly have grown bolder since the last time we spoke, asking me to help unseat the woman I've pledged my life and my service to. Do you really think my integrity means so little that I'd throw it away that easily?"

Ashaya released a flustered huff, but his words came out calm enough. "As I recall, you pledged your service and your loyalty to

Akraja first. What would he say if he saw you now, standing before his son and still defending the woman who stole his crown?"

Muraka let out a short, barked laugh. "*Stole* his crown? You've spent too much time listening to Bhajan and his conspiracies."

The magistrate stiffened, his hands clasped and shaking behind his back. Before he could speak again and make things any worse, Savir stepped forward. "We meant no disrespect, General. I apologize for taking up so much of your time. Perhaps we should go."

She raised her hand. "No, please stay. Ashaya makes a fine point. I did pledge my service to your father, and while I might not go so far as to say the empress was behind the attempt on your life, I wouldn't rule it out entirely. She is…ambitious. To a fault, some would say." She grinned broadly, her teeth bright in the glow of the lantern. "But of course, so am I."

"Well then," said Ashaya, "you'll be interested to know Prince Savir still has a spot on his council for an Advisor of Magic. Or perhaps an Advisor of War, if you'd rather. Once he's crowned, of course."

"Oh, really?" Muraka rolled the words off her tongue like a purr. "Is that true, Your Highness?"

Savir resisted the urge to shoot Ashaya a look. He couldn't deny that he needed the man's help in dealing with political maneuverings since he lacked the skill for it himself, but he'd appreciate at least a warning when it came to major decisions. Then again, why shouldn't he give Muraka a seat on his council? She certainly had the requisite experience. Whether or not he could trust her remained to be seen.

"It's true," he replied.

"How interesting. Well, you've certainly given me a lot to consider tonight, but I do need to ask you all to leave now. I have many duties to attend to, and morning comes too soon."

"Of course," Ashaya said. "Thank you for hearing us out." He turned to leave, but Savir remained rooted in place.

"Is something wrong, Your Highness?" Muraka asked.

He crossed his arms. "What's to stop you from running straight to the empress and telling her about this meeting?"

"I could, but it wouldn't really matter, would it? We all know what's coming. She already suspects you're probing for weaknesses and gathering allies, but she can't do anything to you while you're here on her invitation and under her protection. It's all part of the game, and for now, I hold the cards, so you'll have to wait and see which play I make." She smirked again. "Goodnight, Prince Savir."

The dismissal was clear, and he didn't argue. Ashaya opened the secret passageway behind them and they slipped inside, following the same dark, narrow path as before.

Once they'd arrived back at the entrance to his room, Valkyra fluttered off Savir's shoulder and onto Ashaya's. "Give us a moment."

He clenched his jaw. He hated being dismissed so casually, as if he were simply a boy instead of a prince. If they wanted to put him on the throne, he should be taking a more active role in whatever they planned. "Why can't I stay and listen?"

"The things we need to discuss don't concern you."

"You're lying." He jabbed a finger down the passage from where they'd come. "You planned all of that back there without telling me. I should have been included. Instead, I showed up without knowing what was going on, and I looked like a fool."

"You did perfectly fine, dear."

The soothing tone in her voice only angered him further. He was not some child to be appeased with simple praises and affection. "That's not the point. You need to tell me what's going on. If I'm really the prince, I should have a say."

Valkyra's eyes narrowed. "You *do* have a say, but until you're emperor, we need to be careful. You don't always need to know everything right away, and sometimes it's better if you don't."

"That's not good enough," he shot back. "I want to know what you know. I want to know what you're planning, and I want you to tell me what you're doing before you do it. You went to Muraka to plan for a war we're still trying to prevent. Or at least, I am. Are you with me on that, or do you *want* to see this country tear itself apart?"

"You know I don't. None of us do. But we have to prepare for everything."

"You should have told me."

She gave a long, drawn-out sigh. "Enough, Savir. We will talk about this later. Now go."

He had half a mind to refuse, but that wasn't likely to get him anywhere, and besides, he had a better idea. He spun on his heel and stormed back into his room. With a soft whoosh, the wall slipped into place behind him, concealing the passageway and the two people still inside it.

Immediately, he spun around and pressed his ear to the wall. At first, he couldn't hear anything, so he channeled altma to amplify his hearing. His ears gave a painful pop, and a ringing reverberated through his skull for a few seconds before he managed to get his magic back under control. With a dull ache still pulsing in his head, the sound of two voices finally became clear.

"—didn't seem convinced," Ashaya was saying. "You may need to pay her a visit yourself."

"I can do that," Valkyra replied. "She'll fall in line soon enough."

"Good. Having her on our side will be critical for the war."

Savir seethed. The man spoke of war as if it was inevitable. Maybe he was naive to think he could still prevent that outcome, but he had to try, didn't he? The stakes were too high not to.

There was a brief pause, then Ashaya tentatively asked, "You're sure the boy still doesn't remember anything?"

"No. And he never will."

A knot twisted in his stomach. That wasn't what she'd told him before. Always, she'd reassured him that his memories might come back someday, and she sounded just as certain now that they wouldn't. Why? Which was the truth? Had she only been coddling him all this time, giving him false hope because reality would be too difficult to bear?

Footsteps approached, and he quickly padded across the room to his bed. The passageway's secret entrance slid open, allowing Ashaya to emerge with Valkyra perched on his shoulder. She fluttered over to Savir, and the magistrate bid him a quick farewell before exiting the room through the main door.

Savir rolled over and pulled the blankets up to his chin. He didn't have the heart to look at Valkyra, let alone speak to her. Instead, he retreated to the world of sleep, with its dreams that sometimes felt like memories and voices that almost sounded familiar.

20

ALEIDA

NEWS AND GOSSIP FROM THE PALACE HAD INCREASED SIGNIFICANTLY in the weeks following Prince Savir's arrival, and Aleida listened to as much of it as she could during her daily work hours. Most of the information was useless, and when it wasn't, the details were contradictory enough that she could never be entirely sure what was true. Still, she listened, and together she, Mitul, and Kamaal compared what they learned in an effort to stay apprised of Amar's status and potential plans.

There was always speculation about whether the prince would be taking his aunt's place on the throne. Some said Savir was staying in Jakhat awaiting coronation while others insisted he was already preparing to return to Valmandi. Many voices had grown louder of late, taking their opinions and accusations from quiet, private rooms to parties and public conversations on the street. Several called for Empress Dashiva to renounce her title and allow the rightful heir to take her place. Just as many argued she should name Savir her own heir in place of Jasala to facilitate a smoother transition of power. A few even suggested the prince was a fraud and should be punished accordingly. Mitul always went quiet when that opinion came up, a taut and anxious stillness that belied his constant fear for Amar's safety.

The weeks passed quickly as autumn waned and winter's chill settled over the city. Each day after work, Aleida found herself wandering to the streets where Mitul played music, and when he could, he brought her along as his assistant to the various social engagements he performed at. Kamaal was there more often as well, and his presence always seemed to banish the troubled shadows that lingered in Mitul's eyes, brightening them with light and laughter instead.

Aleida couldn't help but notice the growing intimacy between them. The gestures were small—a hand on the shoulder, a shared joke, the brush of their knuckles against each other, the softness in Mitul's gaze as he plucked a fallen leaf from Kamaal's hair—but they were as bright and burning as the noonday sun. She hadn't really noticed or even seen two people in love since her parents died, and it mesmerized her. There was a certain comfort in the closeness between them that drew her back day after day when before, she'd been content to spend her evenings alone. If Kamaal and Mitul found her company obnoxious or unwanted, they never said so, and instead seemed to go out of their way to include her.

It was their affection for one another that eventually made her pick up charcoal and paper again. She and Kamaal had both come out to listen to Mitul play at his usual spot in this district, and they shared a plate of sugared figs while they watched him from a nearby bench. Kamaal had bought the snack from a young mother and her daughter pushing a cart through the street, but he'd let Aleida eat most of it, insisting he was full. She licked the last of the sugar off her fingers and clapped along with Mitul's small audience when his song ended.

He began to pack up, slipping his coins into the pouch at his waist and then placing his saraj carefully back in its case. Another musician approached to ask if he'd be returning. "No, I'm done for the day," he replied. "You can have the spot if you want it."

The young man thanked him, and a few moments later, his melody began to fill the air. Mitul gave him an appreciative nod and strode across the street to where Kamaal and Aleida waited. "Well, that was the most profitable day I've had in a while. You two must be good luck."

"It's not luck when the musician is as skilled as you are," Kamaal replied. An easy smile settled on his face as his gaze slid to the new performer. "I know this song."

"Ah, yes," Mitul said with a wink. "As I recall, you nearly sent me crashing into your poor sister at her own party."

"I'm a much better dancer now," Kamaal replied confidently.

"Oh, really?"

In response, he tilted his head, stood, and held out a hand. It took Mitul a few moments to accept the invitation, but soon they were standing in the middle of the road, hands on each other's waists and shoulders as their feet moved with a rhythmic grace that looked almost effortless.

Watching them conjured up memories of other songs, other couples, evenings spent laughing and listening to music at the end of a hard day's work. Tyrus' teasing smirk when he talked one of his friends into asking Aleida to dance as a joke, followed by shrieks of mock terror as he ran from her. The memories still hurt and always would, but she found herself smiling anyway.

Something inside her stirred, a familiar urge that, for the first time in weeks, she didn't ignore. The small sketchbook Kamaal carried with him almost everywhere sat open on the bench where he'd left it, along with a few sticks of charcoal. Before she could give too much thought to the absurdity or the inevitable failure of what she was about to do, she picked up the book and flipped to a blank page at the back. Tiny black flecks drifted onto the surface, shaken loose by her trembling hands, but the dryness of the charcoal felt soothing and right against her fingertips.

Her eyes darted between the dancers and the page, and instead of trying to capture every line with perfect accuracy, she moved her hands in quick, sweeping gestures. She could only maintain moderate control over her fingers for a single moment at a time, but it was enough. It had to be enough.

By the time the song ended, she had a page full of shaky lines and smudges she might once have been ashamed of, but all she felt now was satisfaction. There in the center of the page was the shape of two people dancing. It was little more than an impression made from looping scribbles and mistakes covering up more mistakes. But it was *there*, somewhere underneath it all. She could see them.

The sound of approaching footsteps brought her out of her trance, and she jumped, nearly dropping the sketchbook. The stick of charcoal in her hand tumbled to the ground. "Sorry," she said to Kamaal, her ears going hot. What had she been *thinking*, taking *his* sketchbook and scribbling her own less-than-mediocre attempts at art into it? "I shouldn't have—"

"Can I see?"

Heart pounding, she handed it over and stared down at her hands in her lap, fingertips now blackened. Her insides squirmed for what felt like hours as she waited for someone to speak and wondered whether she should apologize again or try to explain. But she *couldn't* explain. She'd simply acted without thinking.

"It's us," Kamaal said. "Look."

Aleida looked up, but he'd been speaking to Mitul and was passing the book to him now.

"So it is," the musician said. "It's lovely."

"It's a mess," she muttered. "The lines are all wrong and I couldn't get any of the details right if my life depended on it."

"Look at it again," Kamaal said, holding the book out to her. "Tell me what you feel."

"Ashamed," she replied without hesitation. "Embarrassed."

He laughed softly, but it was not unkind. "Besides that."

She examined the drawing and tried again, ignoring the churning in her stomach to find what lay beneath. "Happy, I think. Alive."

"That's it."

"Loved," Mitul added.

She nodded. Happy and alive and loved—all the things she'd been remembering when she drew the piece, all the things she'd seen in the way Mitul and Kamaal looked at each other. It was all there, captured even amid its imperfections.

Carefully, Kamaal tore out the page that bore her drawing. She reached for it, but he didn't give it to her. "I think I'd like to keep this, if it's not too much to ask."

"Of course," she replied. "It's yours."

"Then take this." He held the sketchbook out to her instead.

Her brows lifted. "Oh, no, I couldn't. What about all your drawings?"

"I don't need them." He lifted the page he'd torn out. "I'd rather keep the memory of today."

"Are you sure?"

Kamaal chuckled. "Yes. Please, take it."

She took the book from him gently, as if it were as fragile as it was precious. "Thank you."

"Thank *you*. And I expect to see a few more of those blank pages filled soon."

He left them after that, saying he needed to at least try to get some work done before the day was over. Mitul and Aleida headed to their respective dwellings as well, walking together for the first portion of their journey. She held the sketchbook tightly against herself, her mind already cycling through ideas of what to put within its pages. She didn't want to let Kamaal down, after all.

"That was a beautiful drawing you did back there," Mitul said. "I appreciate you sharing it with us."

She shrugged. "It wasn't much."

"Wasn't it? Last I heard, you were saying you'd never draw again. Even making the attempt must have been a big step."

"I guess." Eager to shift the focus of the conversation away from herself, she posed a new question. "Did you mean what you said? About feeling loved?"

"Looking at the drawing? Yes, I thought you—"

She rolled her eyes. "Oh, come on, you know that's not what I'm asking. When you were dancing."

He adjusted the strap of his saraj case. "I'm not quite sure how to answer that."

"It's a simple enough question. Do you think he loves you?"

"Simple, you say? Love is anything but simple, especially given our history."

"That's still not an answer."

"And why do you care so much about my romantic life?"

She wrapped her fingers tighter around the edges of the sketchbook. "It's not like I have much else to care about these days. Certainly nothing pleasant."

This seemed to sober him, and the playful gleam in his eyes vanished instantly. "No, I suppose not." They walked several paces in silence before he spoke again. "Honestly, I'm not sure. I don't know if he can let himself love me, after the way I hurt him."

"But you love him," she said.

The hint of a smile returned to his lips. "Yes. Rather desperately, I'm afraid."

Aleida's mouth scrunched as she fought to conceal her own grin. "I think he loves you, too."

"Oh, really? And what makes you so sure of that?"

She stopped walking and waited for him to stop, too. When he did, she opened the sketchbook and flipped through the last few pages Kamaal had drawn on, allowing Mitul a few moments to take in each one. There were full portraits and partial sketches of individual facial features, the same lanky figure sitting and walking and sleeping, hands in various poses with long fingers pressed against the strings of a saraj.

"Because," Aleida said, "all these drawings are of you."

SAVIR

AFTER DAYS SPENT ALL BUT IGNORING HIS PRESENCE, EMPRESS Dashiva finally arranged a time to meet with Savir privately. His nights were even more restless than usual in the days leading up to their discussion. He tried to get a sense of where Dashiva's mind was at from Jasala, but the princess gave nothing away.

Valkyra lectured him incessantly on how to handle the conversation, warning that he had to be more careful now than ever. "Keep your defenses up, and guard your words closely, especially if you sense she's not being completely honest with you. We're on her turf, and if things don't go our way, we need to be able to leave safely."

Though he was still annoyed with her, he knew better than to disregard her warnings. On the day he was to see the empress, he rose early and paced anxiously until the appointed time arrived, at which point he made his way to the room where Dashiva had asked to meet him. Tarik followed dutifully, of course, and Savir gestured for the man to wait outside. He entered with Valkyra still perched on his shoulder. The empress was already seated at the end of a long table with Jasala positioned to her right.

Savir bowed to them both and took a seat, leaving an empty space between himself and Dashiva. "Thank you for meeting with me, Your Majesty, and for all the hospitality you've shown these last few weeks.

It's been an enjoyable visit, but I do think it best I return to Valmandi soon. My grandparents will be missing me."

"On that, we can agree," Dashiva replied. "Though we ought to discuss what happens next, I think."

Straight to the point, then. Good. He had little patience for word games and political dallying. That was more Ashaya's forte, but he wasn't here now to help navigate such conversations.

"Please," he said. "Speak your mind. I'm happy to answer any questions you have."

The empress' lips pursed. "Oh, I think you've already answered my questions well enough. Except for one, and without Ashaya here to mince words, perhaps you can give me an honest answer." Her eyes narrowed slightly. "What was it that you hoped to accomplish by coming here?"

The answers spun around in his mind, and he almost blurted out the response he knew he was supposed to give: that he'd come to take his rightful place as emperor and gain Dashiva's support in the transition of power that must follow. But that was only what everyone else hoped he'd accomplish—his grandparents, Ashaya, the rest of the council, Valkyra. What he'd hoped for himself had been quite different.

"I hoped to prevent a war," he said evenly, ignoring the prick of claws against his skin. "That's what this is going to come to, isn't it?"

Dashiva canted her chin a little. "There has certainly been talk of war. I must say I'm relieved to hear you don't want that."

"I don't. And I don't think you do, either."

"We don't," Jasala replied, leaning forward. Her mother shot her a quick glance, and she pressed herself back into her chair, lips pressed together in a firm line.

"Unfortunately, it is not for *us* to determine whether war comes or not," Dashiva said. "That play rests entirely in your hands, *Prince* Savir."

It was the first time she'd addressed him by his title, but there was something venomous in the way she said the word. He laid his hand on the table where she could see his birthmark clearly. "You saw the evidence. You know I'm your nephew, and that makes me the rightful heir to the throne."

"I know *you* believe that you are who you say you are, as does most of the country by now. More importantly, King Bhajan believes it. He's taken you in as his own. His long-lost grandson miraculously returned to him." Her voice took on a false sweetness, like a storyteller emphasizing the most important parts of a tale for an audience full of children. "The people even have a song about you, you know. They've been awaiting your noble return for years, and who am I to dissuade them of their hope, misplaced as it may be?"

Savir's jaw tightened, and he had to put conscious effort into not grinding his teeth. He'd been honest with her in saying he didn't want a war, and on that, he thought they could find some common ground. But now she was making a mockery of him, and he couldn't stand for that. "It's not misplaced. You can't deny the evidence we gave you."

She scowled. "I can't deny the evidence I saw with my own two eyes on the night my nephew and sister-in-law were murdered. I knew that child. I saw his poor little broken body myself, and it is not a sight I'll ever forget. I don't know who you are, but you're *not* Prince Savir."

She had to be lying, but openly accusing her of that would only anger her further. "I understand your desire to protect the legacy you've built. Surely, together we can find a way to—"

"Together?" She almost laughed the word. "You are nobody. My legacy is *mine* to protect, and I won't let you steal it from me." She straightened in her chair and took a breath as if to calm herself. "You say you want to prevent a war. If that's the case, you know what you need to do. Lay aside your claim, or better yet, declare your support for me and for Jasala. It's the only way to assure the future peace and stability of our nation."

This was not going the way Savir had wanted. "You can't say you want peace and stability when you're wearing a crown that doesn't belong to you. If a nation's leaders won't uphold the law and follow the rightful line of succession, we may as well embrace anarchy." The words felt like someone else's, rehearsed to perfect delivery, but still hollow.

Dashiva's expression twisted, her lips pulled into a frown that deepened the wrinkles on her face. "Careful, boy. A tongue as brazen as yours is likely to be cut out."

Jasala's brows knit together, and a warning flashed behind her dark eyes. Savir took a breath and tried a different approach—the one he probably should have led with. "If we could come to some compromise, Your Majesty, this doesn't have to end in war. We could rule together, you and I. Or if that's not agreeable to you, then perhaps Princess Jasala and I might—"

Dashiva's hand slammed down on the table. "Enough!"

"Mother, please." Jasala leaned forward and placed one hand over Dashiva's. "Let's hear him out. It might not be such a bad idea."

"No! I will not entertain this nonsense any longer." She clasped her hands together in front of her. The rage that had played across her face moments before settled into a calm repose that was no less terrifying, like a blue sky turning gray before a storm. "I will make no concessions to a thief and a fraud, so let's have a look at what comes next, shall we? You maintain your claim to the throne, and I protect what is rightfully mine. Jakhat and Valmandi go to war, and all the petty nobles around the empire throw in their support for one side or the other." She gave a little shrug. "Or, perhaps they bide their time, waiting to see who might come out on top. It doesn't matter. Either way, the outcome is the same. Piece by piece, our empire tears itself apart. My armies and resources are superior, of course, but Valmandi has enough strength to sustain a conflict for several months at least."

She arched one eyebrow. "Now tell me, Savir, who do you think wins in this scenario? Because I can tell you for certain who loses, and it's not you or I or Bhajan. It's the soldiers on the battlefield and the families they don't go home to. It's the people in this city and in yours who will go hungry when supply lines are disrupted and resources grow scarce. Think about that on your way back to Valmandi, will you? If, that is, you truly *do* want what's best for this country."

With that, she stood, and after a moment's hesitation, so did Jasala, casting a look back at Savir that was difficult to read. He watched them go, his words frozen in his throat and his insides tangled like so much rope.

"You did the best you could," Valkyra said soothingly once the doors had shut behind the two women. "Dashiva's too stubborn to let go of her power so easily. It was always going to come to this, in the end."

"It wasn't supposed to." He'd tried, hadn't he? But perhaps he hadn't done enough. If he were better at being a prince, a leader, a diplomat, maybe he would have known the right things to say and do.

"I know it's not what you hoped for, dear, but we knew from the start this wasn't going to be easy. Now it's time for you to take a stand, like you told your grandparents you would."

Take a stand for what was right and fair—wasn't that what Indira had said? But he was no longer certain what that was. The meanings of the words seemed to shift depending on who he was talking to. It was right and fair that he take back the throne that belonged to him, but wasn't it also right to do whatever he could to prevent the suffering that would come from war, even if that meant laying aside his birthright?

He didn't know what the right choice was, and trying to figure it out was making his head spin. He stood and walked to the window, staring out over the city under a clear sky. White snow already capped the blue-gray mountains to the north. He'd spent the last days of autumn inside these cold walls, and now, winter had come. His soul longed for warmer halls and familiar company, and he suddenly wished very keenly that he was back in Valmandi with his grandparents. If anyone could help him make sense of all this, it was them.

"How soon can we go home?" he asked Valkyra.

She pressed her soft cheek against his. "Whenever you're ready, Your Highness."

22

KESARI

THE JOURNEY FROM DEVEAURAL BACK TO HAYATHU PASSED SWIFTLY. Winter had arrived, and the cooler weather meant travel through the Sular desert had become much safer and easier. Trade routes connecting to Atrea now saw more traffic, and Kesari, Saya, and Lucian encountered a few other travelers on their way, some with important news from Kavora. Prince Savir had apparently returned, but Empress Dashiva wasn't giving up the throne, and there was talk of civil war brewing.

When they reached Hayathu, the news was equally grim. Their first sign of it came from the dozens of new tents surrounding the settlement. "Nomads," Saya explained when Kesari asked about them. "Most of our people live in tribes that roam the desert, following the ghayat herds and living off the land. They often pass through here, but I've never seen so many at once."

They dismounted as they approached the settlement, leading their horses on foot instead. It wasn't long before someone recognized Saya, and she was accosted on all sides by people asking questions, vocalizing their opinions, or whispering behind her back. Kesari had a difficult time keeping track of the young warrior through the growing crowd, and it took all her remaining focus to piece together what she could of their words, most spoken in dialects she didn't know well.

They all seemed to be angry and worried about something, or several things all wrapped together. They spoke of war in Kavora and how that might impact them, how they needed a means to defend themselves and their lands now more than ever. And something had gone missing, stolen in the night two weeks prior by none other than Zefar. Or at least, that's who they were blaming.

It was that piece of information that made everything else click into place, and Kesari exchanged an alarmed look with Lucian. "The records from Shavhalla. He stole them."

"I hate to say it, but I'm not surprised after he tried to take them the last time we were here."

"Yes, but then he was banished."

"So he came back. Risky, although I suppose we should applaud his persistence."

"What do you think he's planning to do with them?"

"No idea. But these people don't seem too happy about any of it."

Saya was steadily making her way toward the masahi's tent in the center of the settlement, not stopping for anyone. Her brothers found her before too long, but even then, she continued on, exchanging only the briefest greeting with each of them. She passed her horse's reins to Halos and motioned for Kesari to do the same.

"You've returned at a bad time," he said as he took the reins from her. "They're feeling extra hostile toward Kavorans right now. It's probably best you don't stay long."

He walked away, and it was only then that Kesari noticed the dark looks being cast her way. Not by all, but enough to make her uncomfortable. At a glance, she appeared Kavoran, and most didn't know or care that she'd been born and raised in Atrea. She hurried to catch up with Saya and followed her into the tent.

Masahi Seda stood with the rest of her council in a semi-circle, along with a few other people Kesari didn't recognize. They'd gathered around a detailed map of the desert and were speaking in hushed voices, but the conversation died down when Saya entered. Seda whispered a few words to the woman beside her, then left the others and pulled her daughter aside. Unsure of what else to do, Kesari followed, and the masahi nodded to her in greeting.

"You've heard the news, I assume?" she said.

"Part of it, at least," Saya replied. "Zefar stole my haseph offering."

"Yes. No one's seen or heard from him since. We've sent a few hunting parties after him, but they have yet to find him. He seems to have left the desert altogether, and he's taken those records with him."

"Do you know what he plans to do with them?"

"No, but he raised a lot of chaos over them before he disappeared. After I banished him, he spread word to the other tribes, telling them you'd found some powerful defensive measure we could use against Kavora. He also said we were refusing to share it, so of course the other tribes came here demanding answers." Her brows knit together, tension evident in every line of her face. "We were forced to tell their leaders exactly what it was you brought back. Some of them agreed it was best kept secret, but with the news coming from Kavora, opinions have shifted."

"Because there's talk of war," Saya said.

"Yes. Things haven't escalated to that point yet, but it's coming, and we've already seen an influx of thieves and intruders on our lands. They're harvesting all the mesala they can find, knowing it will be in high demand for the Kavoran military and their Tarja soldiers."

Kesari hadn't made that connection until now, and it filled her with dread. This was exactly the kind of thing that had prompted Saya to seek immortality for her people. Now it was becoming reality, and the protective measure she'd found for them was gone.

"As you can imagine," the masahi continued, "there were many discussions and arguments about what to do with your offering once the news spread. Soon, it wasn't only our leaders who knew what you'd brought back, but everyone. They demanded we put it to use. Some of our best warriors volunteered to be the first ones cursed. Our Tarja began studying it, cautiously, wanting to ensure we knew exactly what we were doing before we risked anyone's life. It was slow going. Many said we were taking too long, and soon after, the records went missing."

The lines around Saya's mouth tightened further. "Are you sure it was him?"

"Who else would it be? He tried to steal them before."

"Before, yes. When he thought you were going to keep them hidden forever. I don't understand why he would steal them once you were taking steps to use the curse."

"I don't understand half of what he does," Masahi Seda replied gruffly. "But I know enough not to be surprised by his treachery. He's always been a self-serving bastard. His only loyalty is to himself."

Saya scowled. "That's not true. He may never be accepted as a member of this tribe, but he still cares about our family. You've never given him a chance to—"

"You give him far too many chances." She placed a hand on Saya's shoulder and lowered her voice. "I know he cared for you when you felt like you had no one else, but Zefar is a snake. Whatever his reasons were, your offering wasn't his to take."

The warrior gnawed on her bottom lip for a moment. "No, it wasn't."

"We need to get it back. You know better than anyone how dangerous it could be in the wrong hands."

Saya shrugged away from her mother's touch and crossed her arms. "Are you asking *me* to track it down myself?"

"You're the one who brought it here. I would think you'd feel some responsibility for it."

"I do, but..." She didn't finish the sentence.

"But what? Speak plainly."

The muscles in Saya's jaw tensed. "I left those records with you trusting they'd be safe. I'm not the one who lost them, and I have other problems to worry about right now. I can't abandon my friends to go chasing after Zefar."

"I'm not asking you to," the masahi said, and some of Saya's tension eased. "His tracks led north, toward Kavora. You're headed there anyway. He may have even gone there looking for you. If you happen to run into him or find yourself able to search for him, please do what you can. Talk some sense into him, or kill him. At this point, I don't care. Just get back what's ours."

She nodded. "Of course. I'll do my best."

With that, she led Kesari and Lucian back outside, and they quickly made their way to the same guest tent they'd stayed in before. "Do you have any idea why he might have taken your offering?" Kesari asked as she laid her pack next to Saya's bow, quiver, and satchel.

The warrior unwrapped the red sash around her waist and shook out some of the sand that had gathered in its folds. "No, but I intend to ask if we ever see him. Right before I wring his neck. He had *no right.*" Her words became little more than a growl at the end, and her fingers tightened around the fabric in her hands.

"Maybe your mum was right. He might have gone looking for you."

"Maybe, but she was right about him being a self-serving bastard, too. Skies only know what he could be up to." She shook her head. "I've always trusted him more than people think I should, but he's family. I thought I could count on him not to disrespect that, at least."

"We don't know anything for certain yet," Kesari said in what she hoped was a reassuring tone, though considering what little she knew of Zefar, she was more inclined to agree with the masahi about his treachery. But that wasn't going to make Saya feel any better.

The young woman sighed, winding her sash back over one shoulder and around her waist. "Get a good night's rest. We leave at dawn."

ALEIDA

PRINCE SAVIR LEFT JAKHAT WITHOUT WARNING OR FANFARE, HIS departure so sudden it sent new rumors circulating immediately. There was still no official word from the palace about whether the empress was acknowledging him as the rightful heir to the throne, but the way he'd gone so abruptly didn't bode well, and that worried Mitul.

"We need to leave," he announced one evening after Aleida stopped by for supper and a reading lesson. "Amar's gone back to Valmandi, and that's where we need to be. Saya, Kes, and Lucian will be meeting us there anyway."

"Not for another two weeks," she replied. "And we can't do anything until they arrive. You said it yourself. We need a plan."

"I know." He sighed. "But I don't like this. Amar would be horrified if he really understood what he's doing. We need to get to him as soon as possible, and when the others make it back, I don't want them wasting any time waiting for us."

"All right," she said, but something pinched inside her chest. It took her a few moments to figure out what it was. She should have been happy about going to Valmandi. It meant they were one step closer to thwarting Valkyra's plans and delivering the vengeance she deserved. But going there also meant leaving behind something—*someone*—important to them both. "What about Kamaal?"

The worry in Mitul's eyes shifted to something heavier. "It was always going to be temporary, this thing between us. We both knew that."

The flat resignation in his voice hurt her more than it should have, and she tried to shake it off as quickly as she felt it, reconstructing the wall she'd built around her heart. What did it matter that their little group was splitting up? She'd barely known either of them long enough to call them friends.

Still, she had to ask. "Have you told him?"

"Not yet. Tomorrow."

Kamaal had invited them both to his studio for dinner and wanted to show them the painting he'd finished for Empress Dashiva and Prince Savir. He'd planned to take it to the palace earlier in the week, but given what had happened since, that no longer seemed appropriate.

"I don't have to go," Aleida said, unsure whether she really wanted to be there. It was bound to be a gloomy affair, but it might be her last chance to see Kamaal, and she had new sketches she wanted to show him. Still, she was only the tagalong girl Mitul had taken under his wing for the sake of shared purpose. If the two men needed space to say their farewells in private, she could understand.

"You're coming," he said. "You were invited, and he'll want to say goodbye to you, too. Besides, I think I'm going to want a friend nearby when it's over." The smile he gave her was a small, weak thing that didn't reach his eyes. She had the most absurd and sudden urge to hug him but managed to restrain herself.

The following evening, they made their way to Kamaal's studio with a basket of flatbread in hand. Aleida wore her favorite blue tunic with a pair of soft pants and comfortable boots. Mitul was dressed in an equally casual manner but had taken extra care with his hair, all stray strands smoothed back in a loose ponytail. He'd trimmed his beard a little, too, and he carried himself with a stiff confidence that seemed meant to conceal whatever he was feeling underneath.

Aleida did her best to hide her own emotions, or rather, to pretend she felt none. This was only dinner, nothing important, so there was no reason for her to get worked up about it. Most people never got a chance to meet their heroes, but she'd spent weeks in Kamaal's company and had gotten to know him better than she could have ever imagined. It was all too good to be true and therefore prone to disappearing at any moment. She ought to be grateful for her good fortune and leave it at that. It was selfish to want anything more, and foolish to count on it.

But the hollow ache inside her persisted.

When they arrived, Kamaal invited them in with his usual jovial grin and lively gestures. He'd already prepared their meal, and they sat on the floor around the low table to eat, passing each dish until all three had a little of everything. There was a creamy chickpea soup and steamed rice, chicken and vegetables in a spicy yogurt sauce, plus the fresh-baked flatbread to balance it all out. The warm smell of spices made Aleida's mouth water. She was eager to devour it all but took extra time and care to steady her hands as she raised each bite to her mouth.

"That was excellent, Kamaal," Mitul said when he'd finished eating.

Aleida nodded her agreement. The man's artistry with food almost rivaled his skill and artistry with paint and brush.

"I'm glad you enjoyed it," he replied. "I don't often have anyone to cook for but myself."

"Thank you. Not only for the food, but for everything. The painting and all your help with Amar." He offered a small smile. "Getting me through these last couple of months. It means a lot. I don't know what I would have done without you."

"I told you already, no thanks necessary. I was happy to help." He took a drink from his cup and set it back on the table. "Now that Amar's gone back to Valmandi, what will you do? Your friends will be returning soon, won't they? And they'll have a way to restore his memories?"

"That's the plan." Mitul's fingers began to fumble with the cloth spread across the table. "Aleida and I are actually planning to leave for Valmandi the day after tomorrow."

Kamaal's mouth tightened. "So soon?"

Mitul averted his gaze. "I meant to tell you sooner, but I...well, I suppose I didn't want to cast a shadow on our time together."

"I see." His voice wasn't unkind, but it was missing its usual buoyancy.

Aleida glanced between the two men, her insides cracking like ice under the weight of their silence. Goodbyes and broken hearts loomed on the horizon, ready to cut them all down. She'd never believed in fate, and God and faith had failed her, but she'd taken comfort in the idea that there was still enough good in the world to reunite two long-lost lovers. If it all came crashing down in the end anyway, what was the point?

But it didn't matter. *They* didn't matter. Whatever happened between them shouldn't hurt her.

She steeled her heart and shifted the conversation back to more practical matters. "We need to get Amar away from Valkyra. Or find some way to destroy her."

"Do you have a plan for how to do that?" Kamaal asked. "She's a Spirit Tarja Bonded to an immortal man, which essentially makes her unkillable. And it's not as if you can simply slip into the palace and kidnap Prince Savir."

Mitul was still looking down at his plate. "We'll figure something out."

Kamaal opened his mouth to say something else, then frowned and seemed to think better of it. Instead, he reached over and placed one hand atop Mitul's. "I'm sorry. I don't mean to be discouraging. I've never known you to let anything stop you once you've set your mind on something, and I don't expect this will be any different. You *will* figure something out."

Despite the sincerity in his reassurance, Mitul's features remained tense. The silence lingered for a few more seconds, then Kamaal motioned to the sketchbook Aleida had set beside her. "Can I see what you've been working on?"

"Sure." She handed the book over, and he flipped to the center where he'd torn out that first drawing she'd done. She'd since added half a dozen more sketches to the pages that came after, all made of the same loose lines and smudges that were the best her hands could do. None of them were particularly good—at least not by her previous standards—but she was learning to let go of those standards and simply enjoy the process. A pleasant warmth spread through her as she watched Kamaal's smile grow.

"These are beautiful," he said. "You do such a good job of uncovering the purest essence of your subjects without getting bogged down in the details."

That was largely because she was no longer capable of rendering such details, but she appreciated the compliment nonetheless. It was exactly what she'd been striving for, an adaptation she'd chosen to make to accommodate the changes in her hands' movements. If she could eventually turn it into her greatest artistic strength, so much the better.

He closed the sketchbook and returned it to her. "Can I show you what I've been working on?"

"I'd love that," she said, and together, they rose from the table. Mitul followed, and Kamaal led them to a large canvas sitting on an easel in the middle of the studio, where the light pouring in from all the windows would have converged during the day. It was covered with a sheet, and a stool sat nearby with a small palette and several brushes in a cup perched on top. Kamaal gently pulled the sheet back to reveal the painting he'd done for Empress Dashiva and Prince Savir.

The two figures stood side by side against a backdrop of white marble and green foliage. Both looked regal in their fine attire and golden crowns. The empress held a sheathed sword in one hand and a sprig of blooming jasmine in the other, as was the customary way of portraying Kavoran royal figures in paintings. The sword was angled slightly toward Savir, and the edge of the blade could be seen peering out between hilt and scabbard, as if she'd begun to draw it.

Amar's face was easily recognizable. Aleida had sketched it herself many times before, but the way Kamaal had painted him here was compelling. Shadows fell all around him, causing the angles of his face to look sharper. This was contrasted by the light that fell on the empress' side of the painting, where everything appeared softened except for the hard sliver of the sword she held.

"I'm afraid it came out more foreboding than I planned," Kamaal said. "It's probably best I didn't give it to the empress. I'm not sure she'd appreciate the symbolism."

Mitul studied the painting with a dark look in his eyes. "It seems accurate enough. The encroaching shadows, the imposter prince, the conflict that will come if we don't rescue Amar and stop all of this."

Kamaal reached out and linked Mitul's little finger with his. "You will."

The quiet stretched on, and Aleida bent closer to get a better look at the painting. She examined the brush strokes, the colors, the masterful contrast between light and shadow. Once, she'd hoped to paint like this someday. Now, she'd be happy to paint at all, and she would have to find a new style all her own. But that could be a good thing, and it certainly felt better than giving up on her art entirely.

She straightened and glanced over at the two men beside her. Kamaal was still brooding over the painting, and Mitul was watching him intently. The musician shifted around suddenly to catch both of Kamaal's hands in his. The expression on his face was equal parts hope and desperation. "Come with us to Valmandi," he blurted out.

Kamaal's shoulders went rigid, and Aleida's breath stuck in her throat as she waited for his response. But he didn't say anything, only stood there with his lips parted, like he wanted to speak but couldn't find the words.

"Come with us," Mitul said again, softer this time, a question more than a plea. "I don't want to leave you. Not again. But Amar…"

"You have to help him."

"I do." He swallowed and took a step closer to Kamaal. "I wish I could stay here with you. I always wished that. But as long as this curse has him trapped, I can't stand by and not try to free him."

Kamaal raised a hand to Mitul's chin and smiled, but his eyes were sad. The air seemed to grow heavy all around them. Aleida released her breath slowly and let her gaze drift back to the painting, willing herself to be as invisible as possible. This was a private conversation, not something she should be eavesdropping on, but both men seemed to have forgotten she was even there.

"Please."

Kamaal sighed, and the seconds dragged on painfully before he answered. "What you're asking is no easy thing."

"I know."

He let out a halfhearted chuckle. "After all this time, you're back, and I thought we could start something new, for a little while, at least. But it's only the start, and you're leaving again. How is it that we've come right back to where things ended last time?"

"It's not the same."

"It feels like it, to me."

At the edge of her peripherals, Aleida could see Mitul lacing his fingers between Kamaal's. His voice was barely more than a whisper. "Don't make me choose. Please, come with me."

There was another long space where neither of them spoke, finally broken by Kamaal's low, rasping voice. "I can't."

Aleida's shoulders tensed, and she fought the urge to demand he reconsider. This wasn't about her.

So why did it feel so damn personal?

"Why not?" Mitul asked.

"I just can't. Too much time has passed—time that's changed both of us in ways we can't even see yet. We're different men than we were back then."

"Not *so* different."

"Perhaps not. But I can't pretend none of it ever happened. You're still leaving. The only difference is that this time, I have a chance to say goodbye. You didn't give me that courtesy before."

"Because I knew you wouldn't let it be goodbye. I did what I thought was best, and I was wrong, but I didn't want to force your decision or make you give up everything you'd worked for. I didn't want you to resent me for that."

"I know." Kamaal's voice dropped a little lower. "But you made it all about you and what you did or didn't want. You took the choice away from me, left me behind with nothing but a letter."

"You're right. And I'm so sorry for the way I hurt you. I can't go back and change things, but I want to try again. I want this time to be different." His voice broke on the last word.

"Then please," Kamaal said, "accept my answer. Respect my choice."

There was a sharp intake of breath, and Aleida's feet itched to carry her to Mitul's side, if only to show him he wasn't alone. She forced herself to stay where she was.

Kamaal brought the other man's knuckles to his lips. He spoke so softly she could barely hear him. "Our time together has passed. I'll look on the memories fondly, but…I think it's best we say goodbye."

Mitul's eyes watered, and this time, Aleida did go to him. He took a step away from Kamaal, and she closed the gap until their arms touched, just to let him know she was there. She couldn't bring herself to meet the artist's gaze. How could he do this? Not only to Mitul, but to himself. To all of them.

He reached a hand out to her, and with some reservation, she forced herself to shake it. "It's been such a pleasure getting to know you, Aleida. You're going to do amazing things with your art, and I can't wait to see where you end up."

She muttered a quick thanks, but it tasted like ash.

"Goodbye, Mitul."

"Goodbye."

They embraced for a moment, and when they broke apart, Mitul's expression was flat. It shifted as soon as he turned away, heavy and strained, as if tears could start falling any moment and wouldn't stop once they did. When she glanced back at Kamaal, Aleida saw the same look on his face, but he quickly replaced it with a smile when he caught her watching him.

Mitul stepped outside. He didn't look back, didn't wait for her to follow. She hesitated there in the night outside the closed door, still clutching Kamaal's sketchbook in her hands.

She no longer had a family, but for a little while, with the two of them, it had felt like she did. Even though it was new and fragile, it was *good.* She hadn't had something good in such a long time, and now, it was slipping away right in front of her.

This was wrong, and so unfair it made her want to scream, but there was nothing she could do about it.

Her eyes stung, but she fought off the tears. She opened the book to the last few pages Kamaal had drawn on—all his sketches of Mitul. With a yank, she ripped them out, the jerky motion of her fingers creating a ragged edge along the paper. Then she dug out the short, blunt stick of charcoal she'd taken to carrying in her pocket and scrawled a few words beneath one of the drawings. She needed him to know, and to understand that *she* knew what this was between him and Mitul. She could see it as plain as they must feel it, and they were both throwing it away when it should have been protected and nourished.

She read the words one last time.

You love him.

Then she bent and slid the pages beneath the door of Kamaal's studio. Before he had a chance to retrieve them or open the door to question her, she ran to catch up with Mitul.

SAVIR

IT FELT GOOD TO BE BACK IN VALMANDI. THE FIRST THING SAVIR DID upon his return to the palace was to take a hot bath and dress in something comfortable. After that, he joined his grandparents in the dining hall for supper, and they all had a long discussion about his visit to Jakhat.

He told them about his meeting with General Muraka and the potential of her aligning herself to their cause. Bhajan was pleased by this news but remained skeptical, urging Savir to tell no one else until they could be more certain of Muraka's true loyalties. Savir also spoke of his private meeting with Dashiva and Jasala. They were unsurprised to learn the empress had no intention of giving up her throne, and they seemed only mildly disturbed by the threats she'd made. For his part, Savir still didn't want a conflict, and he said as much.

"Maybe it's for the best if I let this go. I don't need to be emperor—not if it means putting this country's people through war."

"We've talked about this before, Savir," King Bhajan said brusquely. "Dashiva can't be allowed to continue her rule when the throne doesn't belong to her. It wouldn't be right."

"I don't see how war is the right answer, either," he snapped. Why was that so difficult for everyone else to understand?

Bhajan's expression softened. "Sometimes there are no right answers, only less wrong ones."

It wasn't what Savir wanted to hear, and he glared down at the plate in front of him, teeth clenched.

"You have a kind heart, my boy," the king went on. "You got that from your mother, and it will make you a fine ruler someday. But first, you must draw on the strength of will to see this through, even when it's difficult, even when it's not what you want. This empire is *your* responsibility. You can't let that go simply because the path ahead is too rough."

"I just don't want to see anyone get hurt because of my pride."

"I'm afraid that's the weight of the crown you wear. But it's not about pride or ambition. It's about integrity and doing what's right, ensuring the stability of our empire."

That was nearly the same argument Dashiva had made. Savir no longer knew which of them was more correct in their assertions, only that he was feeling increasingly like a piece on a Samud board, pulled this way and that by others' hands.

"And Savir," Bhajan said, his expression hardening once more. "Whatever doubts you have, you cannot let others see them. Come to me or to your grandmother if you need support, but to everyone else, you must be unwavering. Is that clear?"

"Yes," he replied, but that didn't ease the qualms still lingering in his mind.

The following day's council meeting was as difficult as he'd expected. As soon as he'd finished telling the advisors about his conversation with the empress, all talk immediately shifted to preparations for war. There wasn't even a question about whether Savir would be better off giving up his claim as the rightful emperor of Kavora. War was inevitable now, and whatever protests he might have made died when he looked to Bhajan and saw the same hardened expression from the night before.

The greatest disadvantages Valmandi faced against Jakhat were in resources and military strength, as Dashiva had so candidly pointed out. General Khan and Lord Vasu, Advisors of War and Diplomacy, led a discussion about which provinces and governing nobles they could count on as allies, as well as which ones might need further persuading. Khatri, the Advisor of Secrets, informed them she'd already set in motion plans to bring others to their side. The level of support they could potentially count on was better than Savir had expected, but it still wouldn't be enough to secure an easy victory.

"We can't put our reliance on assets we don't yet have control of," General Khan said. "We need to focus on building up our own strength."

"What do you suggest?" Bhajan asked.

"Our Tarja battalions are especially promising. We may not have Jhakat's numbers, but we could match or even surpass their power with a little help from the Sular desert."

Savir wasn't sure what he meant by that, but the sly sharpness in Khan's eyes made something in him recoil.

Lord Vasu appeared equally concerned, twisting his hands on the table in front of him. "We've already strained our relations with the Sularans to the point of breaking. Even mere rumors of war have sent greedy poachers and merchants to harvest as much mesala as they can find. More than a few have come back maimed after being caught by the Sularans, and some haven't returned at all."

Savir now understood what General Khan was suggesting, and the uneasy feeling in his stomach intensified. If given to every Tarja soldier in Valmandi's ranks, mesala could greatly enhance their strength in battle. However, the plant was also a vital part of the desert's ecosystem. Taking too much of it would disrupt the Sularans way of life and could even threaten their basic survival.

General Khan inclined his head. "If we were to stop the poaching, would the Sularans agree to let us harvest some of their mesala in a more controlled way?"

"I doubt it," said Lord Vasu. "Once, they might have. But they say the ghayat herds are growing smaller each year, and they blame that on us and our failure to adequately enforce the trade agreements already established."

"We could purchase the mesala that's already been collected," the Advisor of Coin suggested.

"We can, if it hasn't been transported and sold to Jakhat," General Khan said. "I'd feel much better prepared if we could get our hands on our own stock. Perhaps I could send a few small squads to collect some."

"Doing that would only anger the Sularans further," Lord Vasu protested. "And we can't afford to fight a war on two fronts."

"We'd be discreet, of course. The Sularans need never know we were there."

"You clearly don't understand their people or their lands if you think it will be so easy."

"We need every advantage we can get," King Bhajan interjected. "And we need to keep Jakhat away from any resources they might use against us. Send a few squads into the desert, General, but they are only to patrol the border for the purpose of keeping out poachers, merchants, and enemy forces. Surely the Sularans can't object to that."

Vasu's mouth pinched sourly, but he said nothing. Some of Savir's own unease subsided. He still didn't like the idea of encroaching on the Sularans' territory, but at least Bhajan's solution would prevent any further harm.

"And of course," the king continued, "if your soldiers happen to come across some mesala during their patrols, it certainly wouldn't hurt for them to harvest it and send it back here."

Savir's jaw tightened, and he nearly stood from his chair to make his objections known. The shift of his body caused Valkyra to dig her claws into his shoulder so sharply she almost drew blood. He remained seated, trying to put his thoughts to words. He didn't want to openly challenge his grandfather in front of all his advisors, but he had to say something. They couldn't simply rationalize away any wrongdoing on the pretense of securing their borders.

"Are we sure that's the best idea?" he said carefully. "There must be other ways to acquire mesala without angering the Sularans. Or even other resources we can use. Are there any other plants with similar properties?"

Chayani Sha, the Advisor of Magic, shook her head. "None half as potent or as easily accessible."

Savir looked to Lord Vasu for support. "You said we can't afford to fight a war on two fronts. That's what could happen if the Sularans learn our soldiers are stealing mesala."

"Yes, well..." The man seemed far more hesitant now, glancing between Savir and Bhajan as if trying to decide who he should side with.

"So long as the soldiers are discreet in harvesting the flower and make clear their intentions to protect the border, the risk should be minimal."

"Your concerns are noted, Savir," King Bhajan said flatly. "I'm hopeful that this will only be a temporary arrangement. But, as I said before, we must take every advantage we can get."

He left no room for Savir to argue, moving quickly to other matters. The conversation turned toward keeping the army and the city supplied with food and other necessities, as well as the potential economic impact on the region. Eventually, concerns arose regarding their ability to maintain a labor force large enough to sustain the military with supplies, weapons, and munitions—a challenge made more difficult since they also needed to draw from their existing labor force to bolster the army's ranks.

This was a problem to which Savir could see an easy solution. "What about the Visans?" he asked when there was an opening in the discussion. "There must be thousands of them in the camps outside our walls. Some already work here in the city, and if we lifted the curfew or opened other jobs for them, that might help with any labor shortage."

King Bhajan pursed his lips at this and exchanged a look with Vasu, who then spoke to Savir. "We have long maintained that the Visan refugees are Empress Dashiva's problem to handle. After all, the invasion of their homeland was not something we supported or took part in, so why should *we* be the ones cleaning up the mess she left?"

Savir frowned. "I don't understand how that's relevant to the situation we're in now."

Vasu sighed as if annoyed at having to explain something simple to a very small child. "If we suddenly lift all restrictions and allow the Visans free rein in our city, it sends the message that we're accepting responsibility for them instead of holding Dashiva accountable."

"Seems you've been trying to hold her accountable for years and nothing's come of it."

"I agree," said General Khan, who was the last person Savir had expected to back him up. "They could be a valuable asset. Some of them might even be willing to enlist, especially if we frame recruitment efforts around their desire for justice or revenge on Dashiva."

That was not at all what Savir had been angling for, but the other advisors were voicing their agreement now. It was a logically sound idea. Still, there was a certain level of cutthroat cruelty in what General Khan was proposing, recruiting Visans to fight in a civil war for the very same country that had invaded theirs only seven years prior.

"It's a good plan," Bhajan said. "We'll issue a decree right away."

And that was it; he'd suggested something, and they had listened to him. Savir wasn't sure whether he wanted to smile or vomit. They'd twisted the intention of his idea to suit their own needs, but still, they had listened. It was the first time he'd felt like he held any real power since he'd stepped into his role as prince, and that both terrified and thrilled him. With that kind of power, he could make a real difference for good. With that kind of power, he could just as easily set things in motion that would hurt the people beneath him.

He would have to consider his choices and his words far more carefully going forward.

ALEIDA

ALEIDA AND MITUL ARRIVED IN VALMANDI ON THE VERY DAY THEY were scheduled to meet Saya, Kesari, and Lucian at the Saffron Fox. Aleida hoped to find the others already waiting for them there, but when they asked the innkeeper about any guests matching their descriptions, he reported he hadn't seen them, so they rented a room and bought themselves a hot meal to eat while they waited.

Aleida had been pleasantly surprised to learn that the city's many restrictions for Visans had been lifted in the past week. She'd been anxious about coming to Valmandi for that reason alone, and she remembered all too well her brief stint in a cell during her last visit here. She was, however, far less pleased when she noticed the recruitment flyers posted around the inn calling on young Visans to join Valmandi's military.

"Look at this shit," she growled, jabbing a finger at one of the flyers. "I bet they only got rid of all their ridiculous restrictions because they need us to fight their stupid war."

Mitul barely glanced at the poster. "You're probably right." He went back to picking at his food, eyes downcast and shoulders slumped.

Aleida frowned. The man had grown uncharacteristically morose ever since they'd left Jakhat. He often left his meals unfinished, and whenever she tried to pull him out of his gloom with a joke or a conversation or even an argument, he barely responded.

His silence infuriated her. She missed his easy smile and gentle voice more than she'd ever thought she would. She missed his songs. His saraj had remained untouched in its case for the duration of their journey, and when the innkeeper came by their table and encouraged him to play for the guests, he made some excuse about the instrument being broken. If anything was broken, it was Mitul himself, and Aleida could only fault Kamaal for that. If he'd agreed to come with them, things could have stayed the same. They could have been happy. They could have been whole.

Again, she told herself that it didn't matter. It didn't matter that they'd left, or that Kamaal had chosen to stay behind, or even that she'd once again lost the one good thing in her life. They weren't her family, just a couple of strangers whose paths had temporarily intertwined with hers because of their shared goals. When all of this was over, they would go their separate ways, like Kamaal had already, and that would be the end of it.

It had been foolish to let herself become attached in the first place. How many times would she have to experience loss like this before she learned her lesson for good?

The rest of the day passed without the others' arrival. Mitul went up to bed early, but Aleida stayed downstairs where she could watch the inn's entrance for several hours after dark. She nodded off in her chair a few times before finally dragging herself to the room to sleep.

The next day came and went, and still the others did not come. Mitul spent most of that time sleeping, or pretending to sleep, and Aleida grew increasingly frustrated by the delay with each passing hour.

She went to the city's southern gate first thing the next morning. Saya, Kesari, and Lucian would be coming from that direction, and it was better to wait for them there in the fresh air than to stay holed up inside the shuttered inn. She'd debated waking Mitul to talk him into coming with her, but decided against it. He would have protested, and she would have tried to argue with him, and he would have refused to engage in that argument, which would have only upset her more.

She found a place to sit where she could see through the open gate to the road outside. She'd brought her sketchbook and a few sticks of charcoal with her to pass the time while she waited. Her drawings were still messy and so different from how she'd worked before, but she was getting better, learning to lean into what her hands could do rather than fighting for what they couldn't.

She'd filled several pages by late afternoon, glancing up often to watch for a familiar face coming through the gate. Fearing she'd missed them, she returned to the inn, but they weren't there, either. The following day passed in much the same manner.

"We can't keep sitting here doing nothing," she said to Mitul that evening. "We should at least be scouting out the palace, learning more about Amar's movements, trying to figure out a way to get to him. Anything."

He continued staring out the window and said nothing.

The frustration she'd been holding inside bubbled to the surface in a sudden rush, and she slammed one palm against the wall. "Damn it, why won't you *do* something?"

"We can't," he said, his voice listless. "You know that. Not until the others get here."

"I'm not talking about that," she shouted. "I'm talking about you doing *anything* that's not sitting in this room feeling sorry for yourself. Kamaal's gone, all right? He should have come with us, but he didn't, and I hate him for that too, but we have to—" Her voice cut off in a strangled sob, and it was only then that she noticed the tears burning in her eyes. She stood up from the table and made for the door, suddenly needing to be anywhere but here.

"Aleida, wait," Mitul called, but she paid him no mind. The door slammed shut behind her, and she raced down the hall to the stairs, taking them two at a time to the second floor and then the first, where she hurled herself outside to suck in the cold air until her insides stopped burning.

She started walking, thoughts swirling through her head like wind tearing at sails in a storm. She didn't hate Kamaal, not really, though sometimes she wished she could. She was just so damn angry—at him, Valkyra, her weakened hands, and all this waiting. And Mitul, damn him, holed up in his room with his heartbreak, acting like the rest of the world had disappeared. Couldn't he see that she was still here?

She clenched her jaw and quickened her pace. She didn't need him. She didn't need anyone.

Her feet carried her toward the palace, its barred gates closed. She'd seen them open many times in passing during the day and had often thought about simply walking through onto the grounds, as she'd watched so many others do before. That would have been the easy part. Getting inside the palace itself was another matter, and finding Amar without Valkyra knowing would prove even more difficult. And once she found him, then what?

It was still fairly early in the night, and she watched the comings and goings of servants and other palace staff. Many were on their way home after the day's work. They slipped outside through a private door and left the grounds via a small side gate she hadn't noticed before. A few of them were Visan, presumably a new development now that the curfew and other restrictions had been lifted.

As she watched, a plan began to formulate in her mind. It was reckless—an idea she hadn't dared entertain before and probably shouldn't be entertaining now. But she was so tired of waiting. She'd been waiting for months, and every passing day meant Valkyra was closer to accomplishing her own goals while Aleida hadn't made any progress toward stopping her.

She had to do something, even if it was only gathering more information. And if Mitul wasn't going to help her, she would do it herself.

She hopped from her seat and tailed the two Visan servants who'd just left the palace, taking stock of their attire and listening in on their conversation as best as she could. She made a mental note of any details that seemed important, including a list of clothing items she'd need to blend in. It was nothing too difficult to obtain, and she could have it all by tomorrow night. If the others hadn't shown up by then, at least this was something productive to do. Risky, maybe, but she could handle it.

She was only going to look, in and out before Mitul could miss her, if he even noticed her gone at all. What could be the harm? And when she came back with information that would help them rescue Amar, he'd be too pleased to be upset with her.

Aleida spent the next day preparing for the mission she'd taken upon herself. The clothes were easy enough to come by, and her brief surveillance of the palace assured her there were now multiple Visans working there as servants, cooks, and even guards. She might have to do a little improvising to get inside, but the role of palace servant should be an easy enough one to slip into, especially after her experience working in Jakhat. Besides, she didn't actually want to talk to Amar or anyone else important. She only wanted to get close enough to make some observations and gain a little more information.

She left Mitul still sleeping at sunrise the next morning, ignoring the sting of her guilt as the door shut behind her. She'd avoided him all of yesterday and made an excuse about being tired when he'd tried to speak to her that night. Whatever they needed to talk about could wait until she got back. With any luck, Saya, Kesari, and Lucian would be back by then, too.

She made the short walk from the inn to the palace, tying a kerchief around her head as she went. A few servants were already entering through the side gate when she arrived, and she reached into her pocket for the single coin she'd wrapped in a layer of red cloth. With some careful maneuvering and a little luck, it would pass as one of the red metal tokens palace staff showed the guards to signify they had the security clearance to enter.

She slowed her pace until a pair of older women caught up to her, then matched her steps with theirs. With her heart hammering, Aleida positioned herself at one's side, farthest away from the inspecting guard's line of sight, and when the other two women flashed their tokens, she pulled out her coin. She let it show for only a moment, and to her great relief, the guard gave it the briefest glance before waving her inside with the other two women. The air trapped in her lungs came out with a soft exhale.

She stepped into a wide hallway. A pleasant aroma wafted from an open doorway a few paces ahead where more servants were milling about, some carrying in crates of food or stacks of chopped wood while others came out with platters of steaming dishes. The kitchen seemed as good a place to start as any, so Aleida made her way there, ducking past a girl carrying a basket of bread on her way inside.

The scene she walked into was every bit as chaotic as she'd expected it to be. Considering the size of the palace and the status of the people within, breakfast was bound to be a tumultuous affair, and that would serve her well if she could take advantage of the hustle rather than getting tripped up in it.

She surveyed her surroundings quickly, searching for some easy errand that would allow her to sneak into Prince Savir's room. A tray of delicate cups and a ceramic kettle had been placed atop a nearby counter, but that was going to be a tricky job with her hand tremors, and she didn't want to risk dropping it or clattering through the hallways for all to hear. If she could get a basket of bread or something similar, like the girl in the hall had been carrying, that would be easier.

She spotted a shelf full of linens in the back corner. Napkins and tablecloths, most likely, but they might pass for sheets or other bedding at a glance. She stole across the kitchen floor and grabbed a stack from the middle shelf. She was halfway back to the door when someone called out, "Hey, where are you taking those?" but she didn't stop. They could be talking to anyone, after all.

Once back in the hall, she turned right and hurried toward the center of the palace. She kept her eyes focused only on what lay ahead, and as soon as she could, she made her way down another hallway and up a narrow flight of stairs. She had no idea where she was going, but that was okay. She'd need to stop and ask for directions at some point anyway, and if she looked genuinely lost, so much the better.

Another servant gave her a quick nod as they passed. She also passed a pair of women in flowery dresses, but they didn't so much as look in her direction. She was of little consequence to them, practically invisible, which was exactly what she'd been counting on.

After wandering down a few more hallways, she felt sufficiently lost and set about finding someone to ask for directions. Someone who would be sympathetic and willing to help but who wouldn't be too suspicious. She encountered a few more people as she walked—a guard, a pageboy, an elderly woman in silk robes—but none of them seemed like good options. She was about to give up and try to find her way back downstairs when she spotted another servant coming her way. Better still, the man was Visan.

She made her mouth and brows tight in an expression of consternation and quickened her pace to meet him. "Artex save me, I'm so glad I found you," she said in Visan. "I was asked to deliver these to Prince Savir's room, but it's my first day, and this place is so big. I've gotten myself all turned around. Could you help me?"

"Of course," the man said, smiling at her kindly. "Come on, I'll show you the way."

She followed him back the way she'd come. "Thank you. You're really saving me here."

"It's no trouble. My first day was rough, too."

They took an adjoining hallway and descended a flight of stairs, back to the main floor. "What's your name?" he asked.

"Sabina," she lied. She didn't ask for his name, even when he waited a few seconds for her to do so.

"Well, it's a pleasure to meet you, Sabina." He stopped at another hallway branching off to the left and pointed. "It's that way, third door on the right. I don't see his guard outside, so the prince probably isn't in there now. You should be able to go right in."

"Thank you so much."

"You're welcome. I'll see you around."

He left, and Aleida hurried down the hall until she reached the third door. Even though the man had suggested the room would be empty, she knocked, just in case. When there was no response, she entered and set her stack of folded linens on a small table near the door.

The room was nearly as big as her family's entire home had been before the invasion, and it contained enough finery to feed them well for years. There was a large canopy bed in the center and a smaller daybed under the open window. A variety of chests, armoires, and dressers had been placed against the walls and in the corners, the wood carved, stained, and polished beautifully. A tall mirror stood almost directly in front of Aleida, and looking at herself in it, she almost had to laugh at how out of place she seemed.

She wasn't sure what she was looking for, but she began her search in the trunk at the foot of the bed. Inside, she found a few pairs of footwear and a belt with an empty scabbard and holster. The flintlock pistol Amar had carried lay beside it, along with a leather cartridge pouch. The sword itself was still in Mitul's care, tucked away safely with the rest of Amar's belongings.

There was nothing else of note there, so she closed the trunk and moved on to the bedside table. A lantern sat on top of it, along with a few dull-looking books on Kavoran history and economics. There was also a quill, ink bottle, and a few loose papers. Aleida shuffled through these and was about to try deciphering the handwritten notes when a sound outside the door made her flinch.

Footsteps, first approaching the door then stopping in front of it. Shadows blocked out the narrow gap of light seeping in underneath.

She reached to set the papers back on the nightstand, but her fingers wouldn't cooperate when she tried to let go of them, and all she managed to do was drop them. They fluttered down to the floor, and she bit back a curse. There was no time to recover them. The door was already opening.

She dropped flat onto her stomach and pushed herself under the bed. There was a soft click as the door closed behind whoever had entered, and she covered her mouth with her hands to quiet her own ragged breaths. Her heart slammed against her ribcage. She stared straight ahead, past the pair of feet pacing in front of her and into the mirror. A tall figure turned, allowing her to see his reflection clearly. It was Amar, and on his shoulder sat Valkyra, exactly the way she used to perch on Aleida's.

The mere sight of the Spirit Tarja caused a hatred stronger than any she'd ever felt to roil and steam in her stomach. For the briefest moment, it looked as if Valkyra was meeting her gaze through the mirror, and her body screamed at her to fight, scream, run, and stay put, all at the same time. Then the dragon's eyes flicked away, and Aleida quietly pushed herself back a little farther into the shadows. Staying put was the only option.

Valkyra jumped from Amar's shoulder to flutter onto the window ledge. One clawed foreleg motioned to the papers scattered on the floor as he walked over. "You really ought to close your window when you leave," she said in that same motherly tone she used to use with

Aleida. "The wind could send those flying outside next time."

He bent to pick up the pages, and Aleida stopped breathing, willing him not to look in her direction. "I like it open," he said, arranging them into a neat stack.

"At least put those somewhere safer, then."

He straightened and took a couple more steps to the nightstand. There was a quiet shuffle of books being moved about, then he walked over to the armoire on the other side of the room.

Aleida watched him through the mirror again, keeping a close eye on Valkyra as well. He picked out a new set of clothes and began to change. "I heard you and Ashaya talking about that Sularan yesterday. What's that about?"

Her focus sharpened at the mention of that name. Magistrate Ashaya had helped Valkyra to facilitate Aleida's escape from a guardhouse cell when they were still hunting Amar. An old friend, she'd called him then, and Aleida had been upset because Ashaya was also a known friend of Nandini Kumar. That was before she'd known Valkyra and Nandini were the same person, and Ashaya must know that, too. Just how long had they been working together and planning all of this?

"The Sularan wants an audience with the council," Valkyra said. "We're still trying to find out why."

He slipped a new pair of pants over his undergarments and adjusted the waistband. "Tell Ashaya to invite him to the next one. Keeping the Sularans' favor needs to be a priority."

"You're absolutely right, dear. But we can't simply grant an audience to anyone who wants one. We need to know more. Especially since this Sularan seems...peculiar."

"Meaning what, exactly?"

"Meaning I've asked the magistrate to look into it, and he'll tell me if he discovers anything important."

Amar pulled down on the embroidered cuffs of his shirt and checked his appearance in the mirror. "He'll tell *us*, you mean?"

Valkyra sighed. "We've talked about this before, Savir. You don't need to concern yourself with every trivial detail that comes up."

"I'll decide what's trivial and what's not," he replied sharply.

"Of course, Your Majesty. We're only trying to serve you as best we can." She flew back to his shoulder and brushed one wing against the back of his head. "Have I told you how proud I am of the way you've stepped up and taken more responsibility lately?"

"I'm only doing what I have to," Amar muttered, but he seemed to brighten a little at her praise.

Aleida grimaced. Once, she had taken pride in Valkyra's praises too, when she'd thought they were sincere and trusted the Spirit Tarja as a mentor and friend. How blind she'd been back then. She didn't know Amar well enough to consider him a friend, and she'd considered him an enemy so long she might *never* call him friend, but she wouldn't wish Valkyra's deceitful manipulations on anyone.

They went back to the door. It shut with a *thud* behind them, and after a few seconds, the sound of Amar's footfalls faded away. Aleida gave herself a couple of minutes under the bed to return her breathing to a normal rhythm. She'd hoped to avoid running into Amar at all, though perhaps that had been a foolish expectation. Honestly, this whole expedition was foolish, and beyond reckless even by her standards. She needed to get out before anything else happened, but she didn't want to leave empty handed.

She rolled out from under the bed and pushed herself upright. The thin stack of papers she'd been examining before still sat on the nightstand, clamped between two books so as not to allow the breeze to disturb them. Carefully, she pulled them out, reading over the words as quickly as she could. Much of the writing was illegible, scrawled in a messy hand and scratched out or written over again in several places. In between the mess she managed to pick out a few clear lines.

Ruined buildings. Skulls, bones. Green. Forest maybe.

Desert. Sand, windy, orange cliffs. A woman, gold eyes. Sularan?

Music playing, a man singing. An instrument with strings.

Red light everywhere. Tarja girl. Scared.

What were these? Aleida frowned as she tried to make out more of the words and piece it all together, but it seemed so random. The line about music and the man singing—that could have been Mitul. Was Amar remembering these things on his own?

She committed what she could to memory and put the pages back as she'd found them. Now to make her way out of here.

She went to the door and pushed it open, nearly bumping into a young man on his way in. Another servant, judging by the look of him. And probably one who belonged here, unlike her.

Quickly, she stammered an apology. "I'm so sorry, excuse me." She sidestepped, trying to slip past him, but he moved in the same direction. "Sorry," she repeated, stepping the other way.

Again, the young man matched her movement, and this time, he reached out to grab her wrist. "What were you doing in Prince Savir's chambers? Who are you?"

"I was only dropping something off. I'm on my way back to the kitchens now."

"The kitchens are *that* way." He pointed opposite of the direction she'd been headed.

Shit. Why hadn't she left Amar's room five minutes earlier? "Are they really?" she asked, feigning innocence. "I must have gotten turned around."

The man gave her a strange look but would not let go of her wrist.

"You're hurting me," she said.

His eyes flicked to something down the hall, and as she glanced over to see what he was looking at, he raised his free hand. "Hey there! Guard!"

Her stomach dropped as the approaching guard quickened his pace. She tried to wrench free, but the man held her firm, and her sudden movement only made the guard hurry faster. In seconds, both men had her pinned to the wall with her hands pressed against the small of her back.

"What's all this about?" the guard asked.

"She was in the prince's room," replied the servant.

"I was only dropping something off. Please, let me go."

The guard eased back a little, reducing some of the pressure he'd been putting on her shoulder. "If you're a servant here, let's see your token."

Aleida weighed her options. Showing the fake she'd created was a sure way to prove she'd come here under false pretenses. Better to lie about it and hope they didn't search her before she could get rid of the damned thing. "They didn't give me one—not yet. It's my first day. But I can ask about it, if you'll let me get back to—"

"She wouldn't have been assigned to Prince Savir if she's that new," the servant scoffed. "I've never seen her before, and I know every person who attends to the prince. She could be a spy from Jakhat."

"Or worse," the guard said. "You stay here. Don't let anyone else into that room until either I or Tarik return. We'll need to do a full search, but first, I have to deal with this one." He pulled Aleida back roughly and spun her around to face him. "What's your name?"

"Sabina."

He narrowed his eyes as if he didn't entirely believe her.

"I swear, I'm not a spy. I got lost. Can't you just—"

"I don't have time for excuses. Come on." He grabbed her by the arm and began to walk.

Aleida braced her feet against the floor, but he only yanked harder, and she was forced to stumble along anyway. "Where are you taking me?"

"To the cells. Let them sort it out. I don't know what's going on, but I'm not taking any chances when we've got a war brewing." Her face must have betrayed her fear because the next thing he said was, "Don't look at me like that. If you are who you say you are, you've got nothing to worry about. And if not, well, then I guess you already chose your fate, didn't you?"

That was exactly what Aleida was afraid of.

KESARI

HEAVY RAINS AND FLASH FLOODS IMPEDED KESARI AND HER companions' travel through the desert almost from the moment they left Hayathu. The storm itself only lasted a few hours, but the detours they were forced to take to seek higher ground and a passable route made for slow progress.

By the time they reached Sharmok, they were already past due to meet Mitul and Aleida in Valmandi, but they stopped to resupply before moving on. To their dismay, their coin didn't stretch nearly as far as it had only months before. With war looming and people stockpiling what they could in anticipation of lean times ahead, the prices of almost everything had doubled and sometimes nearly tripled. They sold their horses to help offset the cost, even though making the rest of their journey on foot would slow them further.

While shopping, they caught up on the news and rumors coming out of Kavora, which had only gotten worse. Empress Dashiva had officially declared the returned Prince Savir to be a fraud, simultaneously rejecting his claim to the throne and declaring any effort by Valmandi to see him crowned an act of treason. In response, King Bhajan and the prince's other supporters doubled down on their assertions that he was Kavora's rightful ruler, and troops had been moving across the various provinces for the last two weeks, readying for a fight. There was no bloodshed to speak of yet, but everyone agreed that could change at any moment.

Saya also made a point to ask several of the locals about Zefar. Some said they'd seen him a couple of weeks prior, but he hadn't stayed long. They didn't mention any unusual business dealings, which was both good and bad news, depending on which way they looked at it. Saya had expressed fears that he might try to sell the Shavhallan records, but as far as they could tell, he hadn't unloaded them here. Which meant they still didn't know where he'd gone with them, but they could at least make a reasonable guess. The most profitable thing for him to do would be to sell them in a larger city, perhaps to one of the more prestigious Tarja academies. They would surely be willing to pay a hefty price for such a valuable artifact, and they had the coin to afford it.

A few days later, they finally reached Valmandi, tired from a long day's travel and eager for the comfortable beds and warm meals that awaited them at the Saffron Fox. It was past dark when they stepped inside the inn, and when they asked the innkeeper about Mitul and Aleida, he showed them up to their room.

They knocked and only had to wait a few seconds for Mitul to answer. His face was tight and haggard, but it livened a little when he saw them. He embraced Saya first, then Kesari, and the familiar clean, woodsy smell of him made her smile.

"You have no idea how good it is to see you both," he said, inviting them inside with a wave of his hand.

"Where's Aleida?" Kesari asked, looking around the room. The young woman's satchel sat in a chair near the window, but she was nowhere to be seen.

"I wish I knew." His forehead creased as his brows drew together. "She left yesterday morning and still hasn't returned."

"Clearly she meant to, if she left her things here," Saya said. "Do you have any idea where she might have gone?"

"Maybe. I'm not sure. When you didn't arrive on time, she became…restless. And I wasn't paying as much attention as I should have been." The lines in his face deepened, and he wrung his hands together. "I think she may have gone to the palace. She kept talking about it, saying she wanted to scout it out, keep an eye on Amar and Valkyra, start planning for when the rest of you arrived. I told her it was a bad idea, but—"

"The palace?" Lucian interrupted. "What does that have to do with anything?"

Mitul inhaled deeply. "Right. Well, I guess that's the biggest news. We discovered Valkyra has Amar posing as Prince Savir."

A stunned silence hung in the air as they all absorbed this new information. Kesari fit it in with everything they'd heard during their travels. The return of Kavora's long-lost prince was already causing turmoil, but he wasn't Prince Savir at all. Amar was deceiving the entire empire, and he didn't even know what he was doing.

"It's all a lie," Saya said quietly, her brows drawn low over her piercing gold eyes. "The fight hasn't started yet, but it's already hurting my people, and he's not even the real prince. We can't let this continue."

"I know," Mitul said.

"And you're absolutely certain about this?" Lucian asked. "Prince Savir is truly Amar?"

Mitul quickly recounted the events of the last few months, how he and Aleida had begun their search for Amar in Jakhat and eventually confirmed his assumed identity with the help of an old friend. Or at least, that was how he described Kamaal Ruman, but his hand drifted to the silver and turquoise band he'd always worn around his wrist, and Kesari remembered the brief conversation they'd had the last time that name had come up.

He was my partner, for a time. We might have been together for the rest of our lives if things had been different.

What must that have been like, to see the man he'd once loved so many years later? But if there was anything more to tell, he didn't share it with them.

Saya gave him a quick rundown of the most notable parts of their own journey. Mitul was sympathetic to her concerns for her people and the impacts they were already seeing from mere rumors of war, with more and more intruders stripping the desert of one of its most important resources. When she spoke of Zefar and how he'd stolen her haseph offering, Mitul looked more upset than Kesari had ever seen him.

"It seems our problems have only multiplied in our time apart," he said grimly.

Saya nodded. "Hopefully we'll have an easier time solving them, now that we're all back together."

"Not all of us. Aleida's still missing."

Saya frowned and exchanged a look with Kesari. "I don't mean to be cruel, but do we need her? She was never really one of us. Her going off like this only proves what we've known all along—we can't trust her. Maybe it's better if we part ways."

Mitul shook his head. "No. I won't leave her to whatever trouble she's gotten herself into."

Saya didn't look convinced. "We might have a common enemy, but that doesn't make her a friend. We don't owe her anything."

"She's *my* friend." Mitul's voice rose to a near shout. "You barely know her."

"I know enough. She tried to kill us more than once. She's selfish and vengeful and reckless, and we have bigger problems to worry about. We have to get Amar back before things get any worse than they are now."

Mitul's brows pinched at the mention of his brother's name. "Don't you think I know that? I've been worried about Amar every day since Valkyra took him. But he's all right, for now. He's safe. Aleida might not be."

Saya muttered a Sularan curse under her breath and looked to Kesari pointedly, an unspoken request for support. But Kesari didn't know what to say. She could understand Saya's mistrust for the Visan woman, but she also had enough respect for Mitul to honor whatever friendship he'd formed with Aleida. Whether Saya liked it or not, didn't that make her one of them? And they didn't abandon each other.

"At the very least," Lucian chimed in, "we should make sure she hasn't run into Valkyra. If she did go to the palace, that's a possibility."

"Skies, I hadn't even thought of that," Saya groaned. "Fine. I guess we have no choice but to find her. Lucian, maybe you could sneak into the palace and have a look, see if you can learn anything?"

"Of course. I'll go now. With hearths blazing and lanterns lit for the night, it will be easier to blend in."

"Be careful," Kesari said as he drifted toward the open window.

He let out a raspy chuckle. "I'm a ghostly ball of fire that can't be hurt or killed. What's there to be careful about?"

"Getting caught, for one thing," Saya muttered.

"You know what I mean," Kesari said, but he was gone before she'd finished speaking.

"Thank you," Mitul said, looking between the two of them. His gaze lingered on Saya a little longer. "I'm sorry. I'm sure you were hoping we'd be more prepared by the time you got back."

"I'm not sure what I was hoping," she replied. "I certainly didn't expect to find out Prince Savir is actually Amar. It complicates everything."

"I know. But you found Jameson's notes. Kes, do you think you'll be able to bring his memories back yourself, or do you want us to find another Tarja?"

Kesari raised her chin. It was the first time anyone had posed the question to her directly, though she'd thought about it often as she pored over the wizard's notes and discussed his research with Lucian during their travels. Before, she hadn't been sure, but after reviewing Jameson's procedure herself and conquering her fear of the fires in Deveaural, the answer came easily. "I can do it."

"Good. That's one problem solved, at least. Now we just need to get him away from Valkyra long enough to make it happen."

ALEIDA

ALEIDA SHIVERED ON THE FLOOR OF HER CELL BENEATH A THIN, scratchy blanket that barely covered her body, her teeth clenched tight to keep them from chattering. This cell was colder than the one in the palace dungeons where she'd first been sent, and she almost wished she was back there. Her stay had been short, just long enough for the palace guards to question her and decide they didn't want to deal with her. She'd been moved the next day to await a proper trial for the crime of trespassing, and the guardhouse she was locked up in now was indistinguishable from the one she'd found herself in during her previous visit to Valmandi.

Back then, she had prayed to Artex for help, and Valkyra had eventually come to rescue her. Now she knew better than to call on a god who wouldn't answer, and she doubted anyone was coming for her. No one knew where she was. Probably, no one cared enough to come for her even if they did know.

But that wasn't fair to Mitul. He cared, didn't he? He'd always looked out for her, called her a friend, shown her kindness when she hadn't earned it. And to repay him, she'd run off to do exactly what he'd advised against and gotten herself locked up. Locked up in the same sort of place she'd been held prisoner mere months before, because apparently, she was too stupid to learn from her mistakes the first time. It might have been funny if she weren't so damn furious with herself.

Sleep had been near impossible the last two nights, but she tried anyway. She was beginning to drift off when a soft voice spoke from above, and her eyes snapped open.

"Well, you've gotten yourself into a fine mess, haven't you?"

Lucian hovered over her, a tiny flame flickering in the dark. She could barely make out his facial features, but the deep, crackling voice was unmistakable. She was so relieved to see a familiar face that she might have hugged him if he weren't an intangible flame.

She sat up. "How did you find me?" It came out in a stammer between chattering teeth, and her voice was dry with thirst.

Lucian drew a little closer and made himself bigger. The heat that radiated from him was a welcome respite from the cold, and Aleida held her hands up to warm them.

"It wasn't easy," he replied. "Mitul suspected you'd gone to the palace, so I lurked there most of the night, watching and listening. Asked the captives in the dungeon some questions from the shadows, pretending to be one of them. Eventually I heard enough to learn you'd been taken here."

"Mitul sent you?"

"I like to think I nobly volunteered to rescue a damsel in distress, but I suppose he played some role. He was the one who insisted that we not leave you to your fate."

She squirmed. The man's concern for her well-being was more than she deserved.

"So tell me, how exactly did you end up here?" Lucian asked.

She described her venture into the palace, trying to justify what she'd done with explanations that sounded more like excuses. It all seemed so childish now, and foolish beyond even her most reckless reasonings. "They threw me in the palace cells and brought a bunch of the other servants down to vouch for me. Only one of them could, and barely—a man who helped me find Prince Savir's room. I kept repeating the same story, and soon enough they handed me over to the city guard, said they'd let them decide what to do with me. Next thing I knew, I was in here."

"Did Valkyra see you?"

"No."

"Do you think she found out you were there?"

"No." She reconsidered. "Well, I'm not sure. I guess she could have, couldn't she?"

"Yes," Lucian said, drawing out the end of the word like a hiss. "You put all of us at risk, you know. Kes and Saya went through a lot getting what we needed and coming back here, and it all would have been for nothing if you'd been caught."

Aleida tucked her arms around herself. "I wasn't thinking about that."

"Clearly."

"Are they angry?" she asked, though there was only one person's opinion she cared about.

"Saya certainly is. She wanted to leave you in here, and I can't say I blame her. But we can't have Valkyra finding out what you were doing and coming around to ask questions. As for Kes, she's too concerned with getting Amar's memories back to be angry about this."

"And…Mitul?"

He made a sputtering sort of noise that was almost a grunt. "Mitul's got a heart soft enough to let even his worst enemies find their way into his good graces. I'm sure he'll be delirious with joy when I tell him you're alive and well."

He wasn't wrong, and that only made her feel more guilty. "What now?" she asked.

"Now we get you out of here."

She lifted her eyes to meet his, renewed hope sparking through her veins. "Do you know how, then?"

"Not yet. But we'll figure something out. We have to." He shrunk back down and drifted away from her, between the bars of her cell and into the freedom that was beyond her reach. "I'm going to have a look around, see what I can learn about this place that will help us break you out. Any information you can tell me about the guards or their schedule might also be useful, so if you haven't been paying attention, start now. I'll come back later to talk, maybe tomorrow."

He started to float away, and she called after him in a whisper. "Lucian, wait."

He stopped. "Yes?"

"Will you tell him that I'm sorry? Please."

"Tell him yourself when you see him," he said, and then he was gone.

SAVIR

WITH TENSIONS ESCALATING BETWEEN JAKHAT AND VALMANDI, council meetings turned to war meetings and became more frequent and time consuming than ever before. Savir did his best to pay attention, understand the information presented, and weigh in intelligently when his opinion was called for or when he thought he had something valuable to share. For the most part, he was content to let his grandfather take the lead.

An enormous map of the country now covered the table they all sat around, marked with wooden tokens painted different colors to represent various troops and resources. General Khan was shifting a few of the pieces around, explaining as he went along to provide a more accurate picture of their current situation. So far, there hadn't been any real fighting, but troops had mobilized on both sides to take up strategic positions across their respective territories. A few provinces were still trying to maintain neutrality even as Jakhat and Valmandi attempted to sway them to their own cause.

The country's most southwestern province, situated between the Adrati and Mayuka Rivers, was of special interest to both sides. Its rich soil and fertile fields made it the agricultural backbone of Kavora, and it contained most of the country's granaries and other storage facilities. Whichever side controlled the area would have a significant advantage over the enemy when it came to maintaining food supplies for soldiers and civilians alike. So far, leaders in the area were staying out of the fight, but there had already been some minor supply chain disruptions, which were a detriment to the entire country.

The Advisor of Grain wrapped up the council's discussion of winter food storage with several actionable steps she'd be organizing in the coming weeks. From there, Magistrate Ashaya took over the conversation, reminding them all that he and Lord Vasu had a special guest waiting to speak to them. A few minutes later, Lord Vasu returned with another man—a Sularan.

Savir sat up a little straighter in his chair. He'd heard Valkyra and Ashaya talking about a Sularan who wanted to meet with the council, though he hadn't been able to get much more information from either of them. He'd expected a leader of some kind, but this man didn't seem to be anyone of particular importance. Piercing gold eyes swept across each of their faces, and the corners of his mouth were raised in a tiny smirk beneath rough brown stubble. Scars marred his face in the same pattern Sularans painted on their skin during a rite of passage undertaken in their youth, meaning he had not completed that rite successfully or honorably.

An outcast, then. Which made Ashaya and Vasu's decision to bring him before the council even more curious.

"This is Zefar hàs Yaratha of the Sularan people," Ashaya said, gesturing to the man. "He has something very interesting to share with us that Lord Vasu and I thought you all should hear. Something that could help with the war effort."

"Very well then," King Bhajan said. "You may speak."

"Thank you for agreeing to see me," Zefar said, his Kavoran speech accented with the smooth flow of consonants characteristic of the Sularan language. He made a low bow that Savir thought held a certain level of sarcasm. When he straightened, his gaze met Savir's and lingered there a few seconds longer than was respectful. His smirk widened a little. "It's an honor to meet you, Your Highness."

Savir forced himself to stay still, but there was something in the man's gaze that was unnerving. Valkyra's body tensed against his neck, only for a moment, but the soft brush of fur against his jawline made him shiver.

He stared back at the man evenly, giving no response. After what felt like several minutes but was likely only seconds, Zefar's eyes darted away.

"As the magistrate so kindly explained, I have something in my possession that could give you the upper hand in this little civil war you've started." He reached into a pouch at his waist and withdrew a thin, leatherbound book, which he held aloft so they could all get a good look. The advisors seemed confused, and when Savir gave Bhajan a questioning look, the king only shrugged.

Finally, Zefar spoke again. "I have an ancient text from the ruins of Shavhalla. It details a method for using a type of magic that has long since been erased and forgotten—a type of magic that would make any Tarja army who wields it the most powerful in all Erythyr."

King Bhajan cast a stern look at Magistrate Ashaya and Lord Vasu. "I certainly hope you didn't intend to waste our time with tales of lost magic and cursed cities from legend."

"A perfectly legitimate concern," Zefar said. "Which is exactly why these good men went to great lengths to validate my claims before bringing me before you today."

"As much as we could," Ashaya said. "He tells us the book details how to perform a curse."

Zefar clicked his tongue. "Now you've gone and stolen the drama from my presentation." He sounded genuinely disappointed, but only for a moment. "The magistrate is right. The book does contain knowledge on creating a curse—a type of magic powerful enough to dramatically turn the tide of war in your favor. And not just any curse." His voice dropped a level in volume, and he paused a few seconds until several of the advisors had leaned forward in their seats to listen. He tapped one finger against the cover of the book. "These pages reference a curse of immortality."

Murmured whispers rippled through the room at this declaration, expressions shifting between disbelief, awe, and excitement. Savir felt no such thing. Instead, a weight seemed to fall over his shoulders, pressing all the way down into his core. Immortality, as appealing as it seemed on the surface, was something he wanted nothing to do with. When he asked himself why, he had no answer.

"How did you obtain it?" Chayani Sha asked, her sharp voice cutting through the others' whispered conversations.

"It wasn't easy, but I made the journey to Shavhalla myself this last year," Zefar replied. "It is every bit as haunting and dangerous as the legends say. I was lucky to make it back alive."

"Lucky indeed, when so many others have tried and failed before you."

"You think I'm lying." There was a hint of amusement in his voice. "I suppose swearing the truth on my honor as a Sularan wouldn't mean much to you, would it?"

"Why should it? Those scars on your face say you have no honor, even among your own people."

He smiled, a cold, pointed thing that made him look twice as dangerous as he'd seemed before. "Thank you for your time. I think I'll be on my way."

He began to walk to the door but paused when Magistrate Ashaya jumped out of his seat. "Now, hold on a moment. Let's hear him out, please. Your Majesty, you know I wouldn't have brought this matter to you if I thought it was a sham."

Bhajan tilted his head a little, eyes boring into the Sularan. "If this book is truly what you say it is, why would you offer it to us?"

"Why not?" Zefar said with a shrug. "It's valuable, useful. You're wealthy and powerful, and the powerful are often willing to pay well for things that might be useful and valuable ."

"Money, then. That's all you're interested in?"

He raised an eyebrow. "I never said I wanted payment in coin."

"What, then?"

"You have soldiers patrolling the borders of my homeland. They've been taking what doesn't belong to them. I want it to stop."

Bhajan frowned. "They're not taking anything, only preventing others from doing so. I see no issue with that."

Zefar raised his chin. "Whatever you may think of me or my sense of honor, please don't insult my intelligence again. I'm no fool, and neither are you. We both know your soldiers are taking whatever mesala they can find during their little patrols, and they're no longer confining their routes to the border."

Bhajan cast a quick glance at General Khan, who gave a small nod to confirm Zefar's report. "If this is such a great concern for your people, why did they not send their own delegate to address it with us?"

"They have," he replied tersely. "Time and again for the last several decades. Always, they return with new promises from Kavora, but nothing is enforced. Nothing ever changes. Why should they keep trying? Why should they trust those who've lied to them repeatedly?"

It was a fair question, and one that raised another for Savir. "Why are *you* here, then?" he asked. "Why are you trying to change things yourself if you don't think you can trust us?"

"Because of this." He held up the book again. "We've never had anything to offer you before except the very resources you've been stealing. Now we do. *I* do."

"You claim to be doing this for the benefit of your people," Advisor Sha said, "but you're an outcast. What reason do you have to help the people who've shunned you?"

"You're right," Zefar said quietly. "I certainly have no love for most of them. Still, I'd rather not see their lives ruined by the greed and warmongering of the liars in this room." He held the book up once more. "Perhaps this can be a way to hold you accountable for all the promises you've made."

Bhajan's finger traced small circles on the table in front of him, a gesture Savir had often seen from him when he was considering something. After a few moments, he sat up a little straighter and leaned forward. "I'm still not entirely convinced, but I'm intrigued enough to work out some arrangement. We'll take your book, and Advisor Sha will have it examined and studied by our very best Tarja scholars. If they can verify what you've told us and make some use of the information within, we'll withdraw our troops."

Zefar gave the king a placid smile. "That's not going to work for me."

The muscles in Bhajan's neck tightened, but he kept his expression neutral. "Then what do you propose? Keep in mind that we could take it from you by force if necessary."

"Is that a threat, Your Majesty? My, how admirable the hospitality of your court is." He laughed long and loud, uncaring that he was the only one in the room doing so. General Khan stood up with his hand resting on the hilt of his sword, and Zefar put a hand up. "All right, I'm sorry. Yes, you could take it by force. I'd even let you without putting up much fight. You see, I'm afraid this isn't the real book."

"Enough with your games," Bhajan growled. "Stop wasting our time and get out, or tell us what you want."

"I have a few pages I can give you for now," Zefar said. "Have your scholars study them and verify the information if you'd like, but I need to see that you're holding up your end before I give you any more. Tell your soldiers to stop harvesting mesala."

The king brought his hands to rest on the table. "Very well. But we'll keep our patrols. Neither of us want Jakhat or any rogue merchant harvesting mesala, either."

"You mean you don't want your enemies having an advantage you'll now be deprived of."

Bhajan's expression remained impassive. "That's war."

Zefar opened the book and took out a few loose pages. "All right, keep your patrols. But they'd better be effective. If I learn of *anyone* harvesting mesala after this, the blame is yours."

"Very well. General Khan, you'll pass those orders along immediately."

"Yes, Your Majesty."

Zefar held out the pages, and General Khan leaned across the table to take them. He passed them to Bhajan, who gave them a cursory glance before looking back up at Zefar. "Where can we find you when we're ready to talk again?"

"Don't worry about that. I'll find you." The Sularan tucked the useless book back into the pouch at his waist and headed for the door without so much as a farewell. Savir could have sworn he winked as he passed by. The low sound Valkyra made was almost a growl.

Once the Sularan had gone, King Bhajan spoke to Khatri. "I want him followed. Discreetly."

"Of course, Your Majesty," the Advisor of Secrets replied. She stood and slipped out of the room with the silence of a shadow.

Bhajan passed the pages of the book to Chayani Sha. "Do you think he was telling the truth about getting these from Shavhalla himself?"

She tilted her head to one side. "It's hard to say. We haven't sent an expedition for decades, and all the ones I know of ended in disaster. I have a hard time believing he could have gone and made it out unscathed, but it's not impossible. I can only imagine what other treasures are still there, waiting to be recovered."

"Treasures, and long forgotten magic, if this ends up being real," he mused. "We could certainly use more of that. Do you think we could convince a few brave adventurers to explore the ruins themselves?"

"I can think of more than a few who would jump at the opportunity," the Advisor of Magic replied. "I'll make the arrangements."

"Good. Make sure they're generously compensated."

The meeting went on for another hour, by which point Savir was starving and eager for a few minutes alone. Some of the advisors wanted to talk to him privately, but he managed to put them off and made his escape from the room. The hall was empty, and he spoke to Valkyra in a hushed tone as they walked, Tarik trailing several paces behind him as usual.

"The Sularan—he seemed..." He struggled over the right word, some label for the uneasy feeling the man had given him.

"I told you he was peculiar," she replied.

Peculiar indeed, but that wasn't all. "He looked at me like I was supposed to know who he was. *Did* I know him? From before, I mean."

"I don't see how you could have."

He was still trying to place the man when he turned down the hall to his room. A guard stood outside his door. Normally, one would only be there when he was in the room, either Tarik or one of the men who took the night shifts. But Tarik had followed him to the council meeting and still walked behind him, and the shift change wouldn't happen for several more hours. Why was a second man posted at his room now?

"What are you doing here?" he asked the unfamiliar guard.

"I was assigned to watch your room, Your Highness."

"Assigned by who?"

"By him." The man pointed to Tarik.

Savir looked between the two of them. "Why?"

"It was Magistrate Ashaya's suggestion," Tarik replied. "He thought it wise, and I agreed, considering the incident we had a few days ago."

Savir dredged up all he could remember of the past week, but there was nothing that seemed connected. "What incident?" he asked, ignoring the prick of Valkyra's claws against his shoulder.

Tarik didn't answer right away, but of course he wouldn't. He seemed content enough to guard Savir as ordered but clearly hadn't developed any further respect for him over the passing weeks.

"What incident?" he pressed, hardening his voice. "Tell me now!"

It was the new guard who finally blurted out an explanation. "Someone came into your room when you weren't here, claiming to be a servant, but she wasn't one of the usual ones assigned to you, and no one could confirm her story."

He whirled back around to Tarik. "Why wasn't I told about this?"

"It didn't seem important," Tarik replied flatly. "I'm in charge of your security, and I dealt with the situation as I saw fit. We inspected your rooms thoroughly and found nothing out of place. For all we know, the young lady was telling the truth, but the ease with which she accessed your room exposed a gap in our existing security measures. From now on, a guard will remain here even when you're not inside."

The muscles in Savir's face tightened. Once again, he'd been kept in the dark about something that directly impacted him. He didn't have to wonder whether Valkyra had known about this *incident*. If Ashaya had known, she certainly did, too. Another thing she'd chosen to withhold from him, even after he'd asked her repeatedly to keep him more informed. The excuses she kept making weren't good enough, and if she wasn't going to give him a straight answer, he'd get it somewhere else.

"What happened to her? The woman pretending to be a servant."

"She was arrested," Tarik replied. "We questioned her here, then transferred her to one of the guard stations in the city to await trial."

"Which one?"

"Why?"

The other guard sucked in a sharp breath, clearly aghast that Tarik would dare question Savir so boldly, and that was the final straw. He'd put up with Tarik's frosty demeanor long enough, hoping to eventually prove himself and earn his way into the man's good graces. Now, the old guard was openly challenging his orders, and that he could not abide. He was the *prince,* after all, whether or not Tarik himself believed it.

"It doesn't matter why. I asked you a question. Tell me which guard station they took her to."

Tarik's dark eyes flashed beneath furrowed brows, and for half a second, Savir thought he still might not answer. Then he said, "It's on the north end of the city."

Savir nodded. "Good. I want you to ready a pair of horses and meet me in the stables. You will escort me to this guard station yourself. And you will tell no one."

Tarik's jaw clenched. "Surely you can send someone else on this errand. I'll even go myself, if you'd like. It's safer if you—"

"You will do as I command," Savir snapped. "Is that clear?"

He hesitated a moment and seemed about to argue again, but instead, he said, "Yes."

Savir brushed past the second guard, who was still gaping at them both, and entered his room. He strode over to the trunk at the foot of his bed, shifting his frustration to Valkyra. "I assume you knew about this?"

"I did." She hopped down to sit on the lid of the trunk. He glared at her until she moved aside, letting out a long-suffering sigh as she went. "Like Tarik said, it wasn't anything important—certainly not something you needed to trouble yourself with."

Savir dug through the trunk until he found his old belt and ammunition pouch. "I'm tired of you telling me what I should or shouldn't trouble myself with."

"I'm only trying to ease your burdens, Savir."

"I don't need you to ease my burdens." He strapped the belt around his waist, grabbed a cartridge from the pouch, and began to load his pistol. He doubted he'd run into any trouble in the city, but he wasn't stupid enough to wander around unarmed, and weapons had always felt far more reliable in his hands than his own magic. "You want me to be a leader and take on the responsibilities of an entire empire, but you treat me like a child with your secrets. Which is it, Valkyra? Am I a ruler or a mere boy? Because it can't be both at once."

"But it is," she said. "You are a ruler, and a boy. *My* boy. I may not be your mother, but I raised you, and I won't apologize for doing what I've deemed necessary to protect you."

He slipped the gun into its holster and went to the armoire, where he dug out a heavy wool traveling cloak. Hopefully the dull color and simple style would be enough to help him blend in. "I don't want your protection. I want your honesty." He fastened the cloak around his shoulders and turned to look her straight in the eye. "In fact, I *need* your honesty. If you can't give that to me, then I have no reason to listen to you or anything you tell me."

After a few seconds, Valkyra dipped her head and said, "I suppose that's fair."

It wasn't the answer he'd expected, and the fight that had been building in him deflated a little. "Good. Then let's go."

She leapt into the air and flew to his shoulder, soft wings fluttering against his cheek as she landed. "I take it we're off to pay this trespasser a visit?"

"Yes," he said, striding to the door. "I want to know what she was doing here."

"As do I."

"You don't know already?" he asked, his tone only a little sarcastic.

"No, actually. I meant to pay her a visit myself, but I never got the chance. I'm as curious as you are."

He let out a grunt and flung the door open. At least for now they were of the same mind, but he would no longer count on that remaining true.

KESARI

"NOW HOW DO I LOOK?" KESARI ASKED SAYA FOR WHAT FELT LIKE the hundredth time that afternoon. They were in Mitul's room at the Saffron Fox, having gathered there earlier that morning to review and set in motion the difficult task of freeing Aleida.

Saya tilted her head, circling Kesari with an appraising stare. "Better. I can't see anything wrong right now. Let's see how long you can hold it."

Kesari nodded, but only slightly, every ounce of her concentration focused on maintaining the illusion she'd constructed around herself. She'd been practicing them with Lucian for the last two days as part of their plan, which required a great deal of sneaking, deception, and magical precision. If luck was on their side, they'd succeed without anyone realizing something had gone amiss.

The plan itself was simple enough. Mitul had purchased two palace guard costumes from a local troupe of actors, and Kesari had used her magic to make a few cosmetic alterations that gave them a more authentic appearance. The alterations would only last the day, but that was all they needed.

Mitul had worn one of the costumes to the magistrate's office this morning, carrying with him a letter that authorized Aleida's transfer back into the custody of the palace guard. All he needed was a signature, and once he had that, he could walk into the guard station where Aleida was being held and walk right back out with her in tow. He might have been able to carry out the whole operation alone, but they'd decided it best to take extra precautions, which meant Kesari was coming, too. Her magic could be useful if they happened to run into any trouble.

That was where the illusion came in. She looked too young to pass as a guard, and no uniform or hat or any amount of stage makeup could hide that fact—at least not up close. An illusion was a practical enough solution, or it would have been if Kesari had been any good at them. It didn't help that illusions were easier to maintain when one could see what they were doing, and without a mirror in the room, Kesari couldn't see her own face. She'd gotten better in the last couple of days, but her technique was far from perfect, and she couldn't hold it together for more than a minute or two.

"I can see your head," Saya said. "Your real head. And the fake one, actually. It's quite ghastly."

She sighed and let the illusion fall away. "Maybe I shouldn't worry about trying to make myself look taller."

"Not if it's going to end up like that."

She shrugged. "I guess I'll be a very short man, then."

"Better than a person with two heads."

She channeled her altma again, imagining Rajiv's face as she rebuilt the illusion around herself. She already looked a little like him, and it was easier drawing on what she knew to construct her new appearance.

"That's better," Saya said approvingly as she circled again. "Looks more natural."

"I agree," said Lucian as he floated in through the open window. "The paperwork is in order, and Mitul's ready whenever you are. He's waiting near the guardhouse. I can show you."

A sharp knock came before she could reply. "Are we expecting anyone?" Saya asked.

Kesari shook her head and went to answer it. She started to release her illusion, but changed her mind. It might be helpful to test it on whoever was at the door, see if they noticed anything strange.

The broad-shouldered man she found in the hall was no one she recognized, but she offered him a friendly, "Hello." The word came out in her normal, teenage girl voice—a voice that didn't match the young man's face she now wore. She coughed loudly into her hand in an attempt to cover her mistake.

The stranger gave her a look that was equal parts confusion and concern. "I'm so sorry, I was told this was Mitul Rama's room? There must have been some mistake."

"Oh, you're a friend of Mitul," she said, channeling altma into her throat to make her voice sound deeper. It worked, more or less. Now she sounded something like a growling tiger.

"Are you all right?" the stranger asked, eyes glinting with amusement. "Your nose is—honestly I'm not sure what it's doing, but it doesn't look healthy."

Kesari frowned. She'd been distracted trying to make her voice deeper and something must have gone wrong with her appearance. It was probably best not to talk at all when she and Mitul went to get Aleida.

"Oh, skies above, Kes, just drop it," Lucian muttered, drifting forward to hover beside her.

She did, and the moment the illusion faded away, the stranger beamed. "You're Kesari, aren't you? And Lucian."

"Have we met?" she asked.

"No, but I've heard a lot about you."

Saya came to stand in the doorway as well, one hand on her hip as she eyed the man with suspicion. "And who are you?"

"Of course, I'm sorry. My name's Kamaal. Mitul might have mentioned…well, I'm a friend of his, anyway."

A grin slid across Kesari's face. A very good friend indeed, if he'd come all the way here to see Mitul. What was that about?

"You should come in," she said, opening the door and stepping aside to let him through.

"Thank you." His eyes drifted around the room, lingering on a book that lay closed in the center of the table. Aleida's sketchbook, Mitul had told Kesari when she'd asked what it was.

"He's not here right now," she said, gesturing to a chair for Kamaal to sit in. "Lucian and I need to go meet him, but Saya can fill you in while we're gone."

"And Aleida?" he asked.

"We're going to get her, actually. She got herself arrested."

The man drew in a sharp breath. "Is she all right?"

"For now," Saya said. "I might kill her when she gets back here."

He shook his head, dark curls falling across his brow. "I should have come with them," he said quietly, more to himself than to the rest of them. "I won't keep you, but is there anything I can do to help?"

Kesari threw her cloak over the guard's costume she wore. She also grabbed the tiny pouch of mesala and tucked it into her pocket, just in case. "No, but I think you being here helps. I'm sure Mitul will be glad to know you came."

"I hope so. But don't tell him. Not yet. He's got plenty to worry about with Aleida right now, and he doesn't need the distraction of knowing I've shown up unannounced."

It was a strange request; Kesari would have thought Mitul would be happy to know Kamaal was here. But he probably knew better than she did. "All right. See you when we get back, then."

Saya opened the door, nodding to Kesari and Lucian on their way out. "Be safe. And give Aleida a good knock on the head for me when you see her."

"Yes to the first request, no to the second," she replied. When Saya rolled her eyes, she gave her a little pat on the shoulder. "Don't worry. We'll be back before you know it, and you can scream at her yourself."

SAVIR

WHEN THEY REACHED THE GUARDHOUSE, SAVIR DISMOUNTED alongside Tarik, and Valkyra hopped off the front of the saddle to his shoulder. He handed the reins to the old guard. "Wait here."

"I really must insist on coming with you," Tarik said.

"You'll *wait here*," Savir repeated tersely. He would have much preferred to come alone, and now that they'd arrived, he wanted a chance to question the young woman without anyone looming over his shoulder to further intimidate her. Besides, he was nearly as frustrated with Tarik as he was with Ashaya and Valkyra for not informing him of the situation. To give extra weight to his command, he added, "Do not test me on this, Tarik. I have half a mind to tell my grandfather about your insubordination already."

Tarik glared back at him, but the words had the desired effect of keeping him rooted in place.

Savir walked into the guardhouse and approached the first uniformed person he saw. "I need to speak to one of your prisoners."

The woman didn't look up from the rifle she was cleaning. "You got a request from the magistrate's office? No one speaks to the prisoners without an official request."

Savir slipped the gold signet ring off his index finger and held it out to her. "I believe that should suffice."

She glanced at it, then up at him, to Valkyra, and back at the ring. Her brows shot up, and she fumbled to set aside the rifle before standing straight to salute him. "Your Highness, forgive me. We didn't know you'd be coming. How can I serve you?"

He slipped the ring back over his finger. "I was told you have a certain prisoner here, a young woman. She would have been transferred from the palace a few days ago."

"Yes, I know who you mean. A couple of your men just came for her."

"*My* men?"

"Guards from the palace. They said they had more questions for her and they were going to take custody." She pointed to a sheet of paper on the table beside her. The top bore the name and insignia of a local magistrate, and there was a red stamp at the bottom with the same symbol. "That's their transfer request there, approved by the magistrate and all."

Savir's brow furrowed. "Did they leave yet?"

"No, they only arrived a couple minutes before you. They're still in the cells." She jabbed a thumb over her shoulder to another area of the guardhouse. "I can take you to them."

"I'll go myself." He still hoped to talk to the young woman alone. Perhaps a gentler approach would work better than the hostile attitude Tarik and the other guards had undoubtedly taken. He was only curious, after all. She hadn't stolen anything from his room, so what had she been doing there? Or was she truly an innocent servant who'd gotten lost, as she claimed? In either case, he wanted to make his own judgment without anyone else's interference. The fact that two men from the palace were here already complicated matters.

The guard produced a set of keys from her pocket and went to unlock the door. "It's all the way back, then make a right. Should be the fourth cell down that way. You can't miss her. Pale skin, blue eyes, said her name was Sabina. She's the only Visan we've got in here right now."

"Thank you."

"Knock when you're done and I'll let you back out. And stick to the center of the hall. The grabby ones'll snatch at anyone who gets too close."

Savir started down the hall, keeping to the middle between the cells lining either side. Most were empty, but a few faces leered at him through the bars.

When he rounded the corner, his attention was immediately drawn to the red uniforms of two palace guards. The shorter one held open the door of a cell while the taller one led out a third figure—a young woman with pale skin and brown hair bound in a knot at the base of her skull. Savir didn't know her, but the way Valkyra tensed on his shoulder made him certain *she* did.

"Turn back, Your Highness. Now. Before they see you."

"Why?" he whispered, his steps faltering for only a moment.

"Just do it!"

Once, the insistence in her voice might have made him listen. Now, it only made him more curious. What was it about this prisoner that made her so desperate to keep him from her? He kept walking, and the young woman turned. Her hands, bound at the wrist, clenched into fists when she saw him, her blue eyes clear and piercing in a dirt-streaked face.

"Turn back," Valkyra hissed again, pressing her claws through the fabric of his cloak and shirt to pierce the skin underneath.

Savir kept walking, but he let his hand drift to the pistol at his waist. Something about this was obviously making her nervous, and though he wasn't willing to turn around, it was best to be on alert.

Both guards faced him now, and he could make out their features more clearly. The taller one was a man in his forties with graying hair and a neatly trimmed beard, but the other wasn't a man at all. She was a girl, and she looked at least a few years younger than Savir. She carried a lantern in one hand, holding it aloft and outstretched as if trying to see him better. Both guards were staring at him slack-jawed, but the Visan woman watched Valkyra intently.

The older guard took a few steps toward him, and Savir drew his pistol. He didn't take aim—not yet—but arming himself was enough to make the man stop in his tracks. He raised his hands, slowly, his expression shifting between half a dozen emotions Savir couldn't place. When he opened his mouth to speak, only a single word came out—a name.

"Amar?"

"Kill them," Valkyra whispered in his ear. "They shouldn't be here. They're not really guards."

He barely registered her words. There was something about the man's unwavering focus on him and the way he'd said the name that begged curiosity. Who were they, if not guards? And who was this Amar he'd named?

"Amar," the man repeated, not a question this time, but a statement made in reference to Savir. And he was moving again, two more quick strides forward.

Savir raised the gun a little higher. "Don't come any closer."

"It's Prince Savir now, isn't it?" the Visan woman said, her eyes still locked on Valkyra.

"Who are you?" he asked.

The dragon's claws dug deeper. "It doesn't matter. Kill them."

"I know you don't remember me," said the older man. "But please listen. Whatever she's told you, it isn't true. Come with us. We can—"

Valkyra launched herself from Savir's shoulder and flew straight at the man. He raised his arms to block his face from her claws. In the same instant, the fire in the younger girl's lantern exploded out. Flames met fur and feathers, and Valkyra flew into the air with the fireball in pursuit.

"Kill them!" she shrieked to Savir. "These people are enemies of the empire!"

Something closed around her then—not the fire, but something else, a translucent orb of energy conjured from magic. Too late, Savir remembered Tarik's lesson from their sparring match. *Swords and guns aren't the only weapons at an enemy's disposal.*

One of the intruders was a Tarja, and they'd trapped Valkyra inside a barrier.

He should have listened to her from the start. Whoever these people were, they were clearly dangerous, and he was outnumbered.

He channeled his own altma, but before he could release it, the bearded man stepped forward again. He was less than ten strides away now, reaching for Savir with a wild pleading in his eyes. "Come with us!"

Savir raised his pistol to aim at the man's chest. It was an easy enough target, at this range.

"Amar, stop—"

He pulled the trigger.

Part III

The Warrior & the Tarja

KESARI

THE THUNDEROUS CRACK OF THE GUNSHOT ECHOED THROUGH THE halls, leaving Kesari's ears ringing. For an instant, the barrier she'd put around Valkyra wavered, but she fortified it quickly enough to prevent the dragon's escape.

Then she saw Mitul, and it was all she could do to keep her altma from slipping entirely out of her control. He'd staggered back against the bars of a nearby cell, red blossoming across his chest where the bullet had entered.

Aleida screamed his name and shoved past Kesari to run to his side. Amar stood frozen, but there was a look on his face that chilled her. She'd seen that look before, when Jameson had gone through his memories and she'd watched them play out in vivid detail all around her. In them, he was always on some battlefield, with a sword in his hand, blood on his armor, and death written across his face.

He was going to kill them all.

Mitul was incapacitated—*not* dead, *please* not dead—and Aleida had no weapons or magic to fight with. It was all down to Kesari, but she was only a mediocre Tarja still learning to use her powers again, and Amar was an immortal being with centuries of experience as a soldier. They were all going to die, right here and now.

No.

Be safe, Saya had told her just this morning. *Be safe*, Navya had said to her when she left Deveaural. She couldn't die now. She wouldn't, not when there were people counting on her to come back to them.

She reached for the pouch of mesala in her pocket even as Amar stretched his hand toward her. Lightning crackled around his fingers. She barely had time to redirect the altma from Valkyra's barrier into a shield for herself. The lightning spread across it in sparking blue tendrils mere inches from her face. Her fingers fumbled with the strings tying the pouch shut, but after a few seconds, she managed to get it open. She raised it to her mouth and tipped her head back even as Amar blasted more lightning at her.

The powdery substance that hit her tongue had a dry, green flavor, like she imagined autumn leaves must taste right before they fell from their trees. She coughed a little as she forced it down, still fighting to maintain her shield against Amar's attacks. The brutal look in his eyes had only intensified, and Valkyra now seemed determined to inflict as much damage as possible on Aleida, who was using her own body to shield Mitul. Lucian had engulfed the other Spirit Tarja in flames, but it had no impact.

A sudden cold energy swept over Kesari, like she'd fallen through a frozen lake. She gasped, wondering for a moment what Amar had done to her. But the sensation was coming from within, and with it came a calm and a clarity unlike anything she'd experienced before. Her magic was no longer a fickle, wild thing to be delicately coaxed into cooperation. It was a tame and powerful beast loyal only to her, and she knew exactly how to command it.

She divided the barrier she was using to shield herself and sent one half to encase Valkyra. It was so easy she barely had to think about it, and when it was done, she was able to turn her attention to a new task without losing any control over the barrier. She pressed both palms against the floor, shooting energy across the stone to where Amar stood. It lurched up beneath him and he lost his balance, stumbling forward.

"Get him in the cell!" Lucian called. He swooped in behind Amar and expanded to fill the full width of the hall. The man's eyes went wide, and he scrambled forward a little more.

Kesari glanced back at the cell they'd taken Aleida from, the door still open. Echoing shouts and pounding footsteps drew closer. She needed to end this, and quickly.

Again, Amar channeled his altma to create lightning. It danced between his palms, but there was a strain on his face like he was having trouble controlling it. Kesari grinned; she didn't have that problem—not now. She had more control over her magic than she'd ever thought possible.

Before he could strike, she channeled altma into her legs and darted around behind him. He whirled to face her, but a solid kick to the gut sent him staggering, and his lightning fizzled out. A quick shift of energy from her legs to her arms, and she wrangled him into the open cell.

With one hand, she pressed him against the wall. With the other, she summoned the orb-like barrier that still held Valkyra. It drifted in alongside Lucian, and Amar's eyes flitted wildly between them. "Who are you?" he asked, his voice filled with nearly as much confusion as rage.

"A friend, believe it or not." She channeled altma into the stone wall and shaped it around his wrists and ankles to bind him, then created a dome of solid rock over Valkyra inside her barrier. That should buy them a little time, at least. With that, she spun on her heel and sprinted back out into the hall, slamming the cell door shut behind her.

Three guards were already closing in on Mitul and Aleida, swords and rifles drawn and ready for a fight. Kesari pressed her hands to the floor again, sending an even more powerful burst of altma into it. The stone cracked and buckled underneath them, then lurched up to throw them backwards in a heap. Before they could recover, she turned the floor into a wall, cutting off their access to this section of the guardhouse.

She hurried to her companions. Aleida's face was streaked with tears, and Kesari couldn't tell for sure if Mitul was still breathing. Dread tightened around her throat, but she set her jaw and forced it away. Once they got out of here, she could help him. "Come on," she said. "Lift him up."

They flung the man's limp arms over their own shoulders and hauled him upright as best as they could. He made a weak noise somewhere between a gasp and a gurgle, and Kesari nearly laughed with joy at the confirmation that he was still alive. "Lucian, how do we get out of here?"

"I don't know," he said, a rare fear infiltrating his voice. "You just cut off our only exit."

"So blow a hole through the wall," Aleida suggested.

"The whole building could collapse!"

"We have to do *something*! He's dying."

Lucian sputtered and flew off down the hall. "This way, then. Hurry."

They ran after him as fast as they could go, which was quite fast, once Kesari channeled more altma to boost her body's strength. She was able to carry Mitul's weight mostly on her own but still needed Aleida's help to manage the unwieldiness of his taller frame and lanky limbs. A few of the other prisoners called out or even tried to grab at them as they ran by, but they pushed on, spurred by panic.

When they rounded a corner, they came to a dead end, and Lucian pressed himself against it. "This should be one of the exterior walls. Blast through it, and we'll be outside. But be care—oh, skies be damned, there's no way to be careful when you're blowing a giant hole through a building."

Kesari ignored his fretting and took a breath. Her heart raced, and she was still terrified for Mitul, but beneath that was the sure and steady prowess that stemmed from the mesala. They were going to be all right. She would make sure of it. She sent a single, powerful burst into the wall. A tremendous *crack* echoed around them, and a cloud of dust billowed up as the stone crumbled and flew outward. Sunlight blinded her a few seconds later, and she and Aleida carried Mitul outside.

Several people were running away, and it would only be a matter of time before more guards arrived to investigate the source of the commotion. "Where to now?" Aleida asked, her voice frayed and breaking.

"The temple, over there," Lucian said. Its domed roof rose above the other buildings, and he drifted ahead to lead the way, into a busy street with dozens if not hundreds of people going about their business. Kesari created an illusion to disguise themselves as a trio of grandmotherly priestesses out for an afternoon walk. Even with the mesala's help, she knew it wasn't perfect, but it would do at a glance.

Hopefully it would be enough to keep the pursuing guards from spotting them, at least for now.

It felt like an eternity before they reached the temple. She kept checking over her shoulder to see if they were being followed, but so far, they'd been lucky. Mitul's head lolled between them like a worn cloth doll, but he was still breathing. They staggered up the steps to the temple doors, past worshipers lighting incense and praying for altma's blessings. Kesari had never put much faith in mainstream Kavoran spirituality, but now she almost wished she had some incense to light herself, for Mitul's sake.

She let the illusion fall away once they were safely inside. A priestess in black robes hurried forward to meet them. "Skies above, what happened?"

"Please, we need shelter, just for a little while," Kesari said. They couldn't stay here, after all. They were still being hunted, but she had to get Mitul stabilized.

The woman considered their request with pursed lips. "Fine. I'll get the healer. You can take him over there."

She was off before Kesari could tell her they didn't need another healer. On second thought, it might not be a bad idea. The more help they could get for Mitul, the better.

They carried him to the small room the priestess had indicated. It was dimly lit and comfortable, lined with several cushions and probably used for the cleansing rituals that were often performed at temples like this. They laid Mitul down and Kesari immediately got to work. She pressed her hands to his torso and used her magic to seek out the source of the bleeding.

A sudden wave of dizziness swept over her, and she shook her head to clear it.

"Are you all right?" Lucian asked.

"I think so." Her tongue felt thick, and an odd fogginess in her head made everything fuzzy. "It's the mesala, I think."

"You're not used to channeling that much altma. You need to rest."

"Later." She needed to take full advantage of this enhanced power while it lasted. She could still sense it there, a cool buzzing in her core, but it was fading fast. "Go get Saya and Kamaal. Have them meet us here."

He took off, and Kesari returned her focus to the task at hand.

"Kamaal?" Aleida asked. "He's here?"

"Just got here. Hasn't even seen Mitul yet."

Aleida grabbed the unconscious man's hand and made a small whimpering noise that ended in a sob.

Kesari blocked out everything around her, keeping all her focus on Mitul and his gunshot wound. It was the worst injury she'd ever tried to heal with her magic, and a very loud, very large part of her screamed that she couldn't do it. But she had to try, no matter how much it terrified her.

The bullet was lodged somewhere in his chest, and he struggled to breathe. She didn't want to try and remove it yet for fear of making things worse. Instead, she sought out the ruined tissue around the injury and did what she could to repair it.

It was slow going, and difficult, even when the temple healer arrived to assist. Together, they managed to remove the bullet, using a combination of magic and then their own fingers once it was close enough to the surface. Kesari's hands shook as she dropped the chunk of metal onto the floor beside her. A terrible wonder that something so small could cause so much damage.

Mitul's breathing remained shaky and weak, but with every ragged gasp, Kesari's hope grew. She drew on that hope to channel her altma, sending it to the broken places inside her friend and closing them up, stopping the bleeding, repairing damaged flesh. Beside her, Aleida closed her eyes and began to whisper something, still clutching Mitul's hand. Her words flowed out in a rapid stream, a prayer to her Visan god, perhaps.

By the time Lucian returned, Kesari was utterly spent. Her vision swam, and her body ached with a bone-deep fatigue unlike anything she'd ever known. She was half asleep when his voice crackled against her ear. "They're almost here, but so are the guards. There are dozens of them out there looking for us."

"We can't stay," she mumbled. She'd known that as soon as they came here, but at least now, Mitul was stable enough to move. Or so she hoped.

"Kamaal has a horse and a cart. It's loaded up with all his belongings, but there's room to carry Mitul. He says he has a place we can go."

She gave a weak smile. "Thank the skies for that."

On Mitul's other side, Aleida drew in a quavering breath and squeezed his hand a little tighter. Her tears had cut pale lines through the dirt on her face.

"Keep praying, if you think it will do any good," Kesari murmured to her softly. "He needs all the help he can get."

32

ALEIDA

ALEIDA PRAYED.

It was a prayer not of faith, but of desperation, words whispered to a god she wasn't even sure existed anymore for the simple reason that she didn't know what else to do.

Don't let him die. Please, it's my fault. Don't punish him. I don't even know if you're listening, but if you are, if you're real, save him.

She nearly bargained her own faith for the promise of divine intervention, a vow that she'd never doubt Artex again if he would only let Mitul live. But she couldn't bring herself to go that far. It wouldn't have been honest.

Lucian had gone back outside but returned leading Kamaal and Saya. The small room was already crowded, and Aleida stood up to make a little more space. Her hand was still warm from clinging to Mitul's, damp with a mixture of sweat and blood.

The look on Saya's face could only be described as murderous, but Aleida slipped past her to go to Kamaal. When he saw her bloodstained clothing, he gripped her by the shoulders to look her over from head to toe. "Skies, Aleida! Are you hurt?"

"No, it's Mitul. I'm so sorry, I—" Her voice hitched, and she broke down in tears again before she could get the words out. Kamaal pulled her in, and for a moment, she clung to the comfort of his embrace even though it was the last thing she deserved. Then she stepped aside, giving him a clear view of Mitul's supine form on the cushions.

The artist's face twisted in a way that pushed a new stab of guilt through her. He hurried to Mitul's side and knelt there for a few seconds, frozen and silent.

"We need to go," Saya said, helping a shaky Kesari rise to her feet. "The cart's right outside."

The healer from the temple had already brought a blanket and now helped move Mitul onto it. He made no sound, still unconscious. Saya took over from there, gripping one end of the blanket while Kamaal held the other. Together, they lifted and carried him out of the temple by way of a set of stairs at the back. The cart was there waiting in a narrow alley with a space already cleared for Mitul to lay in. They set him down gently, and Saya helped Kesari climb up to sit next to him. She motioned for Aleida to take the front seat beside Kamaal.

He snapped the reins, and the big draft horse hitched to the cart began moving. Saya passed a cloak to Aleida. "Cover yourself up."

She threw on the cloak and pulled its hood over her hair. Hunched forward, she kept a watchful eye on their surroundings, searching for guards as they made their way through the streets. There seemed to be more than usual, probably still looking for the three miscreants who'd attacked Prince Savir and escaped the guardhouse. Aleida held her breath each time one came close.

After several tense minutes, they found themselves in a quieter part of the city, and there were no more guards to be seen. Aleida twisted around to look at Mitul, watching for the breaths that assured her he was still alive.

"How's he doing?" Kamaal asked. His face was creased with worry, an expression so different from his usual unbridled cheer that it almost made him look like a completely different person.

"I think he's all right for now," Saya said.

"Needs a place to rest," Kesari mumbled, and Aleida was sure she was talking about herself as much as Mitul. Her eyes were hooded, and her body jostled with every movement of the cart as if she didn't have the energy to keep herself still.

"We're almost there," Kamaal said. "My sister lives outside the walls. She goes away to visit her husband's family in Pahari every winter, but we can stay there."

"And how are we going to get past *that*?" Saya asked.

Aleida looked to where she was pointing. They were already in the shadow of the city walls, and the usual flow of traffic through the gates had been disrupted by an inspection checkpoint. Guards were stopping everyone coming or going, likely an extra security measure that had begun with the movement of troops and war supplies. They might or might not be looking for Aleida, Kesari, and Mitul specifically, but the fact that they had a wounded man in the back of their cart would certainly raise some questions.

"Kesari, can you make an illusion to hide him?" Aleida asked.

"Obviously not," Saya snapped. "Look at her. She's exhausted."

"Could try," Kesari said weakly, and she stared at Mitul intently. For a moment, the air above him shimmered and a vague shape began to take form. It disappeared almost immediately, and the girl leaned back, shaking her head. "Sorry."

"It's all right," Saya said gently. Her gold eyes narrowed in a sharp glare aimed directly at Aleida. "You've got some nerve, asking her to solve another problem your stupidity got us into."

"Calm down," Kamaal said. "Use whatever you can back there to hide him, and I'll see if I can talk our way out of any major inspection."

There were lots of scraping and shuffling noises as Saya rummaged through Kamaal's belongings, repositioning various items to conceal Mitul as best as she could. She and Kesari moved a little closer to the end of the cart, sitting side by side with their legs dangling out and Kesari leaning heavily against Saya's shoulder. Mitul lay directly behind them, and when Aleida glanced back, even she had a difficult time spotting his face in the disordered mess Saya had created.

"That should do," Lucian said approvingly. "I'm going to make myself scarce for a few minutes, but I'll see you soon."

He shrunk himself down the size of a coin and shot into the air, flickering bright against the sky for a moment and then disappearing from view.

A few seconds later, Kamaal stopped the cart next to a waiting guard and offered a cheerful greeting. "Hello."

"State your name and business," the man replied flatly.

"Kamaal Ruman. I was visiting a friend and picking up some supplies in the city, but now I'm going back to my sister's house."

The guard peered up over the edge of the cart, and his eyebrows rose a little when he saw the paint and canvases inside. "Kamaal Ruman. The famous artist?"

"Yes, though I wouldn't mind dropping the *famous* part. It feels a bit vain, if you know what I mean."

The man's stiff scowl remained fixed. "And who are they?" he asked, gesturing to Aleida and the others. She resisted the urge to pull the cloak forward to better conceal her face.

"This one's my apprentice," he said, motioning to Aleida beside him. "And those two back there are going to be the subjects of my next painting."

The guard went around to the rear of the cart. "These two? The small one looks sick."

"She's tired, I think. It's been a long day."

The guard slowly walked back to Kamaal's side of the cart, peering inside as he went. Aleida watched him closely, waiting for him to notice Mitul. Kamaal's hands tightened around the reins on the bench between them, and she wasn't sure what he would do if they were caught. Would he make a run for it? Would they get very far if he tried?

"All right," the guard said in a lazy monotone. "Go on, then." He waved them forward, and as they rolled away, Kamaal blew out a long breath.

Aleida managed to relax a little as they left the city behind them. They passed the remains of the Visan encampment that had long stood outside these walls. She hadn't seen it for months—not since the last time she'd been in Valmandi while pursuing Amar and his friends. She barely recognized it anymore. A few tents and ramshackle shelters remained, but she could see no people. Most had moved inside the walls or began building on the land outside, something they'd never been permitted to do before. Many had probably enlisted in Valmandi's army, drawn in by promises of food, shelter, coin, and retribution.

Lucian rejoined them when Kamaal turned down a narrow side path, and a few minutes later, they came upon a patch of land that had been cleared of trees with a house and a small field at its center. He brought the horse to a stop in front of the house and hopped off the cart. Saya helped Kesari out, and then she, Kamaal, and Aleida used the blanket to carefully transport Mitul.

It was dark inside, with the dusty, empty feeling homes got after they'd sat unused for a time. Hovering overhead, Lucian made himself larger to better illuminate the space. Kamaal nodded to a room straight ahead, and they laid Mitul on the bed there. Kesari hadn't come in with them, and when Aleida glanced back to look for her, she saw the girl already sprawled in a plush chair next to the hearth, her head resting on one arm and her legs dangling over the other.

"What's wrong with him?" Kamaal asked, gently taking Mitul's hand in his own. "Why isn't he waking up?"

"Kes probably put him to sleep while she worked on healing him," Lucian replied. "So he wouldn't feel anything."

"Is he going to be all right?"

"We'll have to watch out for infection, but once Kes recovers, she should be able to manage that. And he's going to be in pain for a while. But yes, he'll be all right."

Kamaal let his shoulders sag a little. He sat down at the side of Mitul's bed and watched him for a few seconds. They all did, counting his breaths, listening to the rasping sound of them as if waiting for him to stop at any moment. Aleida's stomach lurched at the thought. What would she have done, if he'd stopped breathing?

"We should get him cleaned up," Kamaal said. "He looks ghastly in all that mess, and he won't be comfortable when he wakes up."

"I'll fetch some water," Saya said.

"There's a well out past the fence, and probably some clean towels around here somewhere." He made no move to get up and look for them himself.

Saya headed out of the room, but she paused in the doorway, her limbs tense and fists clenched. Aleida guessed what was coming before she even spoke.

"We should have left you to die in the forest that night we found you."

She didn't answer. She wasn't even sure she disagreed.

Saya whirled to face her. "You almost got him killed! Do you even care? Do you have *anything* to say for yourself?"

She stared down at her feet, her face burning, stomach twisting painfully. Apologizing now wouldn't change anything. Saya would still hate her, and Aleida couldn't fault her for that. She was selfish and reckless, driven to foolish action because she told herself no one else mattered.

How very wrong she'd been.

"You're not going to say anything at all?"

"There's nothing I can say that you'd want to hear," she muttered. "But you're right. Maybe you should have left me to die that night."

"Aleida," Kamaal said, and his voice was so soft and so kind that it shattered the last remaining pieces she was holding together inside herself. She shoved past Saya and ran from the room, out the front door and into the cold winter air, every part of her burning with an anguish that threatened to combust at any moment.

She didn't go far—couldn't bear to go far in case Mitul's condition suddenly changed—but she found a tree at the back of the house with a slight depression in the ground near its base. She curled up into it with her back against the trunk, legs hugged to her chest. New tears threatened to spill down her cheeks, but she squeezed her eyes shut and tightened her arms around herself, somehow managing to hold all the emotion inside.

How could she have been so stupid? For so long, she'd told herself she didn't care, that she had nothing and no one left to lose. But it wasn't true. How had that happened? How had Mitul come to mean so much to her in such a short time? And Kamaal, too. She'd tried to erase whatever connection her heart had built between them, pretended they didn't matter. Because with Tyrus gone, why should *anyone* else matter to her?

But *they* did. And she'd nearly gotten Mitul killed.

Damn him for making her care! She hadn't wanted that—not with him or any of the others. Her sole purpose in joining them had been to stop Valkyra and perhaps gain some small measure of vengeance. But he'd been so patient and gentle and understanding, and for the first time in ages, she'd remembered what it felt like to have someone looking out for her. Without even realizing she was doing it, she'd latched on to the comfort and security that brought like a lifeline in a storm.

And it *was* a lifeline. Without it, how much farther would she have sunk into her grief? How fixated would she have been on her fury, thinking only of revenge and plunging into danger with even more recklessness than she'd shown recently? Because when she put her mind to something, for good or ill, she would pursue it at any cost to herself, never mind what it did to those around her. Mitul and Kamaal had both given her something positive to cling to instead. Only a distraction, perhaps, but one she very much needed.

She didn't deserve either of them, but she wanted them in her life all the same. It had been pointless to pretend she didn't care and didn't need anyone, and hopefully, she hadn't ruined everything and made them realize they were better off without her. She would do whatever it took to prove otherwise.

Footsteps approached, and a shadow fell over her. She only looked up far enough to see the embroidered cuffs of Kamaal's jacket. She couldn't bring herself to look him in the eye, and when he sat down next to her, she turned her face away. "Any change?" she asked.

"No. Still resting. There wasn't much else I could do for him, so I thought I'd come check on you."

The lump in her throat tightened, and she swallowed it down. "I'm fine."

"You're not," he said matter-of-factly. "And you shouldn't be. You've been through quite an ordeal."

That was how he was choosing to phrase it? "I started it. I *should* feel like shit."

"Maybe, but that doesn't make it any easier. Probably the opposite, I'd wager."

Her chin trembled, and she waited a few seconds until it stopped before she spoke again."I wish I'd been the one who got hurt. He should have left me in that cell to rot."

"He'd never do that, and you know it. It's what makes him who he is—the man we both love." He reached inside the pocket of his jacket and pulled out a few folded sheets of paper. When he spread them out, she instantly recognized the sketches she'd slipped under his door that last night at his studio. Her own handwriting was scrawled across the first page.

You love him.

Kamaal tapped the words with one finger. "Thank you for this, by the way. Very subtle."

She let out an amused grunt. "Have you told him, then?"

His grin became sheepish. "Not yet. He'd already gone to get you by the time I arrived, so I'm afraid I'm a little behind, as usual." Before Aleida could respond, he shifted toward the sound of approaching footsteps. "Ah, look. Here's Saya."

The young woman was no longer scowling, which was an improvement, though the look she gave Aleida wasn't exactly friendly. "He's awake. He's asking to see you."

Kamaal's face instantly brightened. "Well that's good news, isn't it?" He stood and offered a hand to Aleida. She grasped it tight, and he pulled her to her feet. Together, they made their way back to the house, their steps softly crunching the fallen leaves underfoot.

Aleida's stomach churned as they drew closer. How was she supposed to face Mitul? What sort of apology would ever be enough?

She was still trying to figure that out when they reached the house. Kesari was asleep in her chair, and someone had thrown a blanket over her. The others made their way to the room where Mitul rested, but Kamaal stayed outside the door, gesturing for Aleida to go ahead. Saya stayed back, too, leaving her to face the man alone.

She stepped inside and stayed there at the edge of the room, looking at him. His bloodied shirt had been removed, and his chest was bare beneath a thick blanket draped over his legs and stomach. A bandage encircled his torso and extended up over one shoulder, covering what Kesari's magic hadn't been able to fully repair. He looked tired, but some of the color had returned to his face, and his eyes brightened with warmth when he saw her. "Come here."

The weak rasp of his voice pinched at her heart. She did as he asked, coaxing her trembling lips into a smile. He turned his palm out to her, and she placed her hand in his. "How are you feeling?" she managed.

"I've been better. You're not hurt, are you?"

He was staring at the blood on her clothes—she still hadn't cleaned herself up—and she shook her head. "It's all yours."

"That's good."

"No, it's not." The fragile dam holding back her emotions burst, and she choked on a sob as fresh tears streaked down her face to drip from her chin. "I'm sorry, Mitul. I'm such an idiot. I don't know what I was thinking. I never should have gone to the palace. You could have died, and it's all my fault, and I'm just so sorry."

He squeezed her hand, and the strength of his grip was a pleasantly surprising thing. "Shh. It's all right."

"It's not." Even now, he was trying to take care of her with his reassurances. It was too much.

"I'm alive, all right? I'm going to be okay."

She wiped at her face with the back of her sleeve. It was already soaked, a disgusting mixture of blood, tears, and snot. "Is there anything you need? Anything I can get for you, or do?"

"One thing," he said in a low, calm timbre. "Promise me."

She leaned in a little closer. "Of course. Anything."

"Don't disappear like that again. I was so worried."

Worried, about her. Because he cared. Because somehow, despite everything, she mattered to him.

She bent to hug him as gently as she could. "I promise." Then, remembering Kamaal, she added, "There's someone else who wants to see you."

"Not Lucian again," he groaned. "He kept making jokes. Hurts to laugh."

Aleida went to the door where Kamaal was waiting and beckoned him in. He approached with slow, deliberate steps.

Mitul raised his head off the pillows a little. "Kamaal? What are you doing here?"

He took up a position opposite Aleida. "This is my sister's house, you know. If anyone has a right to be here, it's me." His teasing smirk morphed into something softer. "I never should have let you leave without me."

Mitul's brows furrowed, eyes searching Kamaal's face. "But you said—"

"I know what I said, and I was wrong." He reached for Mitul's hand tentatively, a single finger hooking around his thumb. "You know me. I often make the wrong choices before I figure out the right ones."

"That's true. But it's all right if you…" He paused to catch his breath. "If you can't do this. You don't have to stay."

"I want to."

Mitul's smile could have thawed a frozen mountain. Aleida caught Kamaal's eye for just a moment, and he winked. She grinned as she backed out of the room, amazed that, despite everything, the world could still feel so right in this single moment.

She could still hear them for a few seconds as she walked away. "Would it be out of line for me to tell you I still love you?" Kamaal asked.

"I still love you, too."

"Good. Because I don't intend to spend another day without you."

SAVIR

SAFE INSIDE THE PALACE WALLS, SAVIR SAT ON HIS BED, PATIENTLY allowing the healer Indira had summoned to inspect him again. His wrists were sore and a little bruised from where the Tarja girl had pinned them with stone, but aside from that, he was fine. Which he'd said, multiple times now. That didn't stop his grandparents from fretting over him, and Tarik stood by watching them all with his arms crossed. His expression was as stoic as ever, but he occasionally shifted from one foot to the other and back again. It was the most restless Savir had ever seen him.

The healer finished his work, and the queen sat down beside Savir. "Does it hurt much?"

He shook out his wrists, which still tingled from the altma that had been channeled into them. The bruises had all but vanished. "No, I'm all right."

"Thank the skies for that." She brushed his hair across his brow and laid her hand against his cheek, her eyes still round with concern.

Bhajan nodded to the healer in dismissal. Once the man was gone, he turned to Savir with crossed arms. "You must never do something like this again. It's not safe for you to be wandering the city, and certainly not without your guards."

"I took Tarik."

"You left him outside while you went to talk to a criminal." He cast a dark look over his shoulder at the old guard, as if it were entirely his fault Savir had encountered such danger. "Honestly, I don't know what either of you were thinking."

"Don't blame him," Savir cut in before Tarik could offer yet another apology. "He wanted to come with me, but I ordered him to remain outside. Even when he tried to talk me out of it, I insisted."

Bhajan crossed his arms. "I thought you were smarter than that."

The disappointment in his grandfather's voice was a harder blow than any other Savir had suffered that day, and he looked away.

"Oh, leave the boy alone," said Indira. "He's been through enough already."

"I don't mean to be harsh," the king said with a sigh. "I was worried. You need to be more careful. You can't afford to put yourself at risk—especially at a time like this."

"I'm sorry. It won't happen again."

"Good." Bhajan clapped a hand on his shoulder and squeezed. "You'd better get some rest."

"Did they ever find them?" he asked. "The prisoner and the ones who freed her?"

Tarik stepped forward. "Not yet. But we have guards scouring the city for them. They'll be caught soon enough."

Savir nodded, and Queen Indira pulled him in for a quick kiss on the cheek. "Goodnight, sweet boy." She stood to join her husband. They left the room, but Tarik stayed behind.

"Is there anything else you need, Your Highness?" he asked.

It was the first time the guard had ever used the formal address when speaking to Savir, the first acknowledgement he'd ever given that Savir was truly the prince. For a few seconds, he was so taken aback that he couldn't formulate a response.

"Prince Savir?" Tarik prompted.

"No," he replied. "I'm fine for now, thank you. Please let me know if they ever find that young woman and her companions."

"I will," he said before bowing quickly and departing from the room. For the first time all day, Savir was mercifully alone.

He walked to the window and stared out at the city below. Lanterns and magically conjured lights created a glowing spatter of color against the night, with the stars and moon shining brightly overhead. It was cold, but it was peaceful, and he stood there for a while, letting his scattered thoughts settle and gather into something he could make sense of.

Valkyra had gone to tell Magistrate Ashaya of the day's events. That had been hours ago, and she still hadn't returned. Despite all they needed to discuss, Savir was still too frustrated with her to miss her. If she'd only told him straight away about the intruder, he could have questioned the young woman while she was still in the palace cells, and this whole mess could have been avoided.

Who was she, anyway, and who were the other two with her? Valkyra had claimed not to know any of them and suggested they were either mad or had mistaken him for someone else. Neither of those explanations were satisfying, but he didn't yet have any better ideas. Only confusion.

The way the older man had talked to him kept circling his mind in an infinite loop. He kept coming back to the earnestness in his voice, and more than that, the surety with which he'd spoken, as if he knew Savir.

Amar.

Who was that? Why did the name resonate within him so deeply?

Perhaps he'd once known an Amar? Someone who had also known the people from the guardhouse. Or perhaps they really were mad, as Valkyra had said. That was more or less why he'd shot the older man, once he'd begun to close in, the wild desperation in his eyes enough to alarm anyone. He'd had every right to pull the trigger.

So why did his stomach roil and his throat ache when he pictured the sudden red bloom across the man's chest?

There was a soft flutter of wings outside the window, and Savir coughed out the knot in his throat. A moment later, Valkyra appeared, soaring inside and then circling back around to perch on the window ledge beside him. "It's quite cold, dear. You really ought to put on a coat if you're going to stand here with the window open."

"I'm fine," he replied flatly.

"You look tired. Why don't you go to bed? You could certainly use the rest, after today's excitement."

"I don't want to sleep."

"That may be, but you—"

"Who do you think Amar is?"

She huffed a little, nostrils flaring. "We've already been over this, Savir. How am I supposed to know what the ravings of a lunatic mean?"

"You knew them."

"What?"

"You said they were enemies of the empire."

"That much was obvious from the moment we saw them, wasn't it? One of them snuck into your room for some undoubtedly nefarious purpose, and the other two were trying to free her."

He shook his head. "They knew you, too. They said you were lying to me."

Whatever she's told you, it isn't true.

She stared back at him, her silver eyes cold and unreadable. Before she could answer, a loud knock drew their attention.

Savir ignored it. "Why would they say that?"

"You should see who's at the door."

"Answer me!"

She didn't, and the sharp rapping came again. He clenched his jaw. There was no reason for anyone to be dropping by at this hour, but perhaps it was some news about the three people from the guard house. With any luck, they'd been found, and he could get the answers he wanted from them.

But when he opened the door, it was only the queen. Her brow creased with an even deeper worry than she'd displayed while fretting over his injuries. "Come, Savir. Your grandfather's summoning all his advisors. You should be there, too."

"Right now?" he asked. That couldn't be a good sign. "What's happened?"

"We've received news of small skirmishes between our troops and Jakhat's. They didn't go well for us."

He cursed under his breath. Until now, the threat of war had been only that—a threat—and some small part of him had still hoped to avoid it. But first blood had been spilt, and the fighting would only worsen from here on out.

"That's not all," Indira continued. "Jakhat's armies are on their way here. They mean to take over the city."

His brows shot up. "How long do we have?"

"Little more than a week, at best. Fortunately, General Muraka sent detailed information about their plans. We'll use that to prepare our defenses."

Savir exchanged a quick glance with Valkyra. So, the general had decided to side with them, after all. Either that, or she was only pretending to. "Are we sure we can trust Muraka?"

"Not yet," Indira replied, "but Advisor Khatri's spies are on their way to verify the information. Now come, and hurry. You should be there before the rest of the council arrives."

He slipped on a pair of shoes. Without waiting for an invitation, Valkyra settled on his shoulder. The weight of her there was more of a burden than a comfort, but he couldn't worry about that now. Whatever trust needed to be repaired between them would have to wait. With Jakhat attacking, they had much bigger problems to deal with than a trio of mysterious strangers.

ALEIDA

After four nights of minimal sleep on the cold floor of a cell, soft blankets and the warmth of a fire in the hearth were a welcome comfort. Aleida slept in late the next morning, and by the time she woke, she felt rejuvenated and optimistic. Kamaal was here, Mitul was going to recover, and she was free. It was a good day.

Mitul was still in bed, but the others were all eating breakfast. Kesari passed her some of what was left—eggs, bread, and hard cheese with a cup of hot tea. She looked much better than she had the day before, though there was still a lingering fatigue around her eyes. Aleida took the only empty spot at the table, which put her directly across from Saya. The Sularan cast her a dark glance when she sat down but said nothing.

"I should check on Mitul," Kesari said, rising from the table. "Make sure everything's still healing properly."

"Yes, but take it easy," Lucian agreed, floating down the hall behind her. "You're still recovering, too."

"How is he?" Aleida asked quietly once they'd gone.

Saya's mouth pressed into a thin line, and her hand wrapped a little tighter around the cup she raised to her lips. For one dreadful moment, Aleida thought something must have gone wrong.

"He's breathing better today," Kamaal said cheerfully. "It will take time before he's fully recovered, but he's on the mend."

Relief washed over her like a cool breeze in summer. "That's good."

"It's lucky, is what it is," Saya muttered, glowering at her across the table. "He could have died, and you—"

"We'd best stay away from accusations and hostility going forward, don't you think?" Kamaal interrupted. He raised an eyebrow at Saya, and his tone was somehow gentle despite the reprimand in his words. "We all share a common goal, after all. A team works best when there's camaraderie, or at least tolerance."

"I'm being tolerant," Saya growled, her shadow falling over Aleida as she rose. "I haven't broken her nose yet." With that, she strode away and out the door, closing it only a little more forcefully than necessary behind her.

Aleida clenched her jaw and went back to her breakfast. She wasn't going to take on Saya's resentment toward her when she already carried enough of her own. If the Sularan wanted to stay mad, fine, but she wouldn't let herself be intimidated by someone who had no respect for her and didn't seem interested in changing that.

"She's just scared," Kamaal said. "Worried about Mitul. I know it would mean a lot to him if you could find a way to make peace with each other."

"She's the one with the problem, not me."

"All the more reason for you to try mending things."

She doubted Saya would be receptive to any such efforts, but she nodded anyway. "Sure."

They ate without speaking for a few minutes. Kamaal finished his breakfast and leaned back in his chair, sipping the rest of his tea slowly. "You know, Mitul said he could hear you talking, back at the temple. It helped, I think, whatever you were telling him."

Aleida scoffed at that and shook her head.

"What?" he asked.

"I wasn't talking to him." She pushed her empty plate away and crossed her arms. "I was praying. It was stupid."

"Why do you say that?"

"I *don't* pray anymore. I haven't since—" Since Tyrus had died, but she swallowed those words before they could come out. "I used to think…I used to *know* Artex was there, listening, watching over me. But I was wrong. No one was ever listening."

"Mitul was, yesterday."

"That's not the same thing."

"Isn't it?" He set his cup down and leaned forward on his elbows. "Your voice comforted him when he was dying, gave him something good to hold on to, and probably played some part in saving him. I'd call that an answered prayer, even if there was no divine intervention from god. Isn't that enough?"

It wasn't, though perhaps it had to be, now that she was living in a world where the existence of Artex or any other god was so uncertain. "I guess so."

"But?"

She sighed. "I don't know. Things were easier when I knew Artex was guiding me. Now I'm not sure that was ever true. And if it was, I don't think I want to worship a god who abandoned me when I needed him most." She traced a knot in the wood table with one finger. "I guess I'm still trying to figure out who I am and who I want to be without my faith."

"A difficult and important task," Kamaal said, "but maybe you don't need to throw out faith entirely."

"What do you mean?"

"You prayed yesterday, and Mitul heard you, even though he was unconscious. You've survived so much and made it this far, so if it wasn't god guiding your path, it must have been something within you." He shrugged. "Maybe we all have a little piece of the divine inside us."

Aleida looked at her hands resting on the table and only trembling slightly. She didn't have nearly enough energy for theological musings right now, but Kamaal's idea was certainly an interesting one. Blasphemous, her old preachers might have said, but not any more so than denying Artex altogether.

There was a shuffling from the hallway and Kamaal stood abruptly. He hurried over to Mitul, who was leaning on Kesari for support as they walked. "Here, let me," he said, wrapping an arm around the musician. "Should you even be up walking around like this?"

"Well, I'm certainly not going to lie in bed forever."

"It's good for him to get a little exercise," Lucian said. "But take it slow. No wild chases around the house or…other strenuous activities." He looked pointedly between the two men, and Aleida stifled a snort at the flustered expression that crossed Mitul's face.

They settled on a bench near the hearth, and Kesari went to fetch Mitul some breakfast. Saya came back inside with an armful of wood and added a log to the fire. "We should make a new plan, now that Valkyra knows we're here and trying to get Amar back. It's going to be tougher, and we can't risk anyone else getting hurt."

Aleida braced herself for another one of the warrior's cutting glares, but it didn't come. Maybe that was her attempt at tolerance, if only for Mitul's sake.

"We obviously can't confront Amar directly," Lucian said, hovering over Kesari's shoulder as the girl sat down. "Not that it was ever a good option, but who knows what Valkyra has told him since yesterday?"

After stacking the rest of the wood in a pile, Saya stood and brushed flecks of wood off her hands. "There will be guards still looking for the four of you. We'll have to keep a close eye out in case they expand their search outside the city."

"I can set some magical warning signals around the house," Kesari said. "If it's all right for us to stay here, that is."

"Of course," Kamaal answered. "I'm sure my sister wouldn't mind, given the circumstances."

"The longer we stay, the more danger we're in," Saya said. "I know Mitul needs time to recover, but we should try to get Amar away from Valkyra as soon as possible."

"Getting him away would be easier if we could restore his memories first," Mitul said. "Though I don't see how we can do that without making contact and putting ourselves at risk."

"Lucian and I have been working on that," Kesari chimed in. "A more indirect way to bring back his memories. We wouldn't have to stay with him to complete the process."

"How?"

"I think I can connect the magic to an object—something important to him. If we can pass it on to him, it should be enough to make him remember."

"The spell will be far less complicated than what Jameson did," Lucian explained. "Especially since he's already remembered his past once before. All we really need is for him to recall his visit to Deveaural and what Jameson did to him. The rest should follow."

"I have his journal," Mitul said. "And his sword, and the kanjira."

"Any one of those could work, but the journal might be best. His own writings could help him make sense of everything."

Aleida walked closer to the rest of the group. "I think he's already starting to remember. When I was in his room, I saw some notes he must have written, things that seemed like pieces of memories. Things about you, Mitul, and maybe Saya, and Shavhalla."

"What else did you find?" Mitul asked.

"Not much. He and Valkyra came in while I was there. I hid under the bed and got out as soon as they left."

"Under the bed?" Saya rubbed at her brow with one hand. "Skies, it's a miracle you weren't caught right then. Of all the stupid—" She clamped her mouth shut for a moment and started over with a new question. "What did they talk about while you were there?"

"Not much. They did mention some Sularan who wanted to meet with the royal council. Someone peculiar, Valkyra said."

At this, Saya's eyebrows shot straight up, and she exchanged a look with Kesari. "Could be Zefar."

"Could be," the girl replied, though she didn't seem half as convinced. "What else did they say about him?"

Aleida shrugged. "Nothing, really. A man named Ashaya was supposed to find out more and report back. I think he and Valkyra have been working together for a long time. They knew each other before she died."

"You're sure that's all?" Saya asked.

"Yes. Who's Zefar?"

"A menace," she growled. "And my uncle, unfortunately. I'm going to strangle him when I find him."

"Do you always resort to violence when you have a problem with somebody?" The words came out before she could stop them.

"You're one to talk. How many times was it that you tried to kill us? Not to mention bullying Jameson into going along with—"

"Saya, please," Mitul said with exasperation.

"Fine." She pushed off the wall and strode to the door, shoulders tense and fists clenched.

"Where are you going?" Kesari asked.

"To see if I can learn anything else about this 'peculiar Sularan.' If it is Zefar, he might still be in the city. I need to track him down before he does anything stupid with those records." She left before any of them could respond.

"Is she talking about the same records she brought from Shavhalla?" Aleida asked Kesari.

"Yes."

Kamaal tilted his head to the side. "I feel like I'm missing something."

"They were an offering for her haseph," Kesari explained. "They hold information about curses. Amar's curse, specifically."

His eyes widened. "You mean how to make someone immortal."

She nodded. "Zefar stole the records and ran. We don't know why or what he's planning."

"Nothing good, probably," Mitul said. "But we need to focus on Amar."

"It's going to take some time for us to get the spell right," Lucian said. "After that, we'll need to get the journal to him, which is going to be a massive challenge."

"Maybe not," Kamaal said. "Valkyra doesn't know I'm connected to any of you, does she?"

"I don't think so," Lucian replied.

"Good. Then I could give it to him. I came to know King Bhajan and Queen Indira quite well when I painted their daughter's memorial. It's been a while since I've spoken with them, but they've written to me often over the years. I'm sure if I let them know I was in the city, I could get an audience."

"And what about Amar?"

Kamaal considered this for a few seconds. "I'll give him the painting I did in Jakhat. All I need is a minute alone with him, right? Just enough time to pass along the journal without Valkyra seeing."

Mitul tightened his grip on the artist's hand. "You don't have to."

"He's right," Kesari agreed. "We can find another way."

"Valkyra will be more suspicious than ever now," Aleida added. "She'll be on the lookout for anything amiss. If she catches you, she'll have guards hunting you along with the rest of us."

"That's a risk I'm willing to take." He leaned a little closer to Mitul, his voice soft but earnest. "Let me do this for you. And for Amar. He was my friend, too."

Mitul's brows were furrowed, and a few seconds passed before he answered. "All right, then. Thank you."

"Of course. I'll get a message written today."

"And we'll start working on the journal," Kesari said.

"And after he remembers?" Mitul asked. "We'll need to make contact with him as soon as possible so we can plan an escape."

"I can handle that," Lucian said, a dark and jagged grin cutting through his flames. "I'll just make a habit of lurking in the palace hearths."

Aleida scowled at him. "That's the first place Valkyra's going to be looking. She'll catch you."

"I doubt that."

"Then you have no idea who you're dealing with."

He hovered a little closer to her, still looking far more amused than the situation warranted. "Yes, she's very powerful and very smart. An intimidating foe, to be sure." His eyes flickered with something impish. "But I'm far more clever and resourceful."

"And arrogant," Aleida muttered.

"That, too, but not without reason. She won't catch me. I bet my life on it."

"You're already dead."

"Kesari's life, then."

The young Tarja scoffed, but one corner of her mouth lifted in a half smile. "Come on," she said to the Spirit Tarja and stood up. "We've still got plenty of work to do before you can go testing your theory."

35

SAVIR

FOR THE NEXT SEVERAL DAYS, SAVIR'S HOURS WERE FILLED WITH ALL the duties and obligations of a prince whose country was at war. There were meetings with advisors and nobles who'd pledged their support, strategies to be laid out and altered as new information came in, and resources to allocate for what would surely become an extended conflict. Spies brought back whatever news they could, and so far, the information General Muraka had secretly passed along was proving accurate. That would give them an advantage in the battle to come, but with Jakhat's larger forces, they were still in for a tough fight.

When Savir wasn't in meetings, he trained for combat far more intensely than he had before, not only in order to join the fight himself but to lead men into battle alongside his grandfather. The latest report was that Princess Jasala rode at the head of Jakhat's troops, and though Savir didn't like the idea of facing off against the cousin who had shown him so much kindness, it was an expectation he couldn't avoid. The logistics of battle had changed drastically in the last few decades with the invention and adoption of firearms, but some traditions still lingered from days when rulers held their power through strength and competence on the battlefield.

Each day left him exhausted both physically and mentally, but sleep remained difficult. His thoughts spun with worry about how this war would impact Kavora and its people, as well as the constant frustration that they'd come to this point, despite all his efforts to avoid it. He replayed his decisions over and over, wondering if there was something he could have done differently to prevent this. All he could come up with was that it would have been better if he'd never come to Valmandi in the first place.

But they were past that now, and he had to do this. There were people counting on him, and taking back his throne was only what was fair and right. If anyone was to blame for the damage that would follow, it was Dashiva, but he would repair what he could when the war was over.

Valkyra had made herself scarce ever since their encounter with the strangers at the guardhouse. Savir suspected she was trying to avoid him and all his questions, but he couldn't worry about that now. When she did check in with him, it was only briefly, and always with the same warnings. "Stay away from the fires. That Spirit Tarja could be lurking anywhere."

"What does that matter?" he retorted one day after hearing the warning yet again. "He can't do anything to me on his own."

"He could be watching, and that's bad enough. We have no idea what harm they meant to do to you, but until we find them, you need to be careful."

"You're being paranoid," he muttered, but he could see the sense in her request and did as she'd asked.

The following day, Zefar hàs Yaratha returned to the palace to meet with the council. He seemed satisfied by the way Valmandi was upholding their end of the agreement and gave them a few more pages of the Shavhallan records. Valkyra had been particularly interested in attending this meeting once she learned Zefar would be present, and she listened intently to the report Chayani Sha gave regarding the study of the records at Valmandi's best Tarja academy. There wasn't enough information to start testing curses yet, but what they'd learned so far had proven to be a promising start, and it was expected progress would continue, as would the council's agreement with Zefar.

When the Sularan left, Magistrate Ashaya followed him out, and the conversation shifted to an update on troop movements and supply routes. Savir's eyes followed the magistrate, and he whispered a question to Valkyra. "Where's he going?"

"I've asked him to enlist Zefar's assistance in dealing with our other problem," she replied against his ear. "He's a mercenary and an assassin—a good one, by all accounts. We're hiring several, actually. Whoever we can find. Perhaps they'll have better luck in tracking down our mysterious friends from the guardhouse."

"Assassins?" Savir raised his eyebrows, then remembered where he was and quickly neutralized his expression. "I thought we wanted to capture them alive."

"If possible. But if not, we need someone who can deal with them. That Tarja girl was…unexpectedly powerful."

"She had mesala," he reminded her.

"Even so. I wouldn't have expected her to best us so easily."

He tried not to let that sting. The girl—little more than a waif of a thing, really—*had* made quick work of incapacitating him. But it wasn't as if he used his magic often, and the skill was still new to him. He hadn't been expecting a fight, or any of the strange things that had happened during the encounter, for that matter. The whole thing had caught him completely off guard.

If they met again, he wouldn't let himself be beaten so easily. And if the assassins killed them all before he got the chance to see them again…well, he had more important things to worry about now, anyway.

After the meeting ended, Valkyra flew off to find Ashaya, and Indira pulled Savir and Bhajan aside. She held up a letter. "I know we all have a lot going on, but we should probably discuss this. I received it yesterday evening."

Bhajan took the letter and held it so Savir could read it with him. It was from Kamaal Ruman, letting them know he'd relocated to the city. He politely requested an audience at their earliest convenience; apparently, he had something he wanted to show them. A gift.

"The head priestess at the temple passed it along," said Indira. "I'm sure Kamaal will be expecting a response soon."

Bhajan sighed and passed the letter back to her. "Skies know we could use a visit from an old friend and a little carefree conversation. I wish his timing had been better, but I suppose it wouldn't hurt for him to come to dinner tomorrow, if he can make it. After that, Savir and I will be riding out to join the military encampment."

Indira touched her husband's arm and gave him a quick kiss on the cheek. "I'll try to get word to him and see if he can come."

Savir held back a frown as she walked away. It wasn't that he disliked the artist, who had seemed friendly enough when they'd met each other in Jakhat. He just wasn't particularly in the mood for company. Dinners with his grandparents were the only times he'd had lately to relax and be himself rather than putting on princely airs for everyone around him. As Bhajan had said, they'd be joining the rest of the army at their camp outside the city very soon, and he didn't want his last good meal in the palace to be intruded upon.

But Kamaal was a friend of his grandparents, and about as unconnected to the current political conflict as anyone in Kavora could be. He couldn't fault them for wanting a single evening's respite from the bleak preparations of war.

He rubbed his hands over the tightness in his neck and rolled his shoulders a few times. He could use a little respite himself, but that would have to wait. For now, all he could do was take a deep breath and brace himself for what was sure to be another long day.

KESARI

TOGETHER, KESARI AND LUCIAN STUDIED, PRACTICED, AND REFINED the magic she would place on Amar's journal to bring back his memories. She started by testing Jameson's original procedure on Aleida, who had volunteered herself for the job and vehemently opposed Mitul's own offer to be the subject of such experimentation. "You still need to heal."

"Oh, stop fussing," he replied. "I'm all right." This was mostly true, though he still walked stiffly, and little winces flashed across his face whenever he moved too suddenly. Kesari continued to do what she could to ease his pain and speed the healing process, but he mostly needed time and rest.

"I only need one of you," she said, even though more would have been helpful. "Aleida will do fine."

With Jameson's detailed notes, it didn't take long for her to repeat the same process he'd used with Amar, pulling Aleida's memories into the room to surround them in lifelike clarity. From there, she started making the alterations they wanted to use with Amar's journal, testing each one as they went and adjusting as needed. First, she brought up Aleida's memories while the young woman was still awake, which proved no more difficult than performing the procedure while she was asleep. After that, they had to work out the bigger challenges of attaching the magic to an object and preventing any sensory projections of the memories that might be taken in by Valkyra or others near Amar. It was slow, hard work, but if she could get it right on her own—or at least, mostly right—she'd have no trouble replicating the spell once she had a little mesala to help her.

Rather than carrying the powdered substance on her person, she'd returned it to her pack. Although she'd fully recovered from the exhausting effects of using it, she shuddered to recall how it had made her feel once its effects wore off. Completely drained, like she was only a ghost of herself. With the mesala in her system, she hadn't been able to sense her own limits. There was only power and mastery, stronger than anything she'd felt before. She'd pushed herself too hard, and once that power faded, she was beyond spent.

But that had been an emergency, and pushing herself to the edge was what had saved Mitul. Exhaustion and discomfort were a small price to pay for that. With any luck, she wouldn't need to push herself so hard again.

She hadn't yet worked out the last few snags in the spell when Kamaal sent his message to the royal palace, but they were out of time and needed to take whatever opportunity they could while it was still available. Troops had been marching out of the city all week, setting up camp to the southwest in preparation for battle. Word was Jakhat's armies marched for Valmandi already with plans to conquer it or lay siege, thereby putting a quick end to their treason. Once the fighting started, getting to Amar would be far more complicated.

The response to Kamaal's invitation came back the next day. "They want me to come for dinner tomorrow night," he announced when he arrived back at the house. "Will the journal be ready by then?"

Kesari exchanged an uncertain glance with Lucian, then nodded resolutely. "Yes. We'll get it done." What other choice did they have?

Mitul rose from his chair and walked to Kamaal. "Are you sure you still want to do this?"

"Absolutely. It's our best option, isn't it?"

"One that puts you entirely at risk."

Kamaal placed a palm against his cheek. "You're so dramatic. There's nothing to worry about. The king and queen love me. Even if something does go wrong, they won't let any harm come to me."

"Just be careful."

"Always."

Kesari and Lucian spent the rest of the afternoon trying to resolve the remaining problems with their spell, channeling altma into various objects and then giving them to Aleida to see if any memories could be elicited. So far, they'd been unsuccessful, but at least none of her memories were spilling over into the room anymore.

They were still working on this when Saya returned from the city, where she'd spent all week looking for Zefar. A cold wind blew through the door as she entered, and she immediately plopped down in a chair near the fireplace.

"Any luck today?" Kesari asked.

"No," she replied glumly. "I'm still watching that Tarja academy someone mentioned, but there's been no sign of him. Any luck for you?"

"Maybe. I think we're on the verge of a breakthrough."

"You've been saying that all day," Aleida muttered, and Kesari might have thought she was complaining if not for the slight upward curve of her lips. She was only teasing, and it was true enough.

Saya looked like she was about to respond with something snarky, but Kesari hurried to reply first, grinning in response to Aleida's teasing. "This time, I really mean it. Maybe. I think."

"Only one way to find out," Lucian said.

Kesari took a breath and placed her fingertips against the paper in Aleida's lap—a smeared and water-damaged drawing her brother had done. She channeled her altma, weaving together the healing magic of the memory spell with the strength and endurance needed to bind it to the page. A faint golden light emanated from her hands and sank into the paper, leaving no trace behind.

The light was the same gold as it had been when Jameson had retrieved Amar's memories, so that at least was a good sign. She held the page out to Aleida, who studied it quietly for a few moments. Her brows knit together in concentration, and Kesari knew even before she asked the question what the answer would be.

"Anything?"

"No. I don't think so."

Kesari sighed and ran her hands through her hair. "Damn. I can't figure out what's going wrong. That should have worked."

"Supper's ready," Mitul called from the table. He and Kamaal had taken to cooking together the last few nights, which mostly involved Mitul trying to be helpful while Kamaal fretted over him and insisted on doing all the work himself.

"Give us a few minutes," she replied, readying herself for another attempt.

Aleida shook her head and stood, the paper still pinched between shaking fingers. "I need a break, and so do you. Come on."

Somewhat reluctantly, Kesari followed her to the table, taking a seat next to Saya. Ever the gracious host and entertaining conversationalist, Kamaal began sharing an anecdote from his childhood as they passed the food around, and Kesari let all thoughts of magic and memory retrieval fade into the background of her thoughts.

They were all finishing their meal when she suddenly noticed that Aleida was crying. She made no sound, but trails of moisture glistened on her cheeks, and her eyes seemed distant. It wasn't until Mitul reached over to touch her shoulder that she spoke, blinking and wiping at her face with the back of her sleeve. "I remembered."

It took Kesari a moment to realize what she meant. "It worked?"

Aleida nodded. "It was something I didn't even realize I'd forgotten. Tyrus' first fishing trip. I think I was only eight or nine. We were playing in the boat, and our father kept telling us to stop, but of course we didn't listen." She smiled faintly, almost to herself. "Tyrus fell out, and I was so scared I scraped my elbow on the edge of the boat trying to haul him back in. He didn't even care. He just laughed, dripping wet and shivering. And then our father started laughing, and I tried so hard to stay angry at them both, but I couldn't. So there we were, out on a boat in the middle of the ocean, laughing like a bunch of loons."

She trailed off for a moment, then leveled her gaze at Kesari. "I haven't thought about that day in years, and now I can remember it like it happened yesterday. Thank you for bringing it back to me."

Kesari blushed and twisted the edge of her shirt around her fingers. "I didn't do much of anything, really."

"You did."

"You did," Saya echoed, and in that moment, a look of what seemed like understanding passed between the two of them.

"It worked," Lucian said, his grin even wider and more jagged than usual. "A little delayed, but it worked. Amar's going to be back with us in no time."

SAVIR

KAMAAL RUMAN WAS ALREADY SEATED AT THE TABLE WITH SAVIR'S grandparents when he walked into the dining hall, though their food had not yet been served. Indira smiled brightly when he entered. "There you are. I was about to send someone for you."

Savir dipped his head at Kamaal, who rose from the table to greet him. "I'm sorry for making you wait. Time seems to have gotten away from me today." He'd lingered in his room longer than planned, wondering if Valkyra was going to return before dinner. She'd gone off on her own early that morning, claiming she wanted to inspect the military encampment before Savir and Bhajan went to join the troops there. She hadn't returned yet, so whatever reports she might want to give him would have to come later.

Kamaal bowed and let Savir sit first before returning to his own chair. "That's quite all right, Your Highness. I arrived a bit early. Your timing is perfect."

King Bhajan motioned to the servants at the door, and they began to file in with the meal the kitchen had prepared. It wasn't as lavish as some of the other meals Savir had seen served when they had guests; rationing and anticipated food supply issues meant even the royal family had cut back on certain luxuries. But that didn't mean the food was anything to complain about, either. There was fish roasted to crisp perfection in a bed of vegetables, seasoned rice, freshly baked flatbread, and a creamy pudding topped with sugared figs for dessert. Savir enjoyed every bite, content to listen and watch as his grandparents kept up most of the conversation with Kamaal.

The artist seemed far more relaxed here than he had in the imperial palace with Empress Dashiva. Perhaps that was because he'd been so focused on his work back then, but there also seemed to be a unique level of familiarity between the artist and the two monarchs. They talked like old friends, and their interactions were some of the most genuine Savir had seen from his grandparents aside from the times when it was just the three of them. It made him like Kamaal a little more, though he was likable enough to begin with. He had an easy sort of confidence about him that was without threat or guile, and he laughed freely and often.

When dinner was finished and the plates had all been cleared away, Kamaal gestured to something leaning against the wall, covered by a white sheet. "I don't want to take up too much more of your time," he said, "but can I show you the painting I did when Prince Savir was in Jakhat?"

Savir rose quickly and had to wait for the others to follow. He'd been mildly curious about the painting ever since leaving the imperial palace and had wondered if he would ever get to see it. He'd always assumed it would be given to the empress when it was finished.

Kamaal lifted the edge of the canvas to unpin the fabric draped over the top. He tugged softly, bundling the sheet up in his arms as it fell away. Beside Savir, Indira let out a soft gasp and covered her mouth with one hand. Bhajan nodded approvingly and smiled at Kamaal. "I've said it before, but your skill never ceases to amaze me."

"It's stunning," Indira said. "You've captured both of them so well."

Savir tried to think of some compliment to give, but if he was honest, the painting unnerved him. In it, he stood beside Dashiva in the same pose they'd held the day Kamaal began the painting. The sheathed sword in her hand was angled toward him, and he'd been cast in heavy shadow whereas she stood in the light.

"What do you think, Your Highness?" the artist asked.

"It's…very nice."

He chuckled. "Why do I get the sense that wasn't a compliment?"

For a moment, Savir panicked, thinking he'd offended the man. But Kamaal waited patiently for a response; it seemed he was genuinely asking.

"Sorry," he replied. "I don't know much about art. You're obviously very talented."

"But?"

Savir hesitated, trying to find the best words to phrase his thoughts. "I suppose I have a question. You may find it rude, but it's not intended to be."

"Speak your mind."

He considered the two figures in the painting and felt his upper lip begin to curl in disgust. He'd been such a naive boy back then, mere weeks ago. "When you started painting this, I thought we still had a chance at peace. Now we're at war, and everything's changed."

"Yes," Kamaal agreed. "It has."

"Did you know we've lost nearly a hundred soldiers already, just in little skirmishes along the river and roads? Jakhat has lost at least that many. Hundreds more will likely die before this is over." He frowned. "I guess what I'm asking is, why does this matter? It's a lovely gift, but it's a painting. What value does it have when so many people are suffering?"

"Savir," the queen said softly, her voice more concerned than scolding. Still, he knew he'd said something he probably needed to apologize for.

"You're right," Kamaal said before he could speak. "It is only a painting, and its value is never going to measure up to the life of even one of your fallen soldiers. But it still matters, I think. Art is important even amid terrible things. Perhaps even more so, then. It's an expression of emotion, and there are certainly plenty of emotions to be felt in any conflict." He smiled. "Even good ones, like the shared hope for peace between two rulers now at war. It's important we remember there was hope for peace and unity before this started. And there can be again."

Savir wanted that to be true, but he wasn't so sure he felt as optimistic as Kamaal. Still, the gift was a sincere gesture. "Thank you. We will treasure it always."

"Of course. It was my honor to finish it for you." He tucked the sheet under one arm and gave a slight bow to the king and queen. "I should take my leave and let you all get back to the rest of your night. Thank you for your hospitality. It was wonderful to see you both."

"And you as well," Bhajan replied. "It's been far too long."

They walked out of the dining hall together, and when they reached the stairs leading to the main entrance, Bhajan and Indira bid Kamaal good night and went on their way. Savir lingered a moment longer, waiting to exchange his own farewells with the artist. Instead, Kamaal said, "If you could grant me a few more seconds of your time, Prince Savir, I have something else I wanted to give you."

He reached into his jacket, and there was movement behind Savir as Tarik took half a step forward with his hand resting on the hilt of his sword. Kamaal withdrew his own hand slowly, holding nothing but a book, and Savir cast the guard an annoyed look while motioning for him to stay put. The man was only doing his job, of course, but did he really think his liege's life was in danger at the hands of an artist his grandparents trusted enough to invite for dinner? Then again, considering the close encounter at the guardhouse, he couldn't blame Tarik for being overly cautious.

Kamaal pressed the book into Savir's hands but did not let go. Leaning in a little, he dropped his voice to a whisper. "This will help you remember everything you've forgotten."

Savir's heart missed a beat. How did he know?

Before he could ask, Kamaal flipped the book open to the back, where several loose papers of varying sizes had been wedged. The one he pointed to bore a drawing of an instantly recognizable dragon. "Keep it secret, especially from her."

Whatever she's told you, it isn't true.

"Why? What do you know?"

Kamaal let go of the book and backed away smiling, as if he hadn't even heard Savir's question. "It was good to see you again, Your Highness. Good night." He turned and trotted down the stairs, humming a jaunty tune to himself all the way down. Then he was out the door and gone, leaving Savir clutching the book that might somehow help him remember his past.

"What did he say, Your Highness?" Tarik asked, falling into stride beside him as they made their way back to his room.

Savir tucked the book inside his own coat and smoothed the fabric over it, not daring to look at Tarik or give any acknowledgement to the suspicion with which he was surely eyeing Kamaal's gift. "He wanted to wish me well with the war."

"And the book?"

"Something he thought I might enjoy."

"You seemed surprised when he gave it to you."

Savir feigned nonchalance with a shrug. "I suppose I was shocked to find him so sympathetic to our cause. And to me. He's from Jakhat, after all."

"I believe he's originally from Valmandi. And of course, he's a good friend of your grandparents."

"Yes, of course," said Savir. "That must be it."

They'd arrived outside his bedroom door, where the night shift guard was already waiting to take over for Tarik. "Do you need anything else before I go, Your Highness?" the old guard asked. He'd started asking this every night, always with the royal address attached to the end. Savir took it to be a tacit acknowledgement that he'd earned at least some respect and loyalty from the man, which was both vindication and relief.

"No, thank you," he replied. "Have a good night."

"Good night. I'll see you tomorrow bright and early."

Apprehension quaked through Savir as he pushed the door open to his room. Tomorrow morning he would ride to the military encampment with his grandfather, but the anxious thrum inside him now was more related to the book Kamaal had given him. He shut the door and was about to pull it out when he caught a glimpse of movement in the corner of his eye.

Valkyra lounged on the bed, her tail flicking back and forth like a cat's. "I saw Kamaal Ruman leave. Did you have a nice dinner?"

Keep it secret, especially from her.

Savir left the book in his shirt, hoping the corners weren't protruding in an obvious way. "Yes, it was lovely." He grabbed his nightclothes from the end of his bed and walked behind a screen in the corner of the room to change. He pulled off his boots first. "How was your evening?"

"Fine," Valkyra said. "The military encampment looks well-organized and secure. They were setting up a tent for you and the king when I left."

Her voice still seemed to be coming from the bed, so Savir quickly pulled the book from under his shirt and jammed it into one of his boots. "That's good," he called back to her.

She went on, providing details about the camp that he probably should have paid attention to but couldn't. His mind raced with questions he desperately wanted answers to. What was in that book, and how had Kamaal come by it, and why was he supposed to keep it hidden from Valkyra?

Those questions would have to wait, but hopefully not for long.

ALEIDA

IT WAS GETTING LATE, AND KAMAAL HADN'T YET RETURNED FROM HIS dinner at the palace. Aleida and the others were still awake, all eager to hear his report. Mitul had taken to glancing out the window every five minutes, until at last the unmistakable sound of cart wheels rolling over the ground drew nearer. He stood and went to the door, flinging it open to let Kamaal inside.

They gave each other a quick kiss, and Kamaal smiled broadly when he pulled away. "I gave it to him. I didn't stick around long enough to see if he remembered anything, but he has the journal now. Hopefully it's only a matter of time."

"That's my cue to go, then," Lucian said.

"Be careful," Kesari replied. One of his eyes flickered out in a wink, and he flew out the door into the dark. He would watch Amar in the palace and make contact as soon as he had some sign the magic had worked.

They stayed up a while longer, listening to Kamaal's recounting of the night's events. The fact that he'd seen no sign of Valkyra made Aleida wonder what the Spirit Tarja was up to. Still looking for them, perhaps, or setting more nefarious plans in motion.

Kamaal and Mitul retired to the bedroom at the back of the house, and Kesari, Aleida, and Saya spread out in the main room to sleep. The house maintained its warmth even when the fire burned low, and

Aleida snuggled comfortably beneath her blankets. She was starting to drift off when she heard Kesari whispering.

"Saya? You awake?"

"Hmm?" the warrior replied sleepily.

"Sorry. I was just thinking, and well, what if this doesn't work?"

"The journal?"

"Yes. I mean, I'm not exactly the best Tarja, am I?"

"That's not true."

"It is," Kesari replied. "I know I've improved, but I'm still just…me. And what if that's not good enough? What if he doesn't remember?"

There was a shuffle against the floor as Saya propped herself up on one elbow, facing the younger girl. "Kes, you're brilliant. I've seen you heal sailors in the middle of a battle and fight stone warriors in Shavhalla. You fought off Jameson himself when he was under Valkyra's control, and you used your magic to steal his research and put out those fires in Deveaural."

"You saved Mitul's life," Aleida said, and they both went quiet for a moment, as if surprised that she was still awake and listening to their conversation.

"You saved Mitul's life," Saya echoed. "You've grown so much. Don't you see that? You're not the scared girl I met in Tarsi six months ago. You're a Tarja to be reckoned with, and I have no doubt that whatever you set your mind to, you can find a way to make it work. Including this. Amar *will* remember, thanks to you."

"I hope so," Kesari replied.

"He will. I know it."

"So do I," Aleida said, fondly recalling the memory Kesari had given back to her the night before. Laughter echoed in her mind amidst seagulls' cries and the soft lapping of ocean waves against her family's boat.

Kesari released a slow breath. Saya caught Aleida's eye, and the corners of her mouth lifted in a smile—a small one, but it was a definite improvement from the glares she was used to.

She rolled onto her other side to sleep, allowing a little of the tension she'd been carrying to melt away. Maybe she and Saya didn't have to stay enemies forever. Maybe they could even grow to respect each other.

Mitul would be proud.

Lucian returned the next morning to give a brief update on Amar. "I don't think he's even had a chance to look at the journal yet," he said. "It's hard to know for sure. I've had trouble getting close to him. Valkyra is keeping a watchful eye on any fires, and even Amar seems to be avoiding them."

"Keep trying," Saya said. "It's important you're there to talk with him as soon as possible, once he remembers."

"I will, but when I left, he and the king were preparing to join Valmandi's army outside the city. Jakhat's forces aren't far off. I'd wager the battle starts before tomorrow's end."

Aleida was unsurprised by this, though the reminder only served to increase her anxiety. They'd spotted a few groups of Valmandi soldiers on the road over the last week, along with a small supply caravan. They'd even debated returning to the city to seek shelter behind its walls, which was what most people in the surrounding area were doing. But with guards still looking for Kesari, Mitul, and Aleida, they couldn't take the risk. Valmandi's army had gathered to the southwest of the city, the opposite direction of where they were. With any luck, the fighting wouldn't come any closer to them than that.

Lucian left again, and Kesari went out to check the magical warning signals she'd set up in case anyone looking for them got too close. Tired of being cooped up inside, Aleida announced she was taking a walk and made her way into the woods bordering the field. It was a cold morning, and her cheeks and nose were numb before too long. She didn't stay out long and was returning to the house when the snap of a branch made her spin around.

"Hello?" she called, not really expecting an answer but hoping her voice would scare off whatever animal might be lurking nearby. She tried not to dwell on the thought that it might not be an animal at all, but a guard from the city who'd finally tracked them down.

No other sounds came. Aleida continued, quickening her pace a little and swallowing some of her nervousness when she spotted the house through the trees ahead.

Something rustled the leaves behind her, and this time when she turned, it was barely in time to see a shadowed figure slip by her. Strong arms gripped her own, and when she tried to fight back, the cold tip of a blade pressed against her throat.

She stopped struggling, breathing hard, unable to see her assailant. Were there more? Were they even now creeping toward the house to arrest Kamaal, Mitul, and the others?

She needed to warn them. If she screamed loud enough, they could hear her from here. She opened her mouth and drew a breath, but the blade's point dug into her skin. Blood trickled down her neck in a warm, sticky trail.

"I would stay quiet, if I were you," a man's voice said. His accent was like Saya's, though not as pronounced. "Who are you and what are you doing here?"

"I should be asking you that."

"Yes, well, I'm the one with the knife to your throat, so I think I'll be asking the questions." His breath was hot against her ear. "What business do you have with the people in that house?"

"None," she lied. "I didn't think anyone was there."

"That's horseshit, and we both know it. You can see the smoke rising as plain as I can."

"I swear, I didn't—"

He cut her off. "You're either here to spy on them or to kill them. Though you honestly don't look like you could kill much of anything."

"I have no idea what you're talking about."

He went on as if he hadn't heard her. "Did Ashaya hire you? I knew I wasn't the only one. What was the prize they offered you, just out of curiosity?"

So it wasn't only guards hunting them anymore, but hired assassins, spies, and mercenaries, including this man. And he seemed to have mistaken her for a competitor rather than one of his marks. Perhaps she could use that to her advantage.

"Money," she said in answer to his question. "A lot of it. We can split it if you let me help you. I'll get closer to scope things out, then come back here so we can plan our attack. They've got us outnumbered, and one of them's a Tarja, but if we work together, I'm sure we can—"

"I've got a better idea. You and I are going to march right up to that house, and I'm going to ask the people inside what they'd like to do about the scum trying to murder them." The blade left her throat, and he pushed her forward. "Eyes straight ahead. Go on, start walking."

She did as he'd ordered, not daring to look back and still trying to comprehend his words. It didn't make sense…unless he wasn't trying to kill them at all. "You're protecting them."

"How very perceptive of you. Hurry up."

"No, this is good. I'm not actually a spy, and I wasn't hired to kill them. We're friends."

"Do you always try changing your story to get out of trouble? You'll have to lie better than that if you want to be believable."

Rolling her eyes, she traipsed onward to the front door. She didn't knock, and when she entered with the stranger right on her heels, the others let out surprised exclamations or stared with mouths agape.

"Hello, Saya." The man put a hand between Aleida's shoulder blades and shoved. She stumbled a little and nearly fell but managed to right herself. "I found this one outside. You might want to think about increasing security, seeing how your friends are wanted by the royal guard."

Mitul immediately went to Aleida's side and pulled her farther into the room. Kamaal placed himself between the two of them and the man who'd accosted her, and for the first time, she got a good look at him. He was much older than Saya but had the same strong, narrow features, along with golden eyes and pale scars raised against brown skin.

"Zefar, you idiot," Saya said. "*She's* our friend. I told you she started working with us after we left Shavhalla."

"*This* scrawny thing?" His upper lip curled. "No offense to you, of course, but honestly, Saya. When you told me about the Tarja who pursued you, you made her sound like a dangerous foe. Now you're telling me you were almost defeated by *her*?"

"She was far more dangerous when she had magic and a Spirit Tarja."

"If you say so."

"What are you doing here? I've been looking for you for days."

Zefar grinned. "I know, and I've been looking for you. A royal advisor hired me and probably several others to track down your friends and kill them. Instead, I came to warn you."

"Which means the others will be coming soon," Saya muttered.

"Yes, but they didn't have the head start I did. You were looking for me first, remember? It made my job much easier."

"Meanwhile, you've been impossibly difficult to find."

"I didn't *want* to be found, not even by you." He winked, and Aleida couldn't tell whether his teasing was good-natured or malicious.

Saya crossed her arms, the muscles in her neck and jaw tightening. "And why might that be?"

"Oh, you know," he replied nonchalantly. "Something about stolen records. I figured you wouldn't be too happy to see me, and I didn't want to deal with the lecture until my plans were finished. But once there was a price on your friends' heads, I couldn't sit back and let you be killed along with them, so here I am. I believe a 'thank you' might be more appropriate than a lecture, at this point."

He was still grinning as if this was all very amusing to him, but Saya remained stone-faced. "You *stole* my offering, Zefar. After you were banished for trying to steal it once before. I vouched for you. I've *always* spoken up for you, and you just..." She made a disgusted noise in the back of her throat. "Why would you do something like that?"

"Because our leaders were wrong," he snapped, all traces of amusement vanishing from his face. "You worked so hard to bring those records back, and they were going to let them sit and rot while the Kavorans continued to plunder our lands."

"It's a curse, Zefar. The repercussions would be too much."

"Maybe so, but they should have at least asked the rest of us." He let out a forced chuckle, shaking his head. "*Them,* I mean. They should have asked the rest of *them*, not us. I don't get a say, after all. And you know what? Maybe that's it. Maybe I got tired of not having a say."

"That doesn't give you any right to steal my offering," Saya said. "I want those records back. Now."

"I can't give them to you. I made an agreement with the royal council—the records in exchange for their promise to stop taking mesala and protect our borders."

Aleida's stomach dropped. If Valkyra had acquired the information Saya had carried out of Shavhalla, she'd soon work out how to create a curse. Magic that powerful could cause this war to become even deadlier than it already was.

"You did what?" The low harshness in Saya's voice mirrored the same dismay in the others' eyes.

"I don't understand why you're so upset," Zefar retorted. "At least this way, your offering is put to good use."

"You put a dangerous weapon right in the Kavorans' hands!"

"One they'll use against each other! They'll weaken themselves while protecting our lands, and by the time it's over, they'll be too busy picking up the scraps to bother with us."

"At what cost? All you've done is postpone our own fight with them, and when it comes again, it will be so much worse. How long do you think it will be before they turn that same power against us?"

He shrugged. "I don't know, but we'll never find out what tomorrow holds if we don't survive today."

Saya groaned and stared up at the ceiling with tense shoulders. "Skies above, Zefar, you have no idea what you've done."

"Oh, give me a little more credit than that," he shot back. "Don't you think I considered all this before I did anything? I gave our people plenty of time to change their minds. They didn't, and I saw a way for us to protect ourselves, so I took it."

"And what about the Kavorans? This war was going to be bad enough already without your help."

"I don't give a shit what happens to the Kavorans. Let them burn their entire country to the ground, if that's what it takes to keep them out of ours."

There had been a time—hell, there were *still* times—when Aleida felt the same. She had little love for Kavora as a whole, but that didn't mean she wanted its people to suffer the same fate as her own. War was an ugly, brutal thing, and far too many innocents paid the heaviest price.

"We're getting that book back," Saya growled, still glaring at Zefar.

"Why? So these people can start plundering our lands again?"

"It's winter. There are no mesala flowers to harvest now anyway."

"That doesn't stop them from digging up the whole plant, and you know it. They'll just go back to what they were doing before, and we'll be in the same destructive cycle all over again."

"We can figure something else out," Saya said, her shoulders slumping a little. "I never should have carried those records out of Shavhalla."

Kesari took a step toward her, gently reaching out a hand to rest on her arm. "Don't say that. You only did what you thought was best."

"I was wrong." She lifted her chin and set her jaw. "But Zefar and I are going to set things right."

The mercenary scoffed. "There's nothing to set right, as far as I'm concerned."

"Isn't there?" she snapped, raising both hands to her hips. "That was *my* offering. I left it under the care and protection of our leaders, and you had no right to steal it. Even if you can justify the rest of your actions, I know you can't make excuses for that one. What kind of uncle steals from his own niece?"

Zefar glared at Saya and spat out a few words in Sularan. Judging from the way Kesari winced, Aleida got the impression they were insulting.

"That wasn't very nice," Saya responded flatly. "You're not going to change my mind on this. Stop wasting time and tell me where those records are so we can get them back."

"As you wish, Masahi." There was a venomous edge to the way he emphasized the words, but if that bothered Saya at all, she made no indication. "I've been giving them to the royal council in pieces. They've had me take the last two parts directly to a Tarja academy for study. The rest I've kept hidden somewhere safe. I can bring them to you tomorrow."

"You'll get them for me now. And I'll be coming with you."

Zefar sighed and let his shoulders relax, all traces of anger masked behind an air of unruffled nonchalance. "Sad, really, how quickly trust erodes amongst family." He stepped aside and made a little flourish toward the door. "After you."

Saya grabbed her cloak from a hook on the wall as she went past. She paused with her hand on the door. "And you need to apologize to Aleida."

He made no protest to this suggestion, but his tone seemed somewhat less than sincere. "Sorry for scaring you. And almost killing you."

"That's all right." It wasn't, of course, but what else was there to say?

"Thank you for the warning," Kesari added.

"Of course," Zefar replied with a smirk. He nudged Saya in the shoulder as they headed outside. "At least someone appreciates me."

SAVIR

THE MILITARY ENCAMPMENT HOSTING THE BULK OF VALMANDI'S forces was nearly a full day's ride from the city, and the sun was setting when Savir and Bhajan arrived at the head of a company of soldiers. The camp was substantially larger than Savir had anticipated. He'd heard all the numbers during council meetings, of course—so many footsoldiers, Tarja, weapons, munitions, tents, and supplies—but there was a big difference between hearing those numbers and seeing them sprawled out across a field here at the edge of the forest. It was an impressive sight, and it bolstered his hope for their victory.

Their latest reports told them Jakhat's forces would be arriving the day after tomorrow, and the plan was to meet them in battle here before they could reach the city. Some of the advisors had advocated for holing up inside the city walls, but General Khan and others argued that doing so would only prolong the fight. This might be their best opportunity to weaken Jakhat's forces, especially since they had detailed information passed along by a powerful accomplice in the enemy's ranks. Savir's arrangement with General Muraka remained a secret to most, but the woman was proving to be an incredibly valuable resource.

The officers riding behind Savir and Bhajan gave orders to their troops, and they dispersed. The king dismounted, handing the reins off to a waiting attendant. Savir did the same, and they strode toward the middle of camp side by side. There were bows, salutes, and more than a few cheers from the soldiers they passed by, and Savir did his best to acknowledge as many of them as he could. Eventually they reached the large, central tent serving as their base of operations. A smaller tent had been erected nearby for the king and the prince to sleep in, and Savir slipped inside to relieve himself of the bag slung over his shoulder. It contained a few essentials along with the mysterious book Kamaal Ruman had given him the night before. He still hadn't had any time alone to look through it, and with Valkyra perched on his shoulder, he didn't dare give it his attention now.

He shoved the bag under a cot covered in warm furs and blankets and went to join his grandfather, General Khan, and several other high-ranking officers. They were gathered around a table inside the larger tent. A map had been spread over its surface, wooden markers showing the positions of their own forces and Jakhat's, approaching from the northwest.

"According to our scouts, they've stuck to these routes here," General Khan was saying. He motioned to the roads cutting through and along the edges of the forest, where the trees were less dense and travel was easier. Then he pointed to a spot deeper within, not far from where they stood now. "We know they're planning to leave a battalion here, in hiding. It's intended to provide reinforcements after the vanguard has weakened our forces, but we already have a full company of Tarja supplied with mesala ready to ambush them."

"Good," said Bhajan. "They'll wipe them out in no time."

An increasingly familiar churning started up in Savir's gut at the coldness in his grandfather's voice. He spoke of those men as if they were the enemy, but they weren't—not really. If he was truly the rightful ruler of this country, then the soldiers fighting for Jakhat deserved whatever fairness and protection he could offer them.

"Have the Tarja capture them instead of kill them," he said. "At least the ones who will surrender."

"A merciful suggestion, Your Highness," General Khan said, "but we can't possibly afford to feed and house so many prisoners."

"Then we'll put them to work. Offer to let them fight on our side. Anything, but I don't want any more bloodshed than necessary. They're still our people—*my* people. Some of them didn't have a choice to fight in this war."

The general opened his mouth like he was about to protest further, but Bhajan spoke first. "You heard your prince. Spread the word to every regiment. We can figure out what to do with prisoners later, but he's right. Killing them won't serve us, in the long run."

General Khan nodded curtly. "As you wish, Your Majesty."

They went over various strategies, using the wooden markers to play out each one and fill in the gaps where Muraka's intel was lacking. The officers present gave their input and were assigned roles and positions based on what would be most advantageous. Bhajan himself was to oversee the vanguard, as was the expected tradition for Valmandi monarchs. General Khan would lead the middle guard, and the remainder of their Tarja forces would be divided between each.

"Savir, you will remain here, with the rear guard." Bhajan pointed to another place on the map, behind the main forces. When Savir frowned and opened his mouth to protest, he touched his arm. "You'll have your chance to command your army in battle when we take the fight to Jakhat's doorstep. For now, I want you someplace your safety can be guaranteed."

Savir forced himself to swallow his arguments, feeling like a small child who'd been sent from the room so the adults could discuss their business. He was little more than a boy, after all, raw and untested. He'd never seen battle, except in his dreams. Vivid though they were, there could be no substitute for the real thing, and if Bhajan was going to lead the main force, he couldn't afford to be distracted by worries about his grandson.

"We should talk about Jasala," said General Khan. "The empress has her leading Jakhat's army."

"While Dashiva hides in the safety in her palace," Bhajan said, his lip curling in sneer. "That may be to our advantage. Dashiva was a ruthless foe, in her prime. But her daughter? I'm not so sure." He ran a hand over his beard and cut a glance at Savir. "You've spent some time with her. What was your impression?"

He still disliked the idea of facing off against his cousin in this fight. She'd been so friendly to him at the palace, even though they'd both known war was looming. She could have chosen to scorn him instead, but she hadn't. "She's smart. Observant. Kind."

"Soft," General Khan said. "That's good."

"She's not *soft*," Savir retorted, his tone sharper than he'd meant it to be. It suddenly occurred to him that Jasala may have only been using kindness as a way to better understand him. After all, wasn't that the best tactic when it came to potential enemies? To know them? He scowled. "I'm sorry. I only meant you shouldn't underestimate her."

"Duly noted."

The conversation continued, but Savir's mind began to wander, and he was startled when Bhajan laid a hand on his arm once more. "We can revisit this later. Come, take a walk with me."

General Khan and the other officers began to talk amongst themselves, with several leaving to attend to the troops under their command. Savir and Bhajan exited the tent with a whole retinue of guards, including Tarik. The king made a gesture, and they hung back at a respectful distance, allowing the two men to converse privately.

"You seem tense," Bhajan said.

"Aren't you?" he replied. "Shouldn't we all be?" This was war, after all, not some leisurely hunting party.

"I only wondered if there might be anything I could do to ease some of that tension." He leaned in a little closer, speaking in a hushed tone. "I could find you some company for the night. Before I married your grandmother, I found it helpful, sometimes. I'm sure there are plenty of young women or men who—"

Heat flushed over Savir's cheeks. "No, I don't need company."

Bhajan chuckled. "All right, then. Just as well. We want you rested, after all." He gave a quick wink, and then his voice became more serious. "I remember my first battle. It was during Emperor Akraja's reign, when we were still trying to establish our rule over the eastern provinces. I was terrified, stayed up all night thinking of ways I might die, even though I was barely at risk with so many soldiers around to protect me. War is so much different for kings' sons than it is for ordinary men, but that doesn't mean it's not frightening. It's all right if you're afraid."

"I'm not afraid," Savir said, and he was almost surprised to realize the words were true. "Not for myself, anyway. I still wish it hadn't come to this."

Bhajan's mouth pressed into a thin line. "I'm sure even Dashiva wishes the same. We're all doing only what we feel we must."

Savir still had his doubts. Was this truly the best course of action? It was like Bhajan said; he was only doing what he had to. But it didn't feel right.

Maybe sometimes, there were no right choices.

"Go find something to eat," Bhajan said gently. "And then get some rest, if you can. Morning will come sooner than we think, and Jakhat's forces won't be far behind."

In some cruel jest from the universe, Savir was awakened what felt like mere moments after he'd finally managed to fall asleep. Valkyra's whisper was grating against his ears, and he blearily tried to swat her away.

"Wake up," she hissed more insistently. "There's a problem outside."

The military camp, Jakhat's army, the impending battle. Savir sat bolt upright, remembering it all, and flung the blankets off himself. "Are they here?" He expected to hear a horn blaring or the sounds of hundreds of soldiers preparing for battle. Instead, all he could hear was Bhajan's snoring from the other side of the tent.

And voices. They were right outside, quiet and rushed. Arguing, though he couldn't tell what about. Valkyra jerked her head toward the sound pointedly.

He stood and walked over to the tent flap, goosebumps rising on his arms as he wrapped them around himself. Outside, two guards stood facing each other. They abruptly ended their conversation when they saw him. One was part of the group that had accompanied Savir and Bhajan to this camp. He didn't recognize the other, but she wore the crisp red uniform of a palace guard.

She dropped into a bow. "Your Highness, I have a message." When she rose, she was holding out a letter, sealed with plain wax and addressed to him.

"From who?" Savir asked.

"Magistrate Ashaya. I was told to bring it directly to you and no one else."

He took it from her and retreated inside the tent. Ashaya had stayed behind at the palace with Queen Indira and most of the other advisors. What could be so urgent that he needed to send a letter, and why address it to Savir rather than Bhajan? He channeled his altma to create a small orb of light and left it hovering overhead as he broke the letter's seal.

Valkyra was watching him closely, and when he unfolded the letter, she shuffled a little closer to read it with him.

You'll be pleased to know one of our mercenaries has tracked down the fugitives we've been searching for. They're staying at a house on a small plot of land west of the city, along with a few others. Two are Sularan warriors, one of whom was described as a man with scars on his face. I'm almost certain it must be Zefar. The fact that he hasn't killed them already means he may be working with them, which is all the more reason to put an end to this as quickly as we can.

Due to the unexpected number of them and the involvement of the Sularans, the man who brought me this news has requested support in dealing with the problem. I'll be riding out there myself with a small group of guards first thing in the morning. We plan to surround them and catch them unawares.

By the time you defeat Jakhat's army, we will have subdued these dangerous criminals, and you'll no longer need to worry about any harm they intended to cause you. May altma guide us both to a swift and decisive victory.

Your humble servant,

Magistrate Ashaya

"I should go with him," Valkyra said.

"We can't leave now."

"*You* can't." Her steely eyes reflected the glow of his magic. "But I can. And I should. I can assess the situation from the air and let them know how to best proceed. Things will go more smoothly if I'm there to help."

He didn't particularly like the idea of riding into battle without her, but there were certain advantages to having her gone. He could almost hear the book in his satchel calling to him from under the bed. "Will you make it there in time?"

"If I leave now."

He pretended to consider this, pretended to hesitate, then nodded. "All right, then. Go."

She brushed her tail over the back of his hand. "Are you sure? Will you be all right here without me?"

Again, he nodded. "I think so. I'll be in the rear guard, and Tarik will keep me safe. Besides, I fight well enough to take care of myself."

She smiled a little. "My dear, brave boy."

He walked to the tent flap with Valkyra perched on his shoulder. Bhajan stirred a little but didn't wake. "You'll try to capture them alive, won't you?" he asked. He still wanted to talk to them and find out what their plans or motives were. "At least one of them. We ought to interrogate them."

"We'll try, but if they fight back with the same force as last time, we may not get the chance."

"Of course. I'm only curious about what they wanted with me."

"As am I."

He clenched his jaw as he lifted the tent flap, the same hot frustration rising at her vague response. She knew more about these strangers than she was letting on, but still, she wouldn't tell him anything.

She brushed his cheek with one soft wing, then leapt into the night, a gray shape fading against the dark. "She gets restless at night," Savir told the guard by way of explanation, then went back in and immediately dug through his belongings. When he had the book in hand, he found a comfortable position on his bed with the blankets draped around his shoulders and the orb of light hovering above. His fingers trembled in anticipation as he turned to the first page.

My name is Amar. Or at least, that is what I've been called these last eighteen years.

Amar. That was what the man had called him at the guardhouse—the man he'd shot. It couldn't be coincidence that the same name now appeared here, in this book Kamaal had given him, along with a warning not to trust Valkyra.

And there was something else about it, too—something that sent a shiver down his spine when he realized it. The handwriting matched his own, as if he'd scrawled it there himself. But surely, that was impossible.

I'm writing this to myself so I can remember.

His heart began to pound. Remember what? What was it this person had forgotten? This person who had the same exact penmanship as Savir himself—Savir, who had also forgotten so much of his past. He read on.

If I die again and forget who I was, I want to have some kind of proof, even if I'm too stubborn to believe it.

What was that supposed to mean? No one could die more than once. And what proof? Perhaps that was referring to the book and the message it contained.

There was more on that first page—words about a man named Mitul, someone the writer trusted. The Visan woman had screamed that name when he'd shot the older man at the guardhouse. Was that why the man had spoken to Savir with such boldness? He may have mistaken him for the writer of this book, this Amar.

After that came a paragraph about immortality, which was curious, but so outlandish he didn't give it a second thought. He flipped through the rest of the pages, most of them filled with the same handwriting. The last several were blank, and stuffed between them were various drawings on loose, mismatched sheets of paper. He pulled them out and went through them one by one.

The first was a portrait of him, not in his prince's attire or crown, but a version of him that brought back memories of days on the road with Valkyra, before he'd ever reached Valmandi. His hair was shaggier than it was now, his clothes were simple, and his face was a bit more gaunt. A few more portraits followed: a young woman with Sularan haseph markings on her face, the man named Mitul, and the Tarja girl who'd subdued him so easily at the guardhouse. Names were scrawled below each one. The Sularan woman was Saya, and the Tarja girl was Kesari. If the names were supposed to mean anything to him, he didn't know what.

He set the portraits aside and flipped through the rest of the drawings. There were several of Valkyra, all in various poses. Another page showed different buildings, their architectural style distinctly different from anything in Kavora. Atrean, he thought, though he couldn't remember ever seeing Atrean buildings and wasn't sure why he'd jumped to that conclusion. There were ships, too, and a few sketches of people who looked suspiciously like pirates.

Forest creatures, flowers, and other plants covered the next page. After that came a series of drawings showing vine-covered ruins, crumbling statues, and bridges made of woven tree roots and branches. A sense of recognition stirred within him, but when he tried to trace it back to a specific source, his mind went blank. It was like one of his dreams, a half-uncovered memory, he was certain, but it slipped back into shadow before he could make sense of it.

He returned to the front of the book to pick up reading where he'd left off. There was a list of names, most scribbled over, but the one at the bottom had been written in bold letters and circled. "Jameson Weatherford," he read aloud. An Atrean name.

He was still trying to decipher the names that had been scratched out when the first horns sounded. They were distant, muffled, and he thought maybe he'd imagined them. Then came another call, and Savir looked up to see a dim gray light seeping beneath the tent where there had been only darkness before. Was it really morning already?

Bhajan rolled over and sat up, eyes wide and muscles tense. Savir snapped the book shut and shoved it beneath his blankets. Another horn sounded, much closer this time and punctuated with a bone-chilling shout.

"The enemy approaches! To arms! To arms!"

40

KESARI

"WE NEED TO DESTROY THEM."

At Saya's words, Kesari stopped scrubbing the dish she was washing and turned to her friend, who stood in front of the window looking out. They were the only two in the house right now. A few soft *thunks* drifted their way as Zefar threw knives into a fence post outside. Kamaal, Mitul, and Aleida had gone to collect more firewood, and Lucian was keeping an eye on Amar at the military camp.

Kesari inclined her head toward the book in Saya's hand. The warrior hadn't let the Shavhallan records out of her sight since she'd gotten them back from Zefar, and until now, she'd given no indication of what she meant to do with them. At least, Kesari thought that was what she'd been referring to. "You mean the records?"

Saya nodded.

"Are you sure? You worked so hard to get them."

"I know. But I think Amar was right all along. He warned me, and I was too stubborn to listen. Magic this dangerous shouldn't be brought back to the world for any reason. I was a fool to seek this out."

Kesari set the dish down on the table and walked over to her. "You were only trying to help your people. Don't blame yourself for that."

She sighed. "How can I not? Especially if the Kavorans are able to create a curse from what he already gave them."

"Well, here's hoping that doesn't happen." She gestured to Zefar out the window. "Did you tell him yet?"

"Why do you think he's throwing knives into that post like he wishes it was my face?"

"I'm sure he doesn't think that." Another wooden *thunk* punctuated her words, and she winced.

"He's pissed," Saya said with a shrug. "He won't stay mad, but for now, I guess I can understand why he feels that way. He went about it all wrong, but I think he really tried to do the right thing for our people, even though they've never done right by him." She held the book out to Kesari. "Before it's gone for good, do you want to have another look? See if there's anything in there that might help with Amar's curse?"

Kesari took it and skimmed through the pages that still remained inside. She'd looked it over with Lucian at least a dozen times during their journey from Shavhalla to Hayathu, and though she couldn't recall everything, she knew there were crucial elements included in the pages Zefar had torn out. Whether it was enough to facilitate the actual creation of a curse, she didn't know, but it seemed possible, especially if Valmandi had their best Tarja scholars studying it. She kept that thought to herself, not wanting to add to Saya's worries.

Her eyes paused on a page near the center—one Lucian had often puzzled over. It gave details regarding the primary source of power for a curse, and Kesari read over the same line he'd recited to the Sularan council in Hayathu. *A Tarja must draw on the blood of their own body and the* jhivan *of their spirit to provide the power needed for an effective curse.* There was also a section about the conditions under which a curse could be broken, and as Jameson had speculated, those were deliberately woven into the curse itself.

She lingered on that foreign word—*jhivan.* Lucian had guessed it was the Shavhallan word for altma and that Amar had simply neglected to translate it in his haste. But what if it was something else? Something that could prove critical in freeing Amar from his curse?

Regardless, the writings on conditions for breaking a curse seemed useful. Kesari tore the page out and flipped to the next. She'd barely gotten a chance to skim the first line when a long, sharp whine pierced the air.

Through the window, she spotted Zefar with his pistol drawn and aimed at a shadowed figure through the trees. A thin stream of red light rose into the sky, a product of the magical alert system Kesari had set up.

She left the book on the table and stuffed the torn page into her pocket. Two gunshots cracked in quick succession, each from a different direction. Saya cursed, leaning forward with her hands on the windowsill. The figure at the edge of the treeline fell. Zefar ran forward, apparently unharmed, and he pulled his knife from the fencepost as he closed in to finish off the stranger.

The front door slammed against the wall as it flew open. Kesari whirled around, channeling her altma in preparation for a fight, but it was only Aleida. Alone.

Saya went to retrieve her bow. "Where are Mitul and Kamaal?"

"Still out in the woods," Aleida replied.

A new shriek rang through the air as another of Kesari's alarms tripped. Saya nocked an arrow to her bow and held it half-drawn. "There's more of them." She raised her bow as she walked to the door. Kesari followed, fingertips tingling with altma.

They hadn't yet made it outside when a ball of fire shot through the open door. Kesari let out a yelp, then spotted the dark eyes amongst the flames. Lucian. "You scared me!"

"I came as fast as I could," he said. "There are half a dozen royal guards around the house, along with at least three hired assassins."

"Only two now," said Zefar, striding in behind Lucian and reloading his pistol. One of the knives tucked into his belt was still wet with blood.

"Valkyra's here, too," Lucian said.

"And Amar?" Kesari asked.

"No. She came with that magistrate—Ashaya. It seems he's the one who organized this attack. No doubt he and the others will be closing in soon. We'll have the best chance of defending ourselves from here."

"What about Mitul and Kamaal?" Aleida asked, her voice high-pitched and frantic.

"I'll go find them," Saya said. "The rest of you should stay here."

Aleida strode forward. "I'm coming with you."

"No! You'll only get in the way."

"I can help! And I can take you to where I last saw them. Come on."

Zefar stopped her in the doorway and held out his pistol. "Take this. You've only got one shot, so if you need it, get close, point, and squeeze the trigger. Think you can handle that?"

The gun trembled in Aleida's hands, but she nodded resolutely and stepped outside. Saya followed, still muttering to herself in frustration. They took a few moments to check their surroundings, then made for the forest at a full sprint, glancing back only once when another of Kesari's alarms whined.

The two guards who had set it off stopped running and knelt beside the fence, raising their rifles to their shoulders. They took aim at Saya and Aleida. Before they could fire, Kesari channeled her altma and sent flames toward them.

For an instant, she was swallowed in a memory, watching the fireball she'd conjured sail off course to strike the clocktower in Deveaural. But this was different. Her friends were in danger, and she would do whatever it took to save them. Her fireball struck the ground beside the two guards, close enough to ignite their uniforms and effectively divert their attention. Kesari did her best to ignore their screaming and watched as Saya and Aleida ran for the trees.

"This might be a good time to use some of that mesala," Lucian suggested. "If there are more, we're going to need every advantage we can get."

Kesari went to retrieve her pack, where she'd stashed the mesala for safekeeping. Before she could reach it, the floor of the house began to tremble. She jumped back as the wood beneath her split and cracked, rising in jagged angles where she'd been standing only a moment before.

Zefar drew a dagger and backed away from the gap forming in the center of the room. With a final shuddering rumble, the floor exploded out in a hailstorm of wood, rock, and dirt. Kesari's cheeks stung as the first pieces hit her, and she formed a barrier to shield herself and Zefar from the rest.

As the last of the debris fell away, a man ascended from the gaping hole. The ground rose with him, and when it stopped moving, he stood on a mound of compressed earth surrounded by the splintered wood of the broken floor. Kesari had never seen him before, but judging by his traditional white magistrate's robes, this was Ashaya. Valkyra perched on his shoulder, her wings fanned out gracefully behind her.

"Hello," she said, drawing the word out with a voice as smooth and rich as fresh cream. "My, what a nuisance you've become, little Tarja. I'm afraid I've underestimated you." The corners of her mouth curved in a demure smile. "That's a mistake I won't be making again."

SAVIR

SAVIR SAT IN HIS HORSE'S SADDLE AT THE HEAD OF THE REARGUARD, watching through the rows and rows of soldiers before him as Jakhat's troops took their positions on the field. Most wore simple uniforms rather than armor, but the morning sun reflected brightly off hundreds of helmets and rifle barrels. Savir's own helmet was a bulkier, heavier thing with a mail face covering—more unwieldy even than the crown he could never seem to settle quite right. He also wore a breastplate and greaves over heavy metal-toed boots. Though the weight of it was uncomfortable, Savir was glad for the protection, and for Tarik's imposing presence beside him. The man was a mountain in red and black armor, his eyes as cold as ever and his focus locked on one single objective: to defend the prince.

Savir's weapons consisted of a sword Bhajan had given him and his own flintlock pistol, one hanging from each hip. There was also a dagger tucked into one boot, though he didn't expect he'd need it. Back here with the rearguard and a dozen soldiers specifically charged to keep him safe, he likely wouldn't see much fighting at all.

Bhajan's head bobbed between the mounted cavalry at the head of the vanguard. Savir had only had a moment with his grandfather before they were both swept off to their duties, and now he wished they'd had a chance to say more. He'd never really thanked the man for all he'd done for him over the last few months. They didn't see eye to eye on everything, but Bhajan was always looking out for Savir, always trying to do right by him, always willing to fight for him. His devotion and loyalty to the grandson he'd only met recently was more than Savir could have asked for.

But now was not the time for such sentimentality. He could say all that to Bhajan later, after they'd survived this day.

The stillness of waiting was punctuated only by the occasional jostling of armor or the soft nicker of a horse. Both sides held steady where they were, and for a few precious minutes, they were all simply pieces on a game board, harmless and unscathed. He breathed it in. It would not last.

A pair of riders separated from Jakhat's front line and rode forward several paces. Moments later, Jasala's voice rang out across the field, amplified with magic so she could be easily heard by all present. "King Bhajan! Turn over the fraud pretending to be Prince Savir, and this can end without violence."

The commanding harshness of her tone was so different from the gentle kindness she'd shown at the palace, and Savir's heart ached with it. Neither of them should be here, facing off as enemies.

When Bhajan didn't respond, Jasala continued. "My mother is willing to forgive your treachery if you surrender now and pledge your fealty once more."

"It is you and your soldiers who've marched here with violent intentions," Bhajan replied, his own voice made louder thanks to the magic of a Tarja who stood nearby. "You dishonor me and Savir both by calling him a fraud. Dashiva's refusal to recognize his legitimacy will be her downfall. We're more than willing to defend our home and Savir's rightful claim to the throne by whatever force necessary." He drew his sword, raising it high in the air so that it gleamed in the sunlight. "Turn back now, or fight! The choice is yours."

A cry rose up behind him and spread through the ranks until it surrounded Savir. He couldn't bring himself to cheer with them. He was still watching Jasala, flitting in and out of his view through the movement of Valmandi's soldiers.

If it had been just the two of them, without Dashiva or Bhajan interfering, could they have found a path to peace themselves? Savir liked to think they might have, but it didn't matter now.

The shouts hadn't yet died down when a series of thunderous cracks ripped through the air. Valmandi soldiers cried out in agony as bullets tore through flesh and bone. Moments later, a second volley was fired, this time from their own side of the field.

From there, the battle erupted into chaos. Smoke choked the air as rifles were reloaded and fired again along with the occasional heavy artillery blast. Tarja worked together to shield their comrades and combine attacks against the enemy. Magical energy of all types and colors flew back and forth, and when Jakhat attempted a cavalry charge, Valmandi's Tarja used their combined power to upend the earth itself. Some of Jakhat's Tarja reacted quickly enough to save most of them from stumbling, and a few almost seemed to fly as they were helped over obstacles on the ground. They met the front line with a violent clash, and the wild screams of injured horses pierced through the din.

Savir held his position with the rest of the rearguard, his own horse snorting and tossing its head in response to the chaos. It was difficult to see much through the smoke, but as some of the wounded began to fall back, the damage became more apparent. Jakhat's forces likely weren't faring much better, if at all, and despite his best efforts, Savir's mind couldn't stop spinning around the sheer human cost of it all.

This was *wrong*.

A rider approached from his right flank and skidded to a stop next to him. She tried to speak, but the words were drowned out by a nearby cannon blast. Instead, she pointed. A flash of blue rose above the forest canopy, where Valmandi's Tarja were supposed to be ambushing Jakhat's reinforcements.

"We need help!" she shouted above the tumult. "They had daravak. Loaded it into some kind of cannon and wiped out half our Tarja's power."

Savir assessed the battlefield as quickly as he could. Valmandi's forces were holding their own, but he couldn't take the entire rearguard and leave them open to an attack from behind. He gave a sharp whistle and signaled to three officers spread down the line. They hurried to him.

"I want you three to stay here and hold this position." He pointed to the company on his right, closest to the forest. "I'm taking those soldiers with me, so keep an eye on our right flank."

"Let one of us go instead, Your Majesty," one of the officers said. "It's too dangerous."

Savir held back a snort. This was all dangerous, no matter where he was, and sitting here waiting for the fight to reach him was only making him anxious. "You have your orders. Tarik?"

"I'm with you, Your Highness," said the old guard.

Before anyone could protest further, Savir dug his heels into his horse's side and rode off, calling out to the company of infantrymen to follow him. They hurried along without question, breaking through the edge of the forest a few minutes later.

Savir, Tarik, and the messenger who'd come to request aid dismounted. The terrain here was too rough for a mounted approach, so they might as well join the footsoldiers. They left the horses and continued with the messenger leading the way to where the rest of her group waited. Soon the sounds of battle from the field faded away, but they were quickly replaced by commotion deeper in the forest.

Before long, they came upon a group of Valmandi's Tarja crowded together behind a makeshift barricade of branches, rock, and earth. Beyond that were dozens of Jakhat soldiers, with more probably hidden in the trees. They fired upon the barricade periodically, and from what Savir could tell, less than half of the Tarja were using their magic to retaliate. The daravak was proving alarmingly effective.

He motioned his soldiers to take cover behind the trees, and when one of Valmandi's Tarja spotted them, she hurried to pass the word to her companions. Before Jakhat had time to recalculate their strategy, Savir ordered his own troops to open fire.

A thunderous volley cleared out several of Jakhat's soldiers, allowing some of the pinned-down Tarja to fall back. Most of the bullets missed their marks. The scent of gunpowder filled Savir's nostrils, and smoke stung his eyes, causing them to water. They weren't going to get very far like this, and it seemed their opponents had realized the same thing. With Valmandi's soldiers now forced to reload, the opposition was forming up for a charge.

"Bayonets ready!" Savir ordered. The call went down the line and they all began fixing the sharp blades to the ends of their rifles. Savir sprinted forward with Tarik matching his stride, both their swords already drawn. At the sound of gunfire, they flattened themselves behind the barricade.

Savir spoke to the officer leading the Tarja soldiers. "Can your men still use their magic?"

"Some of us," the officer replied. "Most who can't have already fallen back."

"Good. When Jakhat's soldiers close in, take out as many as you can. Without killing them, if possible. Trap them inside a barrier, knock them unconscious, I don't care how you do it. I don't want us coming out of this with more blood on our hands than necessary."

The officer nodded, and a cry rose up from Jakhat's soldiers. Savir stood, clutching his sword in one hand and his pistol in the other. He let out a shout as they surged forward. Without any further prompting, Valmandi's troops charged ahead to meet them.

Tarik and the others tasked with protecting Savir closed in around him, fending off any attackers who got close. Savir fired his pistol at a man about to fell one of his guards, then holstered the weapon and used his sword to assist Tarik in fighting off a pair of soldiers. He dispatched the first in a surprise attack from behind, allowing Tarik to take care of the second without much trouble. The man barely had time to nod his gratitude before they were accosted again.

Savir's body moved almost of its own volition, instinct and training taking over in a way that surprised him, considering how little training he'd actually had. He couldn't explain it; he simply *knew* what to do. He knew when to block and when to attack, how to find the weakness in an opponent's defenses, how to respond to a hundred different elements that could turn a fight in his favor.

He lost himself in the battle. Every moment became only about surviving to see the next. Moment after moment after moment, all stacked up until he lost track of them. His hands were red, his armor splattered with mud and blood and gore. He concentrated only on his movements and the air in his lungs, each heaving breath an assurance that he was still alive, still alive, still alive.

It was such a terrible, difficult ordeal, and at the same time, easy. Like he'd been doing it all his life. For a few wild moments, he had the strangest idea that this was only one of dozens of battles he'd fought in.

A man in Jakhat's green uniform lunged for him, and he barely managed to parry the strike. Something in his vision shifted. For an instant, he was somewhere else. A different battlefield. His foes wore heavy armor instead of uniforms.

Pain lanced across his side. He gritted his teeth and shook his head. Were it not for his armor, that might have been a fatal blow. He needed to focus.

The soldier attacked again, his face twisted with malice. He looked like a man Savir had known once, a very long time ago. The name escaped him now, but they'd both been soldiers. Together.

Skies, what was happening to him? That wasn't right. He'd never been a soldier before.

Except he had.

In dozens of other battles.

He inhaled a sharp gasp as his opponent moved in for the kill. Tarik arrived to dispatch the man, and he gave Savir a concerned glance before turning his attention back to their surroundings.

Savir let his sword fall. His vision seemed to warp and spin as hundreds of memories engulfed his consciousness. It was as if the floodgates within his own mind had suddenly opened, drowning him in a tangled mess of images, emotions, sounds, and sensations he couldn't yet sort through.

But he *remembered.*

He remembered so much. Multiple lifetimes' worth of personal history.

"Prince Savir? Are you all right?"

Tarik's voice was little more than a muffled echo, but it gave him something to cling to. He needed to stay present, stay focused.

Stay alive.

Something tore through his leg right above the knee. The joint buckled underneath him, and he screamed.

"Prince Savir!" Tarik cried out. "Hurry, the prince is hurt!"

He was surrounded, then hoisted up and dragged away by those sworn to protect him. Prince Savir, they'd called him, and he laughed now at the ridiculous horror of it all.

The only reason they were fighting this battle was because they believed him to be the rightful heir to the imperial throne. But he wasn't a prince. He had been once, in another time, another place. But he certainly wasn't their Prince Savir.

He was only...

AMAR

AMAR.

Not Prince Savir, just Amar.

The full weight of that realization crushed the air from his lungs and burned across his skin like a wildfire. The air was far too warm. He needed to get out of this armor. He almost wished he could crawl out of his own skin. The very thought of all the damage he'd done was unbearable.

Tarik and another guard had him by the arms and shoulders. They dragged him away from the fight with his injured leg hanging uselessly underneath him. Amar wrenched one arm free and ripped his helmet off, nearly falling over without the extra support. A third guard appeared in an instant to help him recover, and Amar dropped the helmet as they continued on.

His leg hurt fiercely, but the sensation seemed unremarkable amid the turmoil within his mind. He'd started a war. Hundreds of soldiers were now dead because of him, and hundreds of families would be missing their loved ones. All because of the lie Valkyra had led him into.

This was exactly the opposite of what he was supposed to be doing. The words Mahati had spoken all those centuries ago when she'd cursed him came back with sickening clarity.

Your soul shall be bound to the physical world for as many lifetimes as it takes for you to atone for the atrocities of war.

He was supposed to find some way to make amends for all the suffering his father's wars had inflicted. Instead, he'd gone and created more of that suffering in *this* war. In the process, he'd even hurt his own friends—friends who must have been working to save him all this time. The journal, Kamaal's visits, Kesari and Aleida and Mitul at the guardhouse—

Mitul! Oh, skies, he'd *shot* Mitul!

A howl clawed its way up his throat and out of his mouth like some dying animal. The guards exchanged a concerned look with each other and quickened their pace, hurrying him off to have his leg examined by a Tarja healer. But it wasn't a healer he needed.

If he'd killed Mitul, he'd never forgive himself.

"What have I done?" he whispered. His breaths came out panicked and shallow. "Skies, what have I done?"

"Hold on, Your Highness," said Tarik. "We're almost there."

They went around a pair of corpses on the ground, and Amar's stomach heaved. This was wrong—all of it. "We have to stop fighting." When no one paid him any mind, he repeated the words even louder. "We have to stop fighting!"

Tarik looked down at him with pinched brows. "We have stopped. We're leaving the battlefield now. See?"

"Are you sure he didn't hit his head?" the other guard asked. "He sounds delirious."

"Shh!" Tarik hissed. "It's all right, Your Highness. We'll get you somewhere safe and have that leg tended to right away."

They weren't *listening* to him. He planted his working foot into the ground and wrenched free of the guards, wincing at the pain that jolted through his leg when he hit the hard-packed earth. They whirled around, confused, and tried to haul him back up. He skittered away from them as fast as he could.

"This battle must stop! Find Bhajan. Tell them to retreat. We need to surrender."

"Shit, maybe he has gone daft," Tarik muttered.

Amar continued backing away from them but ran up against a tree trunk. There was nowhere else for him to go.

The old guard approached like he was some cornered wild thing, hands raised and voice low. "Please calm down, Prince Savir. We're only trying to help."

Amar's temper flared. "Shut up! Just listen to me. I'm not Prince Savir. This is all wrong."

The frown that crossed Tarik's face was a grim and menacing thing, but he didn't care.

"I think he's lost his mind," the second guard said.

"Might be his injury," Tarik replied, his eyes narrowed in suspicion. "Or the battle. He's never seen war before."

"Stop it, you're not listening!" If they weren't going to help him, they'd have to get out of his way. Amar reached for his altma, but he couldn't get a solid hold on it. Between the recovery of his memories, the pain of his injury, and the horror of what he'd done, he couldn't channel it into anything productive. In frustration, he reached for his pistol instead. It wasn't loaded, but they didn't know that. If he threatened them a little—

A flash of light erupted from Tarik's palm, and a warm sensation pressed against Amar's face. His eyelids suddenly felt very heavy, and the pistol in his hands trembled. It was impossible to hold up. It was too difficult to hold himself up, really. He let the weapon drop and slumped sideways, eyelids drooping.

"What'd you do to him?"

"He's stunned is all." Tarik's voice sounded like a distant echo. "I'll keep him asleep until we can get him out of here and have a look at that wound."

No, that wasn't right. He couldn't afford to sleep now. There was too much to do, too much to fix. He pushed himself back up, or tried to, but his body wouldn't cooperate.

He blinked, only once, and the entire world went dark.

KESARI

KESARI PUT ALL HER EFFORT INTO MAINTAINING THE BARRIER SHE'D conjured around herself and Zefar. Magistrate Ashaya lifted his arms, and with them rose the debris surrounding him. Valkyra watched with that same demure smile, her eyes glinting with a cruel anticipation.

Kesari's heart pounded with the same frantic intensity as it had when she'd faced Jameson, a puppet under Valkyra's control. She remembered too well what it had felt like to be trapped against the ground, utterly powerless and believing—*knowing*—she was about to die, and her friends along with her.

But it had been different with Jameson. Kesari hadn't been nearly as strong as she was now. Or as brave.

She was in control.

The rocks and shards of wood under Ashaya's power began to glow, and Kesari readied herself for the coming onslaught. A blast of wind sent the projectiles hurtling forward. She kept the barrier up, but it weakened against the force of Ashaya's magic. It wouldn't hold much longer.

With a cry, she pushed her shield outward. It slammed into Ashaya, causing him to stumble.

Zefar took the opportunity to rush at him, his dagger poised for a killing blow. Ashaya recovered too quickly. His hand shot out with inhuman speed, wrapping around Zefar's wrist and twisting his arm back until he sucked in a sharp, pained breath. The Sularan struggled, but could not break free of the man's magically strengthened grip.

Kesari channeled her altma again, and orange flames sprung to life around her hands. Valkyra called to her just as she was about to hurl them at their attacker.

"Try anything, and he dies."

She faltered, smothering the flames in a closed fist. Lucian began to float forward, but Ashaya twisted Zefar's arm a little harder. He stopped, glancing back at Kesari. What were they supposed to do now?

Valkyra stretched out her neck to look Zefar in the eye. "I didn't entirely believe it until now, given how much money we offered you for their deaths. But you *are* working with them, aren't you? How long has that been going on?"

"I'm not working with anyone," he spat, still grimacing in pain.

"Really? Well, the girl certainly seems to think you're an ally. Otherwise, why be concerned for your well-being?" She walked forward, down Ashaya's arm and closer to the mercenary's scarred face. "Now tell me, where are those Shavhallan records you've been trading to the royal council?"

"That's not our deal. You get them a little at a time if—"

Zefar's limbs convulsed, and Kesari could see a faint glow emanating from Ashaya's fingertips. He was torturing him. She took a step forward, summoning flames to curl around her fingers again. In response, Ashaya channeled more altma into the mercenary's body. A restrained groan broke through his clenched teeth.

"Stop it!" Kesari shrieked.

"You stay where you are," Ashaya said. "And put out that fire. Now!"

She forced herself to comply, but only with great difficulty. The flames were drawing energy from her anger as much as her altma. She hated that she was stuck here again, powerless, useless. Her nails dug into her palms as she clenched her fists. There had to be some way out of this, and she'd be damned if she didn't find it.

Valkyra spoke to Zefar again. "Our deal ended the moment we learned you'd allied yourself with these miscreants." She cast a dark look at Kesari and Lucian. "Tell us where the records are, and perhaps we'll let you live."

Zefar's eyes slid to Kesari, then down to the dagger still clasped in his hand. It was more than just a casual glance. He was going to do something reckless, but for what? They had him trapped. They would kill him if either of them tried anything.

"Burn them," he said in Sularan.

Before she could even conjure her flames, Zefar let out another pained cry. Ashaya was hurting him again.

"I am losing my patience," Valkyra hissed. "Tell us where the records are. Now!"

Zefar breathed in shakily. His eyes met Kesari's, and there was something pleading in them, but she didn't know what he was asking. Again, he opened his mouth, this time forming the words without giving voice to them. *Burn them.* His gaze shifted to something on the ground behind her.

"The records…" he said, and for a few awful seconds, Kesari thought he was about to tell Valkyra where they were. But his gaze never left hers, and suddenly, she understood.

She'd left the records on the table behind her. Zefar wasn't telling her to burn Ashaya and Valkyra. He wanted her to destroy the book.

She gave him the slightest of nods, and he grinned. His hand tightened around the hilt of his dagger, and with a mighty cry, he tried to raise it. Ashaya stopped him easily, but Kesari took advantage of the brief distraction, new flames flaring in her hand. She spun and targeted the book that had fallen onto the floor. It ignited in an instant.

"Stop the girl!" There was a rush of cool air as Valkyra flew past Kesari to dive beneath the table. She beat at the flames with her wings in an attempt to put them out, but it was too late. The pages were already curling, blackening, crumbling to ash, burning with the intensity of magically fueled flames. With an enraged shriek, the dragon sprang into the air once more and flew at Kesari with claws extended.

She raised her arms to shield her face and channeled altma into a new barrier. Through it, she could see Zefar, still fighting the magistrate's hold on him. It seemed he had the advantage, but in a single instant, Ashaya wrenched the dagger out of his grasp. He plunged it into the mercenary's chest, the blade sinking all the way to the hilt.

Kesari's barrier fell away as Zefar let out a choked sound. He slid onto the floor in a heap and lay there, motionless. Dying.

She'd failed. She should have protected him, but she could barely protect herself. It was like before, with Amar. What good was she if she couldn't keep anyone else safe?

Claws raked across her arms, slashing through her clothes and into the skin beneath. The pain brought everything screaming back into focus, and she blinked against tears as Valkyra swooped in for another attack. She could heal Zefar, if she was fast enough. She'd done it with Mitul. If she could end this fight and get to the mesala in her pack, she could still save him.

She curved the barrier's energy around Valkyra to trap her within. The dragon realized what she was doing and wheeled around sharply to flee. Kesari was faster. Only her voice managed to escape before the barrier snapped shut around her. "Ashaya, stop her!"

Kesari whirled, readying herself for whatever fight he was about to give her. His expression tightened as he looked from the flames in her hands to her face, and she was familiar enough with her own fear to recognize the emotion in his eyes. He was terrified of her.

Good. He should be.

She unleashed the fire. It caught the bottom of his robes and swept upward. He danced frantically from side to side, trying to put it out. At the same time, he reached for something in his pocket—a flask, which he uncorked and tipped upside down. His other hand pushed a blast of air into the liquid that fell out, causing it to mist through the room. Some of it brushed across Kesari's face, the feel of it cool and damp but otherwise unremarkable.

A strange sensation spread through her, or rather, a *lack* of sensation. She tried again and again to send more fire after Ashaya, who was now stumbling backwards over the scattered debris of the house. But the flames wouldn't come, and then Valkyra flew past, free of the barrier she'd been trapped in. She followed Ashaya out the door.

Kesari's panic rose. She needed to find the balance again—mind, body, spirit, just like Lucian had taught her. Breathe in. Breathe out. Acknowledge the fear, the hurt, the anger, but without letting it overwhelm her. Stay in control. She made for the door. She couldn't let Valkyra escape again.

Behind her, Zefar coughed. She stopped, watching the retreating figures through the doorway. There was no guarantee she'd be able to catch them, and even if she did, what then? They might still best her. But she could help Zefar. Of that, she was certain.

She went to him, kneeling at his side to take in the damage. The blade was embedded deep, but he was still breathing, and that was a good sign. Placing her hands gently around the wound, she channeled her altma.

Nothing happened. Again, she became aware of that eerie and overwhelming lack of sensation.

Zefar clutched at her wrists. "You burned them?" he choked out, blood staining his teeth a deep red.

"Yes, hold on. I need to get something."

She tried to pull away, but he wouldn't let her go.

"I have some mesala. I can heal you."

"Kes," Lucian said gently. "You can't."

Old demons flooded into her thoughts. She needed her power now more than ever, but something was wrong. She couldn't even sense her magic anymore.

A sickening realization clawed up her throat, and she let out a cry of desperation as she tried to channel altma again, though she knew it would be useless. There was only one reason Ashaya would have run away like that. His magic was gone, too. The substance he'd misted into the room had made it impossible for either of them to channel altma.

Daravak.

"Stay." Zefar coughed, and blood began to trickle from his mouth. His eyes were wild with pain and fear, and he wrapped his fingers tighter around Kesari's.

She inched a little closer to him, tears blurring her vision. "Shh, it's all right. I'll stay."

"Tell Saya for me," he said, fighting through a gurgling breath to get the words out. "I'm sorry."

"She knows. She's already forgiven you."

Zefar's eyelids fluttered, the gold glint of his irises bright in the sunlight streaming through the window. "I want to go home," he said, his voice weak and barely audible. His grip on Kesari's fingers loosened, but she kept a tight hold of them, running her thumb across his knuckles again and again to let him know she was still there.

Was that what Saya would have done? She hoped so.

Zefar inhaled one last ragged gasp and let it out in a gentle sigh. Then his body settled with the absolute stillness that comes only to the dead.

ALEIDA

ALEIDA CROUCHED BESIDE A FALLEN TREE WITH KAMAAL AND Mitul, all three of them watching their surroundings for any sign of more trouble. Saya stood on the other side several paces away. She loosed an arrow at what they hoped was the last of their assailants. The projectile buried itself in the man's throat, and he went down.

Aleida still clutched the pistol Zefar had given her. She hadn't had cause to fire it yet since Saya's prowess with a bow had provided all the defense they needed so far. The warrior had tasked Aleida with protecting the two unarmed men once they were safely behind cover. "Stay here," she'd said, "and kill anyone who gets too close."

Aleida would have much preferred to have her magic at a time like this. If not for Zefar's gun, she would have had no real way of defending herself, let alone Mitul and Kamaal.

"Is that all of them?" the artist asked, peering over the tree trunk.

Saya walked toward them with her bow drawn, sweeping it this way and that as she scanned the surrounding forest. "Looks like it."

"We should get to the house," Mitul said, rising to his feet. "Make sure Kesari's all right."

They made their way back to the house at a jog, still keeping an eye out for any more assassins. Aleida had lost count of how many Saya had put down, but surely there couldn't be many more of them, if any. She hoped.

They broke through the trees, and the house came into view across the open field ahead. A man ran out the front door, his white robes tattered, burned, and stained with blood. Despite that, his movements were normal, as if he were unharmed, and Aleida's stomach twisted at the thought of what that meant. Had Kesari been hurt?

Whoever the man was, he needed to be stopped. She skidded to a halt with Zefar's pistol raised and used both hands to steady her aim. Her two pointer fingers worked in tandem to squeeze the trigger, which proved harder than she'd anticipated. But she managed it, and the resounding crack and harsh recoil nearly sent the gun flying out of her hands.

The man kept running without breaking stride. Aleida's shot had missed, but Saya took one of her own. She might have hit him, but a white shape streaked into the arrow's path, knocking it off course. Valkyra's wings unfurled, and she hovered there in the air. Saya reached for another arrow, cursing when she found her quiver empty.

"Come back and finish them!" Valkyra called after the man in white, her voice high-pitched and furious.

Aleida relished the sound of her distress. She ran toward the dragon, ignoring the others' cries to stop. This was her chance.

"Valkyra!" she screamed, and something in her leapt with a sick jubilation when the Spirit Tarja's eyes met hers. Valkyra flapped her wings, rising higher with each thrust but making no horizontal movement in any direction. Aleida slowed. She knew what was coming, and she was ready. The man in white didn't matter. She only needed to catch Valkyra.

The dragon tucked her wings against her body and plummeted from the sky. Aleida reached up with both hands, trying to grab a wing, a leg, a tail, anything. Her vision narrowed to the space directly in front of her face, a flurry of white fur and feathers, sharp claws and her own pale hands. Splotches of red soon appeared as well, radiant against a backdrop bleached of color. Her blood, but the pain was little more than a mild annoyance. It would all be worth it if she could just—

Her hand closed around something long and thin, and she pulled down, trying to wrap her arms around Valkyra's unfurled wings. "Help me!" she cried out to the others. "I can't hold her!"

Mitul and Kamaal reached her at the same time, but in that instant and with a single twist of her lithe body, Valkyra slipped from Aleida's fingers. She gave a silvery laugh as she flew up toward the sun, like the whole encounter had been merely a game, and one she'd taken great amusement in.

Aleida let out a cry of rage, reaching up as far as she could, as if that would somehow make a difference. Blood ran down her arms beneath torn sleeves. Mitul grasped her by the shoulders, saying something she didn't care about, didn't hear. Her attention was still fixed on the white blur growing smaller and smaller against the blue sky.

She'd had her. Only for a moment, but she'd had her. And now, *again*, she was gone.

Aleida let out every curse she knew in Visan and Kavoran, and when the words had all run out, she screamed again. Mitul held her silently. A second pair of arms wrapped around her—Kamaal's—and she let herself collapse against them both.

She forced herself to take a deep breath. Valkyra was gone, their attackers defeated, but this wasn't over yet. It was only a matter of time before more came, and they still hadn't seen any sign of Kesari.

Saya's voice came from the house, a strangled, wounded sound that chilled her blood. Aleida could only think of one terrible reason why Saya would be making that sound.

She stood up, noting the panic on Mitul's face and the way he clung to Kamaal's arm. She took his free hand, and together they hurried to the house.

The place was in shambles, barely recognizable on the inside. Dirt and rock and shattered wood lay scattered across the floor, a testament to the chaos of whatever battle had unfolded here. Kesari and Saya knelt at the center of it all, and Aleida was more relieved than she'd expected to be when she saw the girl still alive with Lucian hovering faithfully above her shoulder. His orange glow illuminated a third figure lying on the ground. Zefar.

The man's lips were slightly parted, his eyes open wide, but he was completely still. Saya's shoulders shook as she leaned over the body and pressed a kiss to his forehead. She closed his eyes with her own fingers.

"I'm sorry," Kesari whispered. "I tried to save him, but I couldn't."

"They used daravak," Lucian added quietly. "Even with the mesala, there was nothing she could have done. He died making sure she was able to destroy the records before Valkyra could get them."

"Idiot," Saya murmured, wiping at her face with the back of her hand. "He didn't even want that."

"But you did. He knew that."

Kesari shifted closer to the young warrior. "He wanted me to tell you he was sorry."

Saya's tears continued to fall, but she made no sound. Mitul went to her and laid a hand on her shoulder. She reached for it, interlacing her fingers with his and sucking in a shuddering breath.

They stayed like that for a few minutes, and as respectful as Aleida wanted to be, the danger they were still in made her apprehensive. "We need to leave," she said. "They'll be coming back."

Kesari and Mitul nodded, but Saya gave no acknowledgment that she'd heard.

"She's right," Kamaal said. "We can't stay here."

Mitul bent to speak to Saya in a hushed tone. "I'm sorry. We have to go."

"Did he say anything else?" Saya asked.

"He said he wanted to go home," Kesari replied.

"Good. Then I'll take him." She stood up, and Kesari quickly did the same, her eyes wide and panicked. Saya gave her a sad smile. "I'm afraid this is where our paths divide."

"You're not coming with us?" The younger girl's voice was plaintive.

Saya shook her head. "He deserves all the rites and honors of a warrior, and then I must carry his ashes home to our people. They may never have accepted him, but he was still one of us. His spirit must be set free with the desert winds. It's the only thing I can do for him now."

"Then I'll go with you."

Aleida exchanged a look with Mitul. His brows furrowed in concern; he knew as well as she did what Kesari's departure might mean for them. A Tarja was a useful ally to have when one was facing pursuit and the threat of death at the hands of a powerful enemy.

"You have to stay with them," Saya said. "They need you more than I do."

"But I need *you.*" Her voice shook on the last word.

"Not anymore. You're more powerful and courageous than anyone else I know. I'll feel so much better leaving if I know you're looking after the others. You need to free Amar and end this war before it gets any worse."

Kesari jutted her chin out and squared her shoulders. "Fine. But you'd better come back and find us again as soon as you can. Amar will want to see you."

"Of course."

"How will you find us?"

"Lucian will find me," she replied. "Won't you?"

"Oh yes," he drawled. "After all, what's the point of having a spirit trapped as a ball of fire for a friend if you can't make him go flying all over the country looking for someone?"

"We need to go," Aleida reminded them all, glancing out the window. There was no sign of anyone yet, but that didn't mean they weren't already coming.

"Right. I'll get Zefar's horse." Saya went outside and walked toward the field where the animal had been grazing.

"Let's wrap him in something," Mitul suggested.

Kamaal went to fetch a blanket from the bedroom, and Aleida tucked the pistol Zefar had let her borrow into the holster across his chest. She and Kesari helped Kamaal lift him onto the blanket. They tucked the edges around him carefully. When Saya came back, she and Kamaal carried the bundled form outside and slung him over his horse's saddle.

"Well," Saya said, her eyes still wet and red-rimmed. "I suppose this is it."

Kesari threw her arms around the young woman's shoulders. Mitul joined in the embrace, and a few seconds later, so did Kamaal. Aleida hung back, arms crossed, impatiently shifting from one foot to the other. Kamaal waved a hand at her, and when she shook her head, he began to wave more vigorously. Reluctantly, she went to join the group, and for a few moments, she even allowed herself to enjoy it. The last time she'd huddled with a group like this had been with Tyrus and her parents, so long ago she was surprised she even remembered what it felt like.

It was nice.

But there was no time for sentimental goodbyes, no matter how much they all wanted them. She broke away from the group. "We *really* need to leave."

"I'll get the cart ready," Kamaal said. "Gather whatever you need to bring and we'll get going."

She needed no further prompting, but stopped in the doorway when Saya called out to her. "Hey, Aleida, wait."

"What?" Her jaw and shoulders tightened with the expectation of some lecture or threat.

"Take care of yourself, all right?"

She nodded. "You too."

She went inside, and the sounds of the others exchanging hurried farewells grew faint. Kesari and Mitul filed in not long after and joined her in packing what they'd need for the road. Kamaal took charge of the food stores, much of which he pilfered from his sister's cellar, joking that a little missing food would be the least of her concerns given the current state of her house.

It only took them a few minutes to finish their preparations, but to Aleida, those minutes felt like hours. When they finally left, she was sure Valkyra and a whole host of guards would be closing in on them at any moment, but to her great relief, none appeared.

While Kamaal drove the cart, Mitul tended to the wounds Aleida and Kesari had suffered in their skirmishes with Valkyra. He cleaned them out and applied bandages, speaking in soft, reassuring tones all the while. They hurt a little less when he was finished, and Kesari could do more to heal them once the daravak wore off.

They travelled east, taking a narrow trail through the forest that Kamaal said was used in spring and summer for herding goats. Now, in the middle of winter, they weren't likely to run into anyone, especially given the wet, mucky state of their path. Still, they were careful, always watching and listening for signs of trouble. Lucian scouted both ahead and behind to search for potential obstacles or other dangers, reporting back each time he passed by. He still needed to check in on Amar, but that would have to wait until they were someplace safe.

At one point their wheels got stuck, and they all had to get out and push the cart free. When they climbed back in, Mitul took the bench seat next to Kamaal up front, leaving Kesari and Aleida alone in the back. Fortunately, the road became a little smoother from that point, and they didn't run into any more issues.

The sun began to sink below the horizon, and still, they rolled on. Kesari hadn't said a word since they'd left the house and sat in one corner with her arms curled around bent legs. Occasionally, she flicked out a hand and then stared at it as if waiting for something to happen, and Aleida realized she was trying to channel her altma.

"It will come back," she said when the girl made the gesture again, cringing at the jealousy that rippled through her. Kesari's loss of magic was temporary, but Aleida would never have that power again. And oh, what a power it had been. Of course, it hadn't ever truly been hers to begin with, but she couldn't help feeling it was just one more thing Valkyra had stolen from her.

"Yes," Kesari said, "but it will still be too late. Zefar's dead, and Saya's gone." She sighed. "I wish things had gone differently."

"There was nothing else you could have done."

"I know. I think that makes it worse."

Aleida lowered her gaze. Of course that made it worse. Hadn't she felt the same, after Tyrus died? She'd done all she could for him only to learn in the end that there was never any hope of saving him.

She didn't know what to say. Perhaps there were some things that made any semblance of comfort impossible. All any of them could really do was sit with what had happened, and if Mitul had taught her anything over the last few months, it was that sitting in grief and misery was a little more bearable when someone was willing to sit with you. She scooted across the floor of the cart to Kesari's side and mirrored her posture, knees tucked up beneath her chin.

On the bench at the front of the cart, Mitul and Kamaal had their arms linked together, and Aleida didn't have to see their hands to know how tightly their fingers were intertwined. Her heart gave a panicked little shudder at the thought of what might have happened if she and

Saya hadn't found them before the assassins. But they were still here, alive and whole.

What a fool she was. She hadn't meant to get this attached to any of them. Such bonds became a ruinous weakness when loved ones were killed or put in harm's way, as she'd learned too many times already. The last thing she'd wanted was to create more vulnerabilities for herself or give Valkyra more to steal from her. Now, she'd gone and done just that.

But so what? It was because of them—her friends—that she'd even come this far. It was because of them that she was still alive. And if having people to lose was a vulnerability, so be it.

They could be her strength, too.

AMAR

AMAR WOKE IN A STRANGE ROOM, SNUG AND WARM BENEATH LAYERS of blankets, though the air was frigid. It was dark, but a few lanterns cast enough light to see by, and when he began to sit up, a voice spoke.

"How are you feeling, Savir?"

It was King Bhajan, and Amar suddenly realized that he was not in a room, but back in their tent. Outside, all was quiet, and several hours must have passed for it to be so dark. The battle must be over. He'd missed the rest of it, thanks to Tarik putting him to sleep.

He needed to tell Bhajan everything, but even as he opened his mouth to speak, he caught sight of a small, white shape moving at the end of his bed. Valkyra was back, and she watched him with an intent curiosity that stopped the words in his throat.

He swallowed, weighing his options. If he tried to tell Bhajan the truth now, Valkyra might find some way to stop him or interrupt their conversation before he could fully explain, and then she would know that he'd remembered everything. She might very well have him killed out of desperation just to start their relationship over with a clean slate and manipulate him all over again. That would certainly disrupt her plans, but if it was her only option, she would do it, and he'd be worse off than when he started. He didn't want to back her into that corner.

He needed to end this war, but before that, he needed time to figure out how. Valkyra had planned everything so well, and he'd have to outsmart her if he wanted to succeed in his own goals. Which meant, for now, he'd have to pretend.

"Savir?" Bhajan asked, leaning forward with a concerned look. "Are you all right?"

"Yes, sorry. Still a little dazed, I guess. What happened?"

"We won," Bhajan said. The forced smile made him look decades older than Amar had ever seen him. "You helped with that, leading your troops to support our Tarja. That allowed us to take out most of Jakhat's reinforcements. They're retreating all the way back home, I'm told. I'm sure it won't be the last we see of them, but such a major victory bodes well for us."

"They'll come back stronger next time," Amar said bleakly.

"Probably. I don't think they expected so much resistance this time." He sat up a little taller. "But don't you worry. We'll be ready for whatever they throw at us."

Amar frowned. That was exactly what he was afraid of. The sooner he could put an end to this, the better.

"How's the leg?" Bhajan asked. "They said our best healer tended to it. Should be as good as new in a few days."

Amar hadn't even paid it much attention until now. It felt fine, aside from a small, lingering ache. "It's all right."

"Good."

The gentle concern in Bhajan's eyes made Amar squirm, and he had to look away. The king had shown him nothing but kindness these last several months, and he'd grown rather fond of the man. How heartbroken would he and Indira be when they learned that their real grandson was probably dead after all? Would it be like losing him all over again?

"What's troubling you?" Bhajan asked. "You're even more quiet than usual."

Amar shrugged but didn't answer. He didn't know how.

When the silence dragged on, the king spoke again. "Tarik said you were a bit shaken after you were injured. It's nothing to be ashamed of. You're not the first man to lose his composure in the middle of battle. The first one's always hardest."

Amar held in a dark, grim laugh. If only he knew. This wasn't his first battle by far. "I'm sorry if my actions dishonored you."

"No, not at all. You'll fare much better next time, I'm sure." He rose from his chair. "I should attend to my other duties. You can join me whenever you're ready. It would do the soldiers good to see their prince on his feet."

With that, Bhajan left the tent. No sooner had he gone than Tarik entered. "You're awake," he said. Amar couldn't help noting the way he'd left off the formal title, and he cursed himself for the foolish statements he'd made while still in shock from his wound and the flood of memories regained. He would have to tread carefully if there was any hope of maintaining the guard's trust.

"I am," he said, smiling warmly. "Thank you for keeping me safe out there. And I'm sorry. I know I made things difficult."

Tarik gave a stiff nod. "You did, but that's what I'm here for." He tilted his head to one side. "The things you were saying—"

"I'd rather not talk about it, if that's all right," Amar said, looking down and hoping his panic came across as shame. The last thing he needed was for Valkyra to find out what he'd said, specifically that he'd told everyone within shouting distance he wasn't Prince Savir.

"As you wish," Tarik said. "But I'll say this. It's bad for morale when the troops see a man coming apart like that, let alone their prince."

"I understand," Amar said. "It won't happen again. I promise."

"Good." There was a vaguely threatening growl to his voice, or perhaps that was only Amar's imagination. Now that he could sift through his memories in a more logical order, he easily recalled the guard's words to him the first day he'd been assigned to protect him.

If you stay and I find out you're lying, I'll make sure you regret it.

Amar had no doubt he'd meant it.

"Can I be of any other service?" Tarik asked, and when Amar shook his head, he gave a quick bow and marched back outside.

As soon as he was gone, Valkyra stood and padded a little closer. "You had a rather exciting day while I was gone, didn't you? What happened to staying with the rearguard where you'd be safe?"

He took a steadying breath and chose his words carefully. He still had a part to play, after all. *I am Prince Savir.*

"I didn't have much time to think about it. Our Tarja needed help, and I did what I thought was best." He recalled the boy he'd been mere hours before, so eager for her approval. "You heard Bhajan. I did well. Aren't you proud of me?"

"Of course, dear," Valkyra said, softening a little. "But you must be careful. You're far too important to risk your life so needlessly. Next time you might consider giving orders and letting someone else execute them."

He shrugged, trying to appear far more relaxed than he felt. "Did you and Ashaya find the people who attacked us in the guardhouse?"

"We did."

When she didn't elaborate, he prodded further, anxious to know how his friends had fared. "And? Did you capture them?"

She ruffled her wings in a gesture of annoyance. "No. Unfortunately, they bested us and escaped again. Thanks to Zefar, they knew we were coming, and there were more of them than we anticipated."

"More of them?" he repeated. "What about the man I shot? Didn't I kill him, at least?" Skies, he hoped he hadn't.

"No," Valkyra said, and Amar had to clench his jaw to stop himself from grinning. "He was there, alive and well, along with our dear artist friend."

He blinked, feigning ignorance for a few seconds and then making his eyes wide. "You don't mean Kamaal?"

"I do. I'm not exactly sure how he came to be involved with them, but the fact that he was there means we can't trust him. You must never allow him near you again. Understood?"

"Yes, of course."

She gave her tail a swish and spread her wings. "I hate to fly off again so soon, but I really should get back to the palace. Ashaya's organizing another group of guards to go after them, and I want to make sure we pick up their trail as soon as possible. Will you be all right here on your own?"

"I'll be fine. You'll still try to take them alive, won't you?"

"Oh, Savir," she sighed. "We're well past that, don't you think? I know you want answers, but they've proven themselves far too dangerous. They must be killed before they can cause any more trouble."

Putting himself back in Savir's mind, Amar couldn't find any reason to argue with that. "I guess you're right." His friends had indeed proven themselves not only dangerous but resourceful, and he would have to hope that was enough to keep them alive for now.

Valkyra hopped off the bed and went to the tent's entrance. "I'll be back as soon as I can. Put out those lanterns, and stay away from the fires."

He nodded, and she slipped out beneath the tent flap, leaving him alone with his thoughts at last.

But what if he wasn't alone? She'd been so concerned about Lucian spying on him, but perhaps what she'd really been worried about was that the Spirit Tarja would try to talk to him. He glanced at the three lanterns hanging throughout the tent, searching their flames for some semblance of a face. "Lucian?" he whispered, then again, a little louder. "Lucian, are you here?"

There was no response, and Amar flopped back against the pillows with his arms behind his head. He'd keep trying. Maybe Lucian would come later, after he and the others had dealt with the aftermath of their own battle.

He lay there staring up at the canvas ceiling as his mind sorted through recent events. He'd started the day believing himself to be someone entirely different, and now that he knew the truth, everything he'd experienced these last few months needed to be recontextualized.

The question that weighed heaviest on him was how Valkyra had managed to convince not only him but an entire kingdom that he was Prince Savir. His own conviction had been rooted in who he really was—not Prince Savir, but still a prince, long ago and in another life. Even when everything else had seemed so uncertain, that title felt right, and now, he understood why. As for convincing others, everything hinged on the so-called evidence Ashaya had presented.

The night he'd followed Valkyra out of the inn and eavesdropped on her conversation with the magistrate, they'd mentioned the medallion Amar still wore and Princess Priyani's journal. Valkyra had said the writing matched perfectly, and though he hadn't understood then, he was now inclined to believe they'd forged at least part of it using actual samples of Priyani's writing. Ashaya was a powerful man with powerful connections, and therefore fully capable of acquiring her medallion and her journal. From there, he could have altered its contents to include whatever he wanted—a mention of a specific birthmark, for instance.

Amar glanced down at the small patch of darkened skin on his hand. It had always been there, unremarkable and barely worthy of notice. Now it was one more thread weaving the lies together, along with everything else Ashaya had presented. And that was the real problem—all this evidence had come from the same corrupt source. The magistrate had been Valkyra's accomplice even before Amar met him in Valmandi, but to Bhajan and Indira, he was a trusted advisor. They had no reason to believe he was lying. In fact, they were more inclined to believe him, not only because of who he was, but what he was telling them.

What was it Valkyra had said that night? *People believe what they want to believe. They'll make it true, and that's all we need.*

They had preyed on the king and queen's grief, taking advantage of their deepest hopes in order to deceive them. All so that Valkyra could have her war and unseat Empress Dashiva, the woman who'd once been her friend but eventually ordered her death. She would have put Amar on the throne, and his immortality meant he would rule forever. *They* would rule forever, because she was a part of him now, thanks to their Bond.

He squeezed his eyes shut. How much worse might things have gotten if his friends hadn't found a way to restore his memories?

He lay there a few moments longer, trying to plan his next steps. He felt like a wild animal set free after years in captivity, caught between the urge to act immediately and the uncertainty of what to do. He desperately wanted to see his friends, especially knowing the danger they were still in, and for a few moments, he considered running off to find them while Valkyra was away. But he didn't know where they were, and besides that, there was still the pressing obligation to end the war his deceit had created.

First, he needed to take stock of the damage from today's battle, and he couldn't do that hiding away in his tent. He sat up and found his boots at the end of the bed. After pulling them on, he stood and buckled his belt over his tunic. His cloak and crown lay on a nearby trunk. He threw on the cloak and picked up the crown, turning it in his hands with thoughtful consideration.

It had never fit quite right, and it didn't belong to him. But there were people outside this tent who'd fought for that crown and the person they believed was wearing it. Bhajan had said it would do them good to see him, and if that were true, perhaps he should keep pretending, at least for tonight. The news would be bad enough whenever it came, but it would be especially terrible now, when they still needed to bury so many comrades who'd died in the name of their prince.

He set the metal circle on his head, the weight of it heavier than it had ever been before. Then he squared his shoulders and walked outside, where dozens of eyes immediately fell on him. Soldiers bowed or saluted as he began to make his way through the camp.

How many of them would come to wish they'd raised their rifles to shoot him instead of saluting?

But that was a problem for later. Right now, he needed time to plan his next move and outsmart Valkyra.

I am Prince Savir, he reminded himself again.

But only for a little while longer.

The story continues in

CURSE OF SHAVHALLA BOOK THREE: RIVEN EMPIRE

GLOSSARY

ALTMA – an energy source present in all living things which can be used by Tarja to fuel their magical abilities

ARTEX – the Visan deity, believed to be the creator of all things; sometimes referred to as 'the Artist'

BOND – a magical connection between a Spirit Tarja and a living person which grants the living partner the ability to channel altma at the expense of sharing the remainder of their natural lifespan with the Spirit Tarja

CHANNEL (ALTMA) – the act of drawing altma from one's surroundings and/or within oneself and using it to perform magical feats

CURSE – a specific branch of magic whose affects are longer lasting and more powerful than most types of magic; curses were outlawed in Erythyr several hundred years ago and much of the knowledge about them has been erased or forgotten

DARAVAK – a species of fungus native to Kavora which temporarily inhibits a Tarja's ability to channel altma

GHAYAT – a species of antelope-like creatures native to the Sular Desert that are an integral part of the ecosystem and the Sularan people's way of life

HASEPH – a rite of passage undertaken by all Sularan youth at age sixteen in which the participant is required to seek out and bring back to their tribe something of value so that they may become a full-fledged member of the tribe

JITAARA – The basic monetary unit of Kavora

JHIVAN – a word found in a set of ancient Shavhallan records believed by some to mean *altma* in Kavoran; *jhivan* is also sometimes referenced in myth as a fourth element of magic representing life itself

KANJIRA – a small handheld drum, typically a circular wooden frame covered on one side with a drumhead made from animal skin while the other side is left open

MASAHI – the highest-ranking member on a council of tribal leaders chosen to represent the Sularan people

MESALA – a species of plant native to the Sular Desert which is the main food source of the ghayat and whose flowers can enhance a Tarja's magical abilities; sometimes referred to as 'Sularan torches'

SARAJ – a Kavoran stringed instrument approximately one meter in length, which is versatile for a variety of musical styles and has a rich, reverberating sound

SAMUD – a strategy game favored among Kavoran nobility

SPIRIT TARJA – the spirit of a Tarja who died prematurely; this death causes the altma within them to tether their soul to the physical world either until the altma fades or until the Spirit Tarja forms a Bond with a living partner

TARJA – any person capable of channeling altma to perform magical feats; a Tarja may be born with the ability to use magic or, less commonly, may be someone who has gained those abilities by forming a Bond with a Spirit Tarja

CAST & NOTABLE FIGURES

AKRAJA MUNAR SHARMA – deceased, former emperor of Kavora, father of Prince Savir, sister of Empress Dashiva

ALEIDA CERAN – a young Visan woman orphaned during Kavora's invasion of Vis, older sister to Tyrus, became a Tarja through her Bond with Valkyra

AMAR – a Kavoran man cursed with immortality, currently believes himself to be Prince Savir, long-time friend of Mitul

AVANI MURAKA – an intimidating woman who serves as general of the imperial Tarja military forces

BHAJAN VORA – king of the city of Valmandi within the Kavoran Empire, husband of Queen Indira, father of Princess Priyani, grandfather of Prince Savir

CHAYANI SHA – Advisor of Magic on the Valmandi Royal Council

DASHIVA SHARMA – reigning Empress of Kavora, younger sister of the late Emperor Akraja, mother of Princess Jasala

DEV ASHAYA – Advisor of Law on the Valmandi royal council, formerly a member of Empress Dashiva's Imperial Council

FEROS – a strix belonging to Aleida and Tyrus Ceran who often carried messages between them

HASAN KHURANA – a Tarja healer and farmer who lives in Chatanda, former guardian of Tyrus and Aleida

INDIRA VORA – queen of the city of Valmandi within the Kavoran Empire, wife of King Bhajan, mother of Princess Priyani, grandmother of Prince Savir

Jameson Weatherford – deceased, an Atrean Tarja of great skill and renown, sometimes referred to by his formal title The Great and Honorable Wizard Jameson

Jasala Sharma – official heir to the Kavoran imperial throne, daughter of Empress Dashiva, cousin of Prince Savir

Kamaal Ruman – a famous Kavoran painter, former parter of Mitul

Kesari Eves – an Atrean girl with Kavoran ancestry, sister of Rajiv and Navya, became a Tarja through her Bond with Lucian

Khan – Advisor of War on the Valmandi Royal Council and commanding general of Valmandi's military

Khatri – Advisor of Secrets on the Valmandi Royal Council

Lucian – Kesari's Spirit Tarja, takes the form of hovering flames and is typically about the size of an apple

Mitul Rama – a middle-aged Kavoran musician, long-time friend of Amar, former partner of Kamaal

Nandini Kumar – deceased, former Tarja advisor to Empress Dashiva, now a Spirit Tarja who goes by the name Valkyra

Navya Eves – younger sister of Kesari and Rajiv

Priyani Vora Sharma – deceased, former princess of Valmandi and empress of Kavora (through marriage to Emperor Akraja), daughter of King Bhajan and Queen Indira of Valmandi, mother of Prince Savir

Rajiv Eves – deceased, older brother of Kesari and Navya

Savir Akraja Jai Sharma – son of Emperor Akraja and Princess Priyani, former heir to the Kavoran imperial throne, officially reported dead but believed to be alive by some

Saya hàs Seda – a young Sularan woman completing her haseph, friend of Kesari, Mitul, and Amar

Seda hàs Yusana – Masahi of the Sularan tribe in Hayathu, mother of Saya

TARIK APTI – a stoic guard who has served the Valmandi monarchs for years, assigned to oversee Prince Savir's security

TYRUS CERAN – deceased, younger brother of Aleida

VALKYRA – Savir's Spirit Tarja (formerly Aleida's), takes the form of a small furred and feathered white dragon

VASU – Advisor of Diplomacy on the Valmandi Royal Council

ZEFAR HÀS YARATHA – a Sularan mercenary and an outcast among his tribe, Saya's former mentor

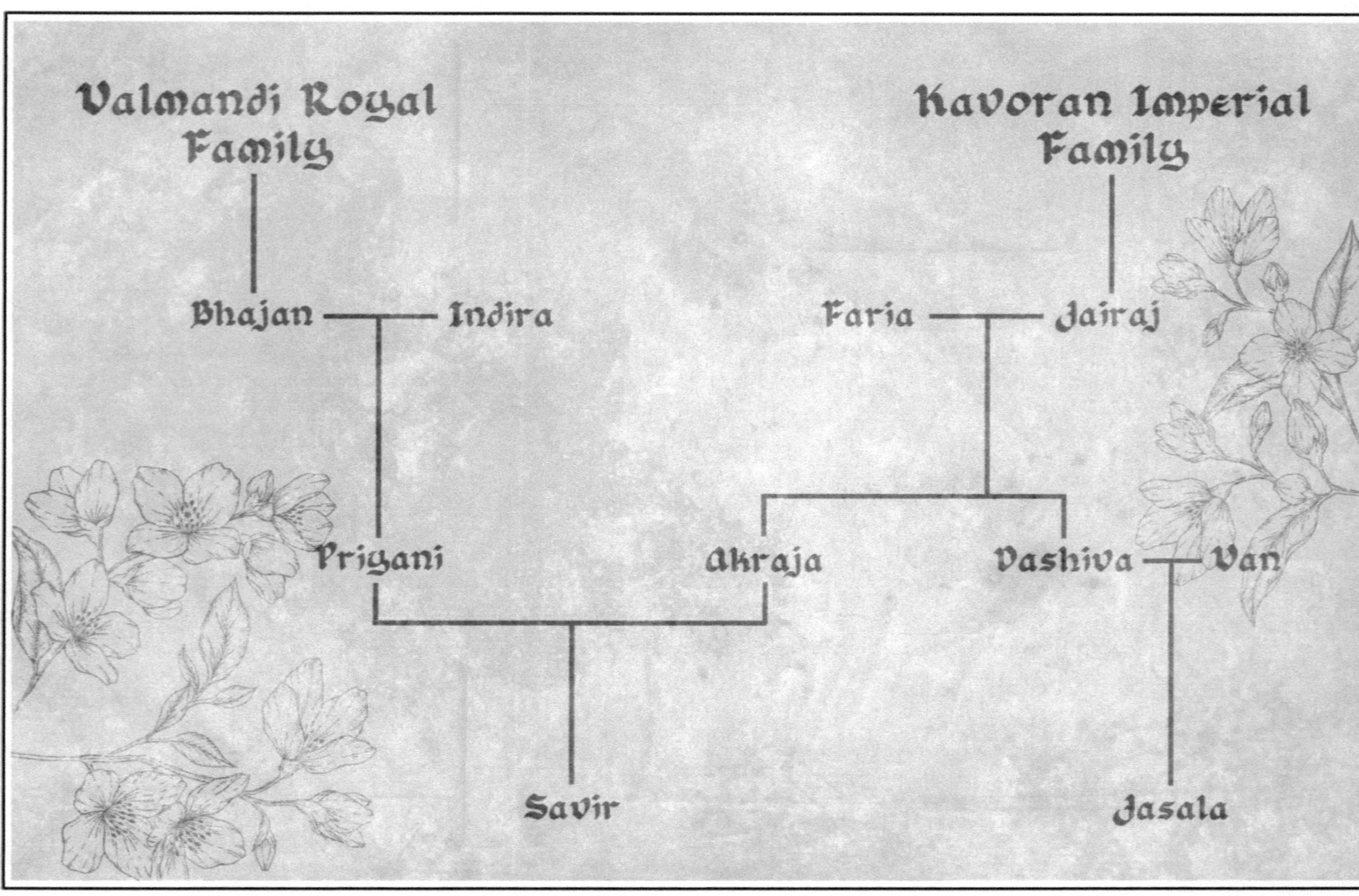
Valmandi Royal Family
Kavoran Imperial Family
Bhajan
Indira
Faria
Jairaj
Prigani
Akraja
Vashiva
Van
Savir
Jasala

DEAR READER

Thank you so much for taking the time to read this book. I hope you enjoyed it. Now that you're finished, please consider leaving an honest review. Reviews are especially important to indie authors and can help others make informed decisions about their reading experience, which allows the book to reach its target audience.

Follow me social media to stay up to date on my writing, and please feel free to reach out. Your questions and comments about the story and characters are always welcome and appreciated.

tahernandez.com
tahernandez@tahernandez.com
Twitter: @ta_hernandez5
Instagram: @ta_hernandez5
facebook.com/tahernandez05

ACKNOWLEDGEMENTS

It seems like with every book I write, the process gets easier in some ways and harder in others, which I suppose is to be expected. However, nothing could have quite prepared me for the challenge that was this particular book. The book itself can only be faulted for about half of that difficulty. The rest of the blame lies with…well, life. Life being messy, as it so often is. With support and encouragement from the following people, I still managed to wrangle this thing into shape.

I had an amazing group of beta readers, critique partners, and sensitivity readers who provided valuable feedback on this story. Thank you to Heather, Stephanie, Taylor, and Michelle for all of your thoughtful insights and suggestions. This story became immensely better because of you.

I also want to thank my family for continuing to support me in all of my creative pursuits, even when that means I get a little lost in a story or a project. I am inspired daily by my daughters' vivid imaginations and capacity to love, and my husband Alex has been my constant shelter in a year full of big changes and self-discovery.

Last but not least, thank *you*, reader, for spending some time in the world of my imagination. Whether you loved it or hated it or fell somewhere in between, the simple fact that you gave it a chance means everything to me.

ABOUT THE AUTHOR

T. A. Hernandez is a science fiction and fantasy author and long-time fan of speculative fiction. She grew up with her nose habitually stuck in a book and her mind constantly wandering to make-believe worlds full of magic and adventure. She was first inspired to write after reading J. R. R. Tolkien's *The Lord of the Rings* many years ago and is now happily engaged in an exciting and lifelong quest to tell captivating stories.

She is a clinical social worker and the proud mother of two girls. She also enjoys drawing, reading, graphic design, playing video games, and making happy memories with her family and friends.

OTHER WORKS BY T. A. HERNANDEZ

THE CURSE OF SHAVHALLA TRILOGY

Tethered Spirits
Revenant Prince
Riven Empire (coming 2024)

THE SECRETS OF PEACE TRILOGY

Secrets of PEACE
Renegades of PEACE
Survivors of PEACE

OTHER STORIES

Whispers of Shadow and Starlight
Calico Thunder Rides Again

www.ingramcontent.com/pod-product-compliance
Lightning Source LLC
Chambersburg PA
CBHW020528310726
48979CB00014B/2247/J
* 9 7 8 1 7 3 4 0 3 3 0 2 1 *